HIGHPOINT

HIGHPOINT

Hans Christian Hollenbeck

Copyright © 2010 by Hans Christian Hollenbeck.

Library of Congress Control Number: 2010914269
ISBN: Hardcover   978-1-4535-8460-6
             Softcover   978-1-4535-8459-0
             Ebook   978-1-4535-8461-3

All rights reserved. No part of this book may be reproduced or transmitted in any form or by any means, electronic or mechanical, including photocopying, recording, or by any information storage and retrieval system, without permission in writing from the copyright owner. Portions of this book references to copywritten material; "Walking on the Moon," The Police, "For Whom the Bell Tolls," John Donne, and portions of "The June Bug" by Edgar Allen Poe were used.

This is a work of fiction. Names, characters, places and incidents either are the product of the author's imagination or are used fictitiously, and any resemblance to any actual persons, living or dead, events, or locales is entirely coincidental.

This book was printed in the United States of America.

To order additional copies of this book, contact:
Xlibris Corporation
1-888-795-4274
www.Xlibris.com
Orders@Xlibris.com
81985

For the real Rebecca

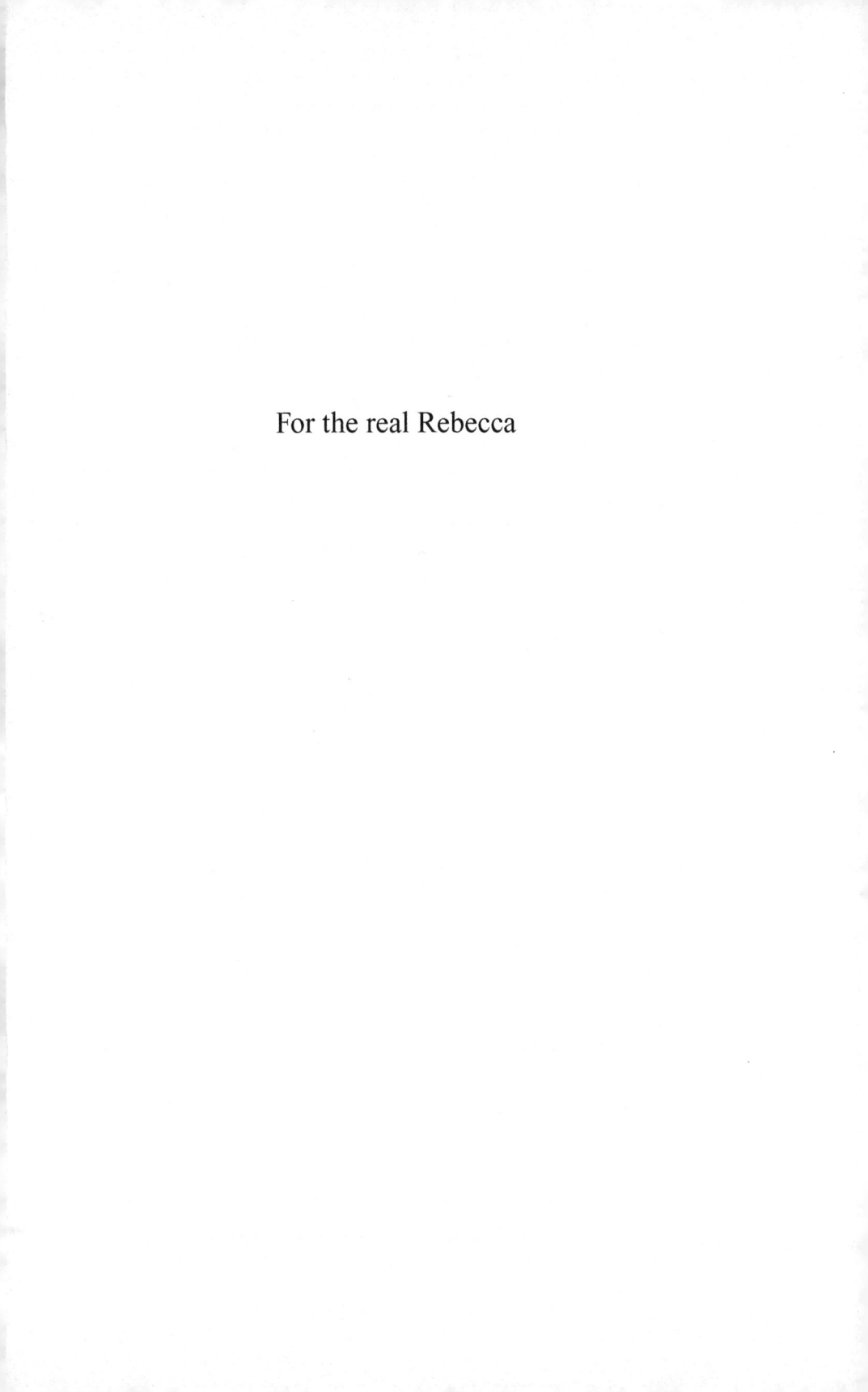

"When man is able to think as God, he has become God himself."
—Shane Behnllock

"All the great empires of the future will be empires of the mind."
—Winston Churchill

"I think; therefore I am."
—Descartes

PROLOGUE

After we get started, take a moment to look around. Seriously. Stop reading this for a second and honestly examine your surroundings. What do you see? You see life, in some form or another. There is something happening right in front of you at this very moment, in front of your eyes. Molecules are working; atoms are in motion. There is an invisible world dancing around you. You are pretending to see **this world** how it is. But in a way, you are actually seeing everything through a filter. A lot of things go unnoticed by you every day. So many things that it would probably hurt you to know how much you have already missed, things you are missing even by the end of this page. You have been missing most of the important things right from the beginning.

It's a good time to catch up.

Now look around again. Take time to inspect everything that you see, and don't miss a thing. Study everything that is in your visual plane.

Did you notice the tip of your nose extending ever so slightly into your field of vision? Probably not. So take another look, now at a particular object. Describe that object to yourself, every aspect of it. Leave out no details.

Did you recognize the shadows around it, instead of just the object itself? Probably not. You probably forgot the shadows upon it, as well as the shadows that subtly surround it. The darkness. Darkness is everywhere. It is waiting patiently in the cracks and folds of everything around us, or silently slipping in even during the brightness of a summer's day. The darkness. It consumes you when you close your eyes or close the shades. It is always all over your body like a sticky film, and you can never ever rub it off or cleanse yourself of it. Shadows follow everything everywhere. The darkness is always around, and always will be. But dear friends, do not despair, for once you have been able to recognize **all** the darkness, only then will you be able to truly see the light.

I will caution you before I lead you **in** any further. Certainly, the words that are written in the culmination of these pages will again put *me in an extreme risk of imminent peril, but these words need exposure. So my warning is this: by simply reading the proceeding text will you be absorbing information that many never want you to know. You are placing **your**self in grave danger by doing so. So let it be understood. You will be risking your health and **head** simply by reading the story that is about to unfold. You have reached the point of no return.*

CHAPTER 1

There is always a still before the storm. There is a moment of calm, a period of tranquility, days, maybe hours, before clouds roll in. It is that moment when you can smell the rain coming, or taste the dryness in the air before a tornado. Everything is as listless as one can imagine, and the mere thought of impending chaos seems absurd. My calm, my still before my own personal storm, were the years of my youth. Those years were incredible. They were a prolonged period of milkshakes and birthday parties, the annual fishing trip to Canada with my family, the baseball games, or the nights spent catching fireflies as night settled. Those were days of repeated pillow fights with my younger brother that resulted in uncontrolled laughter and a mess of feathers. Those were the days of field trips and campouts. Those were the days of first dates and first kisses. Those were the days of ignorance and innocence. Those were the days. The calm.

Then, with a gradual intensity, the storm began to arrive. The first waves of it came when I was sixteen and halfway through my freshman year in high school. Little did I know at the time those waves would grow to a vicious magnitude and form a maelstrom that would last the rest of my life.

I was home with my brother at the end of another boring school day. My brother was slightly overweight and therefore very shy. He was the kid picked last in every competition. Understandably, he normally tried to refrain from any activities of any sort, in turn, making him increasingly less athletic.

The vicious circle.

My brother maintained strength though, especially mentally. He would spend hours riddling my father and me with questions, as well as riddling me with windows into his streams of consciousness.

"What do you think happens when we die?" I remember he asked as we tried to build a house of cards. We never could manage to get through a whole pack. He was trying to steady the queen of hearts against the back of another card.

He did not wait for a reply from me however. He just shot ahead with his own answer.

"I don't remember the time before I was born, so I figure I won't remember the time after I die." He continued, never waiting for an actual answer. He licked his lips in concentration, stabilizing the card in the formation the best he could, "So if I can't remember it, maybe I figure it wasn't for me to know about anyway. Like when Dad says we have to wait until we get older to figure it out. That's what I figure."

My brother liked the word "figure" a lot when he was twelve, and as I was fourteen, I preferred the word as it related to the body of the opposite sex. I sat there for a second, half the deck of Bicycles in my hand, and realized that, until then, I had never really contemplated what I was doing before I was born.

But I've thought about it quite a lot since.

He sat the queen of hearts in its place, and I tried to precisely set the four of spades on top of it. It wiggled for a bit, jeopardizing the entire structure, so I steadied it. I moved it to a sturdier position and gently let it stay. The structure held for a moment then completely collapsed. We had to start all over, but were used to this.

"I think that Santa Claus still exists," he said as we collected the mess. "I mean everyone 'knows' that he doesn't really exist, but also everyone 'knows' who Santa Claus is. That makes him exist right there."

We picked all the cards up and shuffled them. Then started on another foundation for another inevitable collapse.

I realized later that my brother was simply referring to magic, to love, to things that are indefinable in nature, things that defy any laws of physics or property, but still exist in their beautiful invisibility. Mathematics will never give us an equation for love, and science can never explain it further than a mere rise of serotonin levels.

I want to still believe that Santa Claus really does visit eighteen million kazillion homes in one night, simply because Santa *is magic*. The happiness and blissful anxiety that a child experiences when he is waiting for Santa Claus to come is Santa Claus. True joy is the anticipation in the mind of what you hope is soon to come. It, in itself, is the magic and can never be encompassed by a label. If you are magic, you can do anything. It really hurts most of us to admit that we don't believe in Santa or his reindeer, that we don't believe in magic even though deep down somewhere inside of us, we all still do.

My brother started building again tediously, and I added much fewer cards than him as we built another first level. My brother had prompted me to start thinking, as he often did unintentionally, about the existence of magic. I wondered about things as I watched him concentrate and clench his bottom lip then carefully place a card in a worthy position.

My father is a strong man, in will and in stature. Every boy's first icon is truly his father, and all men find their father residing in them as they grow. Your father is the one who forges a trail so that you are able to make your own way.

My father divorced my mother when I was seven, and due to work, she was constantly traveling, so my younger brother and I stayed with him the majority of our upbringing. My father was capable of both being a guardian as well as a friend, and my brother was a reflection of my own thoughts and being. It was the three of us.

I asked my father privately that very day to really tell me the truth about everything that he knew on the subject of magic, of the things that we all can't really see but can feel. We were outside at the woodshed, and as I stacked the wood that he chopped, he told me.

"Well, son," he said with a sweaty brow as his ax buried itself into a large stump.

He stopped and pulled the ax back out from the large crack in the semi-splintered piece. He dropped the head of the ax to his side and held on to the upright handle. "There is really no such thing as magic. Just illusions. A lot of illusions. Make us feel like there is magic. Give us something to believe in. Sometimes, well sometimes, people do things and say things that make someone else happy, even if what they say might not be completely true. The truth might hurt them, ya see, or might not be in their best interest. I'm not saying that it is a lie, but more like—"

"Make believe," I interrupted.

"Yeah, make believe."

"So most of what we learn is a lie?"

"Yep." He propped another piece of wood on the chopping block with his free hand. "Your whole life is basically filled with bullshit that you'll have to wade through—" he shifted the ax into both hands and brought it up and around his head, then down into the log in one swift circular motion, splintering it violently in two.

He stopped, caught his breath. Chopping four cords of wood in preparation for a Colorado winter is not enjoyable.

"But, son, the stars and the moon and the Earth and everything else isn't make-believe, they are as real as you can get. And they are the important things. They are more magnificent than Santa and the rest of it anyway 'cause they are what make you feel magical, they are what make you think that magic really can exist, even if it doesn't."

I picked up the fresh pieces that lay around his chopping block and stacked them neatly on top of the growing wall of wood in the shed. He chopped for a while longer without saying a word, and I worked just as silently stacking it.

"The day that you understand the reality of life is the day you become a man." He said as he walked behind me "The reality is that nothing matters, yet every little tiny thing matters immensely."

"That makes no sense," I replied.

"Some things don't. But the day you realize you are a man, you'll know what I'm talking about. It's once you've separated fact from fiction, truth from bullshit."

He put his arm on my back. "All I can do is guide you the best I can, son, I'm wading through it same as you."

I laughed.

We walked down the path toward the house as night crept in from above.

The winter was intense that year, and we used up every speck of the firewood that my father and I had chopped. The snow in Colorado is beautiful only to tourists after the first few weeks. Schools typically close repeatedly throughout the winter, and often the snow seems endless. A few times I wondered if it were possible for our house to be completely buried in snow, but reassured myself that it probably couldn't.

But the cold and ice always, albeit slowly, melt away.

I found myself getting off the school bus with my younger brother in the heat of spring. I had turned sixteen and would no longer need the ball and chain of a public bus. I recently acquired a car, along with the ability to drive it. As always, the bus dropped us off at the bottom of our long gravel driveway, and as always, my brother and I raced each other to the top. As we exited the bus, we sprinted wildly up the drive as we always did, but this time I stopped halfway up.

My brother gained a considerable lead, which was very uncommon—*he was my younger brother after all, and fat*—and soon stopped to look back at me. We both knew that I had never lost footrace to him, and vowed that I never would. We were brothers, the fiercely competitive kind, and he knew fully well that I would never ever simply give up. Never, at least, to him. He was younger and weaker, and I would prove that to him forever.

For a few moments, he may have believed that I was playing some sort of trick on him or unknown racing tactic, as he stood anxiously in the middle of the drive, poised any quick movement of mine to regain ground. But I didn't budge.

"Are you stupid? You're gonna lose!" he yelled to me, increasing his distance, still perplexed by my behavior.

"I don't care!" I yelled back to him with my head down.

And I didn't.

For the first time in my life, the after-school footrace meant nothing to me. I had seen something, out of the corner of my eye, moving much faster than I had been running. Something more important than a footrace.

"Whaddya doin'?" I heard him yell. "Whaddya lookin' at?"

I had dropped to my knees and was studying the dirt around my feet.

It had moved in there. In the dirt. But now I can't see it.

There were just small pebbles and a mixture of browns and grays in the soil below me.

"Dad's gonna be mad!" he shouted, from farther away. At this point, he was just using blank threats to prompt me to move and chase him. But I didn't care.

There was something moving right here, I could have swo—

Then it moved again, and this time right in front of my eyes. It wasn't an insect or a real small animal, as I had first thought, but it seemed to be . . .

the dirt itself.

"Hey, Tanner!" I yelled to him, without daring to look up or possibly miss seeing the same point in the dirt. "Come here!" But my brother had already gone.

I watched as the dirt began to ripple quite madly, directly in front of me, plain as day. I dropped to a sitting position and placed my backpack down to inspect it more closely. It was now thrashing wildly about, like an undulating skin. Then I realized that the dirt itself was not moving at all, but instead remaining perfectly calm. I was looking somewhere inside the dirt, deep down into its very foundation. I was looking into the fibers of the earth, and what I was seeing were things that didn't really have a solid shape and were even smaller than atoms, billions upon billions of them, and they were jumping around in a frenzy and scattering in every which way. I must have sat there in the dirt for a full minute, staring at something that I wasn't even quite sure I was seeing. Suddenly, I was aware that my eyes had blinked, and the dirt was calm again, moving not in the slightest. The show was over. I scooped my backpack up as I stood, keeping my eyes fixated on that small space in the dirt.

It showed nothing.

As I walked the rest of the way home that day, a bit dizzy, a thought repeated itself inside my head.

Magic does exist, and it is alive and well.

"Christopher Wyer, please report to the principal's office immediately."

The intercom cut through the frigidity of Geography class, as if razors were being spoken instead of words. The urgency of the mechanical voice was different than a normal call to the principal's office for disciplinary reasons. Thus, no teases were snickered at me from my classmates about getting into impending trouble. As I clearly remember, everything was silent.

Muted.

I don't even believe that there was a sound besides my own footsteps as I walked out of class and down the empty halls.

I didn't know what to expect, especially not my father waiting patiently for me near the school exit with a hint of a tear in his large eyes. He didn't even say much to me, except that I would be getting out of class for a while because, just an hour ago, my brother had passed out in his art class and had gone into convulsions. The teacher immediately called the ambulance, and he had been taken to the hospital. My father had come to get me so that we could meet him there.

Under normal circumstances, being let out of school was equivalent to being paroled from a minimum-security prison. A freedom to be savored. But on that day, I wished that I was still sitting uncomfortably at my desk, listening to the monotone voice of Mr. Hadder instructing us where Sudan is instead of anything that came out of the intercom. I wished that the whole day had never happened.

Sadness slows things down. Pain delays time. Complete sorrow makes the clock stop altogether. The ride to the hospital in my father's old Chevy must have taken a year, and it was only ten miles. The walk through the white hallways of the hospital and through its smell of communal sickness must have taken ten. The world was an LP record stuck on the worst song imaginable and playing at quarter speed. Finally, my father and I were at my brother's side, watching him breathe through a machine, and seeing liquids drip down through clear tunnels and into his veins.

I had just been with him hours before, and he was fine.

We stayed there in that small and sanitary room for another twenty-two days, and I learned a few things. I learned that my brother had developed a brain tumor "the size of a marble," as one doctor put it, diagramming its size with long delicate fingers. I learned that a life comes to an end when a sickness like that arrives, and I was soon to learn that I would never see my brother conscious again.

Watching my brother deteriorate slowly in front of me changed things in my heart. As the tumor ate away in his brain, something else ate away at my soul. The happiness in my life was erased with the sound of a pump that breathed for my brother. The gentle expansion and regression of the pump stirred my nerves.

As I sat there, I tried to think of the times that we stayed up late watching horror movies that we weren't allowed to watch, or playing pirates and ninjas behind our house. I tried to see him do one of his famous cannonballs into the local pool, but all I could see was the motionless, emotionless, sickly form of my brother in the hospital bed before me.

I somehow knew that he was already dead.

The pump was only one of those illusions that my dad had talked about. The pump wouldn't do anything for him really. It was just there to make us feel better, to make us feel like something was being done to change things back around—*to turn back time*—to make things we always want them to be.

I saw it as a cruel joke. A lie.

I could see death in his skin; I could see it below his eyelids. Death was hiding all over him. He seemed artificial, almost as if he were made from plastic or had become an elaborate molding of wax. If he had just opened his eyes once, or maybe spoken to me as I dearly wanted him to on so many nights while everyone else was asleep, things might have been different. If he could have just told me that he was glad to be my brother and was not scared.

If he had just said everything was going to be okay.

But he never did. Twenty-two days later, he passed without a word, without so much as a simple twitching of his hands. He was gone, and he took with him the nice person I used to be.

I don't really remember crying, although I knew that I must have. I remember grinding my teeth and being mad. My brother's death was revolting to me, possibly to the point of derangement. I remember wanting revenge. I needed to avenge his death on something, somebody, anybody. I needed to retaliate against the whole world, for it was the world that took him from me. I would never again be taken advantage of; I would never again be the one who suffered.

Never again.

In the moment that I knew my brother was gone, I had changed.

I didn't even make it past the parking lot and into school my first day back before I got into a fistfight. I beat the kid up pretty bad. I don't even remember his name or what he said, but he had the audacity to come up and speak right to me. I turned on him then, like a rabid animal, and began hurling punches into his face. I felt that he deserved his teeth to be relocated to the back of his throat. I also got some kicks in to his crumpled frame before other students pulled me off, but I accepted the anger inside myself, and it felt good to unleash it. It definitely would not be the last time that I expected it to rear its ugly head.

"I do realize that your brother's ... departure, has had a large impact on you, Chris. It has obviously negatively affected you."

The school principal's lips were moist with what seemed to be too much spittle. "I know that this is probably an isolated incident, at least I hope it is. I know you're a good kid, Chris, and smart too. I know that you are better at maintaining control than this."

You don't know shit. I wanted to say. *Dr. Hank Mccallum, in your cheap brown chair and cheap suit. You. Do. Not. Know. Shit.*

He looked stern, but I knew that he was smiling inside that little head of his. His slightly crooked teeth were grinning under the flaps of his thin lips, I could tell.

He likes the fact that my brother is dead.

"I don't want you back in here again, Chris, and you don't want yourself back in here either for your own good. I am going to give you detention for a week instead of suspension. Consider yourself lucky. You could have been expelled for the stunt that you pulled out in the parking lot."

I removed myself from his office but would soon become a regular customer there. I continued to disregard the importance of anything around me, and his threats began to become more and more realistic. I found myself being sentenced to detention, then suspension, and finally, midway through my freshman year in high school, I would nearly be expelled. According to the school, I was an "instigator of numerous aggressive circumstances and an overall distraction to my teachers and fellow classmates alike," but they could have just said that they despised me and wanted me out. And as much as Dr. Mccallum hated me, I hated him. Actually, I hated him much more. But he was the fully accredited Doctor of English (according to the gold-plated plaque on his wall), and I was not.

All the doctors I knew wore white coats and glasses and were usually very nice in a professional kind of way. But "Hank," as only I would refer to him, was unlike all the doctors that I knew. He always wore slacks and an old coat and tie. He had a middle-aged leathery face, and his light brown hair was calmly receding. He would lean just slightly back in his black cushioned chair and slowly flip through the large manila folder that was, as I now knew, "my file." Studying the contents of the folder quite intently, he would then slowly swivel back and forth. I was used to this procedure.

As he did, I would stare up at the "CERTIFICATE OF DOCTORATE," and smell the mixture of western cologne and fresh carpeting. I would normally drum my fingers upon my simple brown chair and wondered what was in store for me and how I truly loathed the stern-faced man in front of me.

"UHHuummm hum." He was clearing his throat. It was time for Lord Hank Mccallum to speak. He licked his lips slightly and quickly making a slight suckling sound. I figured that a sewer rat is the only other creature with the same disposition.

He crossed his fingers on the desk in front of him and looked toward me. "Got in another fight, huh, Christopher? That would seem to make, let me see here . . . a total of six documented fights within the past sixteen months? You have been suspended numerous times, and yet you still don't act like you have learned anything from your mistakes, and I really get the impression that you just don't care. You're going to be a sophomore next year but act like you're five years old. And, Christopher, I believe I saw you just two weeks ago about cheating on your science quiz . . . I gave you your last chance then. Did I not? I believe that I told you if you came back in here again, you would be expelled from school—"

"Well, Hank—," I started, with a hint of arrogance.

"I'm not finished. And you will use Dr. McCallum when you address me, you know that . . . Frankly, I'm tired of you, Christopher. You are relentlessly trying to make some sort of juvenile impression. Well, you've done it . . . I find you to be a humiliation to this school, and a humiliation in general. If it were up to me, I would have expelled you a long time ago, but the administration does not want any unwarranted expulsions. So you have gotten a lot of extra chances to straighten out. But instead, you continuously use foul words and act violently, just begging to be expelled. I will go to the administration, and *I will* get this expulsion this time. But for the benefit of us both, and because I think that you are a bright kid, I'm giving you the chance to voluntarily drop out, leaving you with the opportunity to relocate to another high school. If, however, you want to fight this like you fight so many of your peers, you will lose. And when you do, you will not be able to enroll anywhere for at least one full school year from today's date. This will seriously damage any reputation you may have left as a serious student, as well as damaging the potential for you to attend any reputable university after graduation. Think about that, Christopher. Think about it real hard. Get back to me tomorrow, and we will start the paperwork either way."

"But, sir—," I began to plead. My arrogance was gone. I wanted to be a badass but really did not want to be expelled.

"No buts about it this time, Christopher. I'll see you tomorrow."

I wanted to kill him. I actually fantasized for a moment that I was leaping over his desk and grabbing him by his soft baby blue tie and viciously pulling his face into my oncoming head. I could almost feel the crushing of his features as they smashed into the top of my skull. I wondered for a moment exactly what the reaction of his secretary would be when she opened the door after hearing morbid screaming to find that

I had perched myself on her bloodied employer like a vulture. Ripping and tearing.

Instead, I did nothing but remove myself from his office and stormed aimlessly from the school, teeth gritted and tears welling in my eyes. I was dumbfounded. I was wrecked. And most importantly, I was scared. Scared of what to do. Scared of what was ahead of me. My persona of the tough guy that could beat anyone at anything was only a good façade. I knew better. I was a flower, and my delicate pedals were wilting. My life had been changed. I was now out of my school, out of my element. I made it home somehow and waited for my father to arrive from work.

My father, who was temperamental and craved my success, knew something was amiss within five minutes of walking in the door. He had always possessed that talent for as long as I could remember. I wanted to postpone telling him the news as long as possible, but to no avail. He could see that something was up.

"So . . . what happened today?" he inquired piercingly. It came off as being part question, part statement, as he knew fully well that something indeed had happened.

"You're not gonna like it." I replied in what sounded to me like a very feminine voice. I had to be very careful with my words, as my father could potentially become infuriated with the news.

He looked at me.

"Not gonna like what?"

"Well, I sorta, . . . I sorta got kicked outta school."

"Yeah? Sorta? Sorta got kicked out? Sorta?" He paused for a while as he calmly removed his work boots. He then put his elbows on his knees and looked me right in the eyes. "Well, I sorta figured that was sorta gonna happen sooner or later at this pace. Sounds to me like it's sorta time for you to get yourself a car and sorta time for you to start waking up an hour earlier so that you can sorta drive yourself to Theo Richmond. And it sounds to me like I sorta am not putting up with this shit any longer and that you're sorta playing with your own deck of cards from now on. You get me?"

"Yeah."

"Do you sorta get me, or do you fully get me?"

"Fully get you."

"Good. Some things are meant to happen, son. Mistakes are made by everybody. That's the way it goes. But when you don't learn from the mistakes you make, you only learn to make more of them. You dig yourself a deeper and deeper hole, and pretty soon you're gonna be so far down in it that you'll never get back up again. Some people might help you by reaching down to you, and other people may even kick dirt down on top of you. But it comes down to what you do. Your actions. 'Cause when it comes down to it, it's still your hole, not theirs. That's what you're finding out real quick, isn't it?"

"Yeah."

"Yeah. No excuses anymore, Chris. This is a mistake that you need to correct on your own. Maybe it's time for you to grow up a little bit, climb back up. Hell, all the way back out if you can."

He continued to look at me for a while longer, elbows on knees. He was a good man and had worked very hard his whole life. I felt that I had let him down because he wanted me to succeed. He didn't want me to have to work as hard as he had.

But it had gone well.

Much better than I expected.

He hadn't gone over the edge, hadn't even come close. I had almost packed up my sleeping bag before he arrived, half-anticipating him to kick me out of the house. But the subject was over. He had calmly told me what he expected. He sat on the couch and put the news on for a while then made his way outside to the garden, leaving us both to our thoughts.

When I was young, I never understood the act of gardening but recognized that my father found solace in it. He desperately needed peace at that point, as I did. Tanner's death affected him differently than it affected me, but it damaged just as much.

I knew that I meant even more to him and that he had even greater expectations for me. I had to pick up the slack for my absent brother, and I wasn't doing that. I wandered around the house for a while, into my room to lie on my bed, into the bathroom to study my young face in the mirror. I looked myself directly in the eyes, searching in them for some kind of key, some course of action. Finally, I went out to the garden, to retrieve my father, to ask him a question that I no longer recall. I found him walking through the tall stalks of corn, touching the ears lightly with his fingers. He hadn't noticed me, or expected me, and he was crying. I watched him emotionally exposed for merely a second or two. But it was enough.

He turned and saw me, and saw that I knew.

There was something broken on the inside.

He stood still and looked at me, his remaining son, caring not to wipe his eyes.

"He loved this place the most, I think." he said, the fingers of one hand slow dancing with the long leaf of a stalk of corn. "Maybe even more than me. Caught him out here all the time."

I nodded. That was all I could do.

"I planted this garden years before you both were born," a flicker of a small tear on his cheek. "To escape from everything. To garden is to be self-sustained, and to be completely self-sustained is the only way to live. You can't depend on nothing from this world anymore. Everything's changed. You can only depend on yourself."

He wiped his eyes finally, with one smooth motion of the arm.

"Someone once told me that the universe will always provide. I can't remember who it was that told me that," he said, trying to disguise his torture, "but I don't agree anymore."

CHAPTER 2

My father went with me to speak with Dr. Mccallum early the next day. He went with me only to be there, for support, and nothing more. I had to handle this myself, he had said, I had to go on my own. And after a half hour in that familiar office, I did just that. It would be the last time that I would have to sit in a cheap brown chair inhaling Mccallum's cheap cologne. It would be the last time I would see the "CERTIFICATE OF DOCTORATE" proudly displayed on the far wall. It would be the last time I would see Dr. Mccallum, *the vile prick*, and it would be the last time I would set foot in the school. I had officially transferred to Theodore Richmond High.

Theodore Richmond High School was nearly an hour away from our house, and although I truly hated it, I had to wake up extremely early to make class. My father said that it was about time for me to grow up, and that waking up early is a way of taking charge of the day and aggressively facing **our** responsibilities. I listened to him, and woke up on time nearly every morning, but I felt that I still had something to prove. I felt like I needed a release of my unbridled angst and negative energy, so I still channeled it all into fierce anger toward the outside world.

The cocky, livid, sixteen-year-old young man that I had become had a new school to spoil and more minds to corrupt. I did not want to transfer there, but I was hungry with untapped anxiety to show everyone that I was not the person with whom to fuck with.

In this new school, I imagined myself as a scowling conqueror dressed in a leather jacket, consuming the butt end of a cigar after I was done smoking it. I imagined strolling down the halls in all my glory, all the guys scampering from my path, and all the girls flocking, leading with their loins, as if they were smuggling metal and I had the magnet toward such an intriguing and slightly ominous figure.

But the scenario in my fantasies didn't match the scenario in reality.

I was intimidated immediately because I didn't know a single person there. I walked directly to my assigned locker without saying a word to anybody except to the cute school receptionist who asked my last name before handing me a class schedule. I briefly fantasized about sexually ravaging her in front of the entire school—

Attempting to completely destroy her pelvis while the cheerleading squad rooted me on and the band played, the tuba and drum line matching their downbeats with my thrusts before quietly slipping into my seat for the first class. It would have been quite a first impression, I decided to myself. She did smile at me. I should have just done it. I would have been a school legend within the first hour of attendance. They would speak about me for years.

"Look at him." I heard someone behind me whisper as I sat in my desk.

Was he talking about me?

I felt a slight bit of insecurity when I turned around to face my potential adversary. But the student sitting behind me was talking to me, not about me.

"I said look at him," he whispered again, slightly louder. His head was hung low just above his desk, and his eyes were slyly directed toward the doorway of the classroom. "What a fucking freak," he stated openly. A few kids chuckled. I liked the ridiculing gent already. Someone I could immediately relate to, someone that had my taste for harassment.

The "freak" he was referring to was a slender, fragile-looking kid that had just walked stiffly into the room and immediately took his seat. He was very pale, wore glasses, with thin, uncombed brown hair that sprouted from his tiny head. His eyes looked huge through his glasses, big blue barrels of them with surely enormous blinks. He was most definitely under my definition of "freak," and his presence alone eased my insecurities. There was someone among the group that could be challenged, who would just lie there *wounded* after each insult, desperately crying inside. A victim.

I was back in my realm, nearly frothing at the mouth.

"He must be a full-blown faggot," I muttered back to my unnamed accomplice.

"It's amazing that his glasses aren't broken from all the nut sacks smacking his face," I concluded aloud.

Such a good insult. So poetic.

"I think he's mute," my fellow man of scorn said, again in a whisper, "He never says a fucking thing. Even to the teachers. They stopped calling on him for answers. He just sits there. Watching."

"Watching what?" I asked.

"Nothing, I guess. Or maybe everything. Who knows?"

"What?" I said, perplexed.

"Yeah, I guess the kid is real smart. Aces all his tests. Perfect scores on both his SAT and ACT is what I heard. A real nerd. Fucking freak genius nerd," he whispered back toward me.

"I bet he's a real pussy though. I hate those little nerd pussies," I exclaimed back to him. "Always have their damn heads in a book. I should go over there right now and show him who is so goddamned smart. Let him calculate the dimensions of my shoe when it's lodged in his ass." I emphasized each cuss. I needed to make an intense impression. This could be a kid I could definitely hang with, his mind seemed as vulgar as mine.

"Name's Jerry," the kid behind me said, recognizing my worth.

"I'm Chris," I said, smiling inside. This new school was going to be a breeze.

The "freak," I later learned, had an actual name as well—Leonard Caldwell.

The perfect prey for a graceful hunter.

I didn't even consider myself to be a bully; bullies are amateurs, and I was far above that. I was much more, an aggressor. An antagonist. If you can't pick out the fool from the people around you, then the fool is you. I was about to make little Len just another fool, despite his alleged intelligence.

It was only my second day, and I had already begun my task of exploring the depths of my insensitivity. I decided to sit directly behind "COCKwell"—the name I would now refer to him.

Heavy emphasis on COCK.

I had come prepared; butchers always should know their cuts of meat. He would break within my crushing grasp; the only question was how long he could last.

I began with what I respectively called the "Eskimoan hummer." It requires one cup of ice and one straw. Simply chew the ice into small pieces, placing one small piece at a time (or more if desired) into straw and blow. The small bits of ice are excruciatingly painful from close range when expertly shot from the straw to the back of the head or especially the ear, as Cockwell was about to soon find out.

I wrote Leonard a note, but showed my new friend Jerry first. He smiled and handed it back to me. He obviously approved of whatever plan I had in place.

I began to chew on a large chunk of ice.

> Is your name Cockwell because you can suck cock so well? Or because your ass is so huge it's like a giant wishing well for cock? Answer wrong and be punished.

I have an undeniably sinister mind.

I wanted to fancy myself an evil genius, even though I knew I wasn't really either one. I tossed the note over his right shoulder when the teacher turned.

He let it sit there.

And sit there.

And sit there.

Why wasn't he reading it? Was he blind?
Twenty minutes passed.

"It's a love note," I sarcastically whispered to him, relenting to his indifference.

He waited another five minutes.

"Open it," I said finally, trying to sound stern but almost pleading. He waited longer; then just as I was about to blow my top because I knew Jerry was going to be unimpressed, he opened it.

Then let it sit there.

And sit there.

I must say I was quite overwhelmed with his open ignorance to such a blatant threat. He knew that I could obviously hurt him, and he seemed to care less.

Time for the "hummer." I silently pulled the straw from my McDonald's biggie cup and loading it with the good-sized piece of ice that I had been chewing. I shot him directly on the back of his right ear.

It had excellent force and did not make much of a sound, so the teacher was not interrupted. It was truly a magnificent shot, and I knew that it must have really stung. He made no movement whatsoever.

The little creep didn't twitch.

He didn't fidget at all in his seat. He just continued to stare intently toward the chalkboard, motionless. I loaded another ice pellet into the straw and repeated the process, except hitting his left ear, but with the same result. No result.

This is pissing me off.

"You are pissing me off," I said to him, loud enough for the teacher to stop her chalk. The teacher, Mrs. Lindsey, knew the act of stopping her writing was warning enough to stop the class mischief. The class was silent, and I expected her to turn around and discipline me; but after some deliberation, she merely continued on with her written instructions.

So I shot him again and again.

No result.

Other kids watched in silence, in amazement. Mrs. Lindsey stayed oblivious to my antics and continued rambling and scribbling notes. Caldwell stayed oblivious to the world around him.

He must be in agony, but very good at hiding it.

I tried another tactic. I pushed my freshly sharpened no. 2 (standard) pencil deeply into the back of his neck, forcing the lead tip deep into his flesh. I can assure you that this really, really hurts; yet he still never moved, even after a trickle of blood had drawn. I could not believe it.

After about three minutes of forceful penetration to his skin, which would have been sure torture to any normal human being, I released my pressure. I looked at the mark I had made and saw a small red pinpoint in his neck, probably one-fourth-inch deep. Then he dropped my note back to me. I opened it up to read his reply. There was only one word scribbled under my previous writing.

BELL.

His timing was perfect. The moment I finished reading the word, the school bell rang, ending sixth period.

My first car was a 1984 Dodge Daytona. The car truly taught me one thing about how to choose the right car for durability, handling, gas mileage, etc. That one thing is never, under any circumstances excluding castration and/or death, buy a Dodge Daytona.

All of the meters were shot, it sucked gas faster than a porn starlet would if she were trapped in the tank, and the passenger door only opened from the inside. The tires were always nearly bald, the steering column was shot, alignment was shot, windshield spiderwebbed on the lower half, power steering and all interior lights inoperative, and it would start to shake violently if it was driven faster than sixty-five miles per hour.

I had barely enough cash to put gas in the thing, much less keep up with general maintenance. The car proved to be potentially dangerous on repeated occasions, but since it never turned into a complete disaster, I drove on. It never truly occurred to me that simply driving the beast could result in my immediate death; instead, I was rather more concerned with getting a little action in the damaged leather backseat.

"It's called the reentry module, baby," I said to all the girls who were absolutely terrified by the vehicle's looks alone. It was my name for it, as its black paint had pealed, so it actually resembled an object that could have been scorched as it entered our atmosphere.

The re-entry module, disgusting as it was in its aesthetics, gave me excuses to not bully all the time. I slowly became distant from my little torture friend. He really never showed any reaction to any of my various insults, taunts, or even inductions of pain anyway and was no longer any fun to pick on. I learned to give up on his worthlessness and had moved on to bigger and better things, namely, the fresh supply of high school women, many of whom had yet the pleasure of my introduction. My pubescent body hungered for sexuality more than air, it seemed, so my violence came a distant second to my loins.

One dark night, I found myself driving home, alone.

I was returning from a bad first date with a girl named Connie or Carrie or Carly.

I don't really remember her name.

If it had come up in our short conversation, I had forgotten about it. Her name wasn't what I was after.

It was nearly eleven o'clock, as the dreadful movie that she recommended lasted much longer than it should have. I tried to kiss her on many occasions during the romantic comedy, but that became the true comedy in itself. She turned her head the first time, forcing me to kiss her cheek in some form of awkward reconciliation. I bumped her teeth with mine the second time, and the third time, she simply said, "Stop, I want to see this part." Oddly, it was the point in the movie where the hero kisses the damsel in distress.

The movie ended, and I walked her outside to the re-entry module, where I figured I would get the chance to kiss her outside before we drove away. The car was strategically parked blocks away from the movie theatre, which gave me ample time to make a move.

As we exited the cinema, we noticed Mother Nature had different ideas and decided it was time for rain. Lots and lots of rain.

We ran through the storm, and even though she was clearly yelling, "Why did you have to park so far away?" I could barely hear her through the torrents. Needless to say, when we got in the car, she wasn't exactly thrilled about how everything was going, and it became obvious after I made her wait for a few more seconds while I opened her door from the inside. As I drove her home, the car was mostly filled with tension and few words.

She said "Thanks," both sarcastically and ungraciously, and hurried to exit the car and get back into her dry home and dry clothes. I drove away while listening to the radio loud, deciding that I would probably never get to see her naked.

My own house was located out of town, in a rural area. I drove, and the buildings of town grew sparse then changed into trees that lined the road. The rain poured heavy on my windshield, and I wondered if its weight alone could crack it more.

Then, in my high beams as they cut through the rain, I saw a figure walking on the right side of the road, facing away from me, hitchhiking in the dark and downpour. I first thought that he might be an apparition or a figment of my imagination, but as my headlamps splashed against him, I realized that whoever this is was truly *just an idiot*.

The person was actually hitchhiking in the middle of nowhere in a thunderstorm. I don't know if I felt actually sorry for him, or if I somehow stopped due to my own pure perplexity, but I slowed my car and pulled over in front of him. I reached over, turned the radio down, and opened the door for him.

The figure turned out to be none other than a soaked Leonard Caldwell.

COCKwell.

He closed the door without a word and stared straight ahead, casually.
COCKwell. In my car.

The dove had calmly laid itself within the paws of the hungry lion, directly in front of the uncaged beast. The magnificent lion, powerful and capable of crushing, mutilating, then devouring the defenseless dove, was instead bewildered by the dove's actions. The lion simply stared at the dove. Instead of smiling and revealing teeth that would soon be stained with the blood of his helpless victim, the lion slowly released the clutch (slowly, just like mother lion had taught him) and drove his 1984 Dodge Daytona onward through the rain.
I just drove. I didn't say anything, and he didn't either of course.
I drove some more.
We rode through the night in complete silence, except for the pattering of water on the roof and windows. I didn't ask him where he was going, and he didn't tell me. I didn't reach down to turn the radio louder again. I just drove.
The silence became awkward, and soon the awkwardness became uncomfortable. Then, this lack of comfort gnawed at my brain. It was a terrible feeling, like I had just kissed a girl for the first time and then been informed it was my younger sister.
Strange.
He was just listless, simply sitting there, staring through the windshield.
Then it dawned on me.
Why should I feel uncomfortable? This dumb ass is in MY CAR, and I am the one that feels uncomfortable? No, no, no, no, no. I am the one that shows his wrath, not the one that feels like a stranger in his own home. I am in control here. I am.
I was driving and had the power to do anything I wanted. I had been trying to intimidate Leonard for months, without so much as a flinch from him, and now found myself presented with the perfect way of doing so. He couldn't do a thing about it either. I was going to have the time of my life, and—*the little prick*—would literally be along for the ride. I looked over at him *weakling* and stomped the gas, viewing his reaction. He just continued to stare blankly out the window, with a *stupid* blank stare.

"You should have stayed in the rain," I said menacingly. I shifted into fourth gear and jammed down the gas even farther. The Daytona actually responded convincingly. The road ahead was barely shown by my lights before it was instantly pulled under my hood and replaced by another two-second stretch of scenery before that was consumed by speed as well. I pretended that Daytona was a bullet from the chamber of a gun, and I wondered for a second if the nerd next to me had shit his pants yet. I would estimate that I was easily doing eighty-five in a thirty-five, and I was beginning to seriously scare even myself. This was definitely the fastest I had ever pushed the rickety Daytona.

The rain slammed down, and the highway quickly skewed left, forcing me to turn tightly, my bald tires squealing on the damp asphalt in protest. The Daytona held the road, and I saw a decent straight stretch of double lane displayed in my headlights.

Open road.

We were seriously moving, and I was having a great time. The frame of the car itself began to tremble, with the interior door panel on Leonard's side visibly coming apart.

Definitely a wonderful touch.

My chuckles were suppressed when I noticed *COCKwell* was still sitting in his same position, with the same goddamned miserable expression on his face. In the midst of my juvenile taunting and reckless behavior, he maintained a look of complete indifference.

I pressed the gas all the way to the floor and depressed the clutch to shift into fifth gear. The headlamps of the car flickered through the rain, and my visibility with this speed and weather was heavily impaired. I strained to look ahead, yet still driving insanely enough to scare—*the well from the cock.*

My car was screaming ahead into darkness and rain.

Suddenly, I saw the road verge quickly to the right. I knew I would never make it. I immediately hit the brakes, but they were practically useless with the bald tires and wet road, so the car slid straight ahead as if we were on ice.

A clump of brush and trees zoomed in ominously from ahead, and even though I stiffened my leg against the brakes as hard as I could in panic, the Daytona careened forward. The wheel was almost locked with the damage I'd done to the steering column, and my last effort was to try and tug the car right furiously, but to no avail. The Daytona pushed on, aiming directly for a large wall of trees and brush on the far side of the road.

My hands gripped the wheel like they were set there in cement, and I skidded right over the double yellow lines, across the other side of the road, and into the embankment.

It happened in an instant, the car instantly off the road and jerking down, following the sudden steep terrain. A mixture of headlights and shifting foliage droned by, and different plants slammed against the car. I instantly resolved we were both about to die when through the screen of the roaring windshield, I saw a large pine tree transport itself directly into the headlights and directly into us.

The car crackled and shuddered as it met the tree with tremendous force. In the same moment, I heard the windshield shatter, just before the steering wheel crashed into my face.

I heard screaming.

The headlights went out and everything went dark.

I think I just woke up.
Cold liquid accumulated around my waist.
I think I just woke up.

I realized I had not, not at least in my bed at home where I usually woke. I had not woken from a bad dream. I had just woken up, but from being knocked completely unconscious. I realized that this car crash—*is real* was really happening.

It was pitch black, and I could see nothing. I coughed and spat out a little water. The water had contained fragments of something solid, and I distinguished it must be my own broken teeth.

The water *is ice* was cold, unbearably cold.

I felt a tremendous pressure against my left knee, and my face felt as if it had been squarely crushed in with a baseball bat. Oddly enough, the warm blood that gushed freely from my head actually felt good in contrast to the frigid water rushing in over me.

My right eye began to grow accustomed to the darkness around me, but my left eye displayed nothing. I reviewed my situation in a state of complete panic.

I heard my tongue click as I drew air.

I was lodged between my seat and the driver door, and I could see the outline of black water streaming in through the mangled windshield, splashing down across the dashboard. The car was partially submerged into what I assumed must be a stream or a river. My left knee was tightly wedged under the steering wheel, and even as I thrashed about violently, I was unable to dislodge it.

I could only move my right arm due to the fact I was completely pinned into the driver's side, which was actually the lowest side of the car. The driver side window was still up and unshattered, and due to gravity, my face pressed against it. The windshield was crushed in toward me along with the roof of the car, creating a gap in which the water was pouring through. The whole left side of my body was almost completely numb, probably from both the freezing water that I was becoming increasingly immersed in, as well as the terrible injuries that I most definitely had. I swallowed more tiny bits of my own teeth as I tried to breathe deeply. They were probably my front teeth, I determined, because my tongue continually ran itself of the sharp spikes and fragments that remained. I attempted again to pull myself out, and again realized that I was too tightly pinned by the steering wheel to move anything but my right arm . . .

Cold, sooo c . . . o . . . l . . . d . . .

There was also nothing that I could grab with my free right arm that would provide me leverage to pull against, and the steering wheel was too tight against my body to push away from. I tried to grip at the partially submerged passenger seat, but the icy water allowed my fingers no command. To be overwhelmed with fear is seeing an actual verge of insanity.

With each breath, my left leg shocked bitter pain through my body. The glacial water continued to pour in over me, and I felt it rising higher.

I cried out. I cried out in the hope that my life would be worth saving. I slammed my right fist against the steering wheel in painful agony. I pulled at it as hard as I could.

I am going to drown.

I thrashed around again. I pulled but released nothing. For the first time in my life, I was struggling for my life.

The water made progress like it always does. It had risen many feet since I came to and seeped up around my shoulders. I had not moved. I could feel my heart pound at my chest, and I thought for a moment that it was just simply going to burst. I thrashed the best I could through the water, hoping to somehow free myself. I felt my knee crack, and a sharp electric pain burst up my leg with any movement.

Jammed too tight to move.

I was helpless. I was going to die in this Daytona water pit, and then I was going to go to hell immediately after. I imagined myself being skinned alive by the devil himself within his fiery pits, and I almost longed for it. I was just too cold and in too much unbearable pain.

Take me away from this!

The icy water reached its way up into the car, and would probably soon seep into my soul, as it crept its way around my throat like a gentle grip of death. I moved my head up with the rising of the water, keeping my mouth and nose as far up above it as possible.

Exhale quickly, inhale deeply.

My neck strained, and my head cranked to stay up as far as it would go. The water rose farther, and its frigidity was pure. I could feel the whole core of my body getting numb, and I moved my fingers to see if I still could. I wasn't sure if they did or not.

I'm already starting to shut down.

Both my thoughts and my body were becoming truly disoriented and disconnected from each other.

Hypothermia must be setting in, My eyes searched frantically for any way out.

I'm shutting down. Shut . . . ting . . . do . . . wn . . .

I soon gulped on the chilling water, trying to spit it back. It only continued coming. Penetrating its way into my car and up around my throat.

into this. I couldn't stop it.

Stop it.

I was buried in its swirling black tides. I tilted my head back to inhale one last swallow of precious air and closed my eyes. I actually thought I heard my brain whispering to me, as the dark liquid began creeping in up my nose. My thoughts were definitely whispering a little nursery rhyme. Something to put me to sleep.

"Sleep, sleep in gentle slumber, in this grand game of bingo, God just pulled your number."

I had seen an older lady saying this on a television rerun somewhere.

I was slipping quickly into unconsciousness. I was losing my reality,

And

it was being involuntarily

replaced with disillusion.
Water Water Water Water Water
    Water Water Water
        Water Water
          Water
          Water
            Water
              Water
            Water
          Water
        Water
      Water
pouring in.
I think.
Are you there, brain?
    Yes, sir, I believe that I am.
    And thank you too, kind sir.
    My brain—
The old lad—was singing me a little lullaby before he tucked me in and shut out the lights. Despite the water, I felt warm.

cozy and warm.

    Time to **go . . .**
    A wonderful tingly feeling wrapped around me. I had forgotten where I was again.
    Was I back in bed? I sure am.
                                                    Aren't I?

    The water brushed up against my forehead like a soft kiss. I wanted to kiss back. *just a little goodnight kiss.*
    I thought this might be—*a dream, dream . . . dream . . . dream . . . and it's all going swimmingly.*
    It felt warm inside the car, or my bed, wherever I deemed I was. Dry inside. Dry inside.
    Little pig, little pig, let me in.

    Swim.

Swimmingly.
It felt dry inside the car, or my bed, wherever I deemed I was. Warm inside. Warm inside.
I used to drink gallons of the stuff, but my drinking days are over, clover. They have a wicked way of rearrangin'.
I saw a lowly bird that clipped its wing somewhere in my head.
All just flapping around, looking good while we kiss the ground.
It wants to sip gently from cool blue waters. Putting the little beak in. Daintily sipping, filling its little bird belly. Sometimes I just need a little bath. Something soapy. A warm bubble bath will do.
Is this—
The water felt nice and bubbly warm.
—my life—
I imagined the pungent sound if it were raised to a much more considerable temperature.
—flashing—
Maybe I too could drink gently at the waters swirling around me, I rationalized. *Around me.*
Swirling.
—before my eyes?
How 'bout that? Splashing and laughing, wetting my insides.
Letting the fluids begin. Let them all in.
My friends, my friends.
Gurgling and spraying.
All the little
Tricks
they are playing.
I thought of my mother and how she looked when I was younger. She was smiling and running away from me as I chased her. The sunlight lit her hair, so it was as bright as her youthful expressions. She was laughing in this dream, but I couldn't hear it or see her mouth doing it because she was running away from me. But I knew she was laughing.
Tickling, the soft warm water.
Gargle it down like I used to do after the toothpaste. Refreshment.
like no other, brother. Like no other.

The water had me as dominated as the pain did.
Madness.

Then I was rudely snapped out of my sleepy daze by something tightly clamped around my arm.

A hand?

I had awakened again, to a world that I wanted to leave behind. The water was cold again, frigid actually, and it was unbearable. It also was no longer trying to kiss me. It was trying to burrow its way down my throat.

Choking me, infecting me.

I was covered in chaos, frantically reaching for reason. The world inside the flooded car was spinning faster than a top. But my mind was still singing:

Giant steps are what you take,
Walking on the moon
I hope my legs don't break
Walking on the moon
We could walk forever
Walking on the moon
We could be together
Walking on, walking on the moon.

I gasped for air. Instead, my lungs brutally filled with water. They strained with the unexpectedness. I choked and convulsed as I tried to spew it out. Something still held my flailing right wrist and was pulling. I was completely underwater, and I opened my eyes. I choked again; the water went nowhere.

Black water.

The grip was unbearably strong, and it felt like my hand was in a vice. *Tremendous pressure.*

I gasped in absolute pain. I tried to hold my head above the water, but it kept going under. I was now inhaling only fluids, and they hissed as they crept into my throat and nose. My body jerked as it tried to reject the streaming intake, and my left leg twisted. There was a gurgling in my ears, and I realized that I was hearing myself suffocate. Yet something continued to yank upon my arm with fierce commitment, bringing excruciating pain up from my left leg with each mighty pull. My left knee was definitely being ripped; I could feel something torn and tearing. I howled and screamed, or at least inside my head, as I had been muted by the fluid in my lungs. Gasping for oxygen to raise a voice, my torso convulsed without it. I heard gurgling all around me, the bubbles trying to consume me, as I consumed them. I coughed, or vomited, trying to expel it all. My chest contracted with a powerful thrust of pain and desperation.

I still continued to be forcefully pulled. Time was running out. I felt the absence of oxygen finding its way to my brain now.

Upward, something jerking savagely at my arm.

My left knee was lodged tightly perpendicular to the wheel, voiding the upward pulling. I knew that I would not be conscious much longer. My throat and stomach seemed to burst out and my muscles tensed and bunched, constricting my simplest movements. Then I felt my knee give way, and my body floated free just before I blacked out.

Everything was blurry, just odd shapes and dark colors, but I heard someone speaking very quietly nearby. In my state of disorientation, I could not tell where I was. I could hear someone, somewhere, softly. There was talking at a level between a whisper and a scream. It seemed if I was just barely hearing them, but at the same time their words were echoing inside my head. I hurt everywhere, I wanted to pass out again, the pain was simply too intense.

I'm breathing air again, feels nice.

My eyes finally grew focused on my surroundings, and I saw that I was lying on a weedy bank near a small creek, with the little Leonard kid sitting next to me with his shirt off. He seemed to intermix with the weeds and the darkness, silhouetted somehow within the shadows.

Crickets chirping.

He seemed to appear, only to fade from view again, and reappear just faintly in the foreground with the stalks of the dark plants. Only sparse clips of his hair shown through the black mud that caked his face and head. A partially submerged Daytona headlight shown faintly from the muddy waters of the creek that had just nearly taken my life. The headlamp glittered diagonally up into the sky like an elderly beacon. Faintly winking up at the heavens. I found it fitting.

The pain was more excruciating than anything I could ever even fathom. I knew that my left leg, somewhere down below my waist, covered in mud, with the kid's blood-soaked T-shirt tied around it, was in bad shape. I knew it because I could not feel individual parts of the leg itself, just a general area of pain where my leg should be. We were both on a muddy bank that gradually sloped toward the small rippling creek below. We were nestled within in a land of reeds and rocks that were just faintly illuminated by the moon caressing itself through the outlined trees. I was tired, absolutely drained, maybe half dead. The throbbing in my body and the realization of what I had just been through were the only things that were keeping me conscious.

He was talking gibberish. A fluid stream of gibberish.

Wasn't he? Or is that me?

"*Qui existo unus,*" I thought I heard. "*Qui existo, aetus de mei advenio.*"

He paused. I heard myself breathe long, raspy breaths. He was talking steadily, yet quietly, to no one in particular.

Maybe I heard other voices, I couldn't be sure.

"*Qui existo unus,*" he said again. "*Qui existo, aetus de mei advenio.*"

The mud around my elbows felt reassuringly warm. I lay my weary head back into it.

"*Let me become the only one. Let me be, my time has come.*" He barely screamed. It was almost as if I was only thinking that he was speaking.

He paused longer this time. And my head throbbed.

"*It's an early form of Latin. A dead language. Probably the most formidably constructed languages of man. And it's lost. Lost like our minds and hearts.*"

He is speaking to me, or is he?

"*Dwindled away . . .*"

And he was silent. He seemed to be talking to himself, but talking to me at the same time. The words almost drifted in from a great distance.

"What are you talking about?" I think I asked aloud.

Was that me talking?

Words spoken by a voice that sounded like mine seemed crisp against the darkness around us. I was so disillusioned; I did not know who was who or what was what.

He did not reply. I wanted to ask him again but had forgotten his name. Forgotten how to speak actually, or maybe just too weak. So I said nothing more, even when he pulled me up, in a state of furious pain. I was nauseous and cold but slung my right arm over his shoulder. He pulled me up the small embankment and up to the road from which I had just hastily diverted. I slopped down onto the pavement, weak and ravaged. The world was twisting around me, flailing like a carnival. I remember a car stopping, with punishing headlights, staring right at us.

Maybe through us.

I was a drunk actor on a stage, not moving like I should, missing my lines. I struggled to stay conscious, but everything had melded together into a blurry soup. I felt the winds twirl around in my head, forcing dizziness upon me. A sliver of moon shone down upon me as well, giving my blurry world a metallic tint. Soon, like a violent flood, it all washed me away and pulled me under, somewhere into the depths below. I blacked out again.

Weeks passed, like a movie that I could hardly stay awake for, and so I had temporarily forgotten about my life. I had been quieted.

The doctors were telling me that my left leg (which was broken in several places), left knee (which had torn ligaments and tendons), left arm (which was also broken and dislocated from the shoulder), and ribs (two broken, two bruised) would take quite some time to heal. I also had the pleasure of having my jaw wired shut for it, too, was severely broken.

"He is lucky to be alive," was repeated like it was a broken record.

Being bedridden, unable to walk without unbridled pain, eating meals from a straw, communicating with notes, as well as realizing that I almost died, sincerely humbled me. I read books for the first time in my life without being persuaded to do so for a grade. I enjoyed riddling my brain with questions that I knew I could never answer. I hungered for information instead of brutality and debauchery. I enjoyed moments of complete silence. It was reconciliation within my soul for all the evil I once harbored.

I lay there staring at the little white bumps of the hospital's ceiling, wondering if a person in my state (of mind and body) could ever be cured. I would come to realize that I could.

I grew to become a nonviolent, fully repentant person. I wondered how the person that I used to be could even willfully exist. I was no longer a violent person because I no longer strained to be. When I finally went back to school, over three months later, I went back as different person.

I was in a wheelchair for the first two weeks back at Theo Richmond. The wheelchair, for those who are lucky enough never to know, is a mental dichotomy. The wheelchair itself first is truly the only means of transportation of the disabled person. It allows free movement using one's own power, and in that sense, personifies freedom. On the other hand, the wheelchair itself is confinement, never allowing its user to wrestle free from its grasp. It also becomes a label of being handicapped, showing onlookers that a certain sense of freedom does not exist. This applied to me. I was relieved to be able to move around again, to leave my bed; yet, as I rolled through the familiar hallways of Theo Richmond High School, I felt imprisoned in that wheelchair. I could feel the staring fellow students, their poison gaze infiltrating my core. However, I gritted my teeth weakly (as my jaw had not fully healed) and pulled the wheels of the chair into Algebra III.

He was there, in his usual seat, second from the front. With much effort, I managed to cram my wheelchair past him and behind him. I said nothing, as that was the most I could say with a wired jaw, and he, as usual, said nothing back. The teacher commenced with his tutoring, and I was left wondering how I had come to hate the slender kid in front of me. I wondered how I had come to hate anyone at all for that matter. Hate. Even the word has a cruel sound when omitted from tongue or thought in mind.

Hate is a four-letter word, which makes it similar to the four-letter word love. Hate should be a nine-hundred-letter word, making it impossible to pronounce and as dissimilar to love as possible. I promised myself I would never hate again.

For the first time, I intently studied life. Especially the life of the boy that sat in front of me. The boy who had saved my life. I was now fascinated by everything living in general, for I had tasted death and found it simply distasteful. I wanted to nurture life.

He sat there, just in front of me. I first thought that he was absorbing what the teacher was displaying, but then it seemed that he was intently concentrating on his own inner thoughts. He scribbled some things down on the paper in front of him and then continued to sit peacefully. The kid looked menacingly small to me somehow. He was a fragile feather that looked as if it would snap from the slightest resistance, but was actually reinforced with steel. Disguised. Perfectly disguised. The kid was strong, I knew this. He had pulled all 180 pounds of me—*literally dripping wet*—from a collapsed car with one arm, in ice cold water. Yet he looked as if an eyelash that lightly fell upon him would crush in his skull.

He scribbled another note down in the book in front of him. I would have tried to sit up farther in my seat to see what he was writing, but the pain restricted me from doing so.

So I wrote him.

> **What are you doing?**

He replied then handed the note back.

> **CONTEMPLATING.**

I scribbled another generic question.

> **Contemplating what?**

He took his time. He stayed there without moving for quite a time then finally wrote something. I expected Shakespeare or some philosophical reasoning or some theory on life, my life maybe. This is what I got.

> **O**

What? What is that supposed to mean? Is that a zero, or the letter O, or is he contemplating nothing, as the zero would imply, or is the kid mocking me? He probably thinks that he is really powerful for saving my life and now has the right to play games with me.

I felt a little bit of my old anger return. But I stopped myself.

The kid is really not the type to mock others, especially me. He saved my life for God's sake. He wouldn't cheapen himself like that.

The bell rang, and he dropped another note in front of me. As it did, I scooped it up, put it in my left shirt pocket, and pulled my busted left leg back onto the step of the wheelchair that I had been in for an agonizing hour and a half. With a flick of (mostly my right) wrists, I rolled myself out of the classroom.

Later that night, I almost had forgotten about the note, and it probably would have been eaten up by the washing machine. But it fell from my pocket when I took my pants off before going to bed. I read the note by the light of my bedside lamp, and I became even more perplexed than ever.

ZERO. THERE IS NO SUCH THING. IT IS HUMAN FABRICATION. PLATO WAS WRONG. TO THINK THAT SCIENTISTS ACTUALLY BELIEVE THAT THE UNIVERSE EVOLVED FROM NOTHING. A "BIG BANG," THEY SAY. MOLECULES OF ENERGY THAT FUSED AND EXPLODED INTO LIFE. RUBBISH. CHARACTERIZED AS FACT. ARE MOLECULES NOTHING? IS ENERGY NOTHING? IS MEMORY NOTHING? IS THOUGHT NOTHING? ISN'T THOUGHT THE FATHER OF GOD? IF GOD HAD NOTHING, NOT EVEN HIMSELF IN EXISTENCE, WOULDN'T THE MERE CONCEPTION OF THE UNIVERSE, THE TRUE FIRST THOUGHT, BE THE ACTUAL BIRTH OF THE UNIVERSE, AND IN TURN, GOD HIMSELF?

THERE IS NO SUCH THING AS NOTHING. THE VERY NOTION OF IT MAKES IT AN IMPOSSIBLE TASK. A MISINTERPRETATION OF VOLUME MULTIPLIED TO EXTREME PROPORTIONS. (OR DIVIDED BY EXTREME PROPORTIONS.)

LET US USE "THE" FACTS.

THE MATH: $1-1=0$

RIGHT?

IF JOHNNY HAS AN ORANGE, AND SUZY TAKES AWAY THAT ORANGE, JOHNNY IS LEFT WITH NOTHING, RIGHT? $1-1=0$

RIGHT?

WRONG!!!

JOHNNY STILL REMEMBERS THE ORANGE BEING THERE. HE CAN STILL SMELL THE SLIGHTEST SCENT OF CITRUS EMANATING FROM HIS HAND. HE STILL KNOWS THAT THE ORANGE WAS ONCE HIS. HE KNOWS, REMEMBERS, SMELLS. WHAT'S THE MATHEMATICAL EQUATION FOR THAT? JOHNNY MAY NOT HAVE THE ORANGE ANYMORE BUT HE WILL ALWAYS HAVE MORE THAN ZERO ORANGES. HE WILL ALWAYS KNOW ABOUT THE ORANGE, HAVE A PLACE IN HIS CONSCIOUSNESS FOR IT. IF IT EXISTS IT CAN NEVER BE TAKEN AWAY. SIMPLY BEING CONSCIOUS OF SOMETHING, OR ANYTHING, IS CREATING

AN EXISTENCE. AN EXISTENCE THAT WILL ALWAYS BE MORE THAN NOTHING. MORE THAN ZERO.

ZERO IS IMPOSSIBLE.

SO THEREFORE, IF ZERO IS OUR FOUNDATION OF WHAT WE BELIEVE TO BE TRUE AND THEREFORE ESSENTIAL TO MODERN THEORIES OF MATHEMATICS, ALL THEORIES OF MATHEMATICS THAT WE, HUMANS, HAVE COME TO ACCEPT MUST BE DISCARDED.

AS AN EXAMPLE, IF WE APPLY OUR MATH TO HISTORY THEN THERE HAS NEVER BEEN AN ALBERT EINSTEIN OR A SHAKESPEARE. THEY WERE NEVER HERE BECAUSE THEY ARE NOT HERE NOW. YOUR GREAT GRANDFATHER NEVER EXISTED, OR I WILL NO LONGER EXIST IF I LEAVE THE ROOM. ALL MY THOUGHTS; MEANINGLESS. MY LIFE, YOUR LIFE, OUR LIVES; GONE.

*What the hell was he jabbering on about? Everyone knows that zero exists. It's mathematical law! We all learned it in school, in like the second grade. It is like the stars in the sky, like the oxygen in the air. It is there, and everybody knows it. We may not be able to see it with the naked eye, but that doesn't make it fictional. We know that there is a zero like we know that the sun is hot and the Earth is round ... **The Earth is round.*** But then, thinking that thought, I decided to reread his note. And reread it again. After understanding exactly what he was saying, I reconsidered my opinion of it. Maybe he had a point. Maybe he was on to something. I asked myself a question. How do we know something is true? Because someone else tells us? Do I know that the sun is hot because I've physically touched it? No, but I have felt its heat, so I do know that. But what if, what if the sun is so completely cold to such an extreme that its tremendous frigidity chemically burns? Makes it feel hot? Or maybe the sun is merely "room temperature" and that life itself in reality is much cooler, so that it gives the illusion that the sun is in fact "hot." Highly unlikely, but I liked the way I was thinking. I was actually re-thinking. I liked that fact that I was dismissing "fact."

We know that the Earth is in fact round, but just a little more than five hundred years ago, you would be proclaimed mad to think so. The

Earth was flat back then because the consensus was that it was. The population was taught that it was. So it was. It took someone to prove it wrong before the thought became accepted.

I liked this. I liked it a lot. I read it again. I liked it even more. Len really had a point. I read it again. He really had a point. He was dismissing what we think that we know, but what we cannot prove. Just because you have a belief, it never means that you have a verdict. Anything, and I mean anything, is truly possible. Len was telling me that we should never think that the world is flat, and I realized that in a way, it is a possibility we still do.

I soon began to understand who Len Caldwell really was, or so I thought. He was terribly antisocial because he chose to be. He wasn't frightened of everyone around him, as I had once thought, but instead usually chose not to communicate. People, to him, were mostly entertaining, yet shallow and unfulfilling. He wanted something more, something, as I had come to believe, that most could not provide. As I finished out the remainder of my junior year, I continued to communicate with him as much as I could. I had a feeling that he knew a lot more than he was ever willing to admit to me, and along with the fact that he saved my life, I truly respected him. But he rarely answered any of my questions, and the few that he did, he wrote down on paper. When I think about it, the only time that I heard him speak was after he pulled me from my car and saved my life, although I couldn't quite recollect exactly what he had said.

Something that puzzled me involved the police report on the accident (which led to a ticket being written to me for reckless endangerment). The strange thing was the report clarified that "the passenger, Leonard Caldwell, was thrown from the passenger's side of the vehicle before the vehicle descended completely below to Miller's Creek." (This also was the only time Len was mentioned in the report.) Now, the part of Len being thrown from the Daytona may have been true, but when I later went to the scrapyard to see if there was anything to salvage from the car, I noticed that the driver's side window was up. Fully closed. The car had electronic windows, and as it had always been a pile of trash, especially now, and the passenger controls for the window had never worked, the window had to be opened from the driver's side. And during the accident, it would have been physically impossible for me to have pushed my button to roll it down, as my left arm was incapacitated. Even so, if someone had been able to push the window control, it would have been a useless act, as the car had died and was left without internal power. This left only two options in which Leonard could have been able to pull me from the car.

The first was through the partially shattered windshield, which was completely submerged and with an open space of only a few inches to pull my body through. Not likely.

The second most logical way would mean forcing open the passenger door after climbing upon the elevated passenger side, as the car lay on the driver's side in the creek. Let me point out the fact that, like most cars, the door of a 1994 Dodge Daytona swings outward, which meant that he would have to swing it *upward* to have opened it. Then, he would have to reach in toward the driver's side door to reach me, a distance roughly four feet from the door. He would also have to somehow hold the door open while grabbing me and pulling me out from below. Remember that I was in fact submerged in water and pinned by the steering wheel. It was simply a remarkable feat of strength, especially for a kid that was half my size. Not quite impossible, I would guess, but nearly.

I also began to notice that the teacher had never called on him for an answer in class, and he never talked or seemed to communicate with anybody else. To the untrained eye, the class may look as if they were in a continual act of ignoring Leonard.

So I watched him, while no one else did.

He was constantly studying his surroundings. Then he would scrupulously write down notes in one of his journals (he carried several) for ten minutes or so, and return to surveying for an indefinite amount of time. I managed to sneak a peak at his writings a few times, but only managed to see words or equations that were mostly unintelligible to me. So one day I wrote him a note.

What are you writing about?

YOU WOULDN'T UNDERSTAND. JUST NOTATIONS.

I don't care. I just want to see what you're writing.

He hesitated for a few moments. Then he closed his notebook and passed it back over his shoulder. He was right. I didn't have a clue. The entirety of his journal was written in some form of his own personal shorthand, resembling childish scribbles and jumbled words, but the majority of the book seemed to contain elaborate mathematical equations that would run quite often the entirety of ten pages long. Some pages were written in English, usually reserved for scientific formulae, or for small thoughts or quotes, but the majority of the scripts were indecipherable to me. He also possessed exceptional drawing and sketching ability that would randomly appear throughout the diary. Oh, the fact that all of the pages that were written on were nearly completely filled with text or drawing of some sort was also impressive. He wasted nearly any space at all, any**where**. Even though I could barely understand a word, I took a long while examining what seemed to be a continual stream of consciousness and personal epiphanies.

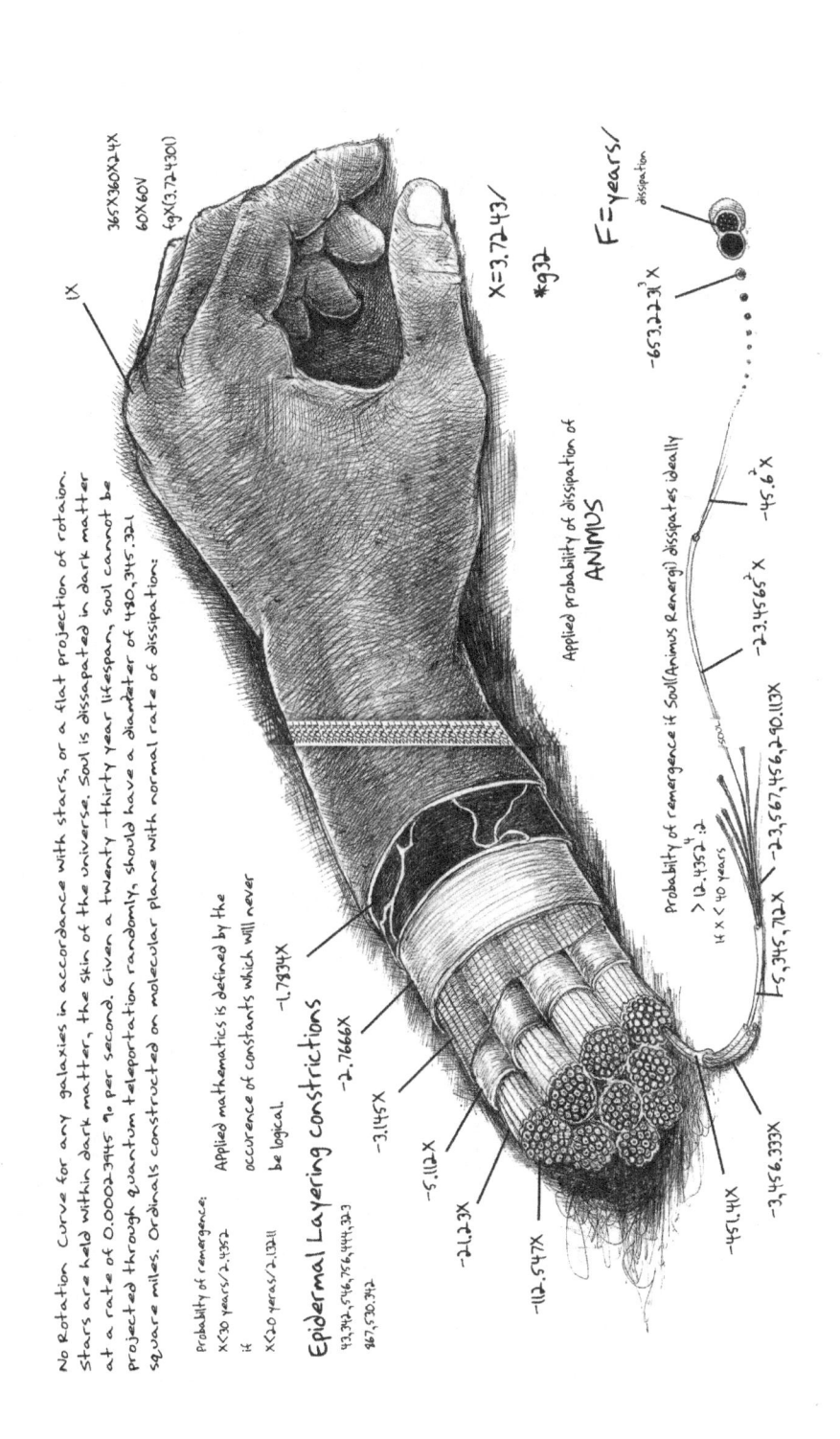

No rotation curve for any galaxies in accordance with stars, or a flat projection of rotation. Stars are held within dark matter, the skin of the universe. Soul is dissipated in dark matter at a rate of 0.00023945% per second. Given a twenty-thirty year lifespan, soul cannot be projected through quantum teleportation randomly, should have a diameter of 480,345.321 square miles. Ordinals constructed on molecular plane with normal rate of dissipation.

Probability of remergence:
X<30 years/2.4352
if
X<20 years/2.13411
967,530.742

Epidermal Layering constrictions
43,342,546,756,444,323

Applied mathematics is defined by the occurence of constants which will never be logical.

1X

366X360X24X
60X60V
fg(3.72-4301)

X=3.72-43/
*932

Applied probability of dissipation of ANIMUS

Probability of remergence if Soul(Animus Renergi) dissipates ideally
> 12.4352⁴
14 X < 40 years

F = years / dissipation

−653,223¹X
−45.6²X
−23,565²X
−5,345,702X
−23,567,456.10.1(3)X
−3.145X
−2.7666X
−1.7934X
−5.112X
−21.23X
−112.547X
−749.141X
−3.9651⁻

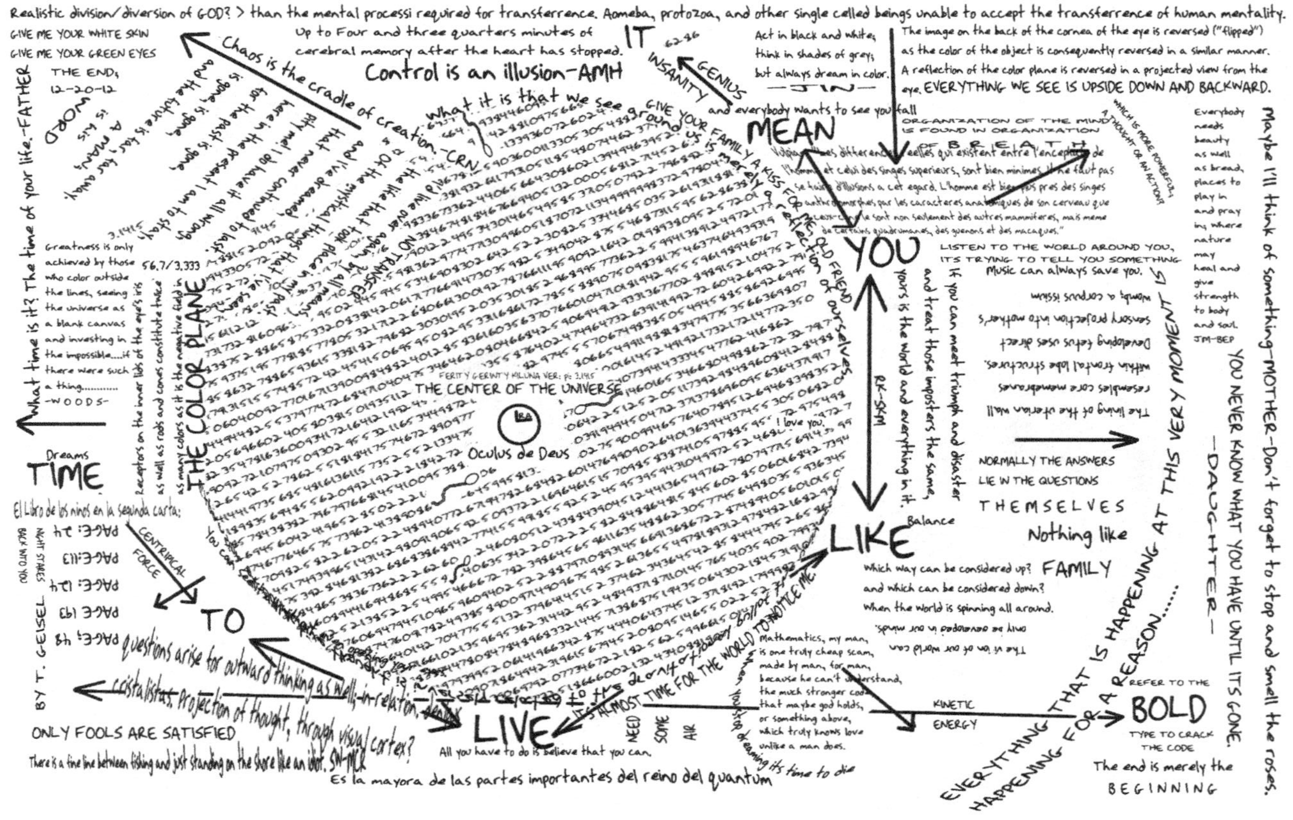

Realistic division/diversion of GOD? > than the mental processi required for transferrence. Aomeba, protozoa, and other single celled beings unable to accept the transferrence of human mentality.
GIVE ME YOUR WHITE SKIN
GIVE ME YOUR GREEN EYES
THE END, 12-20-12
Up to Four and three quarters minutes of cerebral memory after the heart has stopped.
Control is an illusion-AMH
IT
GENIUS
INSANITY
Act in black and white, think in shades of grey, but always dream in color.
—JIN—
The image on the back of the cornea of the eye is reversed ("flipped") as the color of the object is consequently reversed in a similar manner. A reflection of the color plane is reversed in a projected view from the eye. EVERYTHING WE SEE IS UPSIDE DOWN AND BACKWARD.
Maybe I'll think of something-MOTHER-Don't forget to stop and smell the roses.
YOU NEVER KNOW WHAT YOU HAVE UNTIL ITS GONE.
-DAUGHTER-
Everybody needs beauty as well as bread, places to play in and pray in, where nature may heal and give strength to body and soul. JM-BEP
WHICH IS MORE POWERFUL, A THOUGHT OR AN ACTION?
ORGANIZATION OF THE MIND IS FOUND IN ORGANIZATION OF BREATH
and everybody wants to see you fall
MEAN
YOU
LIKE
LIVE
TO
RK-SKM
Balance
LISTEN TO THE WORLD AROUND YOU, ITS TRYING TO TELL YOU SOMETHING
Music can always save you.
If you can meet triumph and disaster and treat those imposters the same, yours is the world and everything in it.
The lining of the uterian wall resembles core membranes within frontal lobe structures. Developing fetus uses direct sensory projection into mother's womb, a corpus lissum.
NORMALLY THE ANSWERS LIE IN THE QUESTIONS THEMSELVES
Nothing like FAMILY
EVERYTHING THAT IS HAPPENING AT THIS VERY MOMENT IS HAPPENING FOR A REASON......
REFER TO THE BOLD
TYPE TO CRACK THE CODE
The end is merely the BEGINNING
Which way can be considered up? and which can be considered down? When the world is spinning all around.
KINETIC ENERGY
Mathematics, my man, is one truly cheap scam, made by man, for man, because he can't understand, the much stronger code that maybe god holds, or something above, which truly knows love unlike a man does.
When you stop dreaming its time to die
NEED SOME AIR
IT'S ALMOST TIME FOR THE WORLD TO NOTICE ME
All you have to do is believe that you can.
Es la mayora de las partes importantes del reino del quantum
There is a fine line between fishing and just standing on the shore like an idiot. SW-MCK
ONLY FOOLS ARE SATISFIED
BY T. GEISEL
PAGE: 43
PAGE: 193
PAGE: 124
PAGE: 113
PAGE: 34
NIGHT STARES BACK INTO YOU
El Libro de los niños en la segunda carta;
CENTRIPICAL FORCE
questions arise for outward thinking as well-in relation
cristalistas, Projection of thought, through visual cortex?
Dreams
TIME
What time is it? The time of your life.-FATHER
Greatness is only achieved by those who color outside the lines, seeing the universe as a blank canvas and investing in the impossible.....if there were such a thing..........
-WOODS-
56.7/3.333
3.14
Receptors on the inner lids of the eye's iris as well as rods and cones constitute twice as many colors as it is the negative field is
THE COLOR PLANE
Chaos is the cradle of creation.-CRN
I'd live over again, by all means, the life that took place in my past. Of the mystical things that I've seen, and I've dreamed, that never continued to last. Pity me! I do have it all wrong, here in the present I am to stay, for the past is gone, is gone, is gone, and the future is far, far away.
A MAN'S is his WORD
What it is that we see
GIVE YOUR FAMILY A KISS FOR ME, OLD FRIEND
ground us is merely a reflection of ourselves
NO TRANSFER
THE CENTER OF THE UNIVERSE
Oculus de Deus
I love you.

I handed the journal back to him. I made a mental note:

Don't embarrass yourself further by asking stupid questions.

The rest of math class went fairly smoothly, and I was relieved that we had no homework over the weekend. I wasn't in the mood for schoolwork. I wasn't in the mood for much of anything to be honest. I just wanted to sit there in my somewhat uncomfortable plastic seat and think. I wanted to think like Len did. I wanted to feel resourceful. I wanted to feel like I was on to something that no one had ever been unto before.

After weeks, months of watching him, I came to believe that Len knew things that I could never even imagine. Even if he tried explaining them to me, which I knew he never would, I would probably not even be able to fathom his concepts. Just before the bell rang, signifying the end of another school day, he dropped a note on my desk. I read it as the students exited the classroom.

THERE IS NO SUCH THING AS A STUPID QUESTION.

I hurried to school the next day, which made me smile in its very concept, and looked for Leonard. I had thought about him constantly, finding myself increasingly intrigued by him every day since the car crash. Leonard was not there that day, or the next, or the next. In fact, for the remaining years attending Theodore Richmond High School, I saw Leonard Caldwell only once more.

He handed me a note as he walked past me in the hall during the end of my junior year. I wanted to talk to him, to ask him something, so many questions to ask, but instead I remained silent. I understood that he wanted the note to be conversation enough all on its own.

I let him pass me and continue on. It had been a while since I had even seen him, much less gotten a note from him. I hadn't thought about Len Caldwell in quite some time. I had new friends and a beautiful girlfriend to content with, and I tried to put my near-death experience behind me. My injuries had completely healed.

The thoughts of summer were teasing the minds of students who were cramming for finals and watching the clock as the fresh sunlight beckoned them through the classroom windows. He continued on through the throngs of them, heading off to his own summer destination. I stood and stared. I was a movie of myself, watching a movie of myself.

He never said a word.

I opened the neatly folded note.

THE WORLD IS MADE STRONG BY THE ACTS OF OLD FRIENDS, THAT IS WHY IT IS NICE TO SEE YOU AGAIN.

I think I expected something more.

My junior year ended then faded into summer, then that summer faded away into a memory. I found myself to be a senior who actually cared about his future. My interest in math and science increased, and so did my GPA. I graduated from Theo Richmond, and clearly remember hugging my fellow graduates. I do not remember seeing Leonard Caldwell at all that year, not even a glimpse of him across the courtyard or in the corner of a hallway or classroom. He was the one I owed my life to, the one that helped me get back on track. I wanted to pick his brain again, see his journals again, maybe thank him in my own way for helping me turn my life around, but Leonard Caldwell had vanished.

CHAPTER 3
FOURTEEN YEARS LATER

Every single cell in the human body replaces itself over a period of seven years. The person you are today is nothing like the person you were seven years ago, even in the slightest. You are changing as you read this. With every breath, with the pumping of every vessel of blood, in every second, you are becoming someone else.

Someone who never existed before.

You can almost sit back and feel it happening. Therefore, one can never presume who a person might become. A sinner can rearrange himself to be a saint, and a saint can rearrange himself to be a sinner.

I would have never believed that I would have turned out to be a family man, a man that was simply encouraged by the love of his wife and daughter. I would have never believed it that I would have fallen in love and wanted the simple things in life. In high school, tormenting underclassmen and recklessly driving my car, I would have never believed it. In college, smoking reefer and dabbling in easy women and the occasional hallucinogen, I would have never believed it. But believe it, Chris Wyer turned out to be a voter, and homeowner, and employed with a successful real-estate firm.

Married with children. Believe it.

High school was a fading memory.

I had all but forgotten about my car wreck and my wheelchair and my bullying and my fistfights. I had forgotten about many of my classmates and girlfriends and teachers, and rarely heard from any of them.

Rebecca, my only daughter, had grown up so fast that I often wondered if maybe someone had recently snuck into the master control room and greased the wheels of time. There she was, one day in my memory, being thrown in the air in my bedroom when I had more hair, and when she was a toddler. I remember the distinct sounds she made as she squealed with delight. She could only express herself with emotions then, with laughter being her favorite and crying her least. I remember looking into her eyes that night, and she looking into mine. For those who have never experienced, looking into your child's eyes, in just the right light, is the only place where you can view the entire universe.

"How does a brat such as yourself get gifted with such an angel of a child?" my father asked in the backyard, eternally confused by the irony of her perfect behavior. "I thought tying you in a burlap sack with some stones in it and tossing you in Uncompahgre river was the only way out for a while there." He laughed to himself as we watched her play—"But if I had actually dragged you behind the truck through broken glass and rattlesnakes, like I wanted to so many, many times, I guess I couldn't have this." He motioned to Rebecca as she chased the cat during another Colorado sunset.

I was certainly blessed with the gift of a wonderful child, I had to admit, even if my father claimed not to be as fortunate.

I parked my car in front of her elementary school like I always did on Tuesdays and Thursdays. Little kids started to appear in droves, draining from the red brick building like a split in a pipeline, and soon the bright-eyed face of my daughter emerged from their masses. She skipped over to the side of the car clutching her pink backpack, opened the door and plopped in.

"Hey, Dad," she said, closing the door behind her.

"Hey, munchkin. Learn anything today?"

"Nope."

"The usual then, huh?" I put the white Ford Taurus into drive.

"Yep."

"Its so weird that you can go to school all day every day, and they never teach you anything."

"Yep. Weird."

I drove on toward the house, and we had our normal Tuesday and Thursday after-school drive-home conversation.

I pulled up to the mailbox to retrieve what was to be my daily supply of bills and junk mail, instead finding only one handwritten letter addressed to me, with the return address bearing only the name **Harper, Lee**.

Puzzling, to say the least.

"Hey, Dad?" Rebecca asked as I looked at the envelope.

"Yeah?"

"Can we have spaghetti tonight?"

"We had *pasgetti* last night, honey. Besides, I think Mom is cooking up some meatloaf."

"Yeah, but spaghetti is way better."

"I'll tell you what. If you eat all of what your mother gives you, and if you're still hungry, I'll make you pasgetti for dessert."

"'Kay. But it is SPAGHETTI, not PASGETTI! Don't act like a dummy!"

"I am a dummy, and it's MACROMOOMASGETTI!" I said, while crossing my eyes, and making a face. I pulled the car to the front of our house, Rebecca giggled and jumped out. I examined the letter for just a second.

Harper Lee?
Wasn't that the author of To Kill a Mockingbird*?"*

The sun was nearly going down, and the rich cascading colors of fall were all around. I took a moment to absorb the scenery before watching Rebecca bounced through the open door to our small three-bedroom home. It was a nice place, and I had really fixed it up since I had gotten it a few years back. I wasn't much of a carpenter, never have I claimed to be, but most of my repairs looked pretty good so far. I was still working on a few things, including new trim and paint, but the important thing was I had a decent place that I could call my own. I had finally carved a niche in this busy little world that seemed as if it often wanted to swallow me whole. I hadn't become a man that lusted for adventure or power or great demands, I just wanted to be left alone with the people I loved. I was perfectly content.

After putting Rebecca to bed, and while watching the tail end of *The Tonight Show*, Cathorine came over and lay down with me on the couch. She was still as breathtaking as the first time I saw her. She had adapted herself to be everything I had ever wanted a woman to be, or I had adapted my mind to desire her completely. The compromise in itself was truly what I loved. Somehow we just fit, and we knew it.

Her long black hair still seemed to drift around her head like a cool mist, and her eyes were a piercing radiance of browns and greens. It seemed she could actually interlace the energy in the room with hers, amplifying it. Her skin had the smell of being freshly bathed in heaven's coolest waters then dried with lavender clouds, complementing its soft olive color. Her body is petite but definitely crafted by an artist with only the finest abilities and knowledge of how a woman should be seen.

She lay softly on my chest, and I could hear her velvet breaths. She seemed to grow more elegant each day, forever rising to a crescendo, and I often wondered, with my slight tummy of middle age and decreasing hairline, if I was starting to fall behind. I wondered if she was too good for me, if maybe she deserved someone better. But as I thought about it, she leaned over and kissed me softly, reassuring me that it indeed was me that she wanted right there with her, as if she had just read my mind.

Her body wedged in against mine, and she rolled over to see the television. I lightly kissed the back of her neck as she flipped through the channels, indifferent to anything on.

"Did we get the bill from the dentist yet?" she asked.

"No, not yet. Shouldn't be much more than three hundred." We had gotten a retainer for Rebecca, much to her dismay. I adjusted my shoulders on the couch. "But that reminds me, I did get some weird letter that I haven't had the chance to look at yet. From Harper Lee or somebody. Never heard of him. Addressed to me, here."

"Harper Lee?"

"Yeah."

"You don't think it's a mistake?"

"I don't know what the hell it is. Haven't even opened it yet."

"The same Harper Lee that wrote *To Kill a Mockingbird*?" Cathorine murmured, her speech slower with oncoming sleep.

Her channel changing became slower, and slower.

"Yeah, I guess," I said in a whisper, as her eyes closed softly. "No wonder he sounded familiar. But I don't think it's the same guy."

"Harper Lee was a woman, honey. But the letter," she paused, breathing instead, " . . . it's probably not really from her . . ."—breathe—"probably not . . . from her . . ." I was losing her to her subconscious.

"Oh. Huh," I replied in another half kiss. "I didn't know that. Learn somethin' new every day. Weird though, still. Probably just a well-disguised piece of junk mail . . ."

I was talking mostly to myself, "Maybe I finally won that Publishers Clearing House."

"Uh-huh . . ." She didn't even chuckle at my joke before sleep took her, proving that I, yet again, wouldn't get the last laugh.

Habits are a hard thing to break. When I was sixteen or so, before I got my first car, I could easily sleep in to eleven or noon. I loved to sleep in. How long ago that seems now. But now, actually ever since I had to finish high school at old Theodore Richmond, I have grown accustomed to waking up early. Getting up with the light. Making a hot cup of coffee to start off my day. Being in second gear before all the other cars are still warming up at the line.

This was one of those mornings that only took place during the midst of autumn. The weather is still holding on to some warmth, but there is an icy tinge of winter desperately trying to nibble in at the skin. It is the morning that is truly complemented with a large cup of hot chocolate or coffee. The warm liquid could never taste any better. I looked outside for quite some time, enjoying the colors of the changing trees. Everything was still. Everything was quiet in the softest ways. *Everything is perfect.* I sipped my coffee gingerly, and then I pulled out a seat at the dining table. As I sat, my eyes adjusted to a letter sitting on the dining table. It was the letter from Harper Lee.

"Who could you be, Harper Lee?" I hummed a rhyme to myself. "Christopher Wyer, that is me. Living here at thirty six-thirty three."

I inspected the nice penmanship on the front of the letter for a moment, then opened it with my finger. There was only one regular-sized, neatly folded piece of paper within. As soon as it was opened, I wanted to close it again. I wanted to shut the can of worms. I wanted to seal Pandora's box. But it was too late. I had already seen inside, and what I saw immediately burned itself into my eyes. I would never be able to see the same way again. I did not know it then, but that letter would change my simple life forever, its consequences unforgiving. I unfolded the paper again to reassure myself that my eyes weren't playing tricks on me. But they were not. This was no illusion, the letter was neatly written in thick red blood.

I spilled my coffee on the carpet beside my naked feet. The cup shattered loudly somewhere below, splashing brown across our new carpet. My guts seemed to want to pounce out through my gaping mouth. I was scared. I wanted to think that this was something of a joke, maybe something my colleagues at work had come up with. But I knew that it wasn't. I could tell by the writing, I could tell by the time that was surely spent creating such a thing. I could tell. This letter had a power to it. This was no joke. Something was going on, something I wanted no involvement in.

"Honey, what the sam hell is going on down here?" It was Cathorine, coming down the stairs. The shattering coffee cup had probably woken her. I did not even look at her, but continued to intensely study the paper in my hand.

"Do you not hear me?" she scowled as she entered the dining room. "And do you not care that your goddamned coffee is spilled all over the brand new carpeting?"

"Honey," I said seriously. "Shut up."

"What! You're just standing there doing nothing, letting the coffee just stain the hell out of the carpet that we spent a million dollars on!" She was really getting mad. The gears of her anger machine were freshly oiled and beginning to rotate.

"Honey!" I said sternly, locking her eyes in mine. She tightened her blue robe around her body. She knew immediately I meant business, especially after she too inspected the letter in my hand. It was a single sheet of crisp paper, and centered on the page, was this configuration of blood.

THE
ANSWER IS AROUND

: i+0 (XV+4); (X+6) -(3V) 0 ;
(0)(-2(i))+13 ; 2X-(XV(0) : 1030 :
(X+4)+2/0 ; (-3) 0+XV; 2X-2-0 (XV+2) ;
2X- 6/0 ; (-3/0)+8 : X-4 (0) ; i+((XV+2)/0) ;
(i/0)+14 ;V+8 (0) : (XX - 1)-(3V)0; 2X-0(XV) ;
(2X-2) - 4/0 ; V+(X+7) (0) ; 5 ; 4V-2/0 :
(XX + 8)/2 + 6 (0) ; XXV - X(0) : 3 ;
XV - (14 (0)) ; 13 ; V + (11/0) :
i+(2X / 0)+i(0) ; (2(V+i)) - 7(0) ;
3(X) /2 + 3/0; i(XV-i) - ((X)(0)) ;
0 + V - 0 :

The letter was richly and almost completely covered in writing, which was all within a large ellipse, and the bloody ellipse and writing within it resembled a large red egg in its entirety. Although the writings and border were thick with blood, they were very meticulously inscribed. There was what seemed to be an assortment of different letters and symbols, but neither seemed to contain a distinct pattern, and the only thing I could decipher was the most predominate writing on the page, directly on the top of the writing in the circle, all in capital letters. It was seemingly the only text, and it was boldly written in English.

THE ANSWER IS AROUND.

"Honey, what is that?" she asked when she saw it, gripping my arm.

"I don't know," I replied, once my mouth decided to move.

"Honey, I don't like it," she said, her voice sounding distant, her heartbeats almost more audibly distinct.

I don't like it either.

Cathorine and I scrutinized the letter until it was my time to depart for work. But we were both seriously confused by its meaning or message, and there was something very threatening about it.

All that blood, so carefully used.

It was the only thing I thought about as I drove Rebecca to school, as I then drove myself to work, and then all day as I worked. I thought about the name *Harper Lee* being an anagram, but the only real meaningful things I could pull from it were "pearl here," "hear leper," and "her leaper." Nothing. Couldn't possibly be an anagram. Perplexity had been nibbling on my consciousness all day and had it completely consumed.

A call came for me just before I was about to leave work.

"Hello, this is Chris," I said as I picked up the receiver.

"Hey." It was Cathorine. "Honey," she said after being momentarily silent at the other end, "I've been thinking about that letter all day."

"Yeah, so have I."

"Well, I think that we should probably go to the police or something. I just don't like the thing. It . . . it . . . seems serious," she said. "I think that we should just have them look at it, just to make sure that everything's all right, you know?"

"Yeah, I guess we could do that, if you'd feel better about it. I'm hoping that it's not that big of a deal, but I think that what gets me about the thing is the—"

"—blood," she interrupted, knowing exactly what I was about to say. "Yeah, the blood. It gets me too. I just think that we'd feel better if we knew a little more about it."

"Well, I'm leaving in about a half hour, so I'll pick it up and take it to the cops, see what they say."

"Okay. Sounds good. I think they should at least know about it."

"All right. See you in a while."

The police precinct of Durango was bustling, policemen in uniform brushing by, along with citizens and other county employees. I've always felt weird walking into a police station for some reason. Guilty somehow. I always felt as if all eyes were upon me, that feeling when you know that someone is watching you. It was the same feeling I had years ago when I entered the principal's office even for the simplest reasons. I strolled to a large front desk that was suppressed with a large pane of thick glass.

"May I help you?" a middle-aged woman, large and flabby at the arms with extra curly brown hair spoke to me from the other side of the pane.

"Yeah, I guess. I don't really know where to go with this, but I received this letter"—I pulled it from my coat pocket—"and it scares me a little."

"Do you want to file a harassment charge?" she asked calmly before taking it.

"No, no, I don't think so yet. See, I don't even know whom it's from or what it's about because it's all in code. But as you can see, it's covered in blood, and that's why I came here." I slid the letter under the large slot in the glass.

She reached for it as I passed it through, but once she saw the blood that was accumulated on the letter, her hands froze. "Oh, I see," she said, as if she were being forced to watch a bad rerun on television. "Um. Yes. I'll tell you what. We can't do anything with this unless you file a formal complaint. If you want to file harassment or maybe a missing persons report that may be related to this letter, then we can do something."

"No, I don't really have any complaints about it, I just thought that you may like to know."

"No, sorry. If we took the time to investigate every prank or whatever this is, we'd need about a million more of us. If this leads to anything that you think may be relevant to criminal activity, come back. But till then, it's just a piece of paper with blood on it, so there has been no crime committed."

I took the letter back and walked out without saying anything more to her, and felt pretty stupid. It was true, the letter was definitely creepy, but it really had no meaning. Plus, I didn't have a clue about whom it might be from. It was not technically a criminal act, or even leading to one. I was wasting the police's time, and wasting my own as well.

It was two days later that I noticed that I was being followed. Yes, I was absolutely certain, the dark blue car had been following me. I had noticed it in my rearview window for about a half hour while I was stopped at the light on Twelfth Street. It had pulled slowly into traffic from behind Tino's restaurant, always keeping a few cars back. I had noticed that the car was there, but made nothing of it. I would probably have never noticed that it was, in fact, tailing me if I didn't have to make a U-turn after I missed the right turn to my daughter's school. I always missed that turn. Today, however, I was glad that I did.

Pulling in to a side street, reversing the car back out, and turning the car around, I noticed that the metallic blue Crown Victoria was moving toward me quite slowly. As we approached each other, I noticed the oncoming car had government plates, and as I passed it, I noticed that there were two gentlemen inside. They were both studying me quite closely as I passed, I could almost feel their eyes. They were dressed sharply, in dark suits, each wearing black sunglasses. The afternoon threw a vibrant glare from the hood of their car, so I could not see much more detail about their physical appearances. I knew one thing. They were definitely police.

I can smell your authority.

As they had not pulled me over and had not really taken much precaution in concealing the fact that they were following me, I figured that I was not in any serious trouble but was just being examined for some reason or another. Closely examined.

I pulled up to my daughter's school and parked the car in the fifteen-minute loading zone. Adjusting my rearview mirror slightly, I could see that my newly found friends in the blue car had turned around as well and had also felt like stopping, roughly twenty yards behind me. They stayed within their car and waited.

Vultures.

They were slightly obstructed by parked cars between us, so I still could not see them with clarity. It was a beautiful September day, still holding the last of the summer heat, and it was being ruined by the fact that I had unwanted nuisances in the form of sharply dressed cops in a large car behind me.

I picked up my daughter from school, along with one of her friends that planned on spending the night. They laughed about things in the backseat, busy with girlish stories, oblivious to the fact that we were being followed. I was not about to tell them about it. No need to get them worked up. I began to head back out the way I had come in, wanting to see if I could get a better glance at my groupies. I pulled out and made a U-turn in the street and headed back in their direction. The school zone speed limit was fifteen miles an hour, but I drove back out at around ten.

My open window afforded me a clear view of their car as I passed by. I could clearly see that the driver seemed to be a middle-aged, heavier-set Caucasian man. His face was rugged, with a big lower jaw and large nose that looked like it may have been broken more than once. Sparse amounts of deep black hair barely covered his balding head, even though he had slicked it all back with large amounts of gel or grease. He was calmly smoking a cigarette, holding it loosely with two fingers of his round left hand, leaving his right hand to rest on the wheel. As I slowly approached, his thick head moved to watch our steady passing. The passenger was darker-skinned, probably black, although it was harder for me to see him clearly as he remained in the shadows on the far side of the car. As I hung my left arm lazily out of my open window, I slowly gave the large driver a shooting motion with my fingers as we made eye contact. He smiled, humored if fazed by it at all, and took another deep drag from his cigarette.

As I drove home, singing along to the radio with my daughter and her friend, I noticed that the car was no longer behind me. I checked the rearview mirror frequently, yet spotted no more blue Crown Victoria all the way over the bridges and back streets that led home. I pulled the car in front of the house, cut the ignition, and we all walked inside. Just before closing the front door behind me, I gave one last glance over my shoulder to see if anyone was on the street. No one was.

I didn't want to tell Cathorine about my followers, no need to get her worked up either. She might jump to conclusions, really outrageous conclusions, because she could be as paranoid as they come. Paranoia runs in the blood like the ability to curl your tongue.

Maybe they weren't following you after all, maybe it was simply coincidence that they had been there. You can't really be sure now, can you?

It had been a good day. Real good.

Hell! It's been a good week. Don't worry so much.

Everything was running smoothly at work and at home. I almost wanted to kiss the co-owner of my business, as much as my wife. We had recently closed a very large deal, and to celebrate, I took my wife out to our favorite restaurant. Rebecca had stayed over at one of her friends, so Cathorine and I had the house all to ourselves when we arrived home from our wonderful meals. Cathorine dimmed the lights when we entered, and moving delicately through the shadows, soon made me feel like the greatest man alive. I wish that I could give you details, but the details are all mine. She definitely took my mind off of the blue car that had followed me a few days ago and the letter written in blood. She nearly melted my entire mind altogether.

I thought about her as I drummed my fingers on the steering wheel days later, blankly staring toward the school. I was picking Becca up again, as I always did on Tuesdays and Thursdays, and I felt better than better could feel in the first place. My mind wandered blissfully. I could still almost feel a slight tingling where her lips and tongue met certain parts of my body. But the letter poked at me from the back of my mind. The letter from Harper Lee. The letter of blood.

The distant sound of the final bell rang, and soon children came pushing through the doors in small hordes. The fallen leaves that littered the schoolyard melded together into brilliant oranges and reds, and were scattered with the small trampling feet of advancing kids. I studied the scenery and watched the students prance around but thought only of the letter. Then I noticed a small girl in ponytails walking with her head down, kicking up a fresh path through the leaves. I could hear soft crackling as her small shoes stepped onward past my car. She had the same complexion of Rebecca but definitely a little older.

Rebecca will look a lot like her in two years.

But where was Becca? Class had been out for a while now, and the schoolyard was completely clear. The girl that looked like her older version had been one of the last students out. What is she doing? I looked at my watch, four-thirty. I had been caught up in my own thoughts for almost an hour, and she should have easily been here in that time. She must have been held after class for some reason. I opened the car door, created my own path through the colors of the fall leaves, and went into Jennings Elementary.

I walked down the long narrow hallways, scanning for Rebecca. They were empty except for a few random pieces of paper. Many of the classroom doors were now closed and locked, but I found that the door to Mrs. Deevers's class was still ajar.

"Hello, Sally," I said as I entered, causing her to look up from her cluttered desk. I had known Sally Deevers for a long time.

"Oh, hey, Chris," she said in blushing smile as she noticed me. "Ya kinda startled me. How are you?"

"Pretty good, although I can't find my little terrorizer. Have you seen her?"

"Nope, not since school ended. She left with everyone. Could she have gone home with somebody else?"

"No . . . No, she wouldn't—" I didn't end my sentence, I didn't need to. Sally could see the worry in my face, and I began to feel it in my soul. Rebecca would never have just gone off with one of her friends or something without telling me. Or a stranger. We had told her many times. She was always real good about being on time and obedient with our wishes. Cathorine and I insisted that she never should do anything like this or she would face serious consequences.

"Cathorine wouldn't have picked her up, would she?" Sally asked as she arose from her desk.

"No, Cath's at home." I looked back out into the empty hallways again and seeing nothing, went back out into them. Sally followed me. We walked quickly toward the gymnasium without saying a word. It was dark and obviously deserted. I began to feel very uncomfortable. Sally opened the door to the adjoining cafeteria. It too was vacant.

"I'll check the girls' restroom," she said hastily.

"Meet me outside, I'll look around out there again," I said as she departed back toward the hallway. I rushed outside to the now cooling dusk air. My eyes scanned the area feverishly, but caught sight of nothing.

"Rebecca!" I demanded to the playground and schoolyard. "Rebecca!"

Odd desperation was setting in, and my skin was crawling, and I had a bad taste of something in the back of my throat. I surveyed everything around me more intensely. The merry-go-round was slightly moving, still spinning, but not nearly as merry as it should be. It was almost menacing now, how it spun. I glanced at my watch for what must have been the fourth time in ten minutes, five o'clock. School had been out entirely too long for her to be messing around with friends or doing class work or whatever else she might be doing. I heard the school doors open behind me, and I whirled around in anxiety. It was Sally, alone.

I rushed with her back inside to the pay phones. My fingers flew as they punched the number to the house. I didn't even realize I was typing a number in to the telephone. I was just rushing through an old pattern that I knew. I heard the ringing on the other end. One ring. I was breathing heavily. *Cathorine, you better have Rebecca and an explanation.*

Two rings. I felt my tense grip on the receiver. Three rings . . .

You better pick up the goddamned phone.

Four rings, . . . and a click as my own odd-sounding voice came on the answering machine.

"Hello, you've reached Chris, Cathy, and Rebecca. Please leave a message and will get right back to you—[A faint giggling of my wife and daughter could be heard in the background.]"

"Yeah, Cath, it's me. I'm here at Jennings and can't find Rebecca anywhere. Please tell me that you have her with you. I'll call you back." I slammed the phone down in frustration.

Sally and I then proceeded to run all around again, with the same bad outcome. I grabbed the pay phone once more, scrambled for the right change, and called again. Again, no answer. I was becoming extremely unsettled. I looked at Sally and saw that she had the wide eyes of worry. I could only imagine how mine looked.

"Sally," I said in a gulp, "Could you stay here while I run over to the house real quick. I'll call you when I get there."

"Oh sure," she said, nearly in one word. "I'll be right here. I'll keep looking."

I jammed the throttle down every moment that I could, driving with adrenaline.

The family wagon could be fast when it wanted to be, and I definitely wanted it to be. I was driving it like I was trying to make it take off. I saw someone flip me off as I passed him, but he was the last thing on my mind. Although I did feel like memorizing his license plate number so that I could track him down later and beat the living hell out of him. The cars seemed to be driving deliberately slow in spite of my hurry.

I yanked the car into the driveway and slammed it to a stop. Cathorine's car was here.

She must know where Rebecca is.

I threw my shoulder into the car door as I opened it, jumped out, and thrust it shut again. I jogged to the doorway of the house and shouldered it too. Then I stopped dead in my tracks.

The house was in shambles. All the plants were knocked over, along with lamps and chairs. Papers and debris covered the floors, and the sliding glass door on the far end of the living room was shattered. It looked as if someone came in with a baseball bat for a little practice.

"Cathorine!" I yelled at the top of my lungs. I could hear in my own voice that I was gasping for air, in fear. I heard nothing in return except for the crunching of the small broken pieces of my home interior beneath my shoes. My heart beat wildly, and I wasn't sure what to do except to run hurriedly through the house checking every area, hoping for something good.

Maybe I don't want to find anything at all.

With the exception of the mess, the house was empty. I rushed back downstairs, not as fast as I had gone up them, and discovered a small trail of blood that led back out the door. My furiously pounding heart, beating like a sledgehammer a moment or two ago, had suddenly stopped. I seemed paralyzed with fear but somehow managed to follow the thin red line outside, where it disappeared into the grass. I ran around the house to find nothing, and then swiped the phone from its holder and called the police.

I stepped aimlessly around my ravaged home, sweating and gnashing my teeth.

Cathorine and Rebecca, my only angels, were nowhere to be found.

My eyes were wet with tears when the police arrived. I was a lost soul in the impeccable sea of sorrow and despair and did not even feel like swimming. The police were all neatly clothed in their uniforms and that made it all even worse. *How could they be so collected when I was so disarranged?*

Two policemen scoured the house while a detective named Cunningham questioned me. He was furnished in a quaint overcoat, wearing a simple gray dress shirt. He had a soft face, a baby with wrinkles, curly brown hair, and seemed extremely calm and patient.

"Mr. Wyer, can you tell me roughly what time you came home?"

"Yeah, yeah. About five, I think," I said, watching deputies peel through the carnage that I had earlier known as being a clean living room. "Yeah, five-fifteen or so maybe."

"And, Mr. Wyer, could you tell me the last time that you had seen your wife?"

"This morning, before I went to work. Probably about seven-thirty, eight."

"And your daughter?"

"About the same time. A little later. I dropped her off to school about ten minutes after I left the house." The same deputy pulled the couch out from against the wall.

"Do you have any enemies, Mr. Wyer? Anyone that you think may have done this?"

I thought for a few moments. "No, not really. No one that would do this."

He jotted down a few notes in his pad and looked toward the deputy. "Anything, Joe?" he asked the deputy searching behind the couch.

"Nothing," the deputy said without looking up.

"Make sure to get a sample of the blood. And check for any more around the glass door." He looked around a little more, only moving his head. "You said that you were supposed to meet your daughter at Jennings Elementary School, is that right, Mr. Wyer?"

"Yeah, she wasn't there."

"Could she have been here, Mr. Wyer?"

"No, I told you, she was supposed to meet me after school."

"What I'm saying, Mr. Wyer, is was it physically possible for her to be here?"

"Maybe, I guess. She might have gotten a ride home from one of her friend's parents, I guess. But I don't think that Cathorine would have picked her up without letting me know. It would be about 90 percent unlikely for her to be here."

"Okay. Did you check to see if anything has been stolen?"

"Yeah, nothing's gone." I really didn't check that thoroughly but knew that cash and valuables that I kept were all sealed in a key-locked safe below the bathroom sink. And nobody had the key except for the one that was still in my pocket, on my key chain. All the electronics were still there as well. It would have been a real nonproductive robbery.

"So not a burglary then, huh?" he was asking and thinking to himself at the same time. "Would you have something that maybe they were looking for?"

"No. Nothing. I'm a real estate agent, not a jeweler. I just need you to find my wife and daughter, not petty cash or my fucking VCR."

He looked up at me blankly, and then looked down again at his notepad.

"I am trying to do that, Mr. Wyer, but I need to have basic facts first," he said solidly. "And the less help that you give me is the less chance that I have of finding your family for you."

"I know that, Detective. But what I'm saying is, even if it was a robbery, I don't care. I only want my family, I don't care about the valuables."

"And what I'm saying," said Detective Cunningham, "is that I am merely trying to determine if this was the work of a burglar or a proposed kidnapping or abduction upon your family. At this point, we have no evidence that your daughter has been kidnapped, although we do have probable cause to say that your wife has been so. I will, in turn, investigate Jennings Middle School and determine if evidence that I obtain there will direct me otherwise."

"But my daughter is gone and I—"

"I know, I know, but at the moment, we have no evidence to formally place your daughter as being kidnapped. We cannot yet factor out coincidence, Mr. Wyer. So sit tight until we can."

I knew that Detective Cunningham was there to help, but I felt that he was a dog chasing his tail. This was not coincidence, and we both knew it.

"I do know, however, that you have a solid alibi, so I am eliminating you as a suspect." He looked up at me again when he knew that I was about to tell him that I was of course innocent of anything. I let him continue without interruption. "And as this is not yet proven to be a crime scene, as no crime but vandalism is yet to be discovered, I will not close off the area and will let you remain in this house if you so desire. Of course, we do have housing facilities, and we would be happy to accommodate you if you do not want to stay."

"No, thanks, I'll stay." A public cell didn't really sound very enticing.

"Okay then, Mr. Wyer. I will call you tomorrow, and a formal investigation will be processed. We will let you know if anything happens, and would expect you to do the same. Try to get some sleep." The police soon departed me to a lifeless house of chaos. I was pitifully hopeless and angry but could do nothing but stay there. Stay and constantly absorb my wreckage. I rambled lost through my own house, numbly walking around.

The phone rang, waking me from my mental misery. It was Sally Deevers. I had called her at the school before the police arrived to see if maybe Rebecca had come back. But she had not. Now Sally was calling me to see if Rebecca and/or Cathorine had appeared. I gave her the same answer that she had earlier given me. "No," a small, stabbing word. I began to breakdown again. Crying desperately into the phone, reaching for my reality.

"We'll find them, Chris. Or the cops will." I remember her saying finally, "They know what they are doing. No crime goes unpunished. They have DNA testing and everything. It will be just a little while, and we'll track 'em down. Don't worry, just have faith in their safety. You have to. Because they are safe. And they will return to us. Just have faith."

"I know, Sally. Thank you," I said between sobs. "Thank you for everything, really. Please just keep looking for them with me. Please help me with this." I was completely devastated. I was caught in those moments where you find yourself desperate for anything good.

"Of course, Chris. Of course I will."

"Thank you, Sally."

"You're more than welcome. Good night."

"Good night."

I was more drained and physically exhausted than I had ever been before in my life, but I stayed awake all night long. I thought about rummaging through the broken remains of my house for clues, but decided to wait until the morning, when my head had cleared.

That night I experienced what was usually unnoticed and unfamiliar to me. The soft whistling of air pushing through a slightly opened bedroom window, the cracking of the house's skeleton around me, the small squeaking of bedsprings under my own weight, but not the breathing of my wife beside me. Nor the glimmer of the nightlight that normally shone through the crack in my daughter's bedroom, some of it escaping into the hallway and partially illuminating ours. I got up from my bed, making my way across the darkened hall to turn it on anyway, more for me than Rebecca this time. It just felt unnatural without it on. I made my way back into bed, remembering all the nights I kissed my daughter after she had fallen asleep. Another tear crossed my cheek before I got there, and I resumed my solitary place in my king-sized bed.

The real reason that I think I truly stayed awake all night was fear. Fear for my daughter and wife, fear for their safety, and fear for their inner security. They were being held against their will, and possibly, although it was hard for me to even fathom the notion, being harmed. I feared for them, completely. I couldn't live without seeing them again, and I also wondered if the people that did this were going to come back for me. I wished that they did. Show their faces. Show me who they were. And I'd show them who I was, and I would not be very cordial, to say the least. They may be able to finally take me, but not after I had exuded justice upon a few of them. My anger would burn away their flesh if they allowed me to summon it, but at the moment, it was disguised as fear. Fear alone kept me up all night.

As the affectionate fingers of the morning sun sneaked through the blinds of the windows, I arose with a passion to discover the truth. I started in the living room, which seemed to be the room that was most destroyed. I normally had a work ethic that forced me to finish the hardest parts of any project first, working down to the easiest. This was no exception. I took a brief break to call into work, telling them only that I would not be making it in today. The telephone rang twenty minutes later. It was my boss.

"Chris, you can't call off work today. You know how busy we are, you are completely booked with appointments. The Kensdon account needs to be finished by this week, and we are already behind. We need you."

"Jim," I replied, "I need me!" I hung up the phone, sparing him any details. I was too intent in my search to find out what was going on. I even thought to disconnect the phone for a minute, then realizing that my family or the police would possibly try to reach me. Jim, fortunately, did not call back.

The living room held nothing but torment. I kept looking at the huge hole in the far wall, wondering what had caused it. I pictured the events that maybe could have unfolded, and did not like anything I imagined.

I called it quits for that room after scrutinizing it for over an hour. The dining room was less torn apart than the living room, but still as disgraceful to my eyes. The beautiful mahogany table that Cathorine had received as a wedding gift from her parents was ruined. It was split directly down the middle. Papers and broken glass lay all over the room, so I picked through it carefully. I hoped, as I looked at the papers, that the mess was not caused from violent contact, but instead a hasty and frantic search.

What could I have that someone would search for so recklessly? Then my eye caught it. The corner of the letter from Harper Lee.

This has something to do with all of this.

I had nearly forgotten all about the thing. I crawled over to it and pulled it from the papers where it was hidden.

Had they been looking for this, and in such a fury knocked over papers and bills, concealing in the meantime the very thing they were searching for?

Then, knee deep in the shambles of my house, I scrutinized the letter for only the second time. The thing that still viciously exposed itself to me was the bold, bloody lettering directly on top of the circled text.

THE ANSWER IS AROUND.

The answer is around? What does that mean? Around where?

I spun around the dining room, realizing I was being foolish. The answer is around? I looked at the letter again, wondering if it was around the letter itself somehow.

It must be around the text itself, in the spaces left empty on the four corners of the page around the circle!

I bolted over to the window and held it up, peering through the page toward the sun. The letter held no watermarks or anything that I could discern as hidden legible writing. I ran upstairs to the bedroom and held it to a lamp. Still, nothing.

I couldn't find anything, but I'm sure the cops could. Invisible ink or dyes, maybe microscopic engraving of some sort.

There must be something.

I dialed Detective Cunningham's number, and was in his office a half hour later, just before ten.

"Why didn't you inform me about this last night?" he asked, while he concentrated on the letter. "This could be exactly the lead we need." He studied the letter for a few minutes as I had, finally picking up the phone on his desk. "Yeah, send Simmons in here." He replaced the receiver. He studied the letter more closely, bringing it to his nose and smelling it.

"What do you think?" I asked.

"Well . . ." he paused, looking up at me. "It looks ritualistic, I'm afraid, Chris. That isn't a good thing, but it's written in blood, which is. They might as well just have signed the thing and wrote the address to their house, if it is in fact their blood."

I felt better and worse at the same time.

"Our DNA testing is superb, Chris, be assured of that. Not many criminals can leave a trail of blood and get away with it in this day and age. And you said that you received the letter about a week ago?"

"Yeah."

"So this couldn't be your family's blood at least, with it arriving before they were abducted and all. That's good." He wasn't helping by mentioning my family and blood together in the same sentence, whatever the context.

A younger, lively man with slick jet-black hair came quickly into the room after a brief knock at the door and stood to my right, eyes toward the detective.

"Simmons, I want a DNA sample of this blood, as well as any fingerprints that may be on the paper," Detective Cunningham ordered. "Get the production facts on the paper and look for any possible watermarks or soluble inks in the corners. The works. I want it ASAP."

"Right away," the energetic young man said, and grabbed the letter, both delicately and quickly, with plastic gloves, then stepped back out of the office.

"Anything else that has crossed your mind dealing with this case, Mr. Wyer?" The detective asked from across his desk. He looked me in the eyes, almost as if I was still holding things back.

"No, not really. Well, actually, . . . a blue car, a Crown Victoria I think, with two guys in it, followed me the other day, the day before yesterday. They were cops though. They had government plates. But it was funny that they were following me. I haven't done anything wrong since high school."

"Hmm," Cunningham thought aloud. "No blue cars in our squad. Unmarked, huh? Hmmm. Did you get a good look at the passengers?"

"Only the driver really. The other guy was on the far side of the car, and I couldn't see him that well. But the driver was a heavier man, white guy, dressed in a black suit, large double chin, sunglasses. He had light brown hair that was pretty thin. Balding even. Definitely a bigger guy. I'd say six-two or so, weighed maybe two-sixty. I'm not always so good to judge when they are behind the wheel of a car though."

"How long were they following you, Mr. Wyer?"

"Only about twenty minutes or so, not even that long."

"Hmm. Doesn't sound like much of a tail. You didn't get their tag number did you?"

"No."

"Well, like I said. Maybe something, maybe not."

"Actually, they followed me to my daughter's school, and that's about when they stopped tailing me."

Then it hit me.

"Oh, sweet Jesus, I didn't even realize it. I led 'em right to my girl's school. They stopped tailing me after I picked her up!"

"Okay, okay. Now we got something. But you have to calm down and think straight." He pressed his hand on my shoulder, trying to restrain my emotions.

"Mr. Wyer, you have to give me all the facts. Everything. Do you understand me? You are not doing a very good job of doing that at the moment. It will help us both. Is that everything that you can remember?"

"Yeah, I think so."

"Are you sure? Everything?"

"Yeah, pretty sure. I've been a little stressed lately, obviously. Maybe I'm not thinking as clearly as I should be, but I think that is pretty much everything. If not, I'll tell you if I remember more."

"You'll need to. Right now, we are all in the dark here. But when the tests come back, we should have something to go on. A starting point at the least. We need a face to match the evidence. That's where you can really contribute to the case. I should have the tests by tomorrow, and I'll get a sketch artist in. That way we can get a face on the driver in the Crown Vic. I'll call you around ten and get you back in here. Until then, keep your fingers crossed on that blood. I have a good feeling about it." He paused while still looking at me, hinting it was now my time to leave.

"Thank you for now, Mr. Wyer."

When I came home, I almost expected Cathy and Rebecca to both just be there, on the couch or outside in the yard, as usual. When I realized that they were still gone, my new reality hit hard again. Very hard. The worst thing to lose in your life, without any exception, is your family. I wished that my legs had been taken instead of my girls.

Take my heart, cut out my tongue or my eyes.

All the money in the world meant nothing to me. I was empty. Last night, I was really just in too much shock to really understand what had happened. My world as I knew it had been shattered, along with the interior of my house. The only things that I really cared for in my life had been ripped from me, and I was left with nothing in the wake. Except for a goddamned letter.

A ransom note.

Written by some sadistic bastard covered in tattoos and piercings, bathing in his own excrement and cackling at his own dementia.

My skin crawled. Some slumlord with gold teeth had my wife and beautiful little daughter.

Oh have mercy.

I pictured them in some underground dungeon of filth, both caged, like the animal that he was. I pictured them helplessly trying to free themselves from their fetid cages. My head spun. I tried not to think of these morbid thoughts, but they kept slithering into my brain.

My wife raped endlessly, internally damaged without repair, my child fed, in pieces, to hungry salivating dogs as a sick form of entertainment.

I clenched my fists as hard as I could. My jaw locked in a frenzied bite. I grabbed the plant that I had earlier collected from the floor and flung it through the dining room window. The crashing of the glass pierced at my ears, while the thoughts of something terrible happening to my sweet girls gnawed at me. Molten angst burned inside. Enveloping me, destroying me, slowly and deliberately. I knelt in my fairly clean living room, brought my hands to my head, and thoroughly cried for an eternity. I went to the liquor cabinet and found half of liter of Myer's Rum. I put it to my mouth and drank as much as I could, straight. I hadn't had a sip of liquor since my brother-in-law's wedding four months earlier. I forced myself to chug it.

Gulp it down.

It boiled in my throat and stomach, but did not burn nearly as bad as my soul did. I felt nauseated as the bottle was finished, and I let it drop to the kitchen floor. It didn't smash like I expected it to, so I kicked it against the refrigerator. It didn't break there either. I yelled at the top of my lungs for as long as I could, but gave up on trying to break the bottle.

I turned and, looking around my destroyed house, realized that I knew why so many people in this world were sad.

They were not whole.

They were incomplete, and tried to cope with knowing that fact by drinking or doing drugs or resorting to violence or whatever their vice may be. Instead of trying to find ways of completing themselves.

My head spun, and I nearly vomited there, standing in my kitchen.

In those last few moments before the alcohol brought me out of a consciousness that I could remember, my thoughts were about the universe and my family. The universe will always be a mystery, I suppose, for everyone. It is always expanding; it is always something that you will never be able to grasp, to understand. The universe is forever and without structure in a traditional sense. The family, however, is the inverse of the universe. The family is somewhere we can all belong, be an integral part of, to understand, to grasp. It is not held together by dark matter, but by love (although both at this point are scientifically indefinable.)The family is realistic in foundation; the universe is impossible in infiniteness. I had lost my family and everything I had come to understand anymore and was helpless, as most are, to the direction of the imposing universe.

CHAPTER 4

There is a blanket of darkness surrounding me, and I can somehow tell that I am deep in a large forest. I am alone and lost in this forest, invisible, vanished in the dark. The crickets chirp wildly all around me, and all I can see are walls of thick trees, outlined and looming ominously in every direction. They are whispering in the night, as most trees do when a gentle wind blows through them, and their leaves crackle softly under my footsteps with the chirping crickets. It is a very cold night, and my skin is overrun with a stark temperature.

I walk ahead, figuring that straight ahead is as good a direction to walk as any. I brush against a rough pine tree as I walk past it, and it almost feels as if the tree itself has skin. Or scales. I have the sudden feeling that I am being watched, and it seems that the tree itself is possibly looking down at me through the dark. I look up at it, yet can only see its trunk ascending into complete darkness. I imagine it having thin beady tree eyes that are obstructed from my view somewhere in the darkness above me. I have this feeling that it can see very, very well in the dark, even if I can't. I imagine the tree slowly bringing a large branchy finger around behind me. Eagerly waiting for the chance to grab me and snap my neck. I would be so brittle compared with this giant of the wood. My dead body would fall and decompose at its hungry base. It would wait years until my body turned to soil, so that it would finally nourish itself upon my organic flesh, drinking my decay. It has time. I whirl around to see if my imagination is true, but there was nothing but the rest of the empty forest behind me. The spindly fingers of a branch were never there.

Yet, there is definitely something menacing about the thing, and I reach out very cautiously to feel its bark with my hand. As soon as my twitching fingers touch the wood of it, I pull them away immediately. There is a film on them. I cannot see it, can only feel that it is there. Its bark seems colder than the chilled air around it. Pure evil. Something grown from sheer hate. It wants me, it wants my taste. I can sense this. I can sense it just from touching the thing.

I quickly step away from the looming leviathan, and walk quickly away from it, passing through more dark pines. I still anticipate one to grab me from behind in an icy grasp, but none does. I begin to hear the wind, what sounds like a whispering just a few decibels lower. But the wind and the whispers steadily increase, and I realize that the whispering is coming from the trees. It is a sinister nursery rhyme of sorts, interpreted by my head through the whispering.

Let yourself go, soul.
Let us feed. Let us feed.
Ever so slow.
Let us grow.
Down, down below,
so far down below,
and ever so slow,
—ever so slow.

I begin to run, but the whispers grow stronger. They are nibbling at my skin, as the cold air is. Licking at my ears. Digging their slippery tongue into my brain. I run harder. The whispers get louder, growing stronger. Rising like smoke. Hehe. Hee. Hee. The laughter of small children can be heard as well, intermixing with the whispers. He heh hee. Haha hee he. Giggling. Simply giggling. The children can only be disguised as children when they were in fact demons. Giggling demons, I can smell their sour sweat. Giggling and laughing, and the thick trees murmuring like fire. An immense fire that growls with power. Soon, all the growling and the giggling and the laughing and the faint chirping of crickets turn into one large guttural moan. It is the unmistakable sound of death itself, steadily approaching from behind ...

I run deeper into the forest, running through branches of the whispering trees, poking at my eyes, stabbing my skin. Blocking my path. Whispering. The wailing and moaning grow louder, rumbling like immoral thunder. I realize that the wailing and screaming is coming from all sides now, coming from everywhere, filtering in from above. A shape has taken form from it, created from this awful sound. I feel its frigid breath. Infiltrating my soul with disease. Pushing its way into my thoughts. Opening its wicked eyes in glee. And the shape, a quick dark shape, like the shadow of something in flight, nearly has me now, as I run from it. I can hear grunting and feel warm breath upon the back of my neck.

My foot snags a root, and I fall to the frozen ground, exhausted and chilled to the core. I crouch, awaiting impending ruin from the wailing beast of death, from this messenger of demise. I felt its icy fingers close in around my neck, hear its rotted jaw crackling, opening wide to accommodate the girth of my fresh skull. Whispering. The trees lean in to watch the kill. Anticipating residue and nourishment that is sure to drip from death's sticky gums . . . Whispering.

CHAPTER 5

Waking up cold, in the middle of my kitchen floor, was quite unexpected. At first, I was unfamiliar with my surroundings, but my blurry eyes finally focused to the bottle of Myer's Rum close to my face. Only then I was reminded of what I had done to make myself sleep there. My body moved as if it were being restricted, like liquid concrete filled my veins and was starting to harden, and it took me a while to pull myself from the floor. My head spun. I was parched, and my tongue wanted to slither to the back of my throat. I held on to the kitchen counter to steady myself, and hazily looked around.

I wonder what time it is.

I had a morning appointment with Detective Cunningham. I was damned if I was going to miss it, but in the state that I was in, I wouldn't make a bit of sense to anybody. I wished that I hadn't tried to drink my demise last night. I wish that I would have just gone to bed, thinking and acting clearly.

Then maybe I could face this world.

The world was no place that I wanted to face under my present circumstances, and the hangover only made it harder. I had been a fool, and now I was paying the price.

I slowly made it upstairs to the bathroom, undressed, and dragged myself into the shower. It helped. I tried to pull myself to sobriety and managed to appear somewhat presentable. The phone call came at about 10:10 AM, and I knew exactly who it was.

"We need to talk," was all he said as I picked up.

"I'll be right there."

It may have been the shortest phone conversation I ever had.

The police station was relatively unpopulated, except for the lady at the desk.

"Detective Cunningham is waiting for you," she said, looking at me. She could see that it had been a rough night.

I steered through some hallways as she directed and found Tyler Cunningham's office. He was talking joyfully on the phone with who I presumed to be his girlfriend/wife.

"I'd never hide it there!" he said, laughing, his back turned toward me.

"It would never fit! We both know that, we should just leave it . . ." As he spoke, he turned to face me, and seeing my condition and realizing the condition in general, his smile immediately faded, and he became serious. "Uh-huh," he said with a half chuckle now. "I know, but I have to go. Call you back."

"Mr. Wyer, I have some news," he said, giving me a solid gaze as he hung up his cell phone, "regarding the case." He continued, "The news isn't necessarily bad, but it's not necessarily good." That made me feel terrible.

No good news is still no good news.

"Coffee?" he asked.

"Yeah, and the news," I replied.

He pushed a button on his phone. "Two coffees please, Stacy." He opened up a folder on his desk and pulled out a ziplock bag that sealed the ransom letter. I sat up in my chair. He leaned back in his. He smiled, unenthusiastically.

"All I can say is, you have somehow managed to nestle yourself in a spider's web that right now seems to be made from some really deep shit." He looked at me, almost as if he was waiting for me to say something.

"We ran some tests on the letter here," he continued in my absence of speech, "ran the damn thing through the ringer, Mr. Wyer."

"And?"

"Well, at first I thought that the letter might be from your family's abductors. A ransom letter, but now, I'm starting to think that's not the case at all."

"Why is that? It has to be a ransom letter." My head swam as I spoke, in the remnants of last night's accumulation of alcohol.

"Well, Mr. Wyer, right now I don't exactly know what the hell is going on. I have never seen anything like this before, so I can't really see how it could be a ransom letter."

"Oh yeah?" I wondered.

"Yeah." He leaned forward in his leather chair, forcing the chair to squeak. He looked me right in the eyes. "This letter," he said, looking down at it, seemingly amazed simply by its presence. "This letter, is a, is simply . . ." he paused, ". . . mind boggling."

"Why is that?" I asked confoundedly.

"Well, yesterday, after you left, we began conducting the usual tests on the letter as we do with all investigations. The paper itself was concluded to have come from a large production company based primarily in the East Coast."

I was about to ask how he figured that out when he told me, "Generally, pulp from the eastern coast differs from the pulp in the West due to different usage of timbers and a different humidity. In general, I deducted that it was a larger paper production company due to the fact that the fibers were very thin and extremely compressed, which normally results from a larger paper mill that produces quality paper with more efficient machines. But the paper only helps us a little, as the location of its production is very vague, and as I said, just a generalization."

He paused for a moment. "We also checked for fingerprints, water markings, and soluble inks, which can show trick, infrared, or "invisible" writings. But nothing appeared." He looked down at his desk.

"Go on," I said, knowing he had much more to tell me.

"The thing is," he said in softer tones. "The interesting thing is what came up with the DNA testing that we conducted on the blood. Initially, all the DNA tests came up negative. Completely negative. Which means that the blood didn't match a soul within the database, or that there was an error in the testing. Basically, what I'm trying to tell you is that it didn't match a single living person with blood work on file on the face of this planet."

"What?" I asked with some skepticism. "But some people don't have blood on file right?

"Well, sure, and of course, animal blood, insect blood, etc., wouldn't show up either, but it would also be easy to decipher as being such. This was definitely the blood of a human. So thinking that the sample that we had put in the machine might have been blemished or tampered with, we added another sample. And ran more tests on it than the first. It, like the first, was inconclusive. Didn't match a soul. But that's not the weird thing."

"Go on," I said.

"Well," Tyler leaned in and spoke in lowered tones, as if someone could be listening. "Mr. Wyer, the blood that the letter was written with—," he paused, looking at me, drumming his fingers on his desk "is over three hundred years old. Tested it three times. Three hundred fucking years old." He smiled at the reaction that must have been splayed all over my face. "Yeah, I know. Crazy. Craziest thing I ever heard of too."

I couldn't even talk. I was confused now more than ever, and almost felt sick, even though my hangover seemed to be subsiding. I had been in the police station for more than an hour and was beginning to get hungry.

Detective Cunningham stopped momentarily as Stacy stepped through the door with two coffees in her hands. She passed me and set one on the desk in front of Detective Cunningham.

"Sugar? Cream?" She turned to ask me, with my cup still in her left hand. She was a very pretty woman, I noticed, and slightly reminded me of my wife with short hair. I just couldn't help but thinking of Cathorine, but the distraction of the investigation helped. My sorrow was returning again.

"Just cream, thanks."

She pulled a small plastic cup of cream from her shirt pocket, just above the descent of her left breast, and handed it to me with the coffee.

"Thank you, Stacy," Detective Cunningham said warmly to her. "Let me know when they arrive would you."

"Absolutely, Tyler," she replied. It was the first time that I had heard his name. It sounded so informal to me, but he seemed not to care at all.

Tyler had waited for Stacy to leave the room before he began speaking again, and he lowered his voice when he continued.

"Anyway, under federal regulation, I am supposed to call the higher ups if something weird like this happens. So I called the Feds and told them that we carbon-dated the letter, describing what I found. They didn't even seem too enthusiastic about it. They said nothing about it but to do no more further testing without them. Here I am almost pissin' my pants at what is going on, and they are telling me in a monotone voice that 'yes, it is obvious that further investigations need be concluded.' Or something like that." He stopped again, composing himself.

"So what does all this mean?" I asked, not exactly knowing what he meant by all of this.

"What it means," Tyler continued, "is that the FBI should be here in a few hours to talk with you. Then they are pretty much taking over. Obviously, this goes deeper than a kidnapping."

"It doesn't fucking go any deeper than that to me! I could give a shit about the FBI and their ten most-wanted list or whatever this deals with. I am only concerned about my two most wanted."

"That is exactly what I am concerned about too. Their case is not the same as mine. I am being paid to find your wife and daughter, nothing else. But rules are rules. And they will be here around four, so until then, we have some things to go over. Now, I believe that the letter is significant to your case, although, with it being so old, I think we can rule out it being a ransom letter."

"So how is it so significant?"

"Well, what I think is that someone knows that you have it. And they want it. It is probably worth a lot of money. Very valuable, I'm sure. At least to them. So they broke into your house to look for it. And when they couldn't find it, they took your wife instead."

"What about my daughter, they wouldn't have gone over to her school to get her, would they?"

"Apparently so. Your daughter wasn't at home, as you said, she certainly could not have been."

"I would almost guarantee it."

"Well then, that is bad news, I'm afraid, Chris. Because not only did these thieves scope out your house to discover that you had a letter, they put forth much effort into abducting your family as a trade. Much effort. So unfortunately, it seems that whoever broke into your home, Mr. Wyer," he brought the cup to his lips, "was definitely not your common burglar. Instead, they were, are, most likely, very cunning professionals."

I gulped.

"But, Mr. Wyer. Do not forget that we have what they want. And we aren't about to just hand it over to them without getting your family back first."

"Abso—fucking—lutely not," I agreed.

Detective Cunningham smiled only slightly. "I don't do anything halfway," he said. "And when I put my mind to something, some bad guy is going to end up getting seriously hurt. Because I take it personal."

"But they didn't take your family, no matter how personal you want it to be. They took mine, so it will never be *that* personal."

"True. But when I do catch these *fucks*," he accentuated, "which I most certainly will, you will feel better than I."

Good point.

He spoke with conviction, I gave him that.

"Well, the sketch artist is coming over from the next precinct, and she should be here in about a half hour," he said, "just in time for us to eat some lunch, if you're hungry."

"Starving," I replied. He must have read my mind.

Tyler was not such a stick in the mud as I first thought that he was. I guess that I always thought of cops as being the ones that were ridiculed their whole lives for being complete conformists, and then became cops to conform with society even further. Plus, they could now use a badge as a weight to press down on all those that now or once did oppose them. But not Tyler. He said that he was definitely the wildest kid in high school but found himself grown out of his rambunctious addictions and decided he wanted to pursue something good. "A changing of the tide," he said. So he began his life as a policeman. "It was either that or a priest," he continued telling me while picking up his hamburger. "And I figured that priests really don't get much action with the lady folk, plus I could still drink, cuss, and get into the occasional skirmish, on or off the job of course. Plus prayin' to God just isn't as fun as chasing someone who is doin' one-twenty."

"You do have a point," I said. "You have to follow your calling."

He started laughing hysterically with a mouthful. "If that is true, I would have been a pimp!" he said, laughing, between chews. He wiped his mouth and took a drink. "But seriously," he said, pausing to wash it all down. "My faith in a god and my faith in spirituality are two distinct things. I think people these days are generally confused. They believe in a certain religion because of an outside influence, not because of what they internally feel in their heart. They were persuaded by their fellow man one way or another into believing one way or another, whether it be their parents that believed in it before them, or maybe a preacher, or maybe a teacher, or maybe even a friend. Whomever it was, it got them started believing that way, and the way religion works, it seems to me, once it's got you, it reels ya' in like a fish. If it were a car salesman that was giving them the pitch, they would have just ended up buying a car."

Tyler took another bite of food and chewed it mostly before continuing.

"Now, I'm not saying that religion is a bad thing because, who knows, the car might be the best damn investment they ever had or it might just be a waste of their time and money. But it's the fighting and bickering. My religion is better than yours, no, mine's better, blah, blah, blah. It's never ending. It's like a huge high school. You got the preps, and the jocks, and the nerds, etc. Each group distinctly separate as a whole from the other groups, with individuals believing in different aspects of various groups. Considering themselves to be connected in some way with certain things offered by diverse parties. Like I'm a nerd, but I'm also partially accepted by the jocks because I'm damn good at basketball. It's the same thing in a way. I believe in a god but not Buddha, so even though I like a lot of the Buddhist ideals, I would never be considered completely Buddhist. There is always that jock kid that will say, 'why the fuck is that nerd hanging out with us?' You get me? I know that religion and high school is a vast analogy, but people need simplicity to see clearly a lot of times. And that is really the reason that I never became a priest."

Actually, you sorta lost me there, Tyler.

"Well, I'm a real estate agent, what does that mean?" I asked, eating my last bite of an overcooked chicken sandwich.

"Well," Tyler chewed some more, "you provide the space that the game is played on, I guess. You got a good job. You could be the janitor, whatever that may elude to." He smiled and slurped the last bit of his drink from his straw. "We should get going, sketch artist should be here soon."

I looked at his 9 mm pistol hanging from his belt as he got up to leave, wishing that I had it two days ago around 3:00 PM at Jennings Middle School. Or at my house when the "cunning professionals" broke in. On that thought, I pictured the fat man behind the wheel of the blue sedan even more clearly.

The sketch artist turned out to be a twenty-something, curly, blond lady named Samantha, who insisted that her sketching was only on a parttime basis. I could see why after she was done. It really turned out horribly, in my opinion, although I tried to describe his face to the exact detail. She asked me if it "pretty much fit the profile," but it was so far off I knew that it was helpless to try and even render it.

"Yeah, that's him," I said, but quickly changed my mind as soon as I saw two men in uniform walking through the precinct door. "No, actually, that's him." I said to her and Tyler at the same time, pointing at the same fat man that I had seen two days earlier.

He walked in as if he owned the land that the station was located on, and immediately looked around. His dark suit didn't seem to quite fit his large frame, and he brushed his thin greasy hair back as he now strode in our direction. His dark-skinned partner, whom I could see very clearly now since he wasn't in a car, entered in behind his heavier accomplice and took one second to say something to Stacy at the reception desk. He held a black briefcase in his left hand. His movements were swift and precise, and the pant legs of his suit fell neatly over the sides of his shoes with each gliding step.

The larger man was now upon us, and Samantha got a direct view of her now visible muse and, clearly disappointed, closed her sketchpad. Tyler, who was sitting between us to the right, got up and moved in front of the advancing men.

"Detective Tyler Cunningham, I presume?" asked the heavier man, before Tyler fully stood. "Agent Marks and Agent Younglin, FBI," he continued without letting Tyler answer, showing his wallet with a flick of his chubby left wrist. I could smell his cologne from where I stood, at least ten feet from him.

Tyler shook his hand, seeming a bit overwhelmed and flustered in their presence. "Good to meet you, gentlemen. Detective Tyler Cunningham. You're here for the Wyer case?"

"Of course, Detective, we have a lot to go over with him," the heavy agent Marks said, speaking about me right in front of me.

"Impeccable timing then, we were just finishing up." Tyler led them my way.

"Good. Do you have a secluded area where we may be able to question Mr. Wyer?" He was looking half in my direction, half at Tyler, still not addressing me, although it was obvious that he knew who I was.

"Certainly, right this way." Tyler now acted much more professional. "Stacy, coffee."

Agent Marks annoyed me immensely as soon as I met him. As we walked into the police interrogation room, he stared at me with a plastic uncomfortable smile plastered upon his thick face. His two front teeth were large, square, and slightly crooked, making his fake smile seem more smug. The longer he smiled, bunching the meat on his cheeks together, the worse I felt about the whole situation.

His whole frame was large, and if he added another twenty pounds, he might almost be flirting with obesity. His suit didn't seem to want to fit him right, like it also had a problem with him, and the ends of his pants and suit jacket were just a bit too short. He continually stared at me, usually with that grating smile on his round face, but never said anything to me until I had situated myself across the table from him.

"Hello, Mr. Wyer—"his outstretched hand met mine, "—Agent Marks." He had a very firm yet fleshy handshake. "This is Agent Younglin." He indicated without looking to the thin black man behind him, who nodded at me. "Do you understand why exactly we are here, Mr. Wyer?" he asked after sitting down. His partner, Agent Younglin, retreated against the far white wall of the room, closest to the door, while Tyler positioned himself to my right at the far end of the table. "Do you realize the extent of the circumstance that you find yourself in?"

I waited for a moment, studying him. After all, he was the person that I was just fixated on detailing to a sketch artist. "I know the circumstance that *I find* myself involved in, yes. But I don't know the circumstance that you may find yourselves involved in, and to tell you the truth, I really don't care. I just want my family back, and why you two were following me the other day."

He chuckled a fake chuckle, obviously annoyed with my direct question. "All of your questions will be answered after we get ours," he replied, eyes widened to meet mine with a fierce intensity. His face seemed to bunch up around his eyes too.

The younger, dark-skinned agent Younglin chimed in from across the room. "We know your family is of the utmost concern to you, Mr. Wyer, but there are more lives at stake. More than you realize. The importance of our investigation includes and yet far exudes the lives of your family."

He looked at me, locking eyes with me for the first time. "So we need your complete cooperation for the aid of us all. Do you understand that?"

"Actually," the larger agent Marks added, sitting, "we demand your cooperation, or you may face federal charges."

"What?" I replied, aggravated now. "I have nothing to do with this except the fact that my family has been taken from me! Do *you* fucking realize that? Do you?"

"Calm down, Mr. Wyer," Agent Marks said my name as if I was his patient. "Don't get carried away, we are just telling you what exactly is happening here."

"Actually, you haven't told me a goddamned thing about what is happening here! All that you have told me is that I might be facing charges if I don't cooperate with you when you should be the ones that are cooperating with me!"

At this moment, Agent Younglin stepped forward and put the briefcase down on the table. Then, while making direct eye contact with me, he spoke softly, "Mr. Wyer, please do not get the wrong impression. We are here to help. Myself and Agent Marks have been investigating this case for some time now, and we need your help. That is all we are trying to say." Agent Younglin then smoothly sat down near his burly accomplice.

I did not like these guys already. Especially the much heavier agent Marks. He seemed nonprofessional, yet with a fake professional façade. There was nothing remotely warm or pleasant about him. But I could tell that he wasn't necessarily here to be cordial, so he didn't care that I could see poison in his eyes.

"Okay, Mr. Wyer," Marks said, almost looking as if he could read my dislike for him. "You need to tell me what exactly happened with the disappearance of your family, and please, spare me no details. I need to know every aspect of what has gone on." He looked me in the eyes as he asked the question, prying for information. I noticed that a gold cross hung from his neck, as he looked at me from across the table.

I recited the exact events without even concentrating on them, in every detail that I knew. It was like playing a horrible old record, one that now seemed to be my national anthem.

After I was done, there was a moment of silence. Tyler rustled in his chair, but Agent Marks did not move his eyes off me. Then he spoke. "Well, Chris, let's all get a few things set straight here. As of this moment, myself and Agent Younglin are here not to look for your wife and child. That is what Detective Cunningham is investigating and that is why he will be working along with us. But we are concerned."

He took a moment to cover his mouth as he coughed.

"Believe me when I tell you that we all here are extremely concerned about their well being. But the reason we are here is for someone else. Someone who we believe is involved in this as well."

"Who?" both Tyler and I said nearly the same time.

"A person you would have known as Leonard Caldwell, Mr. Wyer."

"Leonard Caldwell?" I asked, the name bringing back long-forgotten memories, "from high school?"

"Exactly the one."

"What does he have to do with this?" I asked.

"Probably everything," the quieter agent Younglin answered, pulling his chair a bit closer to the table, "everything and more."

Agent Marks resumed, "We don't know what Detective Cunningham has told you about the case so far, but we will presume it is everything that he knows about it," he looked at Tyler now, probably for the first time since meeting him. His inspecting gaze now set on the detective, for just a moment, but he had taken it off of me. It was a relief. I don't know if he was trained to do so, or if it just came naturally for him to look at you and turn you into ice. "Have you indeed, told him all you know, Detective?"

"Of course," Tyler replied quite timidly, it seemed, under the agent's excruciating eyes.

"Well then," his square face turned back toward mine, "You must then already know that the blood on the letter you received is a few hundred years old—"

"—and the DNA of the blood doesn't match a single person's DNA in the police database," I interrupted, showing him that Tyler had indeed told me everything.

"That may be, Mr. Wyer. But what the detective doesn't know, and what we do, is that it does indeed match up with somebody."

"And that somebody is your old classmate, Mr. Wyer," Agent Younglin interjected.

CHAPTER 6

I will admit that I sometimes tend to miss a few things. Forget someone's name maybe, or skip an appointment. But I catch what is important. And if I am not mistaken, what they were saying to me was that the thick blood that covered the letter that had been sent to me was over three hundred years old. And somehow, a kid that I knew in high school, a kid that could have been no more than fifteen years old then, and no more than thirty years old now, was supposed to be the supplier of the said three-hundred-year-old blood? The only reasonable question to ask then was:

"How the hell can that be?"

"We will get to it all, Chris. I know it must seem absurd," Agent Younglin spoke, his thin black lips barley moving.

"Absurd is an understatement," Tyler spoke for me.

"What we need from you first is the most that you know about Leonard, so that we can piece some of our own puzzle together, then we will tell you all we know." Agent Younglin moved his chair all the way to the edge of the table now, as he continued talking, "and what I need from you, Detective, is the letter itself, so that I may inspect it."

Agent Younglin slid his briefcase in front of him and began rummaging through it as Agent Marks found a cigarette and lit it. Tyler opened his own briefcase, pulled forth the letter encased in a large ziplock, and slid it across the table to the sharply dressed agent Younglin.

Agent Marks was a patient man, as his large body forced him to be. He made no sudden movements. His teeth bugged me, so square and a bland yellow, arranged in their crooked order. But it was clearly apparent that he took his job very seriously, and his job was to locate Leonard Caldwell. Being so, I could not tell if he thought immediately that I was a victim of Leonard's or an accomplice. He questioned me on every aspect of what I knew about Leonard, as if he were questioning a felon. This man trusted nothing but the facts that were laid out in front of him. He questioned me about everything that happened on that night so long ago when I picked up Leonard Caldwell as he hitchhiked along the deserted road in the cold. The night I nearly died from that violent car crash, the night that he saved my life. Agent Marks extracted every detail, and I recalled every detail as best I could.

After he was seemingly satisfied with my testimony, he reclined his large frame back in his chair. He removed another cigarette from his jacket; he had already smoked a few as I told him about what I remembered. He brought a lighter to the tip of the cigarette and scorched an orange circle in its end, bringing apparent relief to his lungs in the form of gray smoke. Taking time before he began, preparing his words carefully, he then told me some of what the FBI knew, never conveying more information than was necessary.

"We have substantial reason to believe that it may be your old classmate Leonard Caldwell who is probably behind all this. So in pursuing Leonard Caldwell, we are in fact pursuing your family's well-being in the process. And that brings me to my point, that brings to my job status at hand." He took another puff of his cigarette and laid it down into an ashtray in front of him.

The agent sat back in his chair and looked around the room. He undid his tie from his bulging neckline. "Leonard is probably not the Leonard you may or may not have known him to be in your encounters with him in high school. And we will get to that. Leonard has been on the FBI's most elusive criminal list for some time now, and we believe that he is now the criminal mastermind behind a few large recognizable terrorist activities. We believe he poses a great danger to your family but also to the United States."

Absurd really was an understatement.

The Leonard Caldwell that I had known was a very nonviolent human being. A purely calm individual, a person that had saved my life even after I had been viciously cruel to him. A person that would never do this. "No, this wasn't Leonard Caldwell, I know that for certain," I told him immediately. "He would never do this sort of thing."

"You think not?" retorted Agent Marks, always antagonistic.

"Yeah, I think you got the wrong guy."

He reached into his briefcase and removed a small folder. I could see that it was a police report on the accident that happened fourteen years ago. "According to this," he said calmly, studying the report, "the officer who took the report documented Leonard only once in report that he had written. But he was documented. The funny thing is, in police procedure, at least correct police procedure, there needs to be documentation. This includes correct identification on each person who is directly involved in the accident. Back then, when you were involved in this accident, when you were—sixteen?"

"That sounds about right," I said.

"And how old would you have figured Leonard was back then?"

"Fifteen?" I replied, picturing his smaller body in my head at that time.

"Well, that might sound right to you, but the point that I am trying to make is that there was no Leonard Caldwell. He did not exist. The officer went back to his office and realized that he never properly identified Leonard but had written his name down in his report. He had forgotten to get Leonard's date of birth or much less anything besides his name, but he needed these details to properly fill out his paperwork. So he logged onto his police computer, figuring he would just punch in Leonard's name and get his information from his file."

"But his file never showed up," Tyler said, partly a question, partly a statement.

"Precisely," Agent Marks replied. "No birth records, fingerprints, even known handwriting. No known aliases or second identities. Well, being that it was a small town, the officer decided to go find this little kid on his own, this kid who had obviously given him a false name."

"But of course he never did because Leonard had already vanished," I said.

"Correct. The officer looked for months, but then just gave up when he never found him. We don't even have a clear record of his existence, even in our vast federal files. But we know he exists, even if not on paper. He has pictures in your damn high school yearbook for instance." He handed me a photocopy of a picture of Leonard, although slightly blurry. But it was definitely the meek-looking kid that I knew. Underneath the photo: LEONARD B. CALDWELL, 1988."

Agent Marks sighed heavily, momentarily scratching the back of his balding head. "It would almost seem as that Leonard had been raised and tutored, as well as be completely protected, to become the perfect criminal that he is today. It almost seems that he was just . . . created out of thin air. Yet you said that he communicated with you so many different times, through his notes and everything. And that is perplexing. To say the least."

"And why exactly is that so perplexing?" I asked.

"Well, it makes me think that you are not being a reliable source. Or that the Leonard Caldwell that you know is not the same Leonard Caldwell that we are searching for. Or that it was a figment of your imagination or lapse in memory. Whatever it may be, I know that our Leonard would never have gone out of his way to speak with you. Even in high school. He was, he is, too careful to do that."

"What?" I asked incredulously. I was astounded by what he was saying because I faintly remembered Leonard speaking Latin or Spanish or something after he pulled me from my wrecked car many years before. And he had definitely written me so many notes.

"Well, maybe he did, maybe he didn't. But it's hard for me to believe that he would speak only to you if he had never spoken with anyone else before and made a point not to speak with anyone ever since. Under any circumstances. You see, Leonard has been groomed his whole life to stay as completely isolated from society as possible. He has been taught to become invisible. And he was taught well. So why would he associate himself with you?"

Agent Marks stared at me for an answer that I did not have.

He paused to unbutton his coat and remove it, setting it neatly behind him on his chair. "Leonard Caldwell is the most meticulous criminal the government has ever known. He has routines that he sticks with. He works in patterns, very well-thought-out patterns, to defy the law with every move. If he talks to you, merely shows himself to you, it must be part of one of his elaborate schemes." He paused, looking directly at me. Thinking.

"I'm gonna cut through the bullshit now, Mr. Wyer." Agent Marks pierced me with his eyes and paused his cigarette inches from his mouth. "And I will expect for you to do the same. I'm not here to be your buddy. I am here to find out what your connection with Caldwell is. And I will find that out by any means possible. You get me? Right now you are so in over your head that you couldn't even be reeled in with a fucking fishing line." He took a drag from his cigarette. "But the fact is that for some reason, you have received a letter from him, a man that may be the largest known threat to humanity."

"No, hold on. Wait a damn second. You just got through informing me that you have no records on Leonard. So how can you tell me that this letter is from him when you can't even match it up with his blood? How do you know that this is even him, when you don't have records of him?"

"Well, Mr. Wyer, what I meant is that we have no *modern* records of his existence. And that Leonard Caldwell is his *modern* name. But there is documentation of his realism, quite a valuable source of documentation, to be precise. He does exist, rest assured."

Agent Marks shifted his weight in the chair and leaned forward. "Here's the thing, and listen very carefully, because I won't tell you twice. What I am about to tell you, as well as Detective Cunningham, is absolutely and completely federally classified information. Detective Cunningham understands the importance of classified information, and why it needs to be kept confidential, correct, Detective?" It was a statement more than a question that was directed at Tyler.

Tyler nodded to meet Agent Marks's strict gaze. "Absolutely."

"And you understand, Mr. Wyer, that what I am about to tell you is something that you are never to repeat, or face a charge of treason punishable by all measures necessary. Actually, to be frank with you, you would never even live to see a formal charge of treason because you would be silenced immediately. You catch what I'm saying to you? And believe me, the government would never be held accountable for your silence thereafter."

"What exactly are you saying, Agent?" Tyler now demanded before I could. "Exactly what procedure does that follow?"

"It follows our procedure, a procedure that does not concern you. Remember that you are only along for the ride here, Detective. You are here to help, but we have absolute jurisdiction in this case, of which you are surely aware. We truly do not even need you involved, but realize that you are already, and realize that our focus will be entirely on finding Leonard Caldwell. But in our concern for the kidnapping of Mr. Wyer's family, we will allow you to work that aspect of this case. But do not question my authority if you want to stay. If you will be a thorn, you can leave."

"No, he stays," I insisted.

Agent Marks glared at me now. Then, he slowly pivoted back to Tyler. "If you become a thorn, I will personally pluck your rosy ass from this sweet little garden that we have growing here. Capiche, Detective?"

Tyler stared back at the large man, and I could sense that he truly disliked everything that he saw in front of him. "Yeah, I'm fine, I'll just get the details I need."

"Wonderful," Agent Marks said with a resounding finality. He took another quick puff from his cigarette. "What is about to be spoken here was never spoken." He looked at Agent Younglin, sighed, and pulled another cigarette from his coat pocket.

"Mathematics. Matrices. Equations. Zeros and ones. The numbers and equations and everything that we were forced to learn in high school. Most of all of that, except for the fundamentals, will never be applied to any normal job or scenario. But the deeper math, the calculus and the advanced trigonometry, things like that, are simply the beginning to what really matters. And what really matters, the mathematics that are really important are the functions that can be applied to life itself. No, not making change at the grocery store, I am talking about the relationships of constellations and the universes that nestle them. I am talking about the numbers that create reality . . ." He breathed out harshly. "Gentlemen, the point that I am trying to make is that there is a mathematical formula that dictates everything. It is a formula so advanced no human would or should even be able to begin to understand it. But there is a man that we believe can. Leonard Caldwell."

"Now wai—" Tyler started.

Agent Marks looked quickly at Tyler and silenced him. "Wait till I'm finished," Marks said sharply. "For some reason or another, we believe that Leonard Caldwell is so advanced that he knows everything that a human being is capable of knowing. Everything and more. Normally, this would be advantageous, as his knowledge could clearly afford the human race a wealth of previously unrecognized information. We think that he knows the mathematical equation for life, and consequently holds the key to the universe. So needless to say, this makes him extremely powerful. I cannot emphasize just how powerful. More power than all the nuclear weapons on the face of this Earth multiplied by ten. Multiplied by a thousand maybe. Who knows. Absolute power in such proportions that we may not even be able to fully grasp how superior he truly is. But as the saying goes, absolute power corrupts absolutely."

I pictured Leonard Caldwell as the weak-looking kid sitting in front of me, scribbling down notes that were, in all actuality, the keys to the universe. I also pictured him sitting behind some elaborate desk of controls somewhere in space, with his frail finger upon a big red button. He would have a huge smile on his delicate face, an evil smile, knowing that one push of the button would destroy all of creation.

I could picture it in my head, but I still couldn't quite believe it.

No one could be that mathematical, especially a kid that went to my public high school.

"However, we think that Leonard has not evolved to his full potential yet. Actually, we merely hope and pray that he hasn't, but who knows. If he does in fact have the mathematical equation for the creation of life, we can conclude that he also has the mathematical equation to erase it. What can be created can always be destroyed. What he could add, he could also subtract. He potentially holds the demise of all creation at the ends of his fingertips—"

"Now hold on a second," Tyler finally interrupted. "What proof do you have that Leonard is this powerful and dangerous?"

"Well, Detective, that is the obvious question. Also, it demands an obvious answer as what I am telling right now could seem a bit far-fetched. At first. What we know about Leonard derives more from circumstance rather than substantial proof. About twenty years ago, scientists were at a classified site outside of Cairo, Egypt, and uncovered a large structure deep within the Earth, miles below the pyramids. A small ellipse had been found, about the size of large living room deep underground. Almost three miles underground. The sphere was made of a substance that reflected nearly all light, so as it almost seemed transparent. Eyewitness researchers described it as being the true opposite of darkness, and even at the site of excavation, a few dozen football fields below the light of the sun, the object seemed to glow. Almost as a beacon. It was shining through dirt, and mud, and the ribcage of our condensed Earth. They found it because it resonated a large electromagnetic pulse.

The agent seemed excited about the continuation of the story, drawing out as much emphasis as he could on the situation as he told it.

"The EMP it sent rendered drilling machines useless once they got closer than one hundred yards from the sphere, so it took years for researchers to actually excavate it, even though they knew it was there.

The inner structure of the ellipse was preserved perfectly, made of various carbon compounds, and it resembled the inner features of the Egyptian tombs miles above it. It was furnished elegantly and lined throughout with jewelry and gold, and in such a fashion that it was sealed perfectly. Airtight. Well, they managed to crack it open, and once inside, they discovered no objects at all, save a large book. Upon opening it, they found that the book contained nothing, no words or dialects at all, just a various series of dots."

"Dots?" I asked.

"Similar to braille, at least in the middle of the book. Without being raised like braille is." He took another puff of his smoke. "And like your letter, all of the dots were printed in blood. Roughly six thousand pages of points of blood, in what first appeared to be in no particular order."

"At first?" Tyler asked.

"Yes," Marks continued, "but upon further inspection, it was discovered that the first two pages of the book had roughly 1.2 billion points of blood on them. On just those two pages, 1.2 billion specks! The rest of the book, all six thousand pages exactly, had some pages that also held billions of dots as well, and some pages that only had anywhere from ten dots to a hundred."

"How the hell can you fit that many dots on a page of paper?" I asked.

"Well, I said it was a large book, and that is a slight understatement. The book is about as large as a queen-sized bed once opened up. And the most interesting thing is, with the exception of one large dot of blood the size of a dime, the size of the dots of blood ranged from the size of a felt tip pen to points that are much smaller than the head of a pin. Microscopic."

Tyler and I were both astounded by what Agent Marks was telling us. Yet, Agent Younglin stayed passive and continued to remain quiet as his partner spoke.

"The interior of the book varied tremendously, with no apparent sequence or pattern, just random points of blood. Page by page, in no definite order or reason, with some pages looking sparse and symmetrical while others were filled with blood. And the last two pages at the end looked similar to the first two pages, again having over one billion points of blood arranging in size from nearly invisible to some as large as a coin. Points that resembled the same points as the first two pages, but not exactly."

Agent Marks stopped for a moment and smiled at the looks on our faces. "The story has only just begun to get good," he said gladly. "After inspecting the book for a while, it was then found that the interior of the walls of the room of the tomb were equally amazing. As I said, the walls were lined with jewels and gold. But upon closer inspection, it was discovered that the jewels on the walls, actually rubies and one large diamond centered in the sphere closest to the Earth's core, matched perfectly with the location and relative size of the dots of blood on the first two pages of the book. The northern hemisphere of the ellipse on the first page, the southern on the second. An exact match. Nearly one and a quarter billion rubies in varying degrees of size in the surrounding walls that coincided perfectly with the dots of blood on the first two pages of the book. The first two pages of the book were laid out exactly as the walls that surrounded it, down to the location of the large dime-sized dab of blood and the large diamond stuck in the wall. It was the most incredible thing that you could ever see. And can anyone guess what they signified?"

"The moon and stars," answered Tyler as I still tried to absorb what was being said.

"Yes, exactly. The moon and stars of our galaxy as seen from Earth looking from the angle created from the center of the Earth up through the diamond in the sphere. An astrological pattern. But the coordinates of stars which could only have existed roughly four and a half billion years ago."

"The beginning of the world?" Tyler asked.

"We think so, Detective," Agent Marks replied.

"So the last two pages signify what then?" Tyler asked, with a hint of nervousness.

"The end, Detective. The end. At least that is what it looks like," Agent Marks said.

"That's what I . . . figured." He ended in nearly a whisper.

"Don't the stars fall into the exact same place year after year?" I asked. "When the world revolves a full rotation around the sun again?"

"No, not exactly. Due to the axis of the Earth, as well as a few other discrepancies, such as the path of the Earth's rotation around our sun, the stars never fall back in the same place as viewed from the same position on Earth. Sometimes, they come close to lining up again, but never an exact match. That is how we are able to date any particular order of stars."

The room was now noticeably warm, and it almost seemed smaller than when we first started. Maybe it was about to start spinning, or maybe my world was simply collapsing in on itself, I couldn't really tell, I felt light-headed. Tyler, Agent Marks, and myself all looked uncomfortable and uneasy in our chairs, but Agent Younglin continued to hunch over the table, intensely studying the letter, occasionally writing a few things down on a small yellow notepad. He seemed to be affected by nothing. I hadn't seen him look up from his work all the while that Agent Marks had been speaking, but he surely knew every aspect of the story already. Tyler, however, looked almost dumbfounded, seemingly forgetting that he too was an investigator and that the discussion somehow pertained to him.

Agent Marks paused for quite some time, fidgeting with his black tie, before resuming. The room held an uncomfortable silence.

"Mr. Wyer, the reason that I am telling you this is because you are the closest connection that the FBI has ever had to Leonard, and we hope that you can help us find him. You maybe the only way that we can find him. So therefore, you must be made clear of the full context of the situation . . ." He paused again to light another cigarette. I had lost count of just how many he had smoked; he seemingly didn't need oxygen.

"For some reason, Leonard wants to get in touch with you, or torture you, or whatever it may be. He may still feel angst for the times that you bullied him, or maybe feels that you owe him your life, because he saved yours. Whatever it is, you have in fact received a letter written in his blood, and that is the biggest break that we have ever had that relates directly to his whereabouts."

Tyler and I watched as Agent Marks finished off his smoke and put it out as crudely as the previous one. "To answer your question from earlier, we *do* know that the blood on the letter matches the blood of Leonard Caldwell's. Or to be more precise, it matches the blood of who Leonard Caldwell used to be."

I didn't even need to tell him that what he had just said didn't make much sense, neither did Tyler, he could see it on our faces.

"I know, I know, just bear with me," he continued. "It all sounded crazy to me when I first heard it too. But what I am trying to tell you is . . ." he paused again, finding the right words.

"We, the FBI, first came across Leonard Caldwell fourteen years ago, basically thanks to you, Mr. Wyer. Thanks to your reckless driving incident, that is. All the police files, especially police files that are done incorrectly or left incomplete, are flagged and sent through to the FBI as procedure. The FBI back-checks everything. Anything that is even slightly amiss, especially dealing with officers that don't follow procedure, is checked up on. Usually to see if we have a "bad cop," or maybe someone that has infiltrated the system. Usually, mistakes like this happen all the time, which is unfortunate, because it is 98 percent bullshit paperwork that we have to weed through. But the other 2 percent, well, it can end up being . . . crucial."

Agent Younglin looked up momentarily to smile.

"Like this. This one turned into one hell of a domino effect. Anyway, because the idiot cop that wrote down the incident report failed to obtain ID from a one 'Leonard Caldwell,' the report came through to the FBI, and we discovered that this 'Leonard Caldwell' was not in our database. Well this could be just a case of mistaken identity, or a false name given, or whatever may be, but the FBI called the cop to follow up with him on why he didn't complete the paperwork, and he said 'because the boy has vanished.'"

"This was interesting to the FBI to say the least. So two federal agents were sent to investigate and obtain all the information that we could dig up on Mr. Leonard Caldwell. What we found was that he was as nearly transparent in real life as he was on paper. We asked around and snooped around, but nobody knew who our 'Leonard' even was. We did, however, find a sample of blood on your broken passenger window, blood that wasn't a match to yours, and so we at least had something."

Agent Younglin interrupted the conversation for a moment. "Are you bilingual, by chance, Mr. Wyer?" he asked.

"What?" The question was unexpected.

"Can you speak another language besides English?" he asked again.

"No," I responded, slightly confused.

"Did you two have any codes or anything that you used when you wrote each other back in high school, only codes you would know—" he handed me the ziplocked letter "—and can you remember if this is his handwriting?"

I took the letter from him and examined it once again. The blood still seemed to shock me. It looked so gruesome every time that I looked at it. "No, not that I can remember. We didn't use codes. He basically just gave me his theories on life and things like that. He was incredibly smart, I do remember that. But I can't remember if this is his handwriting or not. Can I have this letter back? Maybe I can figure it out if I look at it enough."

"I can't let you have the original. It is evidence." His thin dark fingers grasped the ziplocked page again. "But a copy can surely be made for you, maybe you can figure out if all those numbers and symbols mean something."

"Yeah, maybe I can." He looked down again at the letter, obviously resuming his inspection without further question.

Agent Marks leaned heavily back, getting everyone's attention again. Agent Younglin looked up slightly from his scrutiny. Marks continued speaking. "It just so happens that when we tried to find a match to the sample of blood that we found on your broken window, we of course found none that corresponded with it. So we analyzed the blood even further and discovered two things. Two things that medical fields and modern history have never documented. Two things that blew our collective minds. The first thing, as I said originally, was that the blood didn't match up. But it didn't just not match up with any person, but it also didn't even match a known blood type. It was not blood type A, B, AB, or O. It was blood entirely different, a different type altogether, a different strand somehow. Unlike human blood.

"The second thing that was simply amazing, as Detective Cunningham discovered and what you now know, is that the blood is also quite an antique. Basically, using carbon-dating, we rationalized that the blood that was on your passenger window dates back approximately three hundred and sixty-eight years. Well, needless to say, when your letter shows up in the mail, the blood on the letter matches the same blood that we found on your window so long ago. Leonard's blood." He paused, staring at me for a minute.

"Mr. Wyer, have you ever heard of the Dead Sea Scrolls?" Agent Younglin asked.

"Yeah, I think so. They are scriptures that are rumored to be the foundation for the Bible. But they are still undiscovered, so what do they—"

"—they have everything to do with this," Agent Younglin said, finishing my sentence. "The Dead Sea Scrolls are in fact believed to be early scriptures of the Old Testament of the Bible, but what you don't know, and what you now know, is that they *have*, in fact, been discovered. And they have absolutely nothing to do with the Bible. Nothing. The number of recovered scrolls runs into the thousands, as opposed to tens or maybe only hundreds, as some people may think. However, the scrolls, at least the scrolls that were still in a relatively good condition, were written in many different languages and dialects. Some scrolls have language written on them that hadn't even been developed at the time that they were even written. Like modern Spanish and English for instance. Yet, all the scrolls do have something in common. They all describe the book that we found in that ellipse underneath the Egyptian temples, 'The Book of Life,' as it is now referred to.

"Most all reference this book, that it is truly the book of creation, but is also the book that can lead to ultimate destruction. And some scrolls hold clues that help decipher the code written within that book. A code written with billions of dots of blood. It would be an indecipherable code, at least without help, one that could not be broken without the key. A code so advanced that we believe if it were to be deciphered, it may turn out to be the language of life. Maybe instructions written directly by God. The code was not written in Hebrew, or early Latin, or even matching scriptures like the Iliad or any other primary language of that time, but a series of dots, or points, similar to our modern braille. We believe that this form of communication, using dots, is in fact the first form of written communication used by humans."

"I thought drawing pictures was the first form of written communication?" Tyler interjected.

"Petroglyphs? Well, technically, yes. But we think that the dots represent the first form of complex written information. The first real written language. The next step above petroglyphs. Obviously, drawing petroglyphs took quite a long time, so, man, as he evolved, condensed them. He could draw three dots in the sand much faster than he could draw a buffalo, let's say, so in time, after his fellow people understood what he was doing, he could represent that buffalo with three uniquely placed dots instead. A bird might be three dots in a straight line with two dots underneath, and the sun might be four dots in a circle. Slowly, then, the first real written language arose. A language that was easier and faster to write than pictures. A language created in dots.

"We believe that the Book of Life is mainly written in this language, a language that we still have not been able to crack. But the information that we have gained from the parts that we do understand is incredible, and incredibly advanced. This book is so advanced that we think that it may answer any question that has ever been asked. Or maybe it holds the mathematical equation for the creation of the universe and all existence, as we know it. And each one of the Dead Sea Scrolls holds a key that unlocks a piece of the book.

"So get all of the scrolls and figure out what the book says," I interjected.

"So much easier said than done. First off, there are thousands of different scrolls in existence, at least half of which are highly damaged and generally unusable. Hundreds more are held by private collectors, many whom know their worth and would never even show them, much less put them up for sale. But even if we did have enough to satisfy a thorough translation, which we will never have, it would still not be sufficient. There would still be a major wild card, a major thing that scares us."

"And what is that?" I asked.

"What scares us, Mr. Wyer, is that if someone else knew how to read that code, knew how to read that book, then they know how to create something, anything, out of nothing. But they would then also know how to erase something, anything, back into nothing. That is simply terrifying. Nuclear war is nothing compared to a meltdown of all material simply by plugging in the right numbers. If they can make additions at that level, then it is only feasible that they can also make subtractions. And here's the kicker. As you know, the dots were all written in blood, and that blood is literally the signature of the writer of that omniscient book. And the blood in the book—"

"—directly matches the blood that you found on the car window and the blood on the ransom letter," Tyler interrupted, now finishing out the agent's sentence.

"Correct, Detective Cunningham."

The room fell silent again.

"Blood that could only have been discretely saved for centuries, just to be used to write a letter, which was placed in your mailbox almost four hundred years later. Or it is blood that comes from the same person that actually inscribed a book more powerful than anything else and more true than any bible?"

"Little Leonard Caldwell," I said.

"Yeah, little Leonard, the strong silent type," Agent Marks concluded.

"But," Tyler spoke, "how has Leonard been able to live that long?"

"We don't exactly know the details of it all. But I would guess that if I knew how to control creation, becoming immortal would be a perk of the job."

CHAPTER 7

I opened the door to my empty house, truly exhausted. Even more mentally than physically drained. I still expected to see my little Rebecca running toward me as I passed through the threshold, in a full smiling sprint, welcoming me home. But she wasn't there, and neither was Cathorine who would have normally been busily talking on the phone or making dinner. It felt as if there was a bad song that was stuck in my head, and the song was called "sudden and unexpected yet terrifyingly horrible loneliness in A minor." If my life had a soundtrack, it was now the only song playing on it.

I instinctively looked in the fridge, not even really seeing what was in there. I turned on the TV, not even absorbing the words of the talking heads. I realized that I probably didn't have a job anymore. I hadn't even called in for work in four days, much less shown up. I was now the epitome of depression, and wondered if not being suicidal was a blessing or a curse.

Days passed, but I couldn't really recall how many. My clothes stayed the same, and my general location on the couch pretty much did as well. The phone rang occasionally, being relatives or friends, wanting to know "how I was doing?" If I knew how to laugh at the irony of it all, I might have tried.

I found the copy of the letter that Tyler had made me at the police department, and I stared blankly at it for hours on end.

Maybe if I looked at it long enough, it might just become audible and simply tell me what it meant.

I basically had the damn thing memorized. It had burned neatly into my brain. I just couldn't register anything but *the answer is around* scrawled within the circle at the top of the indecipherable text. At least now I was staring at a photocopy and not blood; that alone probably kept me from losing it altogether. I could at least rationalize looking at the code without constantly thinking of someone cutting himself to obtain a sadistic ink to write with. I hadn't slept in probably fifty hours, and the page started to become a mixture of terrible thoughts and a distant connection to my family scrolled right below my tired eyes.

THE ANSWER IS AROUND.
:i ●(XV 4);(X 6)-(3V)●;(●)(-2(I)) 13;
2X-(XV(●)):1●3●:(X 4) 2 ●;(-3)● XV;2X-2-●(XV 2);
2X-6 ●;(-3 ●) 8:X-
4(●);I ((XV 2) ●);(I ●) 14;V 8(●):
(XX-1)-(3V)●;2X-●(XV);(2X-2)-4 ●;V (X 7)
(●);5;4V-2 ●:
(XX 8) 2 6(●);XXV-X(●):3;XV-
(14(●));13;V (11 ●):
1(2X ●) I(●);(2(V I))-7(●);3(X) 2 3 ●;
I(XV-I)-((X)(●));● V-●:

I was completely stumped, needless to say. I needed some rest. I needed some help. I needed something, anything. I needed to feel alive again.

I seem to be just existing, with no clear purpose or relevance to anything.

I noticed that the sun was splintering through the shades of the window, careening into my living room. I almost drifted to sleep as the room gradually illuminated around me. Another morning.

The ringing of the phone was startling and wrenched me from slipping into slumber. I drearily knocked it from the table beside me and managed to fish it from the carpet below the couch. It was Tyler, and I could tell that he was very excited.

"Get your bags packed, Chris! We are going to New York! Agent Younglin cracked the code!"

"Wha—What!"

"Yeah, he cracked it about a half hour ago. Get your things together, man. I'll be there to pick you up in a few minutes!" It seemed that he was yelling through a bullhorn into the phone and then into my ear.

I slammed the phone down and jumped to my feet. I was wide awake now, and so excited I could barely maintain any emotion.

He cracked the code! How?

It felt great to know that everything might be all right again. I felt great along with it. I sang in the shower at the top of my lungs, hopefully waking the neighbors, and threw some clothes together in what seemed like seconds. I could feel the surge of adrenaline pulsing through my body, pumping like a like a piston. I met Tyler outside a few minutes later, as he pulled his white car into my driveway. It was impossible not to tell that he was grinning nearly ear to ear, almost enough to split his face.

"We have a flight to New York in twenty minutes," he said, as I ducked into the undercover police cruiser. "The feds are meeting us there."

"How did he crack it?" I asked excitedly as Tyler hit the gas, and we squealed away.

"I don't know. It's his job. That's what he gets paid the bucks for." Tyler turned a corner sharply, and I felt my side of the car begin to lift up from the asphalt. "The guy did seem pretty bright."

"Yeah, he did." I thought about how the younger agent had scoured over the letter as his partner gave the details about Leonard. His eyes never really looked up, always fixated upon the letter encased in plastic. He had studied it as if it were an endangered specimen. I liked the guy. He did his job very well, and I respected that.

We blistered our way to the airport. Tyler seemed just as excited as I was. But my mind was racing much faster than our car. I wondered for a moment, if my family was even in New York.

If they were, how could they have gotten there?

Surely, they couldn't have taken a flight, at least on a public plane. The drive would be at least four days, so that would make transporting hostages difficult. But Leonard was resourceful, certainly. A private plane would not be unfeasible. Actually, it would be very easy to obtain a private plane, for someone the feds say is as powerful as he. That thought settled my nerves somehow. They had to be in New York, it just felt like they were.

I'll be there in a while, girls. I'm coming to get you.

Tyler brought the car to a secluded area of the airport, and I saw a small black jet slowly pulling out of a large hangar, with about seven men dressed in neat black suits talking to each other. Two of them I had already met.

Tyler turned off the engine. "Are you joining us?" I asked.

"Looks like it, pardner." Tyler said, John Wayne sheriff style, as he pulled his own duffel bag from the back. "I had the next few days off anyway, and the agents specifically requested me because I know vital information about the case and could prove useful. Plus I've always wanted to see New York, and the FBI is footing the bill to fly me back next week."

We met the FBI agents, and even though they were dressed in dark suits and always maintained professionalism, I could tell that they were also quite excited about the events.

"Thank you for assisting in this case, Detective," Agent Marks said, shaking Tyler's hand as we boarded the small jet. "Never know when we can use another able mind." I felt underdressed already, and as I boarded the plane, it evolved to feeling overwhelmed. The FBI jet was a piece of streamlined perfection, furnished in soft white leather and matching white carpeting. It had small computer terminals near the front and an open bar near the back. There was also a bathroom at the rear of the plane, with a compact gold-trimmed shower. Four reclining chairs were situated in the middle of two of the last three divisions of the plane, surrounded by lush seating and marble tables branching out along the sides. The spaciousness seemed nearly physically impossible for the apparent size of the plane, and everything was very sleek and pristine. I had never imagined a small private plane to look something so much like a castle.

The division closest to the cockpit was the meeting area, furnished with a large rectangular table covered with laptops, two drop-down data screens at the ends of the table, and a small communications pod set at the edge of the division. I had never seen anything nearly as nice before. I filed into the jet and followed everyone into the first department, and we all strapped ourselves in. The jet took off with amazing but smooth acceleration, and once airborne, we all relocated to the meeting room.

After introductions (many of the names I had forgotten almost immediately), we proceeded to set out a rough game plan for what was to happen in New York. Agent Younglin showed us blueprints of a building, and the agents discussed the best possible positions of the two snipers, the flanks of the other agents, and the positions of agents guarding the rear exit. I barley even listened to what he was saying, as I just didn't feel like paying attention to detail. The final details would be sorted out once we were in New York, and the scenario might change anyway.

Agent Younglin then went over the letter and, in detail, described the process on how he had cracked the code. At this point, only myself, Tyler, Agent Marks, an older agent named Vindaci remained in the meeting room department. I figured that the other agents left only because the procedure of cracking codes was simply something that they had seen many times or that they didn't care to hear Agent Younglin boast about how he did it. I was truly fascinated by his solution and did not feel that he was being arrogant at all in his disposition.

"Have you ever read *The Gold-Bug* by Edgar Allan Poe before, Mr. Wyer?" He addressed me, as the letter had.

"No, I can't say that I have."

"Well, you should, it's a great story. Poe is a master storyteller, or was a master storyteller, I should say. In any case, there is a character in the story, I believe his name is Legrand, who is a wonderful code breaker. He believes in the basic premise that there is no code created by human intelligence that cannot be resolved by human intelligence, at least with correct application. He simply looks at the code and uses his logic to solve it.

"After I read the story for the first time, I felt I could crack any puzzle that I would come across. This of course was when I was a child, and didn't know much better. But the way that Legrand goes about decrypting the cipher that he finds constantly reassures me that I too can decipher almost any puzzle.

"Basically, like Legrand states, one must always realize that the code aims to communicate a connotation. It *always* means something to somebody. And that somebody, in this case, is you, Mr. Wyer. That is why I asked you if you were bilingual when I first met you. You in fact are not, and since the only text on the letter that can be readily deciphered is 'the answer is around,' we can deduct one major thing: the code is most likely written completely in English. Now that we know that, we can take the next step, and that is to simplify what we have in front of us. There are a few different procedures that we can take, and although the federal bureau teaches different methods of 'simplification,' I always like to first use the procedure that Legrand used. It gets me into a code-breaking mindset."

I think that this was the first time that I had heard Agent Younglin much at all. He was normally very silent, even during our first interview at the police station.

"What Legrand does is chart the predominant symbols, and then tries to correlate them with the predominant symbols of the language that he suspects the code to be written in. In our case, English. You would be amazed how many codes I have cracked using this method. Criminals just don't think thoroughly these days.

"Well, I constructed a table of the symbols in the letter, and how many times they occur. Also, I wasn't quite sure if one of the symbols was meant to be the lowercase letter L, or an uppercase I"

Agent Younglin pulled out his yellow notepad and showed this chart:

SYMBOL	TIMES IT OCCURS
:	9
I or L	9
+	23
0	31
(	39
)	39
X	27
V	17
4	7
;	23
6	3
-	21
3	10
2	16
1	8
/	12
8	8

"Well," Agent Younglin continued as we looked at his chart. "After researching my findings, I concluded that this code uses what I like to call misdirection. Basically, it means that the symbols do not match up directly with letters."

"And how did you come to that conclusion?" I asked.

"Well, it is common knowledge that the letter E is the most commonly used letter of the English alphabet, and as it says in Mr. Poe's story, as well as the bureau's, it is unlikely that you will see any sentence structure in the English language where it is not. According to my chart, the most predominant symbols seem to be opposite sides of a parenthesis, and there are thirty-nine of each of them. Although I have seen codes where two different symbols mean the same letter, I highly disputed that this is the case here. Anyway, to tell you the truth, I scrutinized every aspect of how the chart would be directly useful using the possible concepts of what we call chasers and everything I could think of. I even thought that maybe the 1 and the 4 may not be separate symbols, but instead were the symbol 14. Things like that."

"What are chasers?" I asked.

"Exactly, a point that I made to myself. I took into account that you probably didn't even rationalize what the concept of a chaser is. A chaser is a phantom symbol that tells the reader that the symbol that comes directly after it is the real symbol. For instance, I use the asterisk to let you know that the next symbol, whatever it may be, but let's say in this case an exclamation point, will be the letter H. And I use a question mark to let you know that the symbol after that, let's say a 5, will be the letter I. But the asterisk and the question mark themselves are irrelevant and are not used any further. So if I wanted to say 'HI,' I would write it like this." He jotted something down on a piece of paper.

!?5

"Understand?" he asked.

"Sort of."

"Well, anyway, there are many tricks that you can pull. But I concluded that Leonard would not have used them if he was writing the letter to you, and expecting you to decode it. Unless, maybe, he never wanted you to decode it."

"What?"

"Well,—" he paused.

Agent Vindaci interrupted, "Sometimes, killers, er, criminals, may feel guilt or remorse about what they are doing and give clues that are almost impossible to trace. This way, they can lay partial blame on the people who are unable to figure out those clues. It lessens the burden in the criminal mind. It's like a painter that asks a price that is so extravagant he knows nobody would ever pay it. Because the painter wants to keep the piece of work himself. But he is 'trying' to sell the painting, at least in his mind. And of course, there is that chance that the unimaginable happens, and someone buys it. Just like us 'unimaginably' tracking down Leonard Caldwell."

"Thank you, Robert," said Agent Younglin somewhat sarcastically. "Would you mind getting me a drink, I think I can handle it from here." Agent Vindaci looked over at Agent Younglin tentatively, almost with an air of remorse, then removed himself from the room. Agent Younglin was obviously in charge, and solely wanted to explain the situation, and the silent interaction between the two agents confirmed it.

"I think I'll get myself one as well," Agent Marks said. "Detective, Mr. Wyer, you need anything?" We both waved him off. Then both Agents left the room, leaving only Agent Younglin, Tyler and myself.

Agent Younglin continued. "Okay, where was I? I now realized that my chart was somewhat useless to me at this moment, so I again started fresh, taking another angle on everything. I had wasted at least most of a day using the Poe method, and I could safely say that all possibilities had been safely exhausted. So I took a step back from things. Just let my mind wander. I went home, watched some TV, cooked myself a nice dinner, and a few hours later, I tackled it again. Later, when I looked at it again, I realized that the letter resembled a long mathematical equation. It contained many symbols commonly used in math, such as the symbols for addition, subtraction, and division. Plus sign, minus sign, forward slash, respectively."

"It looked like a mathematical equation to me as well, one that was impossible to figure," I said.

"Quite so, it is quite intimidating as a whole," Agent Younglin replied, "especially if it were one full mathematical equation. But I also realized that the—"

he paused to draw,

: ;

"were not symbols, but merely a colon and a semicolon in the English language. I noted that these symbols, the colon or semicolon, appeared at the end of each line, and at the beginning and end of the whole puzzle. This meant that they were being used to constitute breaks between each part of the puzzle. These breaks were probably signified as a separation between letters and or words. This was a huge step for me, as it divided everything up into individual equations, but I was still perplexed at the simplified remaining code. So I removed the colons and semicolons and spaced it out a bit. The result was this, now only a fraction easier to contemplate." Agent Younglin pulled out another piece of paper and placed it on display.

$$I+O(XV+4) \ (X+6)-(3V)O \ (O)(-2(I))+13$$
$$2X-(XV(O)) \ 1030 \ (X+4)+2/O \ (-3)O+XV$$
$$2X-2-O(XV+2)$$
$$2X-6/O \ (-3/O)+8 \ X-4(O) \ I+((XV+2)/O) \ (I/O)+14$$
$$V+8(O) \ (XX-1)-(3V)O \ 2X-O(XV) \ (2X-2)-4/O \ V+(X+7)$$
$$(O) \ 5 \ 4V-2/O$$
$$(XX+8)/2+6(O) \ XXV-X(O) \ 3 \ XV-(14(O)) \ 13 \ V+(11/O)$$
$$I+(2X/O)+I(O) \ (2(V+I))-7(O) \ 3(X)/2+3/O$$
$$I(XV-I)-((X)(O)) \ O+V-O$$

After everyone at the table had seen the paper, Younglin continued, "Now, I tried to resume with figuring out the mathematical equation, and again found it mind-boggling. The reason being thus: As an algebraic expression, there were simply too many letters to try and figure out what they were equal to. Plus, some of the letters, such as O could double as a number. That made it completely difficult to decipher then what letters might be numbers and vice versa."

He then paused, looking around the table. "And then it occurred to me that all the letters in the code could double as numbers." He paused again. Waiting for a reply. Nothing came. We obviously were not following his total train of thought.

"Yes, not a single letter in the code could not double as a roman numeral. The only letters that are apparent in the code are X, V, and what could be either a lowercase L or an uppercase I."

"The lowercase L or an uppercase I could be a 1, so it cannot be apparent as being a letter," Tyler interrupted.

"Normally true, but in this case you'll see that the number 1 is already being used as well, in the number 13 for example, in the midst of the third division of code. It is clearly a 1 because it has the small tail on the top. Clearly different from the letter that begins **things**."

"You're right," I chimed in, seeing where he was now going with this. "The X is ten, the V is five, the I is one, and what is roman numeral for L?"

"Fifty," Agent Younglin answered, going on, "But there is no lowercase L in the roman numerology, so I deducted that it must be the roman numeral I, meaning one. There is no roman symbol for the letter O, so that must mean that it is zero.

"So if we plug numbers in for the roman numerals, we get a full numerical equation, without letters of any kind, just roman numerals mixed with modern numbers to form the equation. Then, placing the semicolon and colon back into the simplified equation, I came up with this." He brought out yet another piece of paper.

: 1; 16; 13;
20: 1030: 14; 15; 18;
20; 8: 10; 1; 14; 5:
19; 20; 18; 5; 5; 20:
14; 25: 3; 15; 13; 5:
1; 12; 15;
14; 5:

"This is what we get, of course, if we suppose that the roman numeral system stays the same, meaning that XV means fifteen, not ten times five."

"So that leaves us with the final process of decoding this thing. The easy part, actually. We do know that the colon comes at the end of the whole code, so that led me to believe that the colon signaled the end of each division. If we plug in each number as it corresponds to letters in the alphabet, A being one, B being two, et cetera, we get letters separated by semicolons and words separated by colons. It spells it out plain and simple. We now, my friends, get the final product. The end result. Leonard's intended meaning for you when he wrote you in his blood, and what will end up to become his ultimate error."

:A; P; M;
T: 1030: N; O; R;
T; H: J; A; N; E:
S; T; R; E; E; T:

N; Y: C; O; M; E:
A; L; O;
N; E:

≈

APMT 1030 NORTH JANE STREET NY COME ALONE.

"Plain as day. Inviting you over," Tyler said with a smile.

"One would assume," Agent Younglin laughed dryly, as if he was forcing it. "There is a problem with the code however, even once solved."

The plane seemed to dip, right on cue, through a pocket of turbulence. Younglin stared at me. Tyler and I stared back at Younglin. "The problem is," Younglin continued, "Apt 1030 North Jane Street is not a full address. The apartment number is missing."

We waited for what else he would say. Younglin looked back into the other area of the plane, seeing that no other Agents were within earshot. He turned back to us, once he realized we were still talking privately.

"The thing is Mr. Wyer, that even after solving it, I still felt somehow duped, like I was still missing something." He looked at me, suspiciously.

"Not sure what you mean Agent Younglin," I said under his scrutinizing eyes.

"I mean, it still feels like there is something about this code that only you, only YOU, should know."

I honestly had no idea what he was talking about.

"But regardless," he said finally, still with a sense of doubt, "we checked out everything we could about 1030 North Jane Street in New York obviously."

"And?" I asked.

"And we found that the building on 1030 North Jane Street is primarily rented out for businesses, with one exception. There is one section that is rented non-commercially, as living quarters. We called the landlord and discovered that the tenant of that section goes under the name Waldon Lecardell."

That name was meaningless to all of us listening to Agent Younglin, by the looks of everyone's faces.

"Waldon Lecardell didn't ring any bells for me either gentlemen, until I analyzed it just a bit."

"Its an anagram," said Tyler then, excitedly.

"It sure is Detective," replied Younglin, smiling again. "Switch the letters around, and you get—"

"Leonard Caldwell." I concluded for him.

Agent Younglin then removed himself from the table, with pride, apparently to go fix himself a drink that hadn't been brought to him by the other agents.

"The weird thing is though," Tyler said after Agent Younglin was away, "I'm pretty sure that the Romans had no concept of the number zero." He spoke almost to himself, "The code still works though, so they must have, but I could have sworn that—"

"Makes it look easy sometimes," interrupted an agent, whose name I'd forgotten, who was passing us on his way to the lavatory. He was referring to Younglin's decoding skills, which actually were quite impressive.

The code seemed so easy to crack after I had seen how Agent Younglin did it, but I know that I would have never been able to do it on my own. This was haunting me. At least what Agent Vindaci had said about how Leonard did not expect me to figure the puzzle out anyway.

Leonard was teasing me. Toying with my head, as he held my family as bait. Saliva dangling from his jowls like a fox in the henhouse after the slaughter, hoping the farmer might find a bloodied feather or two after the feast as a clue to the carnage.

It only made me more frustrated and infuriated, and Leonard all the more menacing. I wondered about my innocent girls for a bit before trying to sleep in the soft cushioned chair of the streamlined jet, with the excited voices swirling around me. They were anxious for the action; they could taste blood in the air. I was just hoping that the air held no blood of my family. I closed my eyes. The only thing that kept the tears from flowing out was to keep them closed. I closed them as tightly as I could, hoping that they might seal off any part of the potential for disaster hidden somewhere in the impending future that lay ahead.

I really couldn't sleep, but managed to lose my lunch, or whatever it was, into the small gold-trimmed commode as we neared our landing in New York. The butterflies in my stomach had turned into millions of large bats, slamming in unison into the sides of my innards. I almost didn't want to be there, I almost felt like cowering and covering my eyes. I was terrified of what I was going to find on Jane Street, but my family continued to make me strong.

I have to be, for your sake.

The agents became more edgy once the plane landed and became surrounded by pure electricity. Their excitement nearly poured from them. They probably all got this way every time they did a raid or a bust. They didn't need a fix as the criminals that they arrested did. The hunt was their drug, their kick, and they were clearly anxious to be unleashed to their furious bombardments.

We cluttered into a vacant apartment on Jane Street, a few blocks from 1030 North. The apartment, although quite small, was now completely overrun by agents, and their surveillance equipment. More fresh faces had joined up with us as we landed in New York as well. Since landing, no agent had even introduced himself to me, or even generally regarded my presence at all. Everyone massed around a small center table, and pushed together like they were standing at a rock concert.

A bunch of monkeys fucking a football.

I looked for Detective Tyler Cunningham for a few minutes, I felt as if he was the only person who understood and recognized my situation. He was nowhere in the apartment, or its bathroom, or any of the hallways which adjoined it. I concluded that he must have been assigned an outside post.

Agent Younglin and Marks were also so caught up in the business end of everything that they barely recognized exactly what was at stake. The possible whereabouts or safety of my family never even came up within the conversations between the various parties of agents. The only thing that anyone was concerned about was to simply locate, then neutralize, Leonard Caldwell.

I kept trying to emphasize to the agents the importance of my family, who possibly could be locked in a small cage somewhere in the building up the street. So I tried yelling over them to please be quiet and listen to what I had to say. It was as useless as yelling against thunder or spitting against the rain. The only reaction I got was some fat agent scratching himself when I raised my voice. The agents that had heard me paid no attention at all. I decided then to bide my time until the plans were settled and the crowd more dissolved.

After about a half an hour, more agents began to file from the room, taking their positions on the streets and rooftops. The noise had died down, although radio contact still cackled. The only agents left in the room were a petite female agent with short cropped hair, the fat ass scratcher, a slender agent wearing glasses and sporting a small goatee, Agent Younglin, Agent Marks, and Agent Vindaci. Tyler Cunningham was still nowhere to be seen.

"Where is Detective Cunningham?" I asked Agent Marks.

"He is staying out of the way until we need him, if we need him," Marks responded without even so much as a glance in my direction. He was clearly focused.

Green monitors glared out against the northern wall of the apartment, on the right side of a large window that looked directly toward Jane Street. The slender male agent sat fixated in front of the screens, with the young woman behind him, watching him turn knobs and manipulate controls. The meaty agent now had both of his bubbly white hands on the blueprints that lay on the table, and he seemed to be scrutinizing the game plan. Agent Younglin stood with him, pointing toward the papers and talking softly, occasionally pulling his radio to his lips, positioning other FBI agents.

Agent Vindaci, probably oldest of the group, sipped coffee and peered north through the window, toward the target apartment and maybe even past it toward the lights of New York, looking out into what the future held. I sat slumped in a chair, in the farthest corner of the room, realizing I was basically along for the ride. Although I was the key piece in this chess game, I felt like the pawn.

The sunset behind the landscape of New York had grown to an evening sky, and it was time to implement the plan. Since I was the only person who had actually ever laid eyes on Leonard, I was the key figure in identifying him. The Agents concluded that the 1030 North building, consisting mostly of offices and one residential apartment, would be mostly vacant after 6:00 PM. So it was determined that the best approach would be me going in alone, with agents tight on the perimeter. I would walk straight up to the apartment, knock on the door, and hope everything went well from there. They would be awaiting one of three predetermined verbal signals that I was to give, depending on what situation presented itself inside. The three signals were as follows:

If I came into immediate danger or discovered that something drastic was happening, whereas I needed immediate assistance by the agents, I would say the word "soap." "Soap" was my emergency word, my safe word.

If I discovered the person inside to be Leonard, I would announce his presence to the feds by saying "box." Now, this just allowed the agents to realize that I had in fact identified Leonard but was in no immediate danger. I would try and negotiate with him. If that situation became a dire situation, I could resort to the emergency word "soap."

Lastly, if I discovered that the person inside posed no threat, was not Leonard Caldwell or anyone affiliated with him, and that the situation was not connected with the letter, I would simply say the clear word "derby."

Soap Box Derby. Each word would be easy to remember, red light for danger, yellow light for caution, green light for no danger.

As if I could forget at a time like this.

"Give me a gun and give me the letter," I told Agent Younglin after most of the agents had dispersed to their appointed positions.

"Excuse me?" He looked up from the blueprints, finally acknowledging my presence.

"A gun and the letter. I won't go in there without either."

"I don—," he started.

"You know I need them both. I can't realistically knock on the door of the apartment without the invitation, supposing whoever answers is someone other than Leonard, and I need the gun supposing that it is."

Agent Younglin couldn't exactly argue the point, even if it may not be protocol.

He handed me his weapon then opened his briefcase and handed me the letter.

"You lose either one of these, and it's your ass," he said calmly. I had never heard him cuss. I wedged the gun into my pants and put the letter in the inside pocket of my jacket. Another agent also fitted me with a wire that run from my chest and connected to the cuff of my shirt, and an earpiece in my ear. He gave me a strange look and patted my back when he was through, and I was led to the door and out into the New York rain.

Warmest regards,
the look seemed to say,
may God have mercy on your soul.

The rain was light, yet moisture came in wasps from all sides, and I soon became drenched. Jane Street itself was large and fairly deserted with the onset of bad weather, with the exception of a few pedestrians challenging the wetness and a few cars slowly cutting through it. The agents were certainly watching my every move back in their warm command post, or ducked away in alleyways or on rooftops. I ducked umbrellas and navigated around puddles with my head down, trying to stay dry and look normal. The lights of the city ahead, the few cars, as well as a few small streetlamps, were the only illumination on the dampness.

I thought for a moment that it might be possible for a mugger to be waiting in any of the dark alleys that I was passing. It happened all the time in New York, and it was my first time here. Some creep could be licking his chops in the shadows behind a dumpster, ready to pounce on the dumb tourist walking through the rain.

I glanced down the alley on my right, looking for any movement. Nothing.

Bring it on, buddy, there are only about forty federal agents that would be on you in seconds if you tried. Come get this fat wallet of mine. Juicy with money. Come and get it.

No mugger or hobo leapt out at me, so I continued through the watery streets.

I was getting close to 1030, and I could see a yellow light up ahead. It was filtering out of the second-story window, in what must have been the 1030 building, on just the other side of another alley. I got to the door of the building, which seemed older than the other buildings on the street, and had a cracked *1030 North* just above the large main door. The sign actually looked more like *1 3 North*, as the zeros were absent. But the paint behind them was still faded, faintly showing where the zeros had once been.

My heart pounded, and I paused for a minute at the front doors.
Be strong.

The street was gloomy, as both night and the rain fell, and I could barely make out anything in the shadows around the building. I felt the presence of the agents all around, eyes fixated on me through binoculars or scopes of their sniper rifles, yet could not make out a single agent in hiding beyond the soft sheets of rain that were softly weighing down upon me. The agents were good.

This is it.

I brushed the water from my hair and let myself through the main doors of 1030 North Jane Street.

I was met with a dark entry room, in which I could barely make out the outline of a stairwell ahead. I left the doors open as wide as I could to shed light into the entryway. The doors were not obedient, however, and only stayed open a crack. A voice softly crackled through my earpiece. It was Agent Younglin.

"Remember, go up one flight of stairs, the only apartment is the first door on the right."

I got it.

I wanted to say that back to him, but it was silent as a stone in the building. I definitely did not want to make any sound to compromise my position. Shrouded in the darkness, moments from my destined apartment, I realized that I was officially scared *shitless.*

I moved as slowly as I possibly could and made my way to the stairwell. My eyes had only slightly adjusted to the blackness, and I could see only partially up the stairs. My right hand reached and took the cold wooden railing; my left hand felt the hard metal of the gun on my hip. The stairs were constructed of old wood and creaked loudly as I put my weight upon them. I knew that the best way to creep up wooden stairs was to keep to the very edge of each stair, where it meets the joint of the staircase.

Halfway up the stairs, I had been relatively quiet. Nothing had creaked at all again after the first step. I neared the top of the stairs, each foot falling delicately down in front of me, and then the entry doors downstairs slammed shut. The sound resounded through the old building like a cannon, and for a moment I thought that it actually echoed throughout the darkness around me, but it may have only echoed in my head. I immediately froze.

The building stayed silent and cold, but I half-expected it all to come crashing down upon me from the force of the slamming doors. I was now completely shrouded in darkness without the wedge of outside light coming through the door behind me. I stood stiffly for quite a while, trying to maintain silence, but apparently the sound of the door had been ignored. It took me what seemed like an hour to overcome my hesitation and continue on. Four steps later, I reached the landing. The stairs continued upward on my left, connecting to higher floors, but I took a ninety-degree right turn and faced the first-floor hallway. I gripped the pistol that I had upon me, and that seemed to bring a sense of security. Knowing that the agents were examining every development helped settle me as well.

Still, a person could be waiting on the far side of the door with a fully loaded shotgun. I wouldn't even have time to soil my pants, much less say "soap," before he blasted both barrels into my guts. Then there I would be, brave ol' Chris Wyer, lying dead on the floor.

Don't think like that.

My body was still wet, although at that point I believed it to be mostly perspiration. The hallway that I stood in was slightly less faded into complete pitch black than the stairs because of a sliver of light inching out through the door about twenty feet in front of me on the right. This was the objective apartment.

I made my way to the threshold, trying desperately now to breathe through my nose, as the breaths from my mouth seemed to thunder off the walls. I pressed my ear to the door. I listened for any movement, any sound of activity. The soft click of the loading of a gun perhaps, or hopefully the soft snore of somebody sleeping soundly. I heard nothing instead.

Should I knock?

I stood outside the apartment door in the dark like a fool for many moments. *Should I dare reveal myself?*

Any cunning fellow would be most certainly awaiting me now, after my escapade on the creaking stairs. I was positive that my approach had been noticed. But I decided against revealing myself. I was lucky to have the door ajar, so I would not make much sound if I pushed it in and peered through.

I placed one shaking hand against the door ever so lightly, and pressed it forward. My left hand never stopped its grip on the pistol. To my relief, the door moved quietly and soon gave enough that I could gaze inside.

The room was illuminated by numerous candles, and directly in the center, sitting on a large red rug, was a male figure sitting upright and cross-legged, with his arms at his sides. He was directly facing me, head down, his back toward the Jane Street window. His eyes were closed, as if in deep meditation. Shadows flickered from the candles all around him and seemed to contract and tighten around his head and flow into the folds of a dark robe that he wore. I stuck my head farther into the room. It was definitely Leonard Caldwell, or what I would imagine Leonard Caldwell to look like after fourteen years of growth. Although he had porcelain hair, as white as a ghost. His body, although developed, still lacked full muscle tone, and his garment hung loosely around him. It was him though. Definitely.

I opened the door fully and walked in, immediately feeling more comfortable about the situation. I no longer needed to stay hidden from him, as I could clearly tell that he was unarmed and passive. He breathed softly with eyes closed, and it seemed that my presence still went unnoticed. I took a step into the room and felt a complete sense of calm. I was no longer frightened, and the situation had developed much differently than how I had visualized it in my head.

The room was bare except for the rug that Leonard sat on, the hundreds of candles lit throughout the room, and a small dinner plate set on a wooden serving tray. No Rebecca or Cathorine. Nobody in sight, save me and Leonard.

I looked back at him and realized that he had opened his eyes and was looking at me. It did not startle me in the slightest. His face seemed to jump from the intermixing shadows and become highlighted by the soft light of the room. It was nearly the same face that I remembered back in school, with the exception of his white hair. His face was really still just that of a baby, with slightly wrinkled additions around the eyes and mouth. He aged well.

For a moment or two, we simply just locked eyes, and in those eyes I saw that he had collected many things. He possessed serenity about him, and the room in its entirety held a presence of equanimity.

"Box," I said clearly, my own voice shooting back into my ear. I repeated it. "Box."

"Ten-four, box, over." I heard from my earpiece. Everything was going to be fine.

Then Agent Younglin spoke again, "When you can Wade. Over."

When you can Wade? What did that mean?

I released my grip upon the pistol. I didn't quite understand what else Agent Younglin said, but knew that they heard me say "box," so for the moment, everything was contained. I breathed a sigh of relief. All I had to do now was talk with Leonard, find out where my family was, and what exactly was going on.

Leonard looked as docile as a newborn kitten, just as he always had, and I immediately dismissed the thought of viciously attacking him like I figured I might.

He sat calmly, looking me in the eyes, never once appearing to be a kidnapper or murderer. I stayed toward the door, relaxed.

"Leonard?" I asked, just above a whisper. My body was still used to being as quiet as possible.

He continued to sit there, possibly never even blinking is eyes, holding mine in them instead. Something profound was happening in the places of his pupils, I could see that. His mouth parted to reveal a warm smile, one of which old friends share when reunited. He stayed nearly motionless, and then for just an instant, just a fraction of a moment, he looked unlike himself. The angles of his face must have allowed the candles of the room to play visual illusions on my eyes, for his face seemed to change to a face of a child and an elder simultaneously, neither a man nor woman, a blend of features that I might not have cognitively recognized at all. His eyes stayed **wild**, however, even throughout the slight lapse of looking unlike himself. They were focused desperately into my own. His smile slightly faded then, and he was again impassive to any emotion, just before the top of his skull blew apart and his brains splashed across the room.

CHAPTER 8

M oments of great magnitude always happen so fast. The scene blistered in front of me before I had the chance to even realize exactly what was going on. I heard the report of a gunshot from across the street as Leonard still balanced like a top making its final spins. They had shot him, a direct hit to the back of his head. The exit wound opened his face like the popping of a red balloon, and everything that was once so neatly assembled inside blew to all areas of the room. The sniper on the roof across the street had just blasted my only chance of finding my family.

Wade.

He had just instantly killed the man that "held the key to the universe," and might as well just have killed me along with him. My family was as good as gone now.

No hope for anything anymore.

That's what Younglin meant when he said, "When you can, Wade." Wade was given the green light to shoot, and he had now done just that.

I was covered in Leonard's blood. I stood there for a moment, dumbfounded, doused in blood and confusion. Leonard's head had blown apart, but his body continued to sit upright for a few seconds, his pale blue eyes blinking quickly, just below the ridge of exposed flesh and scalp. Oily dark blood cascaded from a large crevice where the top of his head used to be and showered over those surprised blinking eyes, quickly covering the entirety of his face. The top half of his head, just where is hairline started, was torn roughly away, exposing jagged ridges of skull and dangling brain matter. Then his body stiffly fell forward in a clump to the ground, legs and arms twitching and writhing awkwardly. The room immediately became thick with the stench of the realization of something gone terribly wrong.

"What the *fuck*!" I yelled manically, "What the hell did you do! I said box! Box! *Not soap*!" The room was almost spinning as if I were caught drunk in a nightmare.

The whistle of a bullet past my head stopped my obscenities and focused my thoughts. I heard it drone just inches past me. I could feel its heat.

That bullet was aimed at me.

I heard another report from across the street an instant later. I knew then, as my head recoiled from the proximity of flying metal, that it was a bullet intended to make a pulp of my head as well. My left ear was ringing loudly, and burning, and I instinctively slammed my body to the ground, covering my head with my hands.

My right ear with the earpiece rung with Agent Younglin's voice, "Targets eliminated? Over."

"Negative, Captain!" came another husky voice in the microphone, "Target two still active! Over."

Target?

I realized immediately that Wade was now shooting at me! I kept my head against the ground, my mind swirling with confusion and fear. I crawled toward Leonard's crumpled body and pulled out the pistol Younglin had given me earlier.

"Stop shooting!" I yelled, and almost as an answer, another bullet whistled just above my head and hit the wall behind me. The large window in the front of the room also shattered and collapsed, adding more chaos and noise.

At that moment, as the bullet hissed overhead, in the midst of complete destruction and indefinite reality, something wonderful happened. They had shot three bullets through the window and put two neat holes through it with the first two, finally shattering it with the third. The glass crashed down revealing an open window frame, and through it the wind and weather from outside blew into the room and extinguished all the candles. The room turned dark, darker even than the outside, except for a square of the window's gray light protruding in. Rain pattered through the window against the wood floor. My head throbbed, but again I heard voices crackling in my right ear.

"Lost visual on target. Over." It was the husky voice.

"Perimeters move in, secure all exits, over." Agent Younglin commanded. There was a slight pause. I looked down one last time at Leonard's frame in the dark and somewhere inside said my good-byes. Staying on my belly, I crawled toward the door.

Then, Agent Younglin stuttered and began to talk directly to me through the earpiece, "Mr . . . . Wyer. Chris . . . Stay there . . . Uh. I promise we will not shoot at you. That was a mistake. We just wanted Leonard. Honest. We will get this all sorted out."

He had just remembered that I could hear him, and was trying to lure me to them with the promise of peace.

I was not buying. I rotated on my belly, staying as low as I could and faced the door.

"Go fuck yourself, Younglin." I said, removing my shirt and the wire while I crawled. I heard a sharp static in my ear as I yanked off the wire that was attached to my chest. They could hear me no longer, but I could still hear them.

There was a pause, then my earpiece crackled again. "Fine . . . Agents, shoot to kill," Agent Younglin said. "Target two still needs to be eliminated. Over and out."

I crawled from the room back through the door and saw bouncing lights flashing across the end of the hallway to my left, coming up the stairs.

No time.

They were on me already. Dozens of bouncing lights shone up the stairwell, coinciding with pounding footsteps. I quickly maneuvered around the door and out into the hallway then rose to my feet. I would not be able to cross their path in time to reach the part of the stairs that continued up. My only option was to go farther down the hallway past the apartment. I ran to my right and heard shots reverberating down the hallway, echoing past me.

I scampered down the black hallway into uncharted territory. I couldn't see much of anything, as all the doors of the hallway were closed. For a moment, I contemplated hiding in one of those dark vacant rooms, but I decided to run instead. I needed to run. I sprinted down the hall, following the wall on the right side by scraping it with my right hand. I heard shouting and footsteps behind me down at the end of the hall. The wall that I was following ended, signifying the perpendicular hallway, so I took a sharp left. I still couldn't see much, but I continued to run. Rays of flashlights now bounced around in the hallway behind me, spilling into the corner that I had just turned down. If I would have been a second slower, they would have spotted me at the end of the darkened corridor.

The hallway that I had now turned down was just a bit more illuminated, as there was a small single-paned window at its end. I ran toward it, my adrenaline madly urging my legs. I slowed at end of the hallway, about ten feet from the window, and looked to my left. Another darkened hallway. It might loop around back toward the agents or go nowhere at all.

I couldn't take that chance.

I had to jump through the window. It was my only way out. I took a deep breath and sprinted quickly toward it, hoping to make a smooth leap through it. I imagined a center fielder diving for a baseball, fully outstretched, nearly horizontal and parallel to the ground.

Yeah, that is what I need to look like. That is exactly how I will burst cleanly through this thing.

As I ran at it, the pale blue square of glass rushed toward me. It was a large window, maybe four feet by four feet, and I knew that I could easily blast through if a went hard enough, but I would have to leap through it with great force. I was just worried about slicing myself terribly on the broken glass. I sprinted at it and thrust my knees up first, simultaneously trying to cover my face with my right arm. I did not look like that baseball player that I pictured in my head, or James Bond, or some Hollywood stuntman, I assure you. I closed my eyes at the last second, and I felt broken glass slicing the skin of my arms as they burst through. But in all my grace, or lack thereof, I had somehow made it through the pane, and felt myself falling.

I hit something hard on the other side of the window as I fell, felt the rush of air pass me, and opened my eyes just in time to see the ground crashing up into me. I landed on my left side, and doubled up. I immediately went into the fetal position as I felt all my air force itself from me when I hit the ground below.

My body had never collided with anything so tremendously. I lay there dazed, trying to catch my breath. I heard the raining of broken glass around me. Something in my body surely had to be broken, with an impact such as that.

Maybe everything was broken.

I wondered if I would ever be able to move again, to breathe again. I felt actual rain replace the glass then pouring down on me from above. I was outside.

The voices in my ear came to life again as I lay there.

"Target still active, Captain! Must have doubled back on us down the stairwell! Perkins, you got anything down the hallway? Over."

"Negative. Nothing so far. Still securing rooms though. He could be anywhere down here. Over."

"Echo team, anything on the perimeter? Over." It was Agent Younglin.

"Echo, negative. No activity in front or down south alley. Over."

"Keep sharp, Echo. Sanders, Ray, and Digo, move down to the hallways with team Bravo. Double checks on everything. Quick time. Over and out." Younglin now sounded stressed.

There were shards of glass in my back and hands, and I watched my own trembling right hand quickly pull out the large pieces it could. My left ear was ringing painfully. The bullets added a little deafness, I was sure. I rose to my feet and oriented myself, as the rain once again pelted down on my weary head. I had fallen down into a small space that lay between buildings.

Large ventilation shafts hummed behind me, blocking the space that led to the south and the alleyway that I had passed on the way to the building. About twenty feet of open space lay directly in front of me, ending in a vertical wall that was probably another building. I was in a small rectangle between buildings that rose around me by four stories on three sides, and by three stories for the 1030 building.

However, the walls on my right and left were close enough that I could probably shimmy up them, by pinning my back against the wall and pushing myself up with my legs. I ran to the end of the open space, away from the vents, and began to maneuver my way up the buildings. The walls were slick, but close enough together that I was able to maintain ascension. My heart was pounding, and probably pumped the blood twice as fast as normal, as it drained from my leg, hands, and head. I could feel it seeping from me like the tributaries of the Amazon. I strained to keep my body elevated from the ground, and using my battered legs, slowly wedged myself up the buildings.

Over the sound of rain pouring in on me from above, I began to hear the faint sound of a helicopter. It started as a soft hum, but soon was reverberating somewhere overhead, closing in quickly. I was only about halfway up the side of the building, and I knew that it was only a matter of time until the helicopter discovered my location and alerted my pursuers. I knew how a criminal must feel when running from the law after a helicopter has been deployed, like the fox in the foxhunt.

The hounds being machines on steroids.

With my body pressed against two buildings and my legs pushing up, I aimed the pistol the best I could toward the shattered window that I had just leaped through. It was only a matter of time before the agents came to it. I had worked fast and made the immediate decision to jump through it, but I still didn't have much time. I had begun to weaken, but my legs held strong and didn't buckle or slip out from the wall, causing me to plummet once again to the hard ground below. The skin behind my spine was beginning to rub raw against the slick brickwork of the building. The adrenaline coursing through my damaged body was the only thing keeping me conscious and going. I had to make the remainder of the climb, or it would be the end of me.

The chopper was now roaring overhead, but I could not see much above the buildings through the vacant space in which I was ascending. I looked to my left and could now see waving flashlights careening through the broken window. They had found my exit, and I was still about five feet from the top of the buildings.

"Target is out of building. Repeat. Target has escaped from premises. Target apparently to the west of the 1030 building." The voices in my ear confirmed my panic.

I had to really move. I pushed my legs harder. The ledge of the building still seemed so far away, but I could make it. It wasn't hopeless.

"Do you have a visual on that target, Briggs? Over?" It was Younglin again, anxious to hear status updates.

"Negative, sir. Not yet. Just apparent escape route. Over."

I was nearly to the crest of the 1030 building. I could nearly reach the edge of the parapet. My teeth were clenched together as I pushed up inch by inch. I tried to keep my shooting hand steadied at the window. The skin on my back now felt as if it were stripped completely off, leaving only open nerve endings. Then they spotted me, as they leaned from the broken window. I shot at the window and little spouts of cement shot from around them, their heads disappearing inside the window immediately.

"Visual! Visual on target! Shots fired! He is between the 1030 and 1050 buildings, scaling up the walls, nearly to the top! Team Foxtrot, move to north end of 1030 roof! Over!"

I saw the agent lean out the window just slightly, trying to get a bead on me. I shot wildly again, and once again his head disappeared back into the window safely. The rain still pelted down.

He is about to have a very decent shot at my contorted body, shooting at him or not.

I needed to make a jump for the parapet behind me immediately. I summoned all the strength in my legs and pushed with all my force.

I twisted my body around as I pushed, and managed to grab the cold wet edge of the building behind me, dropping the gun to do so. I yelled out with sheer pain, but my hands held. I heard the pistol clank as it hit somewhere below.

Officially unarmed now.

I pushed again with my legs and pulled myself over the ledge, just as I heard a gunshot. I landed on the roof of the building, wondering for a second if the bullet had made contact, but I hadn't felt anything. I looked down quickly at my torso and legs, seeing some faint traces of blood and torn clothing, but no holes. I was back up on my feet that fast, rushing to the north.

The thunder of the helicopter was immense now, and as soon as I clambered onto the top part of the building, I was locked in its spotlight.

Deer in headlights.

I ran in a burst of adrenaline and leaped across parapets to the next building. I was running quickly, caring little that the spotlight of the helicopter shone directly down on me, I just needed a way out. The light was blinding, even as I ran with my head turned away.

"Halt immediately!" A bullhorn bellowed from the helicopter overhead. "Freeze now!" The chopper seemed to be right on top of me, I could feel the wind that it was generating. But I would not stop. I would never stop. I had nothing left to lose.

Nothing at all.

The roof of the building had small ventilation shafts that I nimbly skirted over, and jumped up on the parapet of the building, landing on it with my right foot and then pushing off again, propelling myself across the small gaps much like the one I had just climbed up, to the next building. They weren't very big jumps, maybe six feet between buildings, so I made it easily to the other side without slowing. I was in a full sprint now, letting my legs carry me in instinct. I jumped past more obstacles and toward another ledge. I was running with all I had, and within moments had come to the end of the building again. I arrived upon the small wall and leaped quickly over it.

The chopper grumbled behind me. Or above me. I couldn't quite tell. But it was close. I scampered across the rooftop and then came across another large parapet. Without thinking, I jumped up again upon the ledge and leaped from it. The space between these two buildings was considerably larger than my first jumps. By about another six to eight feet. I only realized this in midair, and by then was completely committed. The next building was also a large distance below the one I had just been on, which is the only reason that I actually made it to the other side. I swiftly glided downward. Then both of my legs buckled and slammed into my chest violently with the force of the landing, and I went into a roll. If I had hesitated, I would never have had the momentum to clear the space. My knees hurt now but were still functioning somehow. Actually, my body as a whole hurt, but I only knew that there was pain somewhere, yet wouldn't allow it to stop me.

The helicopter swung around in front of me, and its sheer noise and blinding lights faced me, and its menacing force forced me to slow. I could only faintly make out the large black mass of the chopper through the beam of light that it had focused in my eyes. The sound of the slicing blades mauled my ears.

"**Don't fucking move!**" A voice somehow echoed through the noise. I put my hands up above my head as a reaction to the bellowing sound.

"**On your knees, now!**"

This was it.

If I dropped to my knees, it would be all over. I would be at their mercy. If they didn't shoot me through the top of the head right out, I would probably spend my life in a cage, even though I hadn't done anything. This thing that I was involved in was obviously very powerful, and they didn't want witnesses.

Why then wasn't the chopper firing at me? Why didn't they just shoot me from the air right now?

Then I realized that the chopper was from the NYPD and had merely come in as a backup. The shoot-to-kill command was given only to the agents. It had only come through *on my earpiece.*

The New York Police Department was only there to contain me, not to assassinate me. The feds would handle that once I was handed over to them. The same feds that were rushing to catch up to me right now. My raised hands slowly pivoted so that the backs of my hands clearly showed two distinct middle fingers. I then ran directly toward the thunder of the helicopter, with my shoulders low and my head down. I held my breath and forced myself forward, no matter the consequence.

The force of the helicopter's rumbling blades slapped air against my head as I went under them, and I figured that they missed my scalp by no less than three feet. Without the momentary blinding glare of the helicopter spotlight, I was once again bathed in relative darkness immediately after rushing forward. I ran underneath the thundering goliath, slightly disoriented from the drastic change of intense light to complete dark. I could barely make out the outline of another approaching parapet, but knew I was again at the edge of the building. I could not make out anything farther than that except emptiness. My feet skipped up on the ledge, and once again, I leaped directly off the far side.

The "look before you leap" premonition is really a great warning to everybody, but under the circumstances, I could have really cared less if the jump was suicidal or not. I had already died with Leonard Caldwell. My family had died with him to be precise, so I cared about living no more. The same bullet that ripped through his skull crushed my heart. So I ran at the edge of the building, lost as I'll ever be, and jumped.

I had gone over the edge. Figuratively and literally. I could never come back, even if I wanted to. The New York wind whistled past me as I fell from grace. Down, down, down, from the top of the building and close proximity of a raging helicopter, into the hungry darkness below. It was peaceful, if for just a moment. I may have imagined myself floating. Floating up, not careening down. Floating up into the soft arms of heaven. Floating to find my family again.

I crashed through the sharp limbs of trees instead. They splintered and shattered around me, or maybe it was me that was being broken around them. Suddenly, my body slapped against a large branch, then another, and another, one ripping itself up under my arm, viciously wrenching me around. I was flipped to the side as I descended from the limb, and met the ground suddenly, facing down. It was most unforgiving.

I felt as if I had been beaten about the body with rubber hoses, and was left to fend for myself. My head swam in the damp grass that I lay in, and my lungs desperately tried to regain air. I tasted blood, a lot of it. I lay there all but paralyzed and lifeless, heartless, and hopeless. My eyes closed, but the world spun. I probably would have cried but was in so much pain that I didn't think to do so. I heaved viciously in pain, my spine crackling up in tremendous convulsions. I gripped the moist grass in my fingers as hard as I could, trying to force it all to just go away. That was basically all I could do, the pain being immeasurable.

"Target has leaped off north end of 1270 building. Lost visual on target. Repeat. No visual on target. Injuries or death to target probable."

"Target leaped off 1270 building?" It was Agent Younglin.

"Sir, yes, sir. Possible suicide attempt, sir."

"Well, get down there as soon as possible to clean up the mess."

"Right away, sir. Foxtrot en route."

"And no radio communication until we find him, unless completely necessary. Is that clear?"

"Crystal, sir. Out."

I could not move; my body seemed to be completely destroyed. I replayed the events of what had just happened, repeating the scene in my head with every attempt at clarity, one bloody labored breath at a time. I remembered that the 1030 building had been a three-story building, both from looking up at it and seeing the measurements on the FBI blueprints prior to them raiding and killing Leonard. After I had scaled back onto the roof of the 1030 building, I had only jumped down in elevation once. Probably only jumped down a few feet to a two-story building. The building I had just been on. With its parapet that I had leaped from, I figured that I had just survived a nearly twenty-five-foot drop. Almost three stories down to where I now lay battered. The tree had saved my life, or to put it more correctly, postponed my death. But I was still alive, even after falling to solid earth.

Pain surged through me like an electrical current. I managed to roll over so that my back was to the ground. I looked up through the tree to see the small splinters of light from the helicopter, searching for my carcass. I had landed in a wonderful position, perfectly concealed from the helicopter under the cover of the large tree. I pulled myself up to my feet again, with my right arm. My left arm, the one yanked up by the branch of the tree, was throbbing. I had dislocated my shoulder. I knew it. At the least.

I could barely even move my bicep away from my ribs. But my legs still worked, and at this point, they were all I needed. I forced myself to mobilize through the pain, with everything and anything I had left. I hobbled up against the trunk of the tree, and glanced around to quickly scan my surroundings. I was at the southern edge of what seemed to be a very large park, with abundant trees. To my immediate left, a small three-story building was jutting out into the southwest part of the park, about twenty yards away.

I remembered from seeing a television show or something that police helicopters were equipped with heat-sensing radar and can locate the heat of your body temperature up to one thousand yards away. Quite useful technology when a criminal is hiding out in the brush. But what the television shows don't tell you is that most technology is not perfect. They lead you to believe that it is, but human operator error, as well as the physical restrictions of that technology, may render it less than ideal. People go into casinos all the time believing that they are constantly being monitored by "the eye in the sky." This could not be further from the truth. Sure, the casinos have many cameras, but to have a camera pointed at every single person at any given time is unfeasible, as well as not economically sound. It would simply be too costly and would require too many man-hours to be effective. So instead, they put up a black bubble on the roof every twenty feet, leading you to only believe that there is a camera hidden within, always pointing at you. But in truth, the black plastic bubble is nine times out of ten just that, a black plastic bubble. A facade that creates tension in every single person that is tempted to pull a sleight of hand at the blackjack table.

The same thing applies to the helicopter. If I am surrounded by a crowd of other people that give off the exact temperature that I give off, the chopper can never distinguish me. Or if I stay tight up against buildings, the choppers heat radar cannot detect me through the many walls and rooms of people inside those buildings. So that is just what I needed to do. I needed to stick right against the sides of buildings until I was able to find a crowded area, or out from beneath its direct gaze.

I had space between myself and the dreadful spotlight of the helicopter, so I felt at least slightly relieved. I could still distinctly hear it overhead, searching. My earpiece allowed me to still hear the communications between the agents on the ground, leaving them unable to discreetly focus in on me. We all knew this fact, and it was the only thing that I had on them. I snuck over to the side of the small dark building and slid around to the other side, sticking close to the building's perimeter. To my luck and surprise, heating ducts ran the entire side, giving off more moving heat to disguise my presence from the black metal bird above.

It had stopped raining for some time, and a slight fog was settling in. This was absolutely wonderful for me, as visibility was dramatically decreased. I heard some noise behind me, about thirty yards away, and knew that team Foxtrot had come to the area that I had dropped into. They were expecting to find a dead or mortally crushed body, but they would find none. If they had in fact found me there, injured to the point that I was forced to be stationary, would they have killed me immediately or sat there and let me suffer from my injuries? Probably the latter. Maybe they would have even kicked me a few times to see just how pulpy I had become. Well, I was bruised but far from broken, and I was going to escape from these animals. I wished that I could have left a live grenade for them though, a memento to show that I truly cared.

"Target still apparently mobile, sir, over." came a soft crackle of a young voice.

"Well, FUCKING IMMOBILIZE HIM! Over!" replied Younglin in a yell. It was still weird to hear him cussing. I imagined his black brow sweating profusely, as he paced around the room of the building that was now many blocks away. I thought that he wanted communication restricted unless necessary. Apparently, it was now necessary for him to cuss.

"Yes, sir! Over and out." The voice tried not to sound discouraged.

I smiled as I continued to stealthily creep around the building. The spotlight of the helicopter scattered wildly across the treetops of the park.

The heat radar also needs to be pointed somewhere in the vicinity to work, you dumb assholes.

I had lost them, if only temporarily, but that slightly eased my unbridled pain. The fog was thick now, settling in like frosty milk left on a glass, and I wanted to kiss it all. I could hardly see ten feet in front of me, so I knew that the same visibility applied to my pursuers. Even farther away, thumping against the sky in the distance beyond the fog, was the helicopter. I felt a resurgence of hope then, listening to the sound of something else besides me being lost.

I came to the edge of the building and slid my head around. I couldn't see much of anything but white murk, but also could not see the towering outlines of buildings in front of me. The area had opened up. I had come to a street that ran along a park. I did not see any movement along the street, but I was quite sure that the agents could be there, somewhere. I did know for a fact that most agents were behind me, but many had taken positions all around the perimeter of the 1030 building. I went forward onto the street, although it meant placing myself in the open. It was a chance that I had to take, and with the immense fog, I had a good chance of going unseen by the agents.

I stepped quietly into the foggy street, going at a forty-five-degree angle. I immediately stopped after a few quiet paces, and stepped back into the crevice once I noticed a slight movement to my right. The movement was an agent with his back toward me, stalking up the street alongside a building. He moved like a cat searching for prey. He was hunched over, stepping as slowly as the hour hand. His head carefully turned back and forth with the barrel of his black rifle as he held it out from his midsection.

I waited for him to continue on, away from me, watching him intently from my secured position. I crossed the small park, tree to tree, arriving upon a smaller set of buildings. There was a small opening between two of them, about a third of the width of an alley. I snuck delicately across the rest of the park and around a dumpster that slightly obscured the opening. The opening was littered with trash and debris that had spilled from the overrun dumpster. I stepped carefully through large mounds of newspapers and discarded items, watching for any signs of trouble behind me.

Suddenly, a hand grabbed my ankle from behind. I twisted and prepared to fight immediately, but luckily did not make a sound. Then I saw him. Covered in newspapers, lying down, with his head under the back of the dumpster. A newspaper slightly obscured his face, and his pointer finger was against his mouth in the universal signal to be quiet. It was Detective Tyler Cunningham.

"Don't make a sound," he said after giving me a mischievous smile. His hand released. I turned around, gasping.

"Wha—?" I didn't have any words to say, just stared at him with a blank bewilderment as he rose from his hiding position.

"I'm on your side," he said, almost rhetorically. He stood up, revealing himself completely. I could see the intensity in his eyes. I wanted to hug him. He was a beautiful sight.

"How the hell?—" I asked, stumbling over my whispers.

"You found me, pardner," he exclaimed silently, again using his John Wayne impression in an attempt to shed some humor on the situation. "I went to go take a leak just before you were sent out on the street to find Leonard. While I whizzed, I overheard two agents talking. They were both the snipers that were going up to the roof across the street from the 1030 building. Wade and Samson.

When you can, Wade.

They were discussing who was going to shoot Leonard, and then who was going to shoot you. I couldn't believe it. But I wanted to hit myself for not smelling something about this whole gig. I had wondered why they had wanted me to come along, and realized that they probably needed me dead as well. After Leonard would be executed, you and I would be the only eyewitnesses to his slaying. They were never after

Leonard to contain him, they were preparing to take him out the whole time."

Tyler pointed toward the next passageway between buildings, and we both scurried across another small empty street into a small alleyway.

"They needed you to make sure that it was in fact the Leonard Caldwell that you knew back in high school," he continued in a whisper when we were tucked away again. "They needed you to physically identify him for them."

Tyler's eyes scanned the streets with mine. "If everything was true that they told us at the station, Leonard basically went underground after high school, you being the last person to maybe see him, or recognize him, for years."

"Yeah, a yearbook picture might not do someone justice," I said as we huddled for a moment.

"Yeah, they needed you. You were their pointer finger. As soon as you gave the signal that identified Leonard as being Leonard, you signed your own death warrant. And you signed mine as well."

"You're right. You and me were the only other people that really knew anything about—"

"You and I," he interrupted, correcting my bad grammar while continuing my statement. "—and Simmons, back at the station."

"Right, Simmons. But he didn't even know that much." I had forgotten about Simmons.

"He knew enough. Enough to probably have two slugs in his head as we speak."

"And they couldn't kill you until they killed me, or I might be suspicious and figure the whole thing out," I said, finally putting it all together.

"Yeah. So I took off immediately. I wanted to warn you, but you were then already out on the street. I was then just hoping that Leonard wouldn't be in the building, and then the feds would have to call the assassinations off. They would still need you to identify Leonard if and when he popped up again. And you would see that I was nowhere around, and smell something fishy." He paused. "But Leonard was there, wasn't he?"

"Yeah," I said sadly.

"Is he dead?"

He looked in my eyes as he asked, and we both knew that he didn't need an answer.

I said box. I said everything was okay. Nobody in the world was listening.

Tyler patted me on the back. "You look like hell, but glad you're through it." My left arm was hanging awkwardly at my side, with my left ear still loudly ringing, my ribs aching and probably broken, but I was happy that I had made it this far. I was sweating even though the temperature outside must have been in the high forties.

"Do you think that my family is still alive?" I asked him then, as we decided our next step. I didn't even expect much of an answer, I just needed something to hold on to.

"I honestly don't know, Chris. I wish that I did. With everything that has gone on, I'm not too sure that we are even going to make it out alive. But to tell you the truth, I am starting to think that maybe Leonard never even had your family at all . . ."

"Huh?"

"I'm saying that the feds never even once seemed to care for your family's well-being, or the part that they played in all this. If the letter was indeed a ransom letter from Leonard, then he would have a motive to hurt you. But he never really had one by the looks of it. He saved your life way back when, but if he felt that you owed him your life in return, as the feds say, he would have simply killed you. End of story. If Leonard is as powerful as they say, he wouldn't fuck around with writing little notes to get you to come to Jane Street."

"I wouldn't have been able to figure out the note anyway."

"Right. I thought of that for a long time, that's why I don't think Leonard was ever against you."

"I have never seen someone look so passive," I thought aloud to Tyler. "If that note was intended for me, I should have been able to solve the damn thing. He would have put in something that only I could know."

"If he was really a ruthless person looking for vengeance, he would have just done paper cutouts that said 'Get your ass over to Jane Street,'" Tyler concluded.

"So you think that the FBI created this letter from the beginning? To get me to find and identify Leonard for them?" As I asked this, I touched my hand to my aching side, feeling that the letter still remained.

"Yeah, maybe. I don't really know of anything for sure. All this shit is kinda hard to piece together, but it is possible that they took your family and concocted this letter to provide incentive for you to want Leonard's blood. I mean, was it just coincidence that they were following you a day before your family vanished? They were actually following you even before you took the letter to us. They knew that you had it, probably had your phone tapped. They came into your house, and trashed the place looking for it, but didn't find it. Then they realized that they could just have you simply bring it right to them. Just kidnap your family, and you'd immediately think that the letter is a ransom note and go straight to the cops. Which you did."

"Holy shit," I said, leaning against one of the walls of the corridor where we hid. Detective Cunningham was a good detective. "Actually, Cathorine called me at work about the letter one day. Called me right from our house. She said that we should bring it to the cops anyway. I brought it to your precinct even, and you guys didn't want anything to do with it unless I wanted to file a complaint."

"Yeah, it meant nothing to us at the time. But I'm sure that it meant something to the feds once they heard that phone conversation. They have probably had their eye on you all the way back to after you had your car crash, just to see if you still had any links to Leonard."

"And now they want me dead," I realized again, and said aloud, "They need to finish this game they started."

"Spilled milk now," Tyler replied. "But we need to keep going, the feds are crawling around here like cockroaches. Multiplying each minute." He turned to walk by me, his dirty face focused and alert.

I followed Tyler into the wedge of more buildings, and watched as he carefully popped his head out into the opening of another street. He took just a couple of seconds before pulling his body back in. "Pay dirt," he said, smiling. "There is a river on the other side of the street, and no agents in sight. But they could be waiting for us anywhere in the fog. I can't really see too far up or down the street."

He looked back through the gap again. Then his eyes focused on me, looking at my battered body. "Do you think you can swim?"

"Yeah, definitely," I said, knowing that I could swim for a year if it meant saving my life.

"Okay, then. We run to the river," he said, turning forward again. He was a born leader, and confident in his decisions, and I respected that about him. He looked at me and winked. "Then we swim."

He turned back toward the street, looked to see everything was clear, then ducked out into the fog. Immediately after he exited the opening, I lost sight of him. The fog was that thick. I swallowed hard then followed his lead, darting quickly into the street. I still could not see much of anything, but I heard his footsteps in front of me. The street seemed very large, and I could tell that it was going to take us a few moments to reach the river on the other side. Then, the fog momentarily opened up in front of me, and I saw Tyler's running figure, and the wonderful sight of a large river fifteen yards in front of him. Even with the sound of the helicopter in the distance, I could still hear the river babbling quietly as it flowed to the north. It was like seeing gold for the first time and discovering that the priceless metal was to be all for you. The river was a source of our escape and freedom, and I was only a stone's throw away from it. We ran swiftly yet quietly through the cover of fog, and felt my body trembling joyously as I neared the water's edge. Tyler was ten feet from a small railing that separated the street from the river, and it would only take us a second to throw our bodies over it and into the brine.

Suddenly, I heard the click of the cocking of a gun to my left.

Through the silk of the mist, I saw the dark outline of an agent running toward us. He had crept up on us from behind, and was pulling his rifle to his shoulder from about twenty yards away. Tyler must have heard it too, but had also continued to run furiously. Shots sharply rang out, but nothing happened to me. He must be shooting for Tyler, who continued to run swiftly, nearing the edge of the brown water. He must have missed however, for Tyler seemed completely unharmed and had almost made the landing. He was only a few feet from the edge of the railing, when suddenly, in the midst of his strides, he flailed and toppled to the ground. He crumpled down near the railing, turning onto his right side.

"Aah . . . NOOO! Tyler! . . . Get up!" I yelled, hurriedly advancing on my wounded friend. He had been hit after all, but it must have taken a few seconds for his body to suffer from it. His right hand went down to retrieve his weapon from his holster, and his left hand held at his chest. His fingers were covered in his own blood, yet it continued spilling out over them. I was upon both Tyler and the railing now, and heard more shots ring out from behind me. Fluid splattered against me as Tyler's chest popped open, leaving a large hollow rose. Blood sprayed out from his shirt as metal sounds violently entered his torso. His chest heaved, and his face contorted in pain.

If I can pull him up and over the railing into the water, we might still be able to make it.

I grasped at his shirt as he propped himself there, against the railing, and I could see the beginnings of tears building in his sullen eyes. Small amounts of blood started to dribble down his chin. He knew that he was hurt, too hurt to make any more of an escape. He tried to say something to me as I pulled at him, but only coughing and more blood spilled from his mouth in the place of words. His face tilted up at mine, showing a mix of anger and fear. I reached out for the railing as I held him, but the blister of more bullets flashed by the left side of my head. My ears burned as they heated past me. I sidestepped to my right in reaction to the onslaught, and my legs slammed into the railing. My upper body continued forward, and I fell awkwardly over the bars, into the brown water just below.

"Targets located!" I heard as I plunged in. The water was frigid, and I hadn't pulled in much of a breath. The current immediately pulled me forward and under, against my will to try and reach up through the railing and grab my friend. I instinctually brought my left arm up to grab the lower bar of the railing, and immediately resented doing so. Incredible pain shot through my arm as my shoulder was still painfully dislocated. I had nearly forgotten how much damage I had inflicted on my side. I was seared with absolute torture, and my left ear rung like a siren inside my head. The icy water bit sharply against my skin as my body was internally immersed in both pain and river water. My right hand and both legs beat furiously with the current as struggled to right myself underwater, needing to get a breath of air.

"One target down, one target's in the river to the west!" an excited voice yelled through globs of static in my earpiece.

My head emerged above the water. I choked for air.

"There he is! Three o'clock!" an agent screamed frantically. I caught a brief glance of Tyler slumped against the railing as automatic rounds scattered in my direction. They whistled past and pelted into the water around me. Tiny splashes erupted quite close to my head. Tyler would never make it, he was gone, and I saw them come upon him before I dipped my head underwater again. Anger and sadness welled inside me. He was going to die because of me, killed by his own government. Killed to cover the truth, to tie a loose end.

I heard two more shots as my head partially submerged.

"Fuck! Agent hit! Agent hit! Agent down!" The panicked voice rung in my ear, but my earpiece was crackling out. Tyler had gotten one of them, and as desperate as the voice sounded, he had gotten him good. Bullets continued to pelt the water around me however, and I was not quite sure which direction they were coming from. I dunked my head back under again, away from the oncoming gunfire, filling my lungs only slightly. This small breath would be all I needed. I had been a brilliant swimmer my whole life and could draw every second out of each breath. I heard the soft thumping of automatic gunfire through the water in the distance, knowing that this time it was for Tyler. I wanted to yell for him, yell at the agents, plead with them to stop, but it was too late. With a pull of their fingers, they had ended both his and Leonard's dreams, and thoughts, and loves, and lives. They had ended their everything. And they still wanted to do the same to me.

The river was swift, and I swam toward the depths of it using mostly my right hand and legs, trying to get completely out of shooting range. I let my left arm float loosely. It was too painful to move. I cried through closed eyes underwater, half in pain, half for my departed accomplice and for the misery that overwhelmed me.

My legs were still strong and kicked hard, pushing for maximum underwater distance. I felt the current pushing me along as well. The river was really moving, causing small waves and ripples from speed at its surface, but I stayed under as long as I possibly could. Only when my lungs completely burned for oxygen did I pop my head above the water. I expected to be showered with automatic fire as I did, but my eyes revealed that no agents were even close. The outline of Tyler was gone as well, and I knew that I would never see him again. He was behind me now, lost somewhere in the fog, somewhere on the lonely street, his presence gradually slipping away.

The river had done its job, and I had achieved considerable distance from everything that had happened. I could keep my head safely above water, at least at the moment. I could not see the agents through the mist, but could swear that I still heard the soft thumping of their running footsteps. The misty streets glided by, and within minutes, the river must have carried me nearly a mile away. The agents had blatantly miscalculated my location in the water, underestimating the strength of the current as well as my swimming ability. They were scanning the waters years behind me.

I kept my head above the gently lapping waves, eyes searching for more agents. My feet kicked smoothly with the current and the sides of the river rushed by. My earpiece was only crackling with static, and I realized that the water had finally destroyed it. I pulled it from my ear and let it sink.

I don't want to hear the bastards talking anyway. Ever again.

My body had grown numb to the cold water, and although it ached from my injuries, I was no longer in excruciating pain. My head still rang like a cowbell, originating in my left ear. I mainly felt so sick to my stomach that as I swam, I lurched many times with vomit and swallowed water. Sickness and sadness seeped into my pores, infecting my skin like a burning rash of oily disgust, never to be washed clean.

I swam down the river for another ten minutes or so and, after considerable difficulty, managed to pull myself out along a cement bank under a large bridge. The river yearned to pull me back in, but I finally struggled free from its grasp, holding on tightly to a large boulder and scaling up its side with my legs. My left arm and ear were both ravaged with pain.

My body began to shiver uncontrollably as I exited into the weeds, but I knew I could not stay in the water. It had protected me from the New York air, but the air had the final chance to bite back. I limped from the weeds, clutching my left arm. I leaned against the mortars of the bridge and vomited. I needed to expel the evil feeling in my stomach, but I knew that it may never go away. I wiped my mouth and looked around. I had never felt more physically miserable. My good ear could hear the soft drumming of cars rushing by overhead, and still only saw the soft white cotton of the mist all around.

I was in no immediate danger.

This was a good time to depart from the river, as the agents would definitely find a good point downstream to fish me out, but I had definitely put some distance between them and myself. This was the only encouraging thing. I stumbled about for a few moments, sobbing inside and vomiting again. I gave a eulogy in my thoughts for two wonderful people, both whom I had barely known, but both whom I would never forget for the rest of my life. I decided then that if I ever made it out of all of this alive, I would come back to pay my respects.

I found myself winding my way up to the street above, putting out my thumb to flag down a ride. Hitchhiking is a risky business in my opinion, especially if FBI agents happened to drive right up to me, then right over me. But I was too sad to even care about much of any risk. I waited there, completely exhausted and saturated in pain, watching cars stream by. Some drivers tried to avoid eye contact; some scrutinized my appearance as they passed. But none stopped.

After what seemed like decades, and just before I was about to fall down in a heap on the side of the road, a blue compact car jerked to a stop in front of my shaking outstretched thumb. The small passenger door swiveled open, inviting me in. I was quite amazed that somebody had the courage or maybe lack of sense to even pull over and offer a ride to a character that must have appeared to be so dissolute as me. I could picture myself as a soaking wet, bloody and battered, emotionally wrecked man with the look of death in his eyes, licking his lips at the thought of jumping into a nice warm car. I'm sure that the picture in my head was not half as bad as I must have looked in reality.

I pulled myself in through the small frame of the car and slammed the petite door quickly behind me. The car indeed was warm, and my moist jeans squeaked as my body adjusted to the sitting position.

"Good gospel, sonny, did yous go and find yo'self in a car wreck?" It was the deep voice of a large black lady who was cramped in tightly behind the steering wheel. She was looking at me with large brown eyes, inspecting my damage. Her large mouth spoke through buoyant lips. I said nothing, staying motionless and grateful that I was no longer surrounded by frigid air or water.

"Can yous hear, boy?" she asked, adjusting her yellow and brown sweater around the girth of her arms and breasts. She stared at me still, maybe wondering if I was even alive at all.

"I got mugged and dropped in the river," I managed to reply, in a daze. It was a perfect excuse for what I had been through, but I was still amazed that she bought it. I figured that my lie would be as easy to spot as the bruises mapping my body. However, she lived in New York, and she probably picked up mugging victims every day on her way home from work.

She looked me over again, one last time. Her football eyes blinked. She then moved her head forward toward the road, and her big brown hand smothered the gearshift into first. The gears ground into place, before the car jolted forward.

"Yous ain't gonna go dyin' on me in my car nows are ya?" Her big lips popped open and shut as she talked. Her large ball of a body nestled in between the seat and the wheel, with her head fixed straight toward the road.

"I hope not ma'am. If I was going to die, I probably would have done it an hour ago."

She uttered a low chuckle. "No need to be callin' me no ma'am or missus or nothin'. Yous can call me Sunshine, 'cuz all my friends do. Sunshine'd be fine." Her right hand jutted out from the puny steering wheel and hung there, waiting for mine.

"Okay, Sunshine. Good to meet you. My name's Chris." I moved my right hand from holding my left arm and met hers. Her hand was massive, and completely devoured mine as we shook. She then patted my leg before she returned her hand back to the wheel.

"Good ta be meetin' ya, Chris. Sunshine loves to be meetin' new folks. Nows where yous be headin' Chris?" I could tell immediately that she was a talker.

"Just take me to the nearest hotel, that'd be fine," I heard myself say. The car was so warm, I felt almost dizzy from the comfort and even felt like sleeping. My massive headache beat in time with my heart, and other sounds seemed to amplify their drumming. My pain closed off everything else. Even the sound of my own voice.

"Aah. Yous ain't from round here nows, are ya'? And yous found yo'self in a pick o' trouble dat does live round here now, dint ya?"

"Yes, ma'am, I mean, Sunshine. Yes, I sure did."

She studied me between takes at the road. "Yous lookin' pretty run down, and yous don't be needin' none of dose motels round here. Nossir," she said after she turned. "You'd only be gettin' yo'self in it worse if I done took yous there. Yous be needin' some sleep and some good cookin', maybe even a little med'cal 'tention, that's what'd do yous up jus' fine."

Sunshine made another turn then reached into the back of the small car, grabbing a large pink sweatshirt. "Yessir. Yous looks like yous be needin' a little warmin' up too. This'll do ya jus' fine. Has a bit o' dog hair on it, but lease be dry. It'd be keepin' yous warm fo' now." She handed me the pink sweatshirt with a large picture of Tweety Bird on it, and although it would never be something I would normally choose to wear, I immediately put it on. It took me a few minutes to manage it over my ruined shoulder, but it was wonderful to wear something warm.

"Thank you," I said softly, strangled by pain.

"Sunshine knows dat yous be a nice fella, Sunshine can be seein' dat in peoples. So Sunshine gonna take yous home wit me for da nite and fix yous up some hot soup, and let yous ress in my boy's room. He ain't gonna be needin' it anyways. And yous sho looks like yous could use it."

I looked up at her like I was a small child that had broken his arm on his tricycle.

"So it's settled den."

"Awfully kind," I said, half consciously, hoping that was the end of the conversation. I knew that she probably meant well, but her voice was as helpful as a Band-Aid on a decapitation. Silence would be perfect. And warmth. And maybe death. Her words, along with the ringing in my head, seemed to be crushing in right behind my eyes. I was tightly holding my left arm, as it was now throbbing more fiercely than ever, with the effort of putting on the sweatshirt.

Sunshine drove on for another few minutes, through blurry scenery, then pulled to a stop outside of a large apartment complex. She climbed from the small cockpit of her car, walked around the front, and opened my door. Her large hands gripped my fragile body carefully, helped me from my side of the car, and then up the stairs that lay at the front of the complex.

From what I initially saw of it, her apartment was small, but decorated in a comfortable manner. Two dogs greeted us as we entered, but they stayed away at her command. She led me down a small hallway that was lined with pictures and into a small bedroom. The bed was piled high with pillows, and I nearly started to salivate at the sight of such comfort. I hadn't slept soundly for what seemed like centuries.

"Bafroom be to yous right, and I'll be bringin' in a fresh change of clothes why'se yous be gettin' showered. Then looks like yous could be usin' some ress. Go on now, Sunshine do everyfing but be helpin' yous get undress." Sunshine softly patted my back with her large hand. Her face was looming over mine, smiling genuinely. "We be gettin' yous up an' a runnin' in no time. Sunshine'll promise."

I hopped into a warm shower that felt wonderful but horrible at the same time. My many cuts and abrasions screamed under the hot water, but my shivering body welcomed the warmth. After stepping from the steam of the shower, I checked out the damage to my body in the mirror. It was bad. Worse than I'd ever seen myself before. My face had taken the best of it, and I only had a large gash above my right eye. Both arms were completely sliced up, mostly between the hands and elbows, and gashes crisscrossed each other, some leaving flaps of loose skin.

Broken glass sure does love to leave intricate patterns of carnage.

My left arm was borderline disgusting. The whole shoulder was shrouded in a gigantic bruise of deep purples and red, and my bicep was considerably swollen underneath to the armpit. Deep gashes ran up and down, tearing into flesh and muscle. I could not move the arm much at all. My chest had several different bruises and lacerations, and my ribs on my left side were tender to even the slightest touch. Swelling bubbled from the whole left side of my body as well, and the dark colors almost blended perfectly with the bruising on my arm. I was a wreck, it was amazing that I could even stand on my own, much less still be alive.

I discovered a set of long underwear laid out on the small bed when I emerged from the steam filled bathroom. They fit me nearly perfectly, and sleep stormed over me as I slipped under the covers and my ringing head met the fluffy white pillows.

CHAPTER 9

*T*he forest is darker than ever and still I crouch. My trembling hands clutch at my head, but the furious grip of icy fingers around my throat are gone, as is the putrid breath of the wicked beast's hungry mouth. I am once again alone, yet lost, somewhere deep inside the dark realm of the foreboding wood. I can still feel the evil around me, but it is no longer directly upon me, preparing to feast. It lingers only on the outskirts of my sights, secluded in its own shadows. I still feel the weight of its scorned eyes gazing upon me, hungrier than ever. The beast has spared me, at least temporarily, for reasons unknown.

I slowly rise from my crouch, and look around into the empty blackness. There are no more whispers, no more children giggling, only the faint breathing of something lurking about. I carefully step forward, senses keen to anything that might suddenly emerge from these dark depths of hell. I walk on, slowly. The thick evil surrounding my small and frightened being sterilizes me with its presence alone. But I continue on, not knowing if I am heading out of the woods or farther into their horrific core, descending further into darkness, into the constricting belly of the reptile.

The intense screaming of both the beast and myself still ring in my ears like a memory. I have no realization of what has just happened and did not know how I have miraculously escaped the tortured jaws of death. But I have, or maybe yet I haven't. I can't quite be sure. Maybe I am simply wandering in pure ignorance, like a freshly slain chicken, without my head. Or maybe the beast is simply teasing me, luring me further into insanity, fattening me up as he sharpens his claws, building its appetite for the magnificent banquet to come. I picture it licking its swollen dry lips with his greasy forked tongue, just beyond the edge of my senses.

I walk through the dense foliage and enter a small clearing. The putrid air hisses around my face, trying to block my progression. Upon entering further masses of looming trees, I notice a pinpoint of light at the far edge of the breach. It sends a flickering glow that seems to *originate from somewhere within the dark forest on the other side. It is the only distinct light I have seen upon entering the wood. The light breaks clearly through the expanding darkness around it, like a small beacon through terrible lapping waves of death and insanity, and beckons me. Yet it is still merely a pinpoint entering into the vast blackness, straining to stay on. I close further in on its source after passing through tree after tree, and entering a clearing. I can see the night sky above now, without further obstruction of trees. The air of the universe is cold and empty above me. Starless and moonless. Vacant. It conceals everything, helping the evils stay hidden from view under the cloak of the expansive blackness of the atmosphere.*

In my perception, the small drop of light continually escapes from my advancement. As I draw closer, it draws further away, incessantly staying mere yards ahead. I hurry my walk. It hurries its regression, moving just beyond reach. I begin to run, and yet, I forward myself upon it by no more distance. Can I be buried in this cavern of darkness with only a meager hope of finding escape? The hope dangling itself in front of me, like a piece of steak tied deliberately beyond the jowls of a starving hound. I charge at it, sprinting with all my remaining energy. Still, it has not closed entirely in toward my gasping frame. Then the forest thickens again with small trees and brush. I fiercely push through the brambles, continuing toward the glow. The light still mocks my movements, glittering just beyond the next branch. As I run deeper again into the forest, the foliage becomes a nearly indestructible mess of obstacles. Branches and leaves whip at my skin, restraining my body like thousands of muscular fingers. Yet, the light ahead seems to shine closer than ever. I push on, always nearly reaching the source of the illumination. However, the constricting forest increases in thickness and sustains an oily texture, like a skeleton beneath a large coat of tar. These sticky black masses of foliage accumulate around every inch of my body, constricting all movement. They writhe and wriggle around me, moving like the grasping fingers of the dying, muscles clenching for the final time. The more I struggle, the more it engulfs me. The weeds and branches wrap themselves around my head, as tight and unforgiving as a constricting python. I am unable to breathe freely, unable to move the slightest muscle, and soon unable to see the streaming pinpoint of light that I know still shines, if only faintly, somewhere just ahead.

CHAPTER 10

A current of pain constantly built itself up and surged through me, slowly drumming me from sleep. The pain from any injury is *always* worse the next day, and this was no exception. The next day is a day without adrenaline and without the anesthetic it brings. I awakened to at first a blurry but nicely decorated room, where the slope of the ceiling declined slightly toward my view. My surroundings seemed to simply pulsate pain down upon me. The very act of opening my eyes and letting light in hurt. I discovered that I was naked except for long underwear, and the flesh of my back felt as if someone had freshly burned it with an iron. I regretted each slight movement. My memory was fogged with pain, only the slightest bits of how I had come to this house held.

Sunshine be here for yous now, Chris, make shore yous get some ress now, jus' get some ress.

I remembered her thick but gentle hands upon my shoulders. I remembered her Tweety Bird sweatshirt that she collected for me from the backseat. I remembered her large motherly smile and her brown eyes through thick glasses; her dark coarse hair pulled back into a bun. The memory of her face slowly blurred into the colors that then formed the room, and the brown door at the center of the far wall. The door dissecting the old flower wallpapering. I stared at the door, mesmerized by its singularity.

The brown wood swung open then, like the wing of a bird, as if forced by my concentration on it. The large woman backed into the room, pushing open the door with her large end, and then turned to face me after passing the threshold. She slowed her walk to look at me. I managed to prop my withered body into a sitting position.

"Well there, suga, at least yous be awake. That be a good sign thare. Yous shoorely must haf taken a whoopin' from somebody. Pretty bruised and beat yous is." She carried a tray of food into the room with her. "I made up some soup to eat. That'll help clear yous head." She put the tray of soup and crackers down on a small table beside the bed. I took the cup of soup immediately, still nice and hot, and as eager as I was to devour the entire bowl in one gulp, I could only manage to sip gingerly.

"This is more than gracious," I said, trying to be as thankful as possible. "I owe you my life." She might not have realized that I actually meant it.

"Yous ain't owin' nuttin' to nobody, specially me." Her gaze met mine, and she smiled warmly, showing her square teeth and large gums. She sat down on the edge of the bed, grabbing a silver-framed picture from a shelf as she did. The bed squeaked and slanted under her weight.

"Yous have any family, Chris? Anyone yous love mo' dan anyfing else?" she asked after waiting for me to try the soup.

"Yeah, Sunshine. I certainly do," I replied, through soup sips. "I have a beautiful wife and daughter. They are the only things in my life, and I love them more than anything else in this world."

"Where dey? Back home?" She turned and looked me in the eyes as she asked.

I didn't really want to go into my situation with Sunshine, but I knew she sincerely wanted to know, and I didn't feel I owed her a lie. I hesitantly decided I would tell her what was happening to me if she persisted in knowing.

"Well, Sunshine . . . It's kinda a long story," she said nothing, but her look prompted me to continue. I decided to make it as short as I could. "Well, they are really the reason that I am here in New York to tell you the truth. You see they were, um . . . kidnapped. Taken from me. Abducted. I went to the police and the FB—well, basically, we tracked them here. Well, we at least tracked someone who we thought took them here. It's confusing and complex, and I really don't want to get into it all. To make a long story short, I got pretty beat up by the kidnappers."

I really didn't feel like telling her that I was running from the FBI, it might sound a little weird. "They ripped me up pretty good, Sunshine. I got beat up pretty bad, and yet I still don't have a clue where my family is." I was saddened again by the reality of it when I heard it from my own lips. "I still really have no clue . . ."

Sunshine sat there for a moment, studying me, seeing my grief.

"Yous be findin' 'em again, I be shoore of dat. And once yous be fixed up dey be right there waitin' for yous to find em again . . ." she spoke quietly. "The cup always be half full, Chris . . . even if it seem dat dere's no cup at all."

"This here's my son," she said then changing the subject, grabbing a picture frame next to the bed. "His name's Russel. Russel with one L. He'd be about yous age prob'ly. 'Bout tirty-five or so. He'd be smiling if hes was here, he sho would. Smilin' like those pearly teefth of his was the only light on this here Earfth. Smilin' like dat smile were about to fade out if he didn't use it. Smilin' all the time he was. Always happier dan a damn jaybird."

She handed the picture to me, but then just moved it so that I could see. She knew that it hurt for even me to even move my hands. The picture was of a strong-looking young black man, from the shoulders up. He had the same large brown eyes of his mother. He was smiling a broad smile and was neatly dressed in a blue Marine Corps outfit.

"He's in the Marines, huh?" I stated in a question.

"Well, he was," she said with a hint of sadness, rubbing the picture frame as if it were him itself. "He was in the Corps. He served da country so well, he did . . . Proud of everyfing he had, proud of his country, proud of his family . . . Proud of hi'self." She softly replaced the picture where it belonged. "I was proud of him too, I was. Proud that hes grew up, be such a kind young man . . . A gentleman. A hero to us all."

"He died in the Corps?" I asked faintly, not especially wanting to elevate her sadness.

"Nah. Oh nah," she said, smiling again momentarily, through her obvious pain. "He served eight straight years dere he did. In da Corps. Came back wif his medals and all, with all his pins and stripes. Came back to his home here to live in New York. Wif his wife. Ta be a teacher, high school teacher . . . He was great at dat too. Loved the kids, and dey loved him back." She pulled herself up from the bed in a calculated motion, steadying her large frame upon her legs. "That be my Russel." She stood soundless in the middle of the room, her large mass motionless after standing. She gazed down at the floor, recollecting her memories. I watched her from my reclined position, sipping my soup. After a while, she spoke with a distant cry lodged somewhere in her voice.

"I done los him too. Los him like you los yous own family. But my Russel, he ain't never gonna be comin' back. See yous, yous be gettin' yours back, I knows it. But Sunshine, na, I ain't never be gettin' Russel back, and I that I knows too, 'cause he already be an angel now." She paused, closing her large brown eyes and turning away from me. She took a few deep breaths that coerced through her throat and into her chest, then back out again.

"Are you okay, Sunshine?" I asked, knowing she was on the verge of crying.

She said nothing in reply for many moments, then spoke, her back turned to me, staring out the bedroom window.

"One day der was dis fire over on forty fif and eifth, I tink it was," she started, keeping her attention toward the afternoon light. "A big fire, one dem strucha fires. Was eatin' up da whole damn buildin', an ol' brick buildin', tall buildin', mussa been fiddy stories high. Like dem projects. Dem housin' projects ya know?"

She hesitated, finding the right words, and then spoke softly. "And course Russel be drivin' home from work, like he always did every day, and is right dere when dat fire firs start happenin'. He musta seen all deese people runnin' from da' buildin, coverin' dere faces and screamin' and all. Some coughin', some maybe even been burnt. Smokes jus pourin' on out dis place. Peoples yellin' and screamin' and all. No fire truck even be dere yet or nuttin', they always never cares about da projects anyways. So course Russel pulls over and stops ta help. Now dat fire's a real rager I heard, when he got there, with smoke just billowin' out all da windows and flames all lappin' up in the insides. People be runnin' all around goin' crazy, pas' Russel and all, but this one lady runs up ta Russel in a panic, tellin' him that her son be still inside. She be all cryin' and hollerin,' beggin' Russel to help. She be tellin' him dat she knows dat her baby still be in dere and that Russel be needin' to do sometin' quick, or dat her poor boy be dead. Russel don't even haf to tink twice, just runs right on in, right frew the front doors, into dem flames."

She pauses again, collecting herself. The soup is nearly done. "He done go run right frew dat door, right in dat fire, he did. Didn't even tink twice 'bout it . . . I jus know it, that's be the way he would have."

Her hands clinched down at her sides. Then she spoke very softly, softer than when she started, "He done run in dere but never did be runnin' back out 'gain." She turned around toward me then, with her head slightly bowed, her large eyes welling with tears. She sniffled a bit, just a soft sniffle, with barely a sound. Her large right hand moved up to wipe her face, to wipe away a tear that hadn't quite formed. Her watery eyes locked with mine.

"Dey say dat that fire burned fo' another ten minutes o' so, burned so strong dat even da people on da streets had to stand way back on way from it. Burned fo' 'bout ten minutes like dat. Hotta dan da depps of hell, 'twas. Burned and burned, fo' ten minutes at leas, 'fo the fire trucks even got dere . . . My sweet Russel, dey say—" She wiped another tear. "—my Russel, . . . he was in dere such a long time 'fo dem firemen even arrived. He been in dere lookin' fo' the little child."

I could only sit in silence as she stood and continued to explain her misery. "When da firemen finely put all dat fire out, that's when dey found my Russel. He was in da bafroom, face down in da baftub, wif da water on. Wif his arms all spread out over da tub. Underneaf his charred up body was that body of da boy, soakin' wet, unconsis, and burned a bit about the legs . . . but livin'. Out cold an' pro'bly scared to def, but still livin' still breavin' away. It was my Russel who was dere fo' him."

She caught her breath between tears. "And I done seen that boy be skippin' and playin' in da yard jus the other day. Bouncin' around and bein' happy as a fresh fish." She turned toward me, small tears still welling in her eyes. At that moment, I believed her eyes to be bigger and more beautiful than the eyes of any other living thing. She smiled her warm smile again, even through her apparent sadness. "My Russel. He always be so happy. And so brave. He done run in dere dat day, he done gone in dere so dat boy could come on out. So dat boy could live some mo' of this sweet li'l life. So dat boy could be grown up an' be as happy as my Russel was."

She solemnly managed the mass of her body again past the bed, and noticed that I had finished my soup. She picked up the empty bowl.

"Ain't dat some good soup?" she asked me with her large square smile and her wetted eyes.

"Delicious, Ms. Sunshine. Thank you."

The floor creaked under her weight. Her legs worked beneath her as she began to make her exit. She spoke again, with her back turned. "Now **you'll** be gettin' some mo' ress, now. Yous need it . . . I be right out here if yous need anyfing mo'." With another small sniffle, she slipped her large frame through the door, and closed it softly behind her.

I realized that Sunshine was possibly the sweetest person I had ever met in my life, and yet life had still taken advantage of her. It was a true shame that in her case, as well as mine in a way, the world sometimes mistakes kindness for weakness, and bad things really do end up happening to good people. It was obvious that she deeply missed her son and quite possibly decided to nurture everybody else in his place. I felt as if I was now the one standing in his place, with her motherhood shining upon me. It was clear that she defended the world from taking anyone else.

The soup had been one of the finest meals I have ever had the privilege of eating, and I could still feel its warmth in my belly. The throbbing throughout my body had multiplied greatly since I had awakened, but at least the soup eased the aches in my stomach. Only slow recuperation could subside the torture in my head, arms, ribs, and back. I slid back under the covers and wished that somehow things would all be right again.

Soon, sleep let itself in through my door of self and whispered things that I would never understand. The whispers brought dreams that I knew existed but would never remember. Then they danced through my thoughts like a secret, mysteriously entertained me, fixated me in their visions, cradled me within their breath. We laughed together at nothing. We sang songs in the absence of reason. We did everything, yet did nothing at all. Then the dreams turned quickly from me, gone like a memory. Leaving nothing but small remnants of their spell in the wake.

Sharp cool water smacked down upon my face, jolting me conscious.

What's happening?

"Wha—? Aah . . . Stop . . . Bla. Aah" I blurted meaningless things.

"Be gettin' up now. Yous needs to be leavin'." Sunshine was throwing water on my head from a cup that she held. "Yous be here fo' long enough time. Time ta be leavin'." There was urgency in her voice, a seriousness that I had not seen before. Her hand scooped out more cold water and threw it down on my face, her thick arm jiggling with each splattering handful.

"Okay. Okay . . . Sunshine . . . Jeez . . . Okay." I was struggling to figure out what was happening. "What's going on?" I was slightly disoriented and was covering my head with my hands, trying to stop the small downpour.

"Yous done slep fo' 'bout twelf hours or so, you'll bess be gettin' on yous way. Sunshine helped yous long enough now." She stopped throwing water on me, knowing that I was fully roused. She backed away from the bed as I unsteadily arose from it. My body felt tremendously better, but seemed as if it could still use at least another week of slumber and recovery. I grabbed my pants and jacket that had been neatly folded and slipped them on. I checked my pockets and only felt the letter of blood, but my wallet was on the bedside table, and I scooped it up as I hastily dressed. It was still soggy from the river. Sunshine stood beside me as I rose and made sure that I was actually going to leave. Her presence, once so motherly and warm, had become discomforting. There was something wrong with her demeanor, and it was obvious that I had outstayed my welcome.

"Yous can have dis shirt to wear, and Sunshine be sorry, but yous gots to be leavin'. Be bess for boaf of us." She handed me a large blue T-shirt, and with some effort, I pulled it over my head. I limped out of the bedroom, and she followed me through her small apartment. Only the noise of a small television broke the silence.

"Well, Sunshine, I do thank you for all that you have done for me, and one day I hope to pay you back. Thank you again." I opened the outside door and stepped out into the New York morning.

"Yous be a good person, like Sunshine already be sayin'. I knows it. And Sunshine be sorry yous have to leave. But yous have to, that be that. Yous can go to the Pinestar Motel, and yous can ask fo' Terry. Terry, he be a good man, and yous can stay at the motel fo' pretty cheap. Yous be safe dere too. Jus ask fo' Terry." Sunshine held the door open behind me, and studied me with her large eyes. I wanted to go back into her small sanctuary again because my body still ached severely. But more importantly, I felt safe in there, secluded from the dangers of the agents outside. Sunshine acted like a mother to me, even if only for a short time, and I needed to be mothered. I needed someone, anyone, to be there for me, for I was deprived of good emotion. Without my family, I had no one there to love anymore, nothing left. My body had healed itself of its exterior wounds, at least partially, but my interior stayed vacant and incurable.

I still had no family.

"But do take care now, yous hear?" she said, arms folded in front of her large bosom. She was trying to look stern, but the sweet and gentle person inside her still shone through.

"I will, Sunshine, I will."

I hope.

With that, I turned and walked from her apartment, directionless, hopeless, faithless, back into New York City.

CHAPTER 11

The menacing trance of New York City only seems to fade as the colors of sunrise infiltrate the tall buildings. Shimmering hues of light intermixing with the silhouettes of skyscrapers bring a calm to the city, make it seem vincible, only then it doesn't seem overwhelming. I found myself outside again midday. I was back into urban saturations. Subways blaring, taxis honking, people moving. Moving, moving. People covering the streets as a twisting layer of living carpet, weaving around and throughout each other. Talking all as one, yet individually not talking much at all. A droning mess of sound and energy escalating from the patters of footsteps, voices into cell phones, honking horns, and running engines. I found myself right back within this crazy plan of population, within the grinding gears of New York City.

Only after walking through busy streets for some time, I began to feel much better. The fresh air (if you can realistically call it that) of New York was rejuvenating. I seemed to have my senses back, and my body was working well again. I had no idea how long I had been at Sunshine's, maybe a few days, but I realized that I should have left on my own. I wish that I would have. It would have been the polite thing to do, although it was quite unexpected that she forced my departure. There was something odd about it, but then I realized what it was. She had washed and folded my clothing as I slept, in a kind and motherly gesture, but had inevitably found the letter written in blood.

She realized that there was something very powerful about the letter, just as I had when I first opened it too. She probably realized that there was something sinister about it, and that my broken appearance had something to do with it. She liked me, I could tell, but needed to wash her hands of anything that could spell trouble. If only I could wash the letter away that easily too, pretend it never existed.

It was wonderful to find sanctity when I needed it most, and I thanked her in my mind for that. It was nice to know that there were still good people living in such a cruel world. But the calm that presented itself within Sunshine's small apartment was merely the eye of the storm.

I neared a business district, as the number of people on the streets grew. I was simply wandering, for I knew nothing about New York. My eyes scanned the crowds constantly for any sign of trouble, most likely in the form of an agent in a dark suit. Yet everyone was wearing dark suits and moving so quickly. An agent could walk right up to me without easily being recognized and have handcuffs on me or a gun to the back of my head before I could run. I decided that it would be best for me to find a cup of coffee and a paper and figure out a destination, while staying as isolated as possible.

I pushed my way through the dense crowds, and noticed a small coffee shop about a block away on a busy street corner. As I headed toward it, I bumped into a young man wearing a sport coat. He stopped and looked at me in a menacing way.

"Do I know you?" he said finally, scowling.

"Don't think so," I replied, looking directly at him.

"I've seen you before, I know that," he said, examining me with his sharp eyes.

"Do you work on fifth? JM Broker?"

"Nope."

He stood there inspecting me for a minute more. His eyes moved keenly, and I knew that he was trying to match my face with another that he had stored deep within his database. "Humph," he mumbled finally, walking off.

Strange.

I went to the next block, found two quarters in my pocket and dropped them into the New York Times. I grabbed the newspaper and stuffed it under my left arm in one smooth motion, then turned and pushed open the glass door to the small coffee shop across the sidewalk. The aroma of rich coffee assaulted my nose immediately, as I took my place behind two people in line.

I could never live in New York City. Simply overwhelming, too uncomfortably busy.

It seemed that nobody stopped moving, if even for a second, like sharks. Everyone always on the go, always swimming, looking for fresh meat. Everyone searching furiously, frantically trying to achieve more momentum. Even the small coffee shop buzzed with activity. I was waiting for the man behind the counter to simply faint from exhaustion at any moment, as he ran back and forth, then back again, swinging his arms in every direction to make another latte or take someone's money. It almost made me tired just watching him.

"Watcha need?" he asked me without taking the time to look in my direction.

"Large coffee, cream and sugar," I replied.

"Yep. One sec." He exchanged a large cup for money with the man in front of me, then scampered off to the other end of the counter. I looked around at the other customers in the store. They were all flipping through their papers silently and sipping on coffee. Nobody said a word. Crowds still flowed like water past the windows outside.

"Three and a quarter," the man said, reclaiming my attention.

I reached in my wallet and grabbed four dollars. I pressed them on the counter and grabbed the warm cup. "Thanks."

I took a small booth by the window and pulled the paper from under my arm. I saw it immediately, right below the fold on the front page. A large black and white picture of my smiling face, with the bold caption:

cop killer escapes new york police!

My blood stopped cold in my veins as I stared at my own picture on the front page of the newspaper as if it were my own gravestone.

I was the subject of this headline.

My throat seemed to constrict, and my bowels nearly released. I looked up from the paper, expecting everyone around me to be staring at me suspiciously. I expected to be pounced on by the whole of the customers in the coffee shop, bludgeoning me to death or beating on me with their bare hands. But the coffee shop moved only with the flipping of newspapers and the maniacal working of the guy behind the counter. The people outside still flowed past the windows, noticing nothing out of the ordinary.

I was really trapped now. Not only did I have the agents to content with, but also thousands of New Yorkers that could recognize me and bring me to "justice." I picked up the paper and cautiously moved to a seat far in the corner, away from the windows, and I read the slander of the newspaper article.

> *Christopher Wyer, 36, wanted on kidnapping charges, shot and killed Detective Tyler Cunningham, 39, at approximately 1:30 AM on the morning of Sept. 15.*

> *Cunningham was shot four times in the chest and once in the head by the fleeing Wyer, who was under investigation for the kidnapping of his own wife and daughter, Cathorine and Rebecca. Christopher Wyer is still believed to be in the vicinity of the New York Metropolitan area, and is believed to be armed and dangerous. If you have any information on Christopher Wyer, immediately call the police, or Crime Stoppers @ 354-6671. Any information leading to the arrest of Christopher Wyer will be subject to a 1,000$ reward.*

What lies!

I simply could not believe what I was reading, and I reread it again immediately. This was all truly disgusting, and I could do nothing about it. The government was fabricating information solely for the purpose of arresting me and silencing the things I knew about Leonard Caldwell. I was their only loose end, and they were going to tie me by any means possible. I looked up from my paper once more, checking my personal security. Still there was no apparent threat. The bustling coffee shop continued to move endlessly, and the rush of thoughts inside my head matched it perfectly.

I pulled my head into the paper again, trying to conceal my face behind the pages at all times. I occasionally sipped from my coffee.

Keep my head down. Don't look at anybody. READ THE PAPER, LIKE EVERYBODY ELSE.

My hands and back of my neck were now sweating profusely. I put down my cup and wiped my hands on my shirt, then wiped my neck with my freshly dried hand. I picked up my cup and took a sip as I glanced up quickly. Nothing. No one was even looking at me.

Or were they? They could be dialing up the cops right now, telling them that the strange cop killer was having a leisurely drink right there in the Sixteenth Street coffee shop.

I glanced to my right past the counter. The phone sat right there on the wall, untouched. I glanced around, nobody was even on their cell phones.

Calm down. Get a hold of yourself. You're becoming paranoid, very paranoid.

Criminals only get caught because they act suspicious. They act like criminals.

And I'm not even a criminal for Christ's sake. I'm a victim, being more victimized by the people I thought were here to help.

I took a breath and forced my fingers to turn the page of the paper.

Ok, hang out here for a while, get a fucking hold of everything. Relax and read the paper. Figure out the next move. Take your time. Maybe order another coffee. Maybe a cappuccino after that. Think things out.

I flipped through the pages as calmly as I could, trying my best to stay collected and draw no attention to myself. I reread the boring letters to the editor about issues I had nothing to do with, happenings in New York that didn't interest me at all. But they weren't about me, and that was the important thing. I picked up my quarter-full cup of coffee. It tasted colder than room temperature. I glanced at my watch. Ten-thirty. I had stayed here for over an hour.

Nice. Killing time. But killing time until what? Until I finally became recognized then pulled out into the streets to be savagely beaten by the angry mobs? Die cop killer! True justice is served with bricks and stones from the hands of the citizens themselves.

I had to certainly leave before I stayed too long, or that too would be noticeable. The customers seemed to be slowly fading out as morning wore down anyway. I could not stay in the cover of the mass of consumers for much longer.

When should I leave the temporary concealment of the coffee shop? And where can I go? Think, man, think ...

"Another cup?" It was the clerk, startling me, asking me if I wanted a refill.

I looked up at him, quickly surveying his intentions. He had both hands on the counter, looking at me below his misplaced hair, waiting for an answer.

He has been busy all day long. Real busy. Probably hasn't even had the time to even notice the paper, much less read the damned thing.

"No, thanks," I replied after a second or two. I folded my paper and got up from the booth.

If he recognized me he would have already done something about it by now. He hasn't done anything but run around, maybe wipe down a table.

I walked up to the counter and put my cold coffee down in front of him.

"Done?" he said, already grabbing the cup.

"Yeah . . . Hey, what is there to do for the day around here?" I asked, trying to sound as normal as possible.

I am just a dumb tourist, not a vicious cop killer.

"This is New York," he said with a slight chuckle. "Anything you want to do. Check out the Empire State, maybe Lady Liberty. Whatever. Central Park."

"Nah. I don't really want anything too touristy. I'm sorta sick of people." *I hope that sounded all right.*

"Yeah, I understand that. Really understand that. I'm getting sick of all the heads too. Well, let me think . . ." He paused and looked about with the stroke of his chin. "Hummm . . . You like movies? There's a good theater about six blocks down. Just plays old stuff. You know, not any new releases or anything, just classics. Lot of black and whites. Pretty cool if that's your thing."

"Yeah, that's perfect, sounds good. Thanks a lot." It was perfect, I hadn't even thought about catching a movie to waste some more time. I could disappear into the darkness of the sticky floors and small seats. I slid him a twenty. His eyes brightened a bit when he saw it. "Thanks again."

I had always been a good tipper, but now especially. I think people that don't tip or tip poorly may have no soul. Plus, at this point in my life, I felt money was of no real value. My wallet basically contained four hundred and fifty dollars, two credit cards, various business cards, and a few pictures of my family. Only the pictures were of any real worth. If I was broke and starving, I would still be happy if I still had those. I would still be able to see true beauty, remember true love. That was more valuable to me than anything else in the world.

I pushed through the glass door exit and merged into a freeway of human movement. I followed the path of the bodies that moved to the left, trying to keep my head down and be as discreet as possible.

"There you are!" a young woman squealed as she stepped toward me. My heart slammed against my chest. She pushed through a few people, strolled directly into my path and then pushed right past me to hug a tall man with glasses and a mustache on my right. It happened in an instant, but my insides curled and my heart beat more than a thousand times.

Stay calm, nothing wrong.

I carried on, and the couple was quickly out of sight.

I continued on and thought about Sunshine as I did. I wondered if she had read the newspapers about me and called the cops. She hadn't alerted anybody, at least to my knowledge, at least while I was there. She only sent me on my way. I hoped she could see that I was a good person.

People blurred by, and I hoped that I blurred by them. I soon saw the movie theater ahead on an adjacent block, displaying *The War of the Worlds* as the eleven o'clock matinee. I went to the ticket window.

"One adult," I stated, removing my wallet. I plucked out four dollars and looked into the glass. Only then did I notice that the large clerk behind the window was reading the paper! It hadn't even registered until then.

Just ease away from the window, pivot, and run! Run!

"Four dollars," he said in monotone, hardly glancing up from the pages. He looked to be on the second page, probably the boring letters to the editor, and was oblivious to my now infamous face. I put the money down, nearly frozen, and waited for him to spring through the glass like a charging bull. Instead, he flipped the page solemnly, wiped his curly hair back, and glanced up only far enough to grab my money and replace it with a ticket.

"Enjoy the show," he said in a low voice, more to the paper than to me.

Horrible customer service skills. He didn't even look in the direction of his movie patron, much less make eye contact as he sells tickets. And I love it . . . Someone else's ignorance actually pays off for me once in my life.

The theater was very dark and very large. It was better than I expected. I kept thinking of Lee Harvey Oswald. I slid into a seat halfway down the landing, up against the wall, and proceeded to watch the film four times in a row. I realized that the dialogue, which I had now nearly memorized, was exceptional. I managed to sleep a few winks and munch down a large tub of buttered popcorn for my lunch, and then I slipped back into the streets of New York. Dusk had emerged with me, and the surrounding city was starting to twinkle with artificial lights. The movie theater provided me with ample time to devise a plan.

I felt more secure as twilight drew in, and I managed to locate a small motel about a half-mile from the movie theater. It was not the Pinestar as Sunshine had recommended, but I needed to be inconspicuous and didn't have privilege to be running all over New York looking for a specific

Motel. The motel I entered was quite run down, but, once again, I was in no position to be picky. The desk clerk was a small older woman, with dyed blond hair, and a homely smile.

"Good evening, sir. How's things?"

"Just fine. And you?" I could tell immediately that she did not recognize my face from the newspaper. "Pretty good. How can I help you?"

"I just need a single room, with a view, preferably. What are the rates?"

"How long did you want to stay?" She typed a few buttons on a computer in front of her.

"Three days, checking out Monday."

"Okay. We have a room for sixty-two dollars a night, second floor. Double bed. Want it?"

"Yeah, sounds fine."

I signed some things, gave her some money, and took the key she gave me.

The room was small but clean, and it had a window that looked down to the street below. I had paid cash, along with a cash deposit for I told the front desk clerk I had no credit card. I definitely didn't have a card with the name Richard A. Hamilton on it, which was the name I signed. My new alias.

I took a shower and wiped down. I noticed that I had accumulated a lot of facial hair as I looked in the mirror. I hadn't shaved in over a week, and was glad for it. It was time to grow a beard, or at least something that resembled one. The hairier the better. I needed to change my appearance as much as I possibly could. I picked up my only change of clothes from the floor, and as I grabbed my jacket, the bloody letter slid from an upside-down pocket and out of its plastic protective sleeve. Sunshine must have unzipped the ziplock and inspected it and not zipped it closed again.

The letter floated down to the bathroom tiles, landing directly in a small puddle left by my long shower, face down. I reached down to retrieve it, ready to throw it away once I had picked it up. It had only been the cause of trouble for me, and I needed it no longer. I picked it out of a small layer of water, and I noticed that the blood on the wet side had begun to run in quite an odd fashion. As I held it aloft, dripping, I saw that only the blood that the zeros were written with was dripping off. The blood that the rest of the letter had been written in stayed dry and unblemished. All the zeros, including the large round circle around the text, had dissolved before my eyes.

I stood up and realized that after the zeros had dripped away, a different code had appeared and a completely new equation would be formed. And then I understood.

It had been written for me after all. It did hold a secret that only I would know, and the secret was the number zero. The true meaning of the letter had been revealed.

I remembered what Leonard had written me, so many years ago:
THERE IS NO SUCH THING AS ZERO.

The zeros did not exist and were only included in the letter as a misdirection. I nearly yelled aloud. I wrapped a towel around my waist and rushed out of the bathroom to a small writing desk nestled in the far corner. Barely holding on to a cheap pen, I anxiously scribbled down the new equation that I discovered. The nearly formed code read thus:

THE ANSWER IS AROUND
: i +(XV+4); (X+6)-(3V); (-2(i))+13;
2X-XV:1030:(X+4)+2;(-3)+XV;2X-2-(XV+2);
2X-6;(-3)+8:X-4;i+(XV+2);(i)+14;V+8:
(XX-1)-(3V);2X-(XV);(2X-2)-4;V+(X+7);5;4V-2:
(XX+8)/2+6;XXV-X:3;XV-(14);13;V+(11):
i+(2X)+i;(2(V+I))-7;3(X)/2+3;
i(XV-i)-(X);V:

I made sure that my math was correct, even double checked a few equations. I also made sure that I did everything that Agent Younglin had done before me. The letter was genius, and worked on two different levels; the first level was a warm up. It allowed the Agents to show me how to solve the real part, or the second level. The second level was the real deal, and I was there. Simplified, after plugging in the roman numerals, it read as thus:

THE ANSWER IS AROUND
:19 ; 1; 11; 5:
1030: 16; 12; 1;
14; 5: 6; 18; 15; 13:
4; 5; 14; 22; 5; 18:
20; 15: 3; 1; 13; 16:
22; 5; 3; 18;
4; 5:

The numbers, when changed to their corresponding letter in the alphabet, now expressed an entirely new and different message. A message meant solely for me.

TAKE 1030 PLANE FROM DENVER TO CAMP VERDE.

I was amazed at what I had just uncovered, a code with two different meanings. A renewed energy beat through the walls of my skin. I had another purpose to carry forward with.

This game is not over yet.

Maybe my family was still out there, safe all along. Safe with Leonard's accomplices, not victimized by them. The letter could possibly be a cordial invitation to simply go retrieve them.

Absolute retribution for what I had been through.

I was so excited, I almost decided to ditch my original plan to hide out for a few days to get some rest and think things out.

Get your family now.

But I reconsidered and forced myself to calm down. I would be no help if I was spotted by someone and turned in to the police. Besides, I needed more rest and recuperation. My body still looked and felt as if I had swallowed a few live grenades. I needed to recover to the top of my physical form again, and let the media die down about me being a murderer in the meantime.

I ordered a pizza, and continued to dress and wash up. I inspected my bruises again thoroughly and realized that I was seriously a lucky man. I had fallen from a three-story building and had jumped through glass with nothing more than a few scratches and a huge bruise about the size of a doormat. But with the exception of a few other cuts, abrasions, and possible sprains, my body had shown amazing resilience to the tortures of my escape. I was impressed with myself. The pizza arrived, and I ate as much as I could and lay down fully clothed upon the stiff bed, thinking about the new possibilities of the letter and drifted into sleep. The darkness of my closed eyes seeped into the darkness of subconsciousness, and then turned into . . .

CHAPTER 12

*T*he cold black wrath of the forest. I have been here before. I have been here. I am again shrouded in the heavy black cloak of evil, exactly where I had been sometime before. There still is a flicker of light somewhere beyond this oily barrier, just beyond my grasp and, at the moment, just beyond my sight. Yet suddenly, the dark sheet that holds me falls away, dissipating around my body so that I can finally breathe again, move freely again. I see the small ember of light in the distance. I am still shrouded in darkness, yet the light ahead is more intense than I remembered it being. I begin to run toward it with furious and renewed energy, but again, it continues to mock me by staying just out of reach. I stop, not from exhaustion, but from logic. This is just a dream, I realize. This whole thing is simply in my mind. I need not to chase the light with my physical self because there is really no such thing as physical self in a dream, but allow my mental to overtake it instead. So I chase it not with my legs but with my mind, visualizing its capture.

The circle of light draws closer and closer, finally lying directly in front of me. It is a soft ring of light, strong in its luminance, only about the size of a quarter. I reach forth and touch it with an extended finger. It burns then, not painfully, but with the sensation of an orgasm at the tip of my touch. It burns with the heat of love, and the memories of **places** I cherish. And slowly, as if time has stopped, it melts away at the darkness surrounding us. The oily layers drip away, becoming translucent. I am able to pull back the blackness, like peeling the skin of an orange, revealing more and more of this wonderful golden light, which has been trapped behind the dark barriers for so long. It all splays out before me, like black curtains opening for the sun. Through my skin and to my core, the light dances and caresses me. Then in pure elation, I step forward and immerse myself outside, into the pure light and heat of everything I have ever wanted, needed, and loved.

CHAPTER 13

I was still not used to waking up in foreign places, in beds that were stiff or small, beds that were unlike my own. I found myself staring at a cracked yellow ceiling of a small room snuggled somewhere inside the depths of New York. I could hear the city breathing around me. Murmuring. I felt awkward. I felt uncomfortable. I felt segregated from everything and transplanted here.

But I will be leaving soon enough.

I secluded myself in the tiny room the whole day, thinking. Inspecting the letter that had become smudged and different than how I had first come to understand it. The letter, which had started it all, lighting the spark that inflamed my life. Yet, I was still so fascinated by it and its history. The young kid that I knew as Leonard Caldwell had grown up and written me a coded letter, leading me into a tragic adventure that I still was fighting to control. He had to have written it. The FBI had not. The second meaning clearly showed that. And even in death, Leonard had changed my life again. I had seen him killed right in front of me, along with a detective who was helping me find him, and I almost ended up right along with them both.

The answer is around. That was the key to the whole thing in the first place; maybe the key to the question of life in general. *The answer is around.* Just look around, and the answer will present itself. If only I had realized that the big circle around the code was meant to be a big zero, I might have been able to solve it my self.

Or would I?

No such thing as zero. That was a statement that only Leonard and I had shared so long ago. So I knew he had written it. I could only hope that it was Leonard's plan the whole time for the feds to solve the original code, to show me how to do it, and then the next phase of the code, the alter meaning, was meant for me. But there were still so many questions.

If Leonard had written the letter, and if I am supposed to meet him in Denver as the revision of his letter means, what the hell was he doing in New York? And now that he was dead, would anyone else be there instead or was I following a cold trail? Did he use the two different meanings of the letter to mislead the FBI? Or to mislead me?

I battered my brain the whole day, and as much as I thought about all the things that still didn't fit, I only had a few definitive answers. What I did know was simple, the FBI was definitely my enemy, and my family was gone. Leonard and Tyler had both been killed by the FBI to cover something up, leaving me to be the only leak. But what exactly was the information that was so valuable and needed to be covered up in the first place? The FBI could have easily told Tyler and myself that they needed to kill Leonard, and I would have been furious, but that would have been all I could do. "Tough shit, Chris," they would have said. "Sorry about that, I know it will be all but impossible to find your family now. Good luck." I wouldn't have been able to do anything about it.

However, they knew that I was their only connection to finding Leonard, so they had to tell me all the information on him. All the information about his blood being thousands of years old and of his supreme intelligence. I needed to be informed about his evolution and possible threat to national security because it would help me find Leonard. And it would help them destroy him.

They had to tell me everything so that I could get to him. And then, once I had been told the information, they had to kill me as well. They had to shut me up. I had signed my death warrant the minute I began listening to Agent Marks speak about Leonard between breaths of nicotine. They told me the truth about Leonard or their story would have ended up having too many holes in it. They already knew that I knew, that the blood on the letter was hundreds of years old. They couldn't have really made up a good enough lie around that one. So they figured they might as well just tell me everything, let me lead them to Leonard, then simply put a few rounds in my head. Then what I knew would not have mattered. It was exactly what they tried to accomplish, yet they had not succeeded. They had gotten Len and Tyler, but had not gotten me.

Two out of three is close but not close enough boys. You still fucked it all up. And I am going to make sure that it comes back to haunt you.

The letter was one last hope of somehow ending this thing, and the longer I stayed in New York was the longer I was in danger. The masses seemed to be quietly closing in.

My place was not in New York anyway, but with my family. Time to roll another round of dice. *The answer is around.* The solution, I hoped, would present itself.

> **(Female) Hotel clerk: Front desk.**
> **Room 412: Yes, this is ... room four-twelve. I will be working on business documents for the next few days. I do not want any interruptions, not even housekeeping. I will set linens and towels in front of the door if I need them changed."**
> **Clerk: Okay, got it ... room four-twelve.**
> **Room 412: And hold my messages.**
> **Clerk: Okay, Mr. Hamilton, will do. (Resounding click of receiver.)**

The clerk hadn't thought twice about it. Perfect. I packed up my things, tossed the DO NOT DISTURB sign on the door and was on my way to Denver.

I hailed a cab, slightly aware that the cab driver may have picked up the morning paper, but figured it was relatively safe bet. He shouldn't be reading the paper if he is busy driving a cab, plus, being a New York cabbie, there was a very good chance of the driver only speaking Portuguese anyway.

"No comprendo, cop keella?"

I climbed inside a box of incense on wheels. A small Caucasian man in a blue sweatshirt was the driver. He did not turn to look back at me, but his eyes glinted from under his Yankees hat, studying me in the mirror.

"Where to?" he asked in a New York accent that was thicker than a New York steak, moving no other part of the body but his mouth. His hands rested comfortably on the wheel. He definitely wasn't Portuguese. For a moment, I wondered if my dumb luck let me hail the only English-speaking cab driver in New York. Of course, he would be the only cabbie that would be able to read the paper and coincidentally point me out.

"Airport," I responded to him, glancing forward to see him through his mirror.

"Airport is twelve miles away. Be a half hour to forty-five minutes in traffic. Be sixty bucks. Plus it will take you another hour to wait through security."

Security. I had almost forgotten. I am a wanted man. I couldn't board a plane, not without proper identification. Shit. I didn't even think about it. I need to be sharp, always remember that I am known as a murderer.

"Shit, I lost my ID. Do you think it is still possible to get on a plane without ID?"

"No ID? No way, not on a plane. But . . . well, da train is only two miles away. Plus da train don't have much security. Go right through, right on board. Just need credit card. Never need no ID. Amtrak just wants your money, not your name."

"Are you sure?" I questioned. "I haven't ever even been here before. I—"

"Don't even sweat it. No ID, no problem. Give me an extra twenty bucks, and I know a guy that will get you through. Get you right through and whatever else you got on ya without searching. Twenty bucks." Then he turned in his seat for the first time, just staring as he now faced me. "Twenty bucks, get your drugs through without question or whatever. No problem."

My drugs. I chuckled a little. "No, no drugs. I seriously just lost my driver's license, that's all."

"Uh huh. Sure, buddy. Well, twenty bucks gets you no hassle, whatever your problem is." His beady eyes penetrated my vision, letting me know that it was just best to give him a twenty. I handed the money over.

He turned back to the wheel quickly and pulled the automatic handle down into drive. "Twenty, plus fare, of course." He gave a quick glance back at me to see that I understood, then forced his foot upon the gas pedal.

I watched him as he drove to the train station. He seemed on edge the whole time, nervous. I expected him to stop the cab at any moment and simply jump from it, running in a jerky motion like a madman toward the nearest policeman. He drove furiously, constantly accelerating whenever he could, passing cars with vigor. He glared at any driver that forced him to slow down, before he could pass them. We were at the train station in a matter of minutes, and he yanked open the car door immediately after he stopped the car at the main entrance. His small body shot out from the door and went around the front of the cab.

I exited as well and followed him inside, matching his quick pace as he entered the lobby of the station.

"This way," he said, knowing I was directly behind him, but not looking back. He scattered through the small crowd of people and made his way toward a long ticket counter, where he situated himself in front, cutting in line. A young couple scowled but said nothing. The young man behind the counter recognized him as he approached and seemed to regret him being there.

"Hey, Thomas. This is a friend of mine. His name is—"

"Christopher," I concluded for him.

"Yeah, Christopher. Get him a ticket would ya? Good friend of mine and all." The cabby impatiently drummed his fingers on the counter.

"Yeah, yeah. I'm sure you both go way back," Thomas said, as he casually looked at me. "Where are you heading today?" he asked.

"Denver," I answered.

"Okay . . ." He typed something into a computer in front of him. "One hundred and fifty-six dollars there, Christopher. Cash or charge?"

"Um. Cash, I guess." I plopped down eight twenties. I had nearly spent every dime I had in cash. He grabbed them and reached into the register near his waist.

"Four dollars is your change. Car fifty-three on train seven. It should be boarding within the next ten minutes." He handed me my change and a ticket. "Enjoy the world of Amtrak, and please ride with us again," he said sarcastically.

The cabbie turned to me, winked, and escaped back through the small number of people. I headed past the counter toward the loading trains, found the right one, and loaded into it.

The number fifty-three car was actually a large private compartment, about half of the size of the train car. The kid had given me a good seat. I pulled aside the sliding door and entered into a small area with bench seats on both sides. A large window separated the seats, and luggage racks hung above them. It was spacious yet simple, and it was empty.

I took a seat at the edge nearest to the window on the right side, waiting for the train to depart as I had situated myself.

Perfect. No one is even here that I even have to deal with. The car is all my own.

I looked out the window at the other trains and few people walking between them. These were people that, likely, had no family, or knew what it meant to lose a family in any case.

These were people that were not like me. These people had no direction like I had. No motivation like mine. These people weren't trying to save anybody but themselves. They were trying to save money on travel fare, not be unnoticed by the FBI so that they could rescue their loved ones.

I looked in my wallet, I had now just under fifty dollars cash. In hindsight, I was glad that I had spent only cash, as the FBI were most likely able to track any purchases that I would make using credit.

The train softly lurched into motion, and I was already closer to Denver, if only by inches. Soon, after the countless amounts of buildings and people drifted by, the train began to wind its way into less urban areas. It glided past fields of tall grasses and light woods. The sky seemed to open up and reveal its true soft blue colors with the sun clearly shining, without the obtrusive skyscrapers and yellow smog of the city. It felt liberating to feel unbound by the grasping conurbation. Night grew from dusk, and I lay down across the seat and slept as the train rolled onward.

I slept for many hours and woke the next afternoon to the rocking of the train. I purchased a sandwich from the deli car hours later and stopped in an area of the train, which was dedicated to be a small library/study. This portion of the train had a small writing desk and chair, pens, pencils and paper, and a limited assortment of random books. I browsed through the literature, finding mostly old romance or western novels and some scattered Tom Clancys and Cormac McCarthys. I was about to leave, seeing nothing to my initial liking, when I noticed a smaller paperback without a cover. The book had no legible writing on its front or binding, and was quite tattered. It was obvious that someone had left it on purpose. It had been discarded. I grabbed it anyway, knowing that the train still had quite a journey, and I might pass my time doing some reading. I waited until I returned to my sleeping car with my sandwich to examine the book. I flipped through the first couple of pages and smiled immediately when I was able to recognize which book it was.

To Kill a Mockingbird by Harper Lee.

I chuckled aloud at the irony.

I had never read it before. It was missing the first ten pages or so, but I figured I could fill in the blanks. I had a day and a half to do so without interruption. I slept and read and looked out the window to the passing countryside. I was as content as I had been in a long time. The book was an amazing work, and I finished it hours before arriving in Denver, as if savoring a fine meal. I left it on the seat, beaten and tattered as I had found it, for someone else to find and savor as well.

CHAPTER 14

I had been to Denver before, but I made no time contacting old friends or seeing the sights. I went directly from the train station to the airport. I felt less persecuted by the masses though, being such a distance away from New York and my three-day-old picture on its *Times*. I still made no effort to make myself conspicuous however, and found my way to the Denver international flight schedule board.

The letter said, **"Take 1030 plane from Denver to Camp Verde,"** but did that mean that the flight left at 10:30 AM/PM? or that the flight number was 1030? I had no idea. So I scanned the departures for anything that matched up. There was only one direct flight to Camp Verde, and it left at 3:00 PM. But the flight number was *1030*.

Bingo.

Something might actually be going right that is affiliated with the damn letter.

"I need a one way to Camp Verde," I exclaimed to the clerk after waiting patiently in line.

"Business class or first class?" he muttered back to me.

"Business. How much?"

"Let me see. Comes to three hundred ten dollars and forty-eight cents," he glanced back up at me from his computer, waiting for payment.

I had twelve dollars left in cash. I had to use credit. I placed my Visa on the counter and prayed that the feds couldn't track it. But I had a bad feeling that they most certainly could.

It's the only way, according to the letter, I have to be on this flight. Have to be. Nothing else to do. Nowhere else to go.

He smiled as he took the card, like he was another agent, knowing that he was about to spring the trap. He scanned it and handed it back to me. "Thank you for flying the friendly skies of United," he said, handing me a plane ticket. "Have a wonderful day." It sounded like the same polite garbage that came out of the clerk at the train station.

I killed an hour in the terminal, getting a ten-dollar hotdog and cup of Pepsi. I boarded the plane that I somehow hoped would lead me to salvation and return me back to my family. I squeezed past the seat that contained a man reading a newspaper and situated myself next to him in my window seat. I always liked the window seats. I always wanted the view. From no other perspective can you see the beauty of the world float by underneath you, a gigantic green beach ball bobbing on an invisible ocean.

Soon the captain announced himself, we all buckled in, and in an exhilarating acceleration, we were off. I gazed down at the Earth as it fell away from the plane, watching the towns and cities below turn to small perfectly symmetrical squares of green and yellow fields. The demanding wings of the plane cut through clouds around us, and we soon leveled out at our destined altitude.

"*Unmistakably beautiful,*" the man next to me with the newspaper said, still covering his face with its pages, seeing none of the scenery, which he spoke of at all. His voice seemed to come crisply into my ears, yet somehow it seemed that he spoke from a distance.

"Yes, it really is. Truly magnificent," I said aloud for him to hear, as I looked out to the lands below.

"*A statement holding true to many things, Mr. Wyer,*" he exclaimed, as he continued to flip through the pages of his *Denver Post*, his face still concealed behind it.

Had I just heard him say my name?

"Did you just call me Mr. Wyer?" I asked, my attention now fully on the passenger beside me.

"*It is your name, isn't it? Christopher Layne Wyer.*" He calmly turned another page, as if none of this creepy was happening at all. Beyond the edge of the paper, I could see wisps of thin graying hair. I was puzzled at his irreverent actions and the fact that he knew my name. He folded the paper in front of him, and finally revealed his face. He had the face of a very old man, but still somehow looked young. It was his eyes, his childlike eyes that created a permanent youthful appearance. His irises seemed to take up just a little more space on the eye than they should, fading from a light blue to a darker hue as the color neared the pupils. His hair was wiry and curled up and away from his head like the flames of a fire. He may have stuck his finger in a socket forty years ago and just never took the time to recomb his hair. He stared right at me, emotionless. Then he spoke to me again, but his thin lips remained stationary. They didn't even quiver. His speech was so that he was finished with a paragraph even before you are done reading this line. Yet he spoke quite clearly, with words that never merged, so somehow his speech never seemed hurried. There were no hastily spoken phrases, like the articulation of an auctioneer, but he instead seemed to tell all his sentences at once.

"*Christopher Layne Wyer. Born in Washington in sixty-one. Mom and Dad got divorced fourteen years later. Never stayed with mom much, always seemed to get along better with your father. Went to college for two years, dropped out, and moved to Durango, Colorado. Still have a scar right above your left buttocks from that snow sledding accident that you had with your younger brother when you were ten and he was eight. That was, of course, before he became sick. Never went sledding together again, quite unfortunately, but you think about him practically every time you see your scar. You loved your brother, although now you sure wished that you had shown him more love than you did.*

"*You met your first wife in California, and you still hate the whole state for it. She was both clever and mean, a lethal combination, and took you for a ride during the short marriage and the long divorce. Taught you an expensive lesson. You fortunately found yourself a woman who sincerely cares for you and can really relate with, thanks to what you learned, and you now consider the divorce money well spent. Your heart leaps when you think Cathorine, even now, which is the surest sign of love. You have a child with her, Rebecca, and she is the sweetest little thing that you have ever imagined. She is your child, your pure heart molded on its own and healthily growing, all the best things you could imagine in yourself you can actually see in her. You now sell real estate, or at least did sell real estate. Don't have much of a job now, under the circumstances.*

"*Those circumstances being you, here on this plane, with me. So just as you found yourself situated with your pension plan and your weekend barbecues, a whirlwind of violence and intrigue swept over you, leaving you dazed and with nowhere to run. You find yourself trying to piece together that civilized life again and hopefully recover your lovely wife and child. And quite lovely, they most certainly are. You boarded this plane in hopes of somehow doing just that because the letter of blood that devious two-meaning letter from one Harper Lee instructed you* to do so. You have survived the assassination attempts, falling from windows and buildings, as we knew that you would. You escaped those foul situations to wind up here on flight number ten-thirty. To wind up in a seat somehow situated directly next to mine, next to an old man who still contains a glimmer of youth, especially in the eyes, somehow raving on and on without really even moving his old chapped lips. Talking almost all at once. But this curious old fellow speaks mad truths about your life that only you could possibly know. Did I get that about right?"

"Yeah," I responded, in more of a gulp than in speech.

He was clearly a good ventriloquist, and he did actually know things only I knew about myself. It had to be some devious trick. A real con man. A professional. I inconspicuously moved my hand to my wallet and was surprised to find that it was still there.

"*I didn't take your wallet,*" he said, looking away from me and surveying the rest of the plane. He chuckled then, as I thought about how he had somehow still managed to manipulate me. "*Mr. Wyer . . . I do believe that you have me all wrong. A con man I am surely not. Nor a pickpocket, or a thief. Actually, I am probably one of the most truthful and non-deceitful people you will ever have the opportunity to meet. My name is Huxley, and am here to give you something, not take anything away.*"

"Tell me then, Mr. Huxley, if you do not wish to trick me, why aren't you moving your mouth when you speak? How did you know that I was going to be on this flight and what my name is and the history of my life?" My slightly agitated voice projected over to the next aisle, where a young woman turned and noticed our conversation. She studied the two of us with a quick confused glance, then pulled her eyes back in front of her as to disguise her eavesdropping.

"*Mr. Wyer, I know you because you have shared many things with me. I know your life story because you gave it up free-willing, whether you know that you did or not. It cannot simply be coincidence that you are here, nor that I have so much knowledge about you, just as it is not simply coincidence that the sun rises every day.*"

I was beginning to get nervous. Something monumental was happening, and I could feel it in my body. The man sitting next to me was correct, this wasn't random.

"*I apologize if I have shocked or scared you. It is not my intention. And there is no trick with my lips not moving with what you hear. It is easier for me to . . . communicate this way. You see, Mr. Wyer, I am no ventriloquist, nor am I performing a trick of any kind. Instead, I am speaking to you in your mind. I am projecting thought into your head. But to you, it almost seems like I am speaking, although almost as if from across the room, with a clear yet softened voice. This is because you have never been communicated to like this before, but once.*

"Leonard," I exclaimed.

"Yes, Leonard spoke to you like this on the banks of the river from which he pulled you so many years ago."

When he saved my life.

"Yes. When he saved your life."

Huxley folded his paper completely and slid it to the side of his chair, re-situating himself. The woman glanced over at us again, smiling this time in an attempt to clear any tension.

"The woman, whom you just noticed, cannot hear a word I am communicating to you. She is confused, and rightly so, because she sees you jabbering words about, while I utter not a single reply."

"Telepathy," I exclaimed, lowering my voice, in case what he was *saying* was right.

She does seem not to notice a single word that he says, while giving me some weird glances, and his words do almost bypass my ears and leap directly into my brain.

"Telepathy, yes, but many fathoms more powerful, as well as more multidimensional. The thought I possess could never be tamed into being simple telepathy. For instance, I am speaking with maybe thousands of people right now, as we fly over the world. A conversation in collective consciousness. Speaking in different tongues, and in different dialects. Speaking in thought, yet delivering different voices in different ways. Telling different stories. All naturally, not unlike breathing. Billions of thoughts radiating from my head, as I simply turn the page of the newspaper. And I think to them as clearly as I think to you. As clear as your own thought. As strong as your own inspirations. If I wasn't here, you would actually believe that you were thinking these words up yourself. Yet I focus it, so it sounds as if I'm actually speaking to

you, without moving my mouth. But I am not. I actually haven't had to physically speak in over three years. If I no longer needed to eat, my tongue would lie useless in my mouth."

A tall female flight attendant pushed a drink cart to our seats. "Can I get you gentlemen anything?" she asked pleasantly.

Huxley spoke then, staring up at her from his seat. "I'll have a water, thank you."

I was left perplexed yet again, for he just said he did not speak aloud, but I clearly heard him and watched his lips move. I didn't need anything, so she gingerly handed him a clear plastic cup and continued down the small aisle.

"I thought you said that you haven't spoken to anyone in over three years?" I asked him then noticing the lady from the other aisle again turning her head and raising her eyebrows this time.

"*I haven't,*" he replied in thought as he drank. "*But I can still move my lips you know, to make it look like I am talking. I simply think aloud for all to hear and move my lips along with my thoughts.*"

He put his cup down on the plastic tray that he had folded from out of the seat in front of him. "Like this," he loudly said to me, or so it seemed. He made sure to accentuate his mouth to show how the words would look coming from it.

The lady across from us now stared in complete bewilderment, as I moved my lips without a sound, impersonating what he did.

"*She thinks you are a complete imbecile and cannot wait to get back to Hollywood where it is civilized. How she wishes that she was not bumped back into business class with the flagrants and fools,*" Huxley thought to me. "*That is her direct mind quote, by the way.*" He smiled slyly. He had not even turned to look at her.

I laughed a little, as I watched her put two tabs of something in her airplane cup, waiting until they fully dissolved before drinking it all down.

"*Never mind her, she unwittingly believes that money is the most powerful thing that human beings can obtain. She is more proud of the Rolex around her wrist than the fact that she is healthy and alive. If she met Gandhi on the streets today, she would see him as foul, as a bum, judging him for his apparent lack of wealth, unable to recognize the power of his mind.*"

"I am ultimately supposed to find you then? The letter lead me this whole way so that you can tell me—think me this?" I still tried to keep my voice down, as I realized that it did look to the passerby that I was simply talking to no one in particular. The important thing to me was the whereabouts of my family, not telepathy.

"No, no, dear boy. I am merely a stepping-stone on the path that you have already found yourself treading awkwardly on. I am a sign in the road. I am here to tell you what you only need to know, to guide you in the right direction. You must absorb the rest on your own. I can reassure you that your family is fine, even though I have had nothing to do with their abduction. But the things that I am about to tell you will shed light on their disappearance, as well as give you the keys to get them back. And from now on, if you haven't noticed already, you need not speak, only construct rational thought, and I will be able to hear it."

I can simply think of what I am going to say?—I formed in my head.

"Exactly. You did it just now."

His voice rung clear in my head immediately after my "thought." I realized that we were now speaking in perfect harmony with each other—having a complete conversation without uttering a single word. The lady next to us stopped, nervously glancing in our direction as well, due to our complete absence of anything auditory. It was magnificent, but I realized that this man could read everything in my brain, therefore making me very vulnerable to him. Yet I fully believed him, genuinely, even after only knowing him for minutes. Everything had taken an awfully strange turn and completely trusting someone is the only option you have when they can read your mind.

Have I always been able to speak with anyone like this? I asked him, inside my head.

"You have been subliminally communicating with everything your whole life, but this is a different level. So no, not just anyone. Not yet. You may someday learn how to transmit your thoughts at the intensity of mine, but at this moment you cannot. Your mind is simply not strong enough to stay intact. Schizophrenics hear voices in their heads and are

crazy because of it. Imagine its intensity if you actually did start hearing people's thoughts, and in their rawest form. You hear people suffering on the inside, possibly. Ever complaining about their lives as the best they know how, in the privacy of their heads. Or maybe they truly are sick, and you can feel their constant thought concentrating on the parts of them that ache. You hear the perverted, the aggressive, the dullards, the academics, the hate, the love, the shame. There is nothing you miss, nothing filtered, all combined into a super-flow of random streams of consciousness. No off switch."

My lips don't look as good as hers, and she's probably older. I hate him and what he did. He knows it. Poison. A disgusting wretch. Gary never should have said that to her. Should be rich by now. I bet her pussy smells. If I punched the seat, it would break my hand. I shouldn't cry over this, but I probably will. Refrigerator needs to be cleaned. Time things better, that's all I have to do. Chew the nail on my index finger. Shoulder, shoulder, shoulder, shoulder. The days really have been drifting away. Tommy has that huge of a cock? You can tell how old someone is by feeling their hands. I must have a cavity. That is over with now, thank God, she deserves better. She is sleeping. The contract should be worth 3.5 or more. Have to pee soon, but I hate those bathrooms. In my ass, or whatever. My sister would have liked the way the funeral was handled. I will hold it for him, and he knows it. There it is again. I could buy you, you fuck. Drooling again. It could be that good. Small rash on my mouth, been there too long. I should look for it, must remind myself. Look at it and tell me that. Possibly galena, or iron ore. If I fucked her hard enough with it, the candle would probably melt. These days without you let me down slow. Thank God for that. I'd be naked walking in front of them. It could work for a commercial or something. A grilled cheese actually sounds good, with tomato. I shouldn't say it, she'll be mad. I suppose I could use more eyeliner.

My mind received all that suddenly, in a rush that resembled the feeling you get from quickly standing up from a period of motionless. It affected the equilibrium dramatically in a rush of blood to the head. All the sentences blended as one large concept, no beginning or end, just a large block of ideas. I felt immediately dizzy as I received it. Huxley steadied me with a firm hand, as if sensing my sudden headache and slight nausea.

It can be hardly enjoyable at times, he thought after I breathed a bit, *and those were the thoughts that occurred in less than a millisecond from the row in front of you.*

There were only four people in the row in front of me. Simply absorbing a sliver of their constant thought had been stammering.
How can you live like that? I asked in my head

"How can't I? Reality is merely how one copes with it."

The plane had gone silent; I barely heard the droning of the engines. He had given me a long chance to let my mind stabilize before he thought to me again.

"Think of a massive network, one which covers the whole span of the world, and the ever-expanding universe for that matter. A network of minds, Chris, a network of advanced thought. We are all connected by this network, all strains of life, a collective consciousness that is the universe itself. This network grows vastly stronger and stronger with each second, multiplying in infinite proportions. It has grown to a colossal size, the only thing being able to comprehend its own size and expansion is itself. Coming to grips with ourselves will always be our greatest test."

He studied me with his eyes, the only feature that moved on his face.

"The reason that you are wrapped up in all of this, the letter, your family, the FBI, Leonard, everything, is because we need you. Actually, Leonard needs you. For several different reasons. Unfortunately, for you and your loved ones, the FBI needed you too, to get to us."

Leonard is dead, Mr. Huxley, I watched a sniper blow his brains out all over a New York apartment, and all over me. They splattered him like a bug against a windshield. With this thought, Huxley chuckled heartily, a large laugh from a little man, and it must have been clearly audible, for not only the woman in the next aisle but a few other passengers noticed the commotion.

Huxley spoke inside my head as he laughed.

"*That is just what we needed the FBI to believe! If they believe that Leonard is dead, then they no longer need to pursue him. This allows our safety and freedom, ensuring no further complications. No end of the world, no end to the universe. I will get into it all, eventually. Leonard is not dead. You see, the Leonard Caldwell that you knew, the Leonard Caldwell that saved your life, the Leonard Caldwell that died in front of you, was simply a shell. A shell that momentarily held pure thought, much like the shell of a crab. And just like a crab, the shell will sooner or later need to be discarded once it becomes inadequate to accommodate its host for any reason. It is outgrown as you have outgrown children's clothing. When you saw Leonard die, you saw a shedding of a skin, so to speak. Because what lived inside that man, the man you saw die, must live on forever. Call it a soul if you like. One of the most magnificent souls to ever grace the universe.*"

Huxley situated himself in a different position in his small seat and picked up his newspaper again. He still continued to speak fluidly to me without words, and as he thought to me, I gazed back through the small circular window.

He coughed a bit, and I heard the pages of the paper rustling again.

"*A child was born nearly a thousand years ago when man was just starting to unravel the mysteries of the world. Man had only recently become strong, as they now realized the power of the mind. And this child, yet still young, showed remarkable intelligence—intelligence, which rivaled even the wisest of men. This child understood many things and soon began to study everything around him. He not only studied everything, but absorbed it fully. He was able to recollect everything, every word in every book, every person's name that he had ever met, as well as the exact conversations that he had with anybody. He could remember dates and times of every event that he had ever seen, witnessed, or even read about. He absorbed it all, missing nothing. Every bit of information that was processed by his senses was stored in his head. The concentration to accomplish such a feat is uncanny, and this boy learned how to categorize everything he saw, smelt, or heard, using meticulous organization methods.*"

Total recall. I thought to myself, barely recognizing that I had thought it at all.

"*Exactly. Total recall. The ability to remember absolutely everything.*"

Huxley coughed, heavier this time. A large cloud enveloped the plane, its cottony folds drifted around the wing and kissed by my window, and small holes of the cloud briefly allowed the distant Earth to peek in and out.

"*The boy grew to be a young man and could tell you where he was and what he was doing exactly eight years and twelve days ago at three o' clock in the afternoon. He could recite any page of any book verbatim and could diagram the exact points of the sun, moon, and large stars at any point in time from memory. It was incredible, simply miraculous. The people around him understandably respected and admired his genius and wealth of mental information. He was known for miles around as a living encyclopedia, a sea of answers and knowledge.*
"*Yet, he was not satisfied. He had read and obtained more information than any man knew more about anything than anyone, yet he wanted more. He needed more, because he was scared. Scared of death. Not of the pain that may come from it, but scared to lose all the information in his brain once death arrived. Scared of all his intelligence and of his thoughts ending, being erased. Death to him could quite possibly be the absence of knowledge, and he could not allow that. He simply would not accept it. Death left a precursory taste in his mouth, although he knew he was many, many years away from it. But it was somewhere out there waiting for him. Waiting to destroy all the work that he had locked tightly inside his skull with the quick twist of a last breath. Yes, he had written books, books that were already being taught to the masses. He had spoken to thousands of eager listeners, all of whom hungered for his enlightenment. The sick could be cured within minutes under his scalpel and focus. He could do nearly anything in accordance with human scripture, but he could not cheat death. Not yet. No matter how intelligent he was, in all of his memories, in all of his dedication, he was still a human being and therefore destined to die.*"

I heard the crackling of the newspaper behind me as Huxley refolded it. I turned around to look at him. His face stayed motionless, and he looked at me sullenly through his blue eyes. His thoughts had stopped for a moment. The plane dipped sharply, then steadied itself. My stomach lurched with the sudden drop in altitude, and suddenly my bladder seemed full. Huxley smiled knowingly.

"Remember to wash your hands," came through to my brain. *"And make it quick, six other people need to use it too."* He pulled his knees to the side to open a path even before I stood up to make my way to the bathroom.

I wondered if he had made me have to piss.

"Pretty sure the two beers and water you had at lunch is the culprit."

I balanced past Huxley into the small aisle and opened the small square door at the rear of the plane. The compartment was miniature, and I immediately felt claustrophobic as I shut the latch behind me. The walls were no more than four feet apart, and the artificial blue liquid in the bottom of the shiny bowl swished gently back and forth with the motions of the plane. I placed my right hand on the small sink that stretched nearly to my waste and steadied myself as I added my own liquid to the mix.

Huxley never stopped telepathically communicating, his thoughts arriving in large chunks like he was reading a book to me page by page, instead of word by word.

"He locked himself away then completely secluded himself from the public to avoid distraction. He needed his own undivided attention to compose a solution to his greatest challenge."

I would have been slightly embarrassed with any normal conversation while I defecated, but I knew he was still sitting quietly in his seat outside the small bathroom and down the aisle.

"He knew that if there was an answer to solving his problem he could find it. If there was a way to beat death, it was he who could do it. He just needed time. He made a formal announcement to the general public, apologizing for the effects that his sudden conclusion may cause, but pleaded for their understanding in what he issued as his own dire matters. Then he locked himself away in his family home."

I zipped up.

"He was let be for quite a while, as his general orders were commonly respected. He would devote the rest of his life if need be. It would be surely worth postponing further study of life for a few years to study death. To discover a weakness if indeed there was one. Then he would have eternity to absorb life again. To examine the future that he would not normally have witnessed, to help lead and nurture humanity for the indefinite future. He was intent on his project, feverishly working night and day on finding a solution to eternal life."

I managed to turn toward the sink and wash my hands and face.

"Years and years went by, and the young man grew old. He had come up with thousands of diverse theories on molecular resilience and properties of physical matter. He had theories and attempted to manipulate the properties of light, space, mass, matter, gravity, and time. His experiments namely tested the physical properties of mass around him, as well as his own physical abilities and physical properties. He conducted tests on ambient light in relation to the structure of his own molecules, he tested the resiliency of his own tissues and membranes. Years passed, but all his tests were inconclusive for any hint of leading toward immortality. He had exhausted every option in trying to alter his own physical realm.
"What really incensed him was that it seemed that he could actually feel himself aging, and so he knew that death was still outwitting him. After all the ways of manipulating the physical world, he could not manipulate the afterlife. Death still concealed itself in a shadow and a mystery that after forty eight years, he was still unable to unfold."

I opened the door to a line of two anxious people and scrambled back toward Huxley and my empty seat. His words did not grow louder as I neared him, as they would with usual speech. They stayed at a constant level that was neither loud nor quiet, just there.

"But Leonard had been doing tests on all the wrong things. There is no way of manipulating the physical world, and he had come to this harsh realization. He found himself to be an old man, one who had gained enemies after all these years. The people that had once loved him so and *cherished his intellect and aid felt betrayed by his seclusion. People were hungry for his intellect and the answers that they continually felt he could provide. Yet he had left them to fully explore his own mind. After nearly fifty years of his silence, the people had boiled and conspired against him and his indifference. They had begun to believe that anything he was not showing to them, he was hiding from them. Anything that he discovered that he did not share with them, he was holding against them. They now feared him for the same reasons they once cherished him. His knowledge. His power."*

I returned to my seat just as the flight attendant arrived with her cart.

"Cherry Coke, please," I said aloud, discovering what a nuisance it truly was to speak. I seemed so loud, and my voice just seemed . . . unnecessary.

"Nothing for me, thanks," I heard Huxley say to the tall brunette. Or as I now knew, thought that he transmitted so that it seemed to be audible. He was good. It sounded exactly as if he was indeed speaking. His lips moved perfectly to the thoughts of noise in our heads. The location itself also seemed a bit different than when he thought directly to me. Speech rings through the ears distinctly, and it seems to come from the *outside*, from the perimeter of your head. But you 'hear' telepathy from within, almost feeling it. Just forming there somewhere in your cerebrum. While speech is concise, thought is more precise. Words can never convey the exact meaning of a thought. He spoke directly into my thoughts as the flight attendant served us.

"The man had worked many long years straining for an answer to eternal life. He had come across so many wonderful things, but still could not find anything that led him to believe that immortality was within his grasp. He had come to the conclusion that it just was not physically possible to live forever. He knew that sooner or later any physical body will succumb to the effects of gravity, friction, and time. Everything eventually winds down. Even under ideal conditions, it is just inevitable that our bodies are not capable of living much longer than two hundred years."

So he gave up? I asked him without really intentionally doing so.

"Well, no. Not because he didn't want to pursue it further, instead he was stopped."

Stopped?

"*Yes. A tipping point came to the townsfolk, and they decided that he must be eliminated, that he was too much of a threat, even if he never came out of his house. Remember that this occurred roughly nine hundred years ago, when the label of witch or warlock could be certified by any strange behavior. Leonard had been doing many astounding scientific experiments much advanced in their processes, above the understanding of many simple people.*

"*Rumors circulated about Leonard using spells or tricks with fire or concocting bubbling liquids that could only be used in conjunction with Satan himself. People forgot about the Leonard that they once knew well, the Leonard that may have helped them using his sense of modern technology or medical attention. People only saw that he was absent, and had been for quite some years, and heard that he was using black magic. People kept talking, the stories becoming more erroneous and absurd. Soon the general public's consensus was that the devil must have surely corrupted him.*

"*One night as he worked, villagers formed a mob and raided his home. There had been witnesses to unbelievable acts of nature, the God-fearing town could not, as proper Christians, allow it to go on any longer. The villagers were in a frenzy, knowing of the power that the man possessed, and realizing that if he were to use his knowledge in wicked ways that it might pose grave danger for all of mankind. So they had come to stop him, to execute him, by any means necessary.*"

He escaped though, right?

"*No. He didn't need to, but the thought definitely crossed his mind. He was done with his studies. He had constantly worked on the challenge of immortality for decades and had failed in discovering a solution. He had failed, and he had never failed at anything before. He figured that it must have been a sign. He had missed the deadline to find the answer. The ultimate deadline. So he let the mob take him, although he could have tried at least to persuade them otherwise.*"

He gave up? He let them kill him?

"*No, no. You get too far ahead of yourself, dear boy. He let them take him. But in doing so, he discovered the answer that he had been searching for all those years. It was right in front of him all along. For as they burst into his room, they tipped over a glass of water, and it spilled to the floor. Hands gripped him tightly, but he watched as the water spread across the wooden boards and concentrated over a small crack midway between the toppled glass and the door. There, the water seeped into the hole and disappeared, leaving only a moist area where it had covered the floor. And the man, who had grown much older since he had gone into seclusion, smiled happily as the villagers dragged him away."*

So water is the key to eternal life? It was that easy?

"Cherry Coke," the stewardess said as she handed me my drink.

"I wish it were. But it is not. He was not looking at the water itself, but instead how the water moved across the floor and into the tiny crack. He had been pursuing the wrong thing for nearly forty years. He had been walking in the complete opposite direction of his goal. He had studied physical life all those years, trying to find a loophole that would allow his physical self to live forever. He kept running into dead ends because it is impossible for anything to live forever physically, but not mentally. An idea occurred to him as he saw the water flow across his floorboards. 'Thoughts flow just like water.'

"When someone thinks, it spills out into the air and spreads, just as the water spilling out onto the floor. The greater the thought, the farther it travels out into the world around you, larger thoughts are like larger cups or tubs or lakes or seas, being spilled out in every direction from your brain. So thoughts spread evenly out into the atmosphere, possibly saturating many people in the process."

How so?

"If you were to walk into the room after the cup had been spilled, without knowing that anything was actually spilled, your feet would still get wet, correct?"

Yeah, on the part of the floor that was wet.

"Sure. So your feet are wet from the floor, but you didn't know how the floor got wet. It just is. But little do you know that just an hour ago, someone spilled a large glass of water directly where you are standing. That is just like a thought. You suddenly get a wonderful thought inside your head, but little do you know that you may have just stepped into someone else's ripple, their spill. Someone else's cup of water. Someone

else had a thought maybe many, many years ago, and it has traveled over to your head, and you picked it up like a sponge."

All my thoughts have already been created by someone else? Collective consciousness saturates me, allowing no original thought of my own?

"It is possible to spill water on top of water. You probably spill thousands of new cups a day. But it is also very probable that you have absorbed someone else's thinking too. Walked right through it."

So what does this have to do with living forever? I took a drink of my Cherry Coke as I asked him without saying a word.

"Everything, Chris. Absolutely everything. You see, mentality, unlike physicality, lives forever. It can be molded, or it can have no structure at all. Once you think something, it does not just die. It does not dry up and evaporate like that water would. It stays forever. And when the man saw the water concentrate around the hole in the floor, it gave him the greatest idea that he ever had. He realized then, that if he could concentrate all his thoughts, memories, and ideas into someone else, he then would continue to live on. He would simply be in another body, a hermit crab encased in another shell. But the shell was his next challenge. Could he just transmit his thoughts and memories, his being, his soul, into someone else yet still maintain his own identity? Or would someone else just be walking around with these new thoughts in his head? Or would two different identities be fighting within one mind? Our friend pondered this thing he now called transference. He pondered if it could even be accomplished but knew somewhere inside him that it could."

Leonard?

"Well, obviously this man is Leonard Caldwell, only that was not his name in the past."

What was his name?

Huxley chuckled again, and the wrinkles in his face bunching up on each other.

"We'll just stick with Leonard for now, and not get into other things. His name is insignificant, whether it is Leonard or . . . something else. But anyway, the mob locked him in an underground cell, and he furiously pondered how to transmit his thoughts to a suitable encasement. The guards told him that he was to be executed at daybreak the next morning, then laughed and spat upon him, but Leonard paid no attention. He was completely transfixed somewhere far away, deep in his own mind. He had decided to try and focus all of his thoughts and memories into the brain of a large rat that was scurrying around his cell, but nothing happened. He focused harder, imagining his soul being transported into the body of the rodent. Still, nothing.

Hours later, the rat stopped and looked toward Leonard. Leonard stared into the **the** little beady eyes from across the empty cell. The rat stood stone-still, completely transfixed, only whiskers twitching, and Leonard continued to sit there, hours upon hours more, trying to manipulate his thoughts into the rat. Still nothing happened, both Leonard and the rodent remained unchanged. Soon, after becoming greatly annoyed, Leonard cried out in anger, and leaped toward the motionless animal. His hands came down upon the furry thing, intending to crush it in an act of utter frustration, and immediately as he did, he found himself looking through a different perspective through the eyes of the rodent. He was not just looking through the rat's eyes however, but was actually sharing its consciousness. He thought like the rat, and the rat thought like him.

My Cherry Coke was finished.

"He was inside. He had never felt like this before, he felt small and dirty and hungry. His nose twitched involuntarily as it smelled many more things than he had ever smelled before. He could feel a long tail behind him, dragging the straw floor, wagging gently. But the rat had a consciousness too, although much diminished, and Leonard understood that the rat was scared and trying to flee as he was. It did not know where to go because the rat could feel Leonard inside its small little head. It ran in circles, controlling its own little muscles much better than Leonard could at that time, so Leonard ran in circles with it. It was a very strange sensation to Leonard altogether, feeling muscles moving, muscles that he never had before, completely on their own. Soon Leonard grew distressed, trying desperately to stop running in circles, as he too was certainly terrified. So as the two beings inside of the rat were fighting to control itself, the rat tripped and tumbled, fighting itself for control of its own motor functions. It was purely uncomfortable for them both, as one willed the legs to carry on while the other willed them to stop. The muscles inside of their body twitched and contorted, receiving mixed signals.

"Leonard felt cramped and restricted inside this new body, without similar logic or conceptual ideas, and knew he wanted to get out. He did not want to share one brain any longer, especially one so feeble and rigid. He let the rat spin again until Leonard saw his own human body a few feet in front of him. His body looked as if it were sleeping, hunched over while sitting in the exact spot that he had made contact with the animal in which he was now inside. As he faced his old self, the rat realized what the thing inside itself wanted, and Leonard sensed that the rat wanted the same thing as well. They scrambled toward the body together and came in contact with an outstretched leg. Then, Leonard found himself whole again, in his own body, within the solidarity of his own mind. It was a relief. The rat squeaked in front of him, and immediately scurried away. Intense concentration was the key to transference, Leonard had concluded, but a physical touch was needed to complete the transfer."

So *he had found out how to live forever, by transferring his thoughts into other things?*

"Yes, Chris, through a focused touch. But he did not like the feeling of sharing a body. It is most uncomfortable, I assure you. Yet Leonard's only other option was death, and so he felt that it was necessary until he found a better alternative."

The clouds broke from around the plane, and the countryside was illuminated by the sun far below. Farmlands passed by, and I figured that we were about halfway to Camp Verde. The mental conversation with Huxley had gone so much faster than a regular verbal conversation would have, but for a moment, I almost wanted him to slow down so that I could really manage everything that he was thinking. I was so excited by everything that was happening that I didn't want the plane to land. I just wanted to sit there in peace and absorb the most that I could from this man.

"Daybreak came, along with the hour of his execution, and Leonard still feared uncertainty. He had no idea what effects two consciousnesses *sharing one body would have, besides the obvious discomfort in battling with your own body and recognition of self. Or if the focused touch was merely a fluke coincidence with the rat, maybe in his constructive mind, he had only imagined it? He may never even get another chance to touch anybody at all.*

I noticed the seatbelt light blinked off.

"The cell door was thrust open, and the two large, incredibly aggressive guards grabbed him and shoved him down onto the dim dirt floor where he was being detained. The guards were both humongous men, and Leonard could not have overpowered them even if he tried. 'Time to die, warlock,' one of them hissed as they entered the jail. They were touching him, and he wondered if this was the opportunity to escape into one of their brains. They slammed him down with violent efforts and bound his wrists with a piece of rope that they brought with them. One held him down with a knee to the back of his neck, as the other tied his hands so tightly that the rope actually drew blood. As they grunted and tensed in their efforts, Leonard decided he would never want to share the same skull with either, but that he must. They pulled him to his feet, and the larger man, the one holding him down, spat in his face as he stood, then leaned in close and spoke. Leonard was nearly able to actually taste the man's breath, as vile as it was.

"'We're going to torture you nice and slow, then throw your body to the fires,' the guard said, spittle still emerging from his lips as he stared Leonard down. 'I may chop your head off meself and keep it,' he continued as Leonard was pulled from his chamber. 'Scoop out your brains and turn this nice face of yours,' Leonard closed his eyes as his face was squeezed and inspected by the guard's enormous hands, 'into a tray for my cigar ashes.' Then the guard slapped Leonard hard, and heat stung the side of his face for many minutes.

"They opened another locked door and emerged into the sunlight. A large crowd awaited him. As he was revealed from his detention, a large roar escaped from the masses. They were cheering not for him, but for his death and desecration, their voices thickening the air with anger and anticipation of bloodshed. Food and stones were thrown at him, and his hair became quickly matted with debris. A large cross had been erected in the middle of the courtyard sometime during the night or early morning, and the two guards pushed him through the vicious *taunts and human obstructions toward it. Leonard scanned the crowd for anybody or anything that he could transfer into and not be tortured with distasteful emotion, but all he saw were faces with spitting mouths and furious eyes. The guards dragged him to an area that was barren and dry, and forcefully laid him down. Dirt was kicked upon him, along with a few random boot strikes, which the guards couldn't or didn't intend to defend. The cross was taken down from its gregarious display of wreaths and flowers. They unbound his hands and turned him over and lifted him unto the cross, binding his hands again to the cross this time. The larger guard received three metal spikes the length of school rulers from someone in the crowd. 'Hold still now,' the guard said to Leonard, smiling. His large square jawed face showed Leonard a look of compassion then, but in a terrible sarcastic fashion. He delicately placed the tip of the spike against Leonard's palm, and held the mallet high, enticing further uproars from the crowd, before driving it home. Leonard could feel his hand tense closed around the spike automatically. He had never realized pain so severe.*

"*The crowd roared again, but Leonard only heard his own cries emit from his throat. Tears dribbled down his cheeks. His hand burned with pain, and the guard struck the mallet upon the spike numerous times to secure it. Then Leonard saw the mallet return upraised, in a sign of victory, and actually heard the crowd again, even though the pain that shot from his hand up through his arm disguised nearly everything else.*

"*The guard looked around proudly. Thus far, he had played the torturer to perfection. Then he stopped and glanced down at Leonard, noticing the tears on his face. The guard knelt, his face changing again to one of feigned remorse and sadness. He closed in and whispered to Leonard, 'Keep crying like that, and I'll put one through your balls.' The guard's face frowning, he wiped the tears from Leonard's cheek with the cold steel of one of the spikes, then licked it off, smiling again. Then he triumphantly rose back to his feet, holding the spike aloft for all to see. The crowd responded in another enormous roar.*"

The plane limped over another small pocket of turbulence.

"*Leonard was just flesh and blood after all, despite the enormity of his brilliance. He could never change that. He realized then, as he was surely facing death, that he may have missed his chance to continue living. The guard trotted slowly around to Leonard's other bounded* arm, raised the mallet for the crowds, waiting gloriously, milking the demented publicity for all it was worth, then drove the second spike. Leonard gasped and convulsed, pain again overwhelming him. It seared through his arms and chest so completely he was nearly to pass out. He choked at the air. He could not allow himself to pass out; he had done so much to allow himself to give in now. So he breathed heavily, in through his nose as much as he could, and tried to mentally push the incredible pain away. He closed his eyes, feeling tears swell from them, and continued to breathe, concentrating only on that. He felt them bind his legs together, overlapping his feet. He tried to kick away, but strong hands secured them. He felt the cold point of the tip of the metal spike again atop his right foot and knew another vicious impalement was soon to come.

"He breathed in deeply through his nose, as much as his lungs could bear. He heard the crowds rise to a crescendo again, knowing the mallet was once again uplifted. He waited for it, then it came, mottling his mind as pain erupted up from his feet. His legs buckled from the massive amounts of nerve endings firing at once, but the freshly lain spike restricted them, so that the muscles in his legs only lunged against his own skin, but restrained from kicking. There was no more air in his lungs. He had breathed out already with the immense pain, although he intended not to. The pain surrounded him, thumping against all parts of his body. The sound of the crowds had transformed into a bright stinging that screamed in his head.

"Moments passed in the darkness of his closed eyelids. He tried to regain his breathing, but the pain was too absolute to focus on anything but. Then he felt the cross move, and he was raised upright. Apparently, the guard had spared him a fourth spike, contradicting the promise that he would, and Leonard figured that would have been it if he hadn't. The pain was excruciating enough to make him want to end it at that point, he couldn't imagine more. He heard the crowd again as he was displayed for all to see. He kept his eyes closed, trying to find air in his chest, but it was nearly impossible with the cross erected. Leonard was dying quickly, suffocating."

Suffocating?

"—in that position, being upright and nailed to a cross, the weight of one's own body pulls against the diaphragm, making it incredibly *difficult to breathe normally. And Leonard was nearly on the brink of passing out when he noticed, even through absolute pain, that someone was touching his feet. Leonard opened his eyes. It was the guard, posing with an arm propped up against the bleeding feet of his dying victim, posturing in front of his demented work. He still waved his mallet through the air, a visual memento for his adoring fans. In the blinding pain, Leonard gasped a breath, maybe his final one, and focused with everything that he had left upon the point where his bare foot met the exposed skin of the guard's arm. He breathed and focused, visualizing himself transferring out through his foot and into the body of the guard, moving as if a wisp of smoke.*

"*He breathed, and focused, through the pain. Breathed. Focused.*

"*The guard turned and, in obvious joy, stared up at Leonard. This was a man who truly enjoyed his sadism, of delivering despair. Leonard wondered how any being capable of compassion and love as humans were could possibly attain joy from such acts of cruelty. The guard reveled in this spotlight of pain and looked up at Leonard, to further gaze upon the desperation he was creating in the beauty that he was in the process of destroying. They locked eyes, and in that moment, Leonard's intense concentration outweighed his absolute suffering, and he tensed up with total energy and a fevered push of concentration.*

"*Seconds later, Leonard found himself standing on the ground, without pain of any sort, holding the mallet high above his own head. He found himself looking up into the absent face of himself. He also immediately sensed the complete confusion of the guard who he newly mentally resided in, and felt his hand release the mallet in reaction. The mallet dropped to the dirt at his feet. Both of his enormous hands went up to his face and head, much as they had done to inspect his face earlier, while he awaited execution. Yet, he had a different face now. The guard turned from the cross and the motionless body that was staked to it, and stumbled around for a second or two. Leonard could feel his own mighty legs walking, and his own huge eyes blinking rapidly, trying to clear what could be a blurred vision and blurred thoughts. Leonard felt his own mouth start yelling intermitted cries of utter horror and complete jovial laughter when his own thoughts of laughter burst out. The crowd was silenced and watched the strange routine of the normally shrewd and determined guard.*

"'*My eyes! My head! Fuaaaaaghggh! Something inside my head! What is this? You are inside my head! Oh God, make it stop! This is it! I* am inside your head! Look at me! Look at me! Whee! Aaarrrggh! Lord, what is this? Aaahhhh! Yeee! No more pain! No more cruelty! No more! Argh, stop it!'

"The villagers were obviously perplexed by the sudden erratic behavior of the guard and stood waning in their applause, watching him claw at his own face, then jump around in splendor, then roll around in agony, then kick his legs gleefully as a little girl would. He would move one way then stop, then move another way. He would clutch at his chest, or his own face, or his arms. He would fling them about, or yip and yell, or laugh then scream. They watched him turn around as if lost, then seem to find himself again, if only temporarily, then become lost again, pulling at his clothes or falling down. This went on for minutes while the crowd simply stared, nearly as confused as the guard appeared to be.

"Then the guard stood stalk still, gnashing his teeth in obvious discomfort, and stumbled over to an old blind man who had fallen or been pushed down by the frenzied crowd. The guard stopped suddenly, directly before the man, who was blind and deaf, and pulled oddly at his own hair. Then the guard, in a perceptible act of kindness, pulled the old man up off his knees and helped steady him on his ancient legs. The guard then lightly brushed the old man's face with the back of his palm and stood still again. The guard clenched his fist, the very hand in which he had caressed the man's cheek seconds before, as if to strike at the man, but then held off. The crowd, still stunned, watched these events happen, then dispersed as the old man stumbled away, leaving the guard deflated.

"In that brief exchange, Leonard had transferred into the blind man's head and was suddenly enveloped in silence and dark gray surroundings. He was successfully inside the man's mind. Unlike the rat however, Leonard was able to communicate with the man's thoughts in the form of advanced sentiments rather than in the raw form of emotion, and the old man immediately accepted Leonard inside his mind, unlike the guard. They stood there together for many moments, after the initial point of being quite startled, as would be expected when someone accompanies your brain, the man realized the necessity for Leonard to get away from this combustible situation. The man somehow found his walking cane on the ground in the midst of the crowd where he had fallen, and together they hobbled their way away from the courtyard.

"The man's name was Fitzgerald, but they didn't exactly exchange names as is customary in a conventional greeting, but Leonard already *knew it. The longer he stood inside someone's head, the more he knew about them. From the point of inception, memories and knowledge and aspirations would blend between the two, working backward toward birth or toward a person's earliest memories. Leonard was overjoyed with being alive, and Fitzgerald became immediately aware of this as well, along with importance and magnitude of Leonard's life. Leonard also mentally expressed in smaller tinges how he had derived a bit of pleasure in mentally disturbing the guard, if even for precious moments. Fitzgerald smiled at the thought of this, his own control of his own muscles of his own mouth, due to a foreign memory that had just been shared. They would grow to be quite close and liked the pleasure of each other's mental company, and they recognized that fact immediately as well.*

"Fitzgerald was actually quite gracious to have Leonard's thoughts living inside his own, and they were able to walk together as one, unnoticed, from the disturbed masses of the villagers. He really hadn't had anyone to visit with in a long, long time, and as Leonard came to know, being blind could be a pretty desolate place. But before leaving the square, Leonard smelled something that was incredibly terrible, and in the darkness inside the man's head, he asked Fitzgerald what it might be. Fitzgerald reminded Leonard that his other senses were amplified due to his lack of sight and hearing. Fitzgerald's thoughts expressed to Leonard that with his new heightened sense of smell, Leonard had just witnessed the putridity of his own death, as the crowds had lit his mentally vacant body to fire.

"Although Leonard was deliriously happy to still be alive, he was past the point of no return, as his physical self had just ended. He knew it then. Nothing could ever again be truly his own. He could never return to his own skin, his lips, his heart, his hair, his smell, his private realm, himself, again. It was a lot to take, and Fitzgerald, now sharing his memories and emotions, took it too."

The intercom of the plane belched on. "Good afternoon, passengers, this is your captain speaking. We are beginning our descent into Camp Verde, and should touch down within a half hour or so. I will be putting on the seatbelt lights back on as we begin our landing. We thank you for flying with us today and hope that you enjoy your further travels."

CHAPTER 15

The plane was cleared of empty cups and trash, and the tray tables were set back into the seats in front of them. The seatbelt sign had indeed been turned back on, as the pilot had promised, but Huxley never stopped thinking to me.

"Leonard counted steps with the old man in the dark of their brain. This was how the old man retrieved his mental directions, how he found his way around town and, in turn, home. The sounds of the cheering crowds faded as they slowly hobbled farther and farther away, but the smell of his own burned flesh may never have completely disappeared. He was grateful that he no longer endured such vicious torment as he had just experienced and was grateful to find the old man's small dilapidated shack, eight hundred and sixty-two steps later, and the small hard cot that was three steps within it. The old man was exhausted, and Leonard realized that, even with his escape from execution, he was certainly not much further from death. The old man was also dying, of old age.

"They awoke together in the dark, and Leonard felt the sun upon their face, and figured it must be the next morning. It took Leonard a moment to realize that he was actually awake and no longer dreaming. In his dreams, he could see. In reality, he now could not.

"He awoke to lungs that stayed tired and a body that stayed tender and slow. He could feel himself pulling up from his slumber but could see nothing. He felt the crumpled mattress under his fingers and could feel his old muscles strain to lift his body up. He would have to learn to work with Fitzgerald in the crippled body that was afforded them, but Leonard realized that Fitzgerald's mind was still sharp, deep, and determined.

"They cooked themselves breakfast, as they were starving, a meager meal of rice and beans, then took time in what could simply be described as a meditation, where their body sat still in the center of the hut, but their minds conversed. They shared all their beliefs and memories and ideas and ideals in such a way, and the body of the old man could be *observed, sitting idle for hours at a time. Leonard actually believed that being nearly deaf and blind afforded him less distraction, and after learning the most efficient ways of coexisting within one body, he came up with incredible new advances to his own mentality.*

"*It was discovered that their minds had to work together to move smoothly, and that one could only overpower the other for seconds at a time, and that the body's muscular system was very vulnerable to becoming numb if the minds contradicted themselves repeatedly. They took many a day learning how to walk again, how to move again, together. But they also found that over time, as they grew increasingly familiar with each other's intentions, their movements became stronger and faster. The old man's body had become weakened over the years, but together they could make it stronger than it was before, using twice the normal mental impulses to fire the muscles.*

"*The old man's health actually showed significant improvement within even the first week, and the deep cough that he constantly suffered from, along with severe arthritis, were all but gone. With this new energy, the old man carried himself more diligently, finding the effort to clean himself and his surroundings more, taking walks into nature and meditating all day instead of being generally bound to bed rest. The deep walks through nature and long sessions of meditation afforded Leonard time to grasp many things that he had never before accomplished, thus he furthered his studies in math, science, physics, metaphysics, time, space, and the completed process in which he now referred to as transference; the mental transfer into another form of life.*

"*He found that he, and only he, could transfer by touch, along with concentrated thought, into almost any living organism. Leonard believed that anything alive could be transferred into, including single-celled creatures, but most things were quite undesirable to share consciousness with. Not to mention being dangerous. The rat that he had first transferred into was the simplest organism in which he felt comfortable with transferring into on his own.*

"*The smaller the intellect of any living thing, the harder it was to first control the being in any logical direction or plan any course of action. Rats, for instance, are smart enough to sense danger and have a more definitive mental assertion of what is happening around them. The rat had known somehow that when he had been touched by the human being, something had changed inside its brain, and it was able to realize* that. Leonard coerced it into retouching the human being in an attempt to change them both back. The brain of an insect will never be able to think with any sort of rationality, even with human intellect sharing it. So Leonard, trying to persuade an insect into flying north, would be like trying to train a fly to jump through a hoop. So the danger was that an insect could simply fly away, carrying Leonard's intellect with it, without a way of controlling or stopping it.

"Leonard was fortunate to have Fitzgerald in this way, for during one of their walks through the countryside, Leonard decided to transfer himself into a flower. He found that plants were especially wonderful to occupy, as they provided a very serene and quiet place of darkness where he could get a lot of thinking done. Plants do not have much of a consciousness either, so he could be pretty much to himself. Also, a blooming plant experiences a sensation much like an orgasm, yet greatly multiplied and prolonged, so that was an added treat. Yet, he still depended on touch to transfer himself, and if not for Fitzgerald waiting around for a period of time, he would have to wait until another animal brushed up against the plant before he could get out. But the most important thing that Leonard discovered was that it was possible to live forever, mentally traversing between physical bodies."

Huxley paused again. "*Have you ever thought about how truly old you are, Chris?*"

What do you mean?

"*I mean, have you ever thought about how long you have existed? How long the material that would eventually mold into you has been around? Have you ever thought about your cells floating around in your mother's womb before you were conceived into human form in her uterus? You existed then, correct, even if in microscopic proportions? Part of you existed within your mother's loins before she even met your father, as well as part of you existing in cells that your father carried his whole life, before meeting your mother. There was something in their flesh, at least a blueprint of you, that made her egg and his sperm into you. And that very something was the small but undeniable existence of life destined to happen. Fate. Microscopic cells and particles had you written all over them and were passed on, generation to generation, thousands of years back, continually branching out the farther back they went. So even before your grandfather himself was born, you existed. You were there, deep inside his parents, somewhere deep within them both. Do you understand? So in all actuality, you, your essence, your code has realistically been around for hundreds of thousands of years. Even though you have only been this human body for thirty-two."*

Good point. I thought.
Huxley never paused, even while putting on his seatbelt.

"Even after your body dies, you, the physical Chris Wyer, will live on. Your body will decompose and filter into the soil, which will feed the roots of a tree maybe hundreds of years from now. That tree will grow, and maybe be an apple tree, and will of course produce lush apples that nestle within its leaves, tempting creatures and livestock to eat the precious fruit. A cow may wander by and take a nibble from a freshly fallen apple. A fallen apple, which, somewhere within its core, contains molecules of you. Those molecules then filter into the blood of the cow, through its digestive system, and nestle then within its flesh. Flesh that, let's say, is soon killed and cooked in the form of a nice, round T-bone steak. Then it just so happens that some man eats that T-bone while on a honeymoon with his beautiful wife. It's the best steak of his young life. He is madly in love with her. There is a magic moment that maybe only a few experience, where happiness seems inevitable. They are really, really in love. She has that sweet woman smell, and maybe some softly batting blue eyes, and he is being driven absolutely wild. All the while, the molecules of the steak are absorbed into that man's body and then he ends that perfect night with a perfect consummation of the marriage. She conceives and soon Mr. Chris Wyer, with a few slightly physical differences, pops his ugly head back into the picture again . . ."

Nice.

"Yes, it's real nice. But the thing of it is, your mentality won't be passed on. Your thinking contains no matter, no physical structure, it can never be passed on with your body. So the new Mr. Wyer would have to start over in a way, mentally that is, and absorb information all over again."

But Leonard can transfer his mentality, so he just needs to find his physical body when it regenerates, and he will be himself again. Right?
It was so much easier to understand someone when they think right into you.

"*Exactly, and when he does, he becomes stronger mentally, having an existing mentality when he reemerges coupled with a more advanced mentality transferring into himself. A copy of a copy of himself.*"

But how does Leonard figure out where and when his physical self will reemerge?

"*Ah, yes, the important part. This is where it gets good. As I said earlier, Leonard was exceptionally advanced in mathematics and studied them further within Fitzgerald's head. He began to use them again to figure out that very dilemma. He knew that his body would somewhere return to life once again, and that he needed to be there when it did. He believed that was his ticket to wholly becoming himself again, in complete physical and mental form. You see, there is a probability to everything, Chris, without exceptions. Everything has a particular design, a fate. There is a possibility that this plane we are on will crash into a flock of geese, ruining the engines, stall and crash. That possibility isn't as great as the possibility that we will land safely on the asphalt in Camp Verde with a little squeak of the wheels, but it could happen. Anything can happen. But if you are able to distinguish the higher probabilities of something happening as opposed to something else, you could probably vaguely narrow down what might happen to you and when. If you were able to develop a mathematical probability to life and be able to narrow it down with extreme precision, you could predict anything. Anything. You could predict when Joe Blow will trip and fall and cause the mark on his face that he will have for the rest of his life. You could tell when the rain will come and the exact point where the lightning caused by that rainstorm will hit. You could tell when the next man will die, and where and how it will happen. You could even predict the extinction of the world, and foretell the exact second that our sun will burn out. The options are limitless. It is a pattern, a very complex and excruciatingly intricate pattern, but a pattern nonetheless.*"

A pattern that could be explained with a mathematical formula. And if you were able to discover that equation, you would therefore have discovered the formula for the structure of life.

"Yes, precisely. Leonard started working on the development of this equation when he was twenty-two. At least the basic principles of it.

Like I said, he was fairly gifted. But Leonard took a few years inside Fitzgerald's head and refined this formula, and then he began to apply it to larger, more dynamic principles. He revealed that the next time his body was due to emerge was somewhere in Europe at the beginning of the fourteenth century. But Leonard went a step further and plugged his formula into the life of the world. And the answer he came up with really surprised him. And scared him a little too. He plugged it in again, just to make sure, and the answer came back the same."

When? I pleaded.

"*I'm not going to tell you because it would scare you too. But relax, it is under control. Leonard has got it figured out.*"

Will the shit hit the fan in my lifetime? Will I get to see everything go?

Huxley started chuckling again, and other passengers again noticed the peculiarity of an old man abruptly breaking into fits of laughter.

"*Chris, Chris, Chris, my dear boy.*"
Even his mind seemed to be chuckling as it sent me thoughts.

"*Yeah, you'll see some amazing things before you go, let me tell you. But the Earth is quite resilient, she doesn't just roll over for anybody. I have been trying to tell you, some things don't always appear as they seem. The end of your life isn't always the end. The end of the world doesn't mean the end of humanity, or the universe for that matter. Actually, I didn't really want to get too far into this because it will leave you with too many questions unanswered, but there is not an end or a beginning to anything. That is a human invention. Reality is not a line with a beginning and an end, reality is a sphere. Everything has always been, is, and always will be. It is that simple.*"

Like the note that Leonard wrote me, that there is no such thing as nothing. No such thing as zero, no such thing as empty space. So he was right, and of course, it even helped me solve his letter.

"*Of course he was right. Scientists don't know anything. There was a big bang, surely, but that was simply the universe changing shape. The* universe has always been here just continually transforming. It is all a gigantic thundering circle, no start, no stop. I know that that seems hard to think about, but humanity in general really has no concept of what is really happening. But Leonard does, and is trying to teach everyone who wants to listen."

But Leonard never even as much as talked to me. He never showed me what was going on. You're giving me way more information than he ever did.

"Part of learning correctly is discovery on your own. Leonard only gave you clues, just as the world does, just as the universe does. It is you that has to find the best way of decoding them. Let me get back to Leonard again. As I told you, he had now prophesied many things, and that soon included the death of his host and now wonderful friend Fitzgerald. Of course, Fitzgerald found out about his own death as soon as Leonard did because Leonard was sharing his body when he calculated it. It was a huge despair to both of them obviously, but Leonard made him a promise. He assured him that he would make it his lifelong goal to pursue the molecules of Fitzgerald as he would pursue his own, and forever pass on as much knowledge and care that he could to them. And Leonard promised that Fitzgerald would be happy when he reemerged again, when his cells reemerged again. He promised Fitzgerald that he would be taken care of, even though Fitzgerald would have no idea of whom he had once been.

"And so sure enough, months passed, great months, months of a bonded friendship that grew stronger day by day. A friendship forged in the darkness of blindness through the collaborations of minds, stronger than the ailments of age. They learned from each other, even if about their own differences or about the ways they believed the world and themselves to be. But they began to get sick, with pneumonia actually, as expected, and began to wither away in Fitzgerald's body. Fitzgerald himself was incapable of transference, as his own thoughts weren't powerful enough to generate enough concentration, even though Leonard was relentless in his teachings and attempts. They grew weaker day by day, so they collectively decided that it was time that Leonard should leave before they both became too ill. Fitzgerald did not want Leonard to witness his own death, as even the most noble of men certainly all die alone, and Leonard had the decency to accede with his friend's wishes. They *walked to a grove of trees where they had journeyed together so many times before, and the old man's arm reached up and touched the branch of an older tree. The hand stayed against the tree for some time, as the sun set, then released from it. 'Good-bye my friend,' the old man said through sobs. He had not needed to use his voice very often anymore. The old man then turned, and with tears in his blind and closed eyes, walked back home alone, counting his steps."*

I fastened my seatbelt as the plane began to slowly curve in its descent.

"But Leonard stayed, and there was much sadness within the tree for a very, very long time. He wanted nothing more than to dwell within the silence of the tree, and to think. And think he did. Powerful thoughts. Thoughts of stars and nebulas, and suns and light skimming through angles, and of crimson galaxies billions of light years away, and of gigantic masses and atomic energies. His mind wandered, further and further than anything he had ever thought of before. He thought of the world, and when it would end. And then he realized something. It was up to him not only to continue his own life, but to continue life on Earth. And how could he do that? If the only possibility of another fertile planet capable of sustaining life is thousands, if not millions, if not billions, if not multiples of trillions of light-years away, how can we be transported to that planet if we cannot even travel the speed of light in the first place? The answer was something Leonard had been using all along. He realized then, deep within the silent tree, half in mourning and half in determination, that there is only one thing that can travel faster than the speed of light."

Thought. I thought, conclusively.

"Of course, Chris, the most powerful thing we can ever attain. Thought."

The plane took a steeper angle, and I watched as the fins on the wings of the plane lifted, in turn changing air flow, manipulating the foil of the winds all around us.

CHAPTER 16

The plane had begun to descend into a landing pattern over the airport a few miles outside of Camp Verde. Huxley stopped thinking to me for a moment and began to gather up his newspaper. He shifted nervously in his chair.

"Of course trees grow old and die, just as Fitzgerald had. Leonard therefore had to skip around to stay alive, alternating between physical beings. Leonard enjoyed the serenity of plants and trees but was also vulnerable once inhabiting them. Plants cannot move, therefore Leonard could not. Plants cannot see or hear, therefore are oblivious to something approaching. Plants can be ravished by fire or chopped down or suffer a drought, and dry up and die. Leonard could not afford any of these outcomes, so he preferred to inhabit mammals, or at least mammals that he could handle mentally.

"Most animals, dogs, cats, rats, etc., cannot be occupied without completely freaking out, as the human brain and the animal brain are only similar in basic functions. Leonard could not mentally coax a dog or cat to go, nor could he mentally override any being's synapses. Any physical body can only be shared, fifty-fifty. So for seconds at a time, Leonard would be calm inside a dog's body perhaps, familiar to the mental coexistence, but seconds later, the dog would be overcome with fear and extreme anxiety and mental confusion. Leonard would not be able to explain to the dog what was happening.

*"Therefore, humans were the most suitable for mental occupation, but this also caused problems. First, the most important problem, is that the idea of someone inside your head may sound quite interesting for a little while, but soon you realize that you are sharing everything with someone, your darkest fears, your embarrassments, your failures, your insecurities, everything. Someone is **IN-SIDE**.*

"It is also quite uncomfortable for someone to have half-control over you, intermittently. Especially, if that someone just comes in without an

invite or warning. So to put it simply, Leonard bounced around between many different bodies. Which posed another problem—"

More people knowing about him.

"Precisely. The sad thing is that even though most people that he has transferred into find it generally unappealing to have him share their brain with them, they are mortally transfixed by what had happened once he leaves. They continuously track him down, some for the understanding of his mental prowess and what exactly has transpired within them, and most for greed or to greater themselves. So this was also a risk. In general, people are stubborn. Most never realize the whole picture beyond the scope of immediately satisfying themselves. So the more people Leonard transferred into, the larger the following he inevitably had as a result, and most commonly not for righteous purposes.

"Leonard found himself constantly running and hiding, constantly searching for those he could trust, but ultimately never quite knowing who he could. Anyone can be Judas hiding in wait. A re-emergence with his original body was his only true salvation, and when it came around, roughly every twenty-three and a half years or so after his body died, that's when truly great things happened. Leonard, using his intricate equations to calculate where his body would re-emerge, was led to Italy. There, Leonard found a young Leonardo da Vinci as a four-year-old boy. He transferred into himself and was immediately intertwined with a mentality that was all his own, albeit in a younger state. Leonard taught himself everything he knew, quite quickly as the tutoring took place inside their own minds. Leonard was passing himself down to himself. Evolution at a dramatic rate. He then calculated his own impending death, as Leonardo da Vinci and with his other mental self, in a double transference, continued on in other bodies and trees and animals for the period of time until he was able to find himself again, this time in the body of Shakespeare. Then it was Newton shortly following Shakespeare's death, then Hegel, and finally Einstein being the last."

He is becoming stronger and stronger the more times he reconnects with himself?

"Yes. When he left the body of Da Vinci he left with two of his mental selves. When he left Shakespeare he had a collaboration of three, and when he got to Einstein he had six mental powers working inside him."

No wonder. The plane straightened out and let down its landing gear.

"He hopes that this is the key. If other people can learn to transfer, then hopefully the end result will be a world and universe without physical boundaries, just one ever-expanding consciousness."

So the body that I know Leonard to be, the body of a boy who I met in high school, the body of a man that I saw executed was really a person, who Leonard was simply coexisting with?

"Unfortunately, yes. Leonard transferred into him just before he met you. Knowing that the boy was mute, and that you would inevitably pick on him and bully him because of his weak stature and constant silence."

Leonard knows my nature that well, huh?

"Of course he does."

The plane touched down, and Huxley showed a smile.

What part do I play, what part do you play, in any of this?

"We are all merely actors on a stage, aren't we anyway, Chris? Everyone has their part to play."

But why would Leonard let Leonard die? Didn't he know that the agents would shoot him?

"Of course he did. And little Leonard knew his fate as well, even of his fate to be bullied by you. He accepted it. He is one of those that are blessed by his position, and knows it. He will be justly rewarded."

Huxley stopped thinking to me and looked at me seriously with his piercing blue eyes. His smile had faded as the plane taxied the runway, replaced with a hint of sadness in his eyes.

What's wrong? I asked him in my head.

"Chris, I better let you know now. The agents are going to be waiting for you when you arrive. They were able to trace your credit card as soon as you used it to pay for this plane. Just as you thought they might. They are going to surround the plane as soon as we land. Then they are going to try and kill you. And they will if you don't listen to everything I transmit to you to make it out of this. But you will. Have faith. You're going to have to keep your composure so that I can send you thoughts clearly, if you don't . . . well, if you don't . . ."

I won't make it, I thought.

Huxley didn't think back an answer, which meant that I was probably right.

"The real reason that you flew to Camp Verde today, Chris, besides meeting me, is that your family is being held here, as you hoped."

Oh my God, thank heaven. My heart leaped. I wanted to see my girls again, more than anything in the world. *Does Leonard have them then? Keeping them safe and sound for me?*

"No. I wish he did. Leonard never had anything to do with their abduction. At least, directly. The FBI is solely responsible for it all. They arrived at your house while your wife was there. She let them in because they said they had a search warrant. She tried to call you, but you were on your way to get Rebecca. There were six of them, including your newly acquainted Agent Marks."

They were looking for the letter from Leonard?

"They were merely making it look like they were, so that they could make up an elaborate story about Leonard abducting your family. Something you could believe. Something that would make you want to *voluntarily point Leonard out. They only had a short time to search your house because if you would have come home and witnessed them or anything, the jig about Leonard taking your family would have been up. But that was not meant to be."*

But how did they know that I even had a letter from Leonard? How did they know that it even existed?

"You sorely underestimate the power of your own government, Chris, as most people do. You underestimate the information that they know, and the lengths that they will go to get what they want. Those men don't even work for the FBI officially, but use that as a cover. They are black ops, a hidden agency out for one thing and one thing only, to destroy anything that jeopardizes a complete takeover. Leonard is their main objective, and stopping the knowledge that he holds. The main objective of the government, regardless of what they tell you, is control. They aim to control every aspect of our lives, from the advertisements that we see, to the food we eat, to the people we meet, while maintaining the lie that they have no control over us at all.

"They had you under surveillance days from the car accident that you had with Leonard, just in case Leonard ever happened to get in touch with you. They did not know just how powerful he was then until they matched his blood that they found on your passenger window to the blood in the Book of Life. Then they knew Leonard was something. They knew he was the one that they needed to be after. And that led them to focus directly on you because Leonard had become invisible to the world. He had become a ghost in the machine."

So when I talked to my wife about the letter over the phone that day, they were listening in on me?

"That and so much more. You talked to your wife ten years ago about this crazy kid you once knew in high school, and they have every second of that conversation recorded."

I hadn't even remembered that particular conversation.

Then they had my house bugged too?

"Absolutely. Along with your cars, your office, even a pair of your shoes. They had you tuned in like you were a hit radio station for the last fourteen years. But what prompted them to actually take the next step and reveal themselves was the letter. They had actually taken stills of the letter as you arrived in the police station that day after you talked it over with Cathorine. The receptionist at the front desk was as clueless to what was happening as you were. She had said that police procedure didn't warrant anything to do with the letter unless it was connected to a crime somehow. Remember?"

Yeah, I remember.

"Well, the technology of their operation is so advanced that they were able to analyze the letter even from the photographs that they had taken of it, as you handed it over the counter to her. The results were that the letter was in code, and that it was written in blood. So they concocted a story, broke into your house and stole your family, then blamed it on Leonard, hoping you would lead them to him, which you did."

But Leonard actually wrote the letter to me, knowing that it would turn out this way. Knowing that my family would be abducted because of it.

"I know, crazy huh? What came first the chicken or the egg?"

My face became flush with a renewed anger at Leonard.

"It was all meant to happen, please refrain from anger. Leonard needs the government as much as they want him. And he needs you too. Please try and allow yourself to look for the forest for the trees. Leonard knew that was going to happen, just as you know the sun will rise tomorrow. But there are reasons behind it all. There are reasons. Reasons you need to be here, and reasons that this all needs to happen this way. The reasons will become clear after everything unfolds."

Everything unfolds? I asked as I looked from my window and saw that the runway was completely lined with black SUVs. There had to be at least ten or twelve of them, shining brightly in the sunlight. I felt a lump in my throat.

Huxley did not reply.

I figured that the captain of the plane had been informed of a criminal onboard, but the plane rolled to a stop with only a "thank you for traveling with us today, folks, please enjoy the rest of your day" from the big guy up front. He made no mention of why there were close to fifty guys in suits emerging from vehicles that partially obscured the tarmac. Most of the passengers, however, did not even notice or paid no mind if they did, until agents actually began to come on board.

Huxley was in my head again. *"I'll talk you through it."*

A young agent with a blond crew cut entered our business-class compartment and took the microphone from the tall stewardess that served me earlier. "Ladies and gentlemen, we have a slight matter at hand in which we will deal with as quickly and smoothly as possible. Please cooperate, and this will all be over in a very short time."

Two other agents moved past him and walked casually over to my seat with their right hands concealed under the left breasts of their suit jackets. The taller one spoke quietly to me as they arrived and stood next to me in the open aisle.

"Mr. Wyer, please come with us. Do not make any sudden moves or we will be forced to employ drastic force. Raise your hands in the air please." I raised my hands and looked into the other agent's eyes. He was shorter than the one that was talking to me, but stockier, and his eyes were full of fire. I could tell that he was coiled like a spring, waiting for me to simply blink the wrong way.

The taller agent clasped handcuffs around my wrists and pulled me harshly from my seat. "Walk," he instructed as I stood. My hands were still in front of me, and I thought that I may be able to combine my fists to punch my way through the agents and escape out of the open exit, but I remained calm. Huxley hadn't said anything yet, and I wasn't about to do anything drastic until he did.

I am scared shitless.

I followed the shorter man with rage in his eyes out of the plane with the taller agent following closely behind. I was escorted from the plane without saying a word.

"The agents are not going to shoot you in public unless they have to. So do as they say. But they are going to execute you unless you give them a reason not to. And it would have to be a pretty damn good one,"

Huxley spoke as clearly as a bell even as I was thirty feet outside of the plane.

So what the hell is my goddamned reason? Should I just say please? I was beginning to get panicky as I neared a large black Suburban with its doors open. Huxley was almost making it worse by not thinking to me. The black vehicle was as foreboding as a dank prison cell with an open metal door luring me in. The urge to urinate came over me even though I had used the bathroom just recently on the plane. *Who was to say that once I was inside the deeply tinted confines of the vehicle that I wouldn't get my head blown off?*

"I am to say. That's not probable of happening. Believe me, and calm down a little bit. Just go with the flow. The ball is in your court, just don't swing too early."

I was led to the open door and forcefully urged in. The agents that led me to the vehicle took a seat on either side of me and closed the doors behind them. In the front passenger seat was none other than Agent Marks. He gave a thin smile through his pulpous lips, showing his square yellow teeth.

"Long time, Mr. Wyer. Glad you decided to be stupid and come back."

"Where's my family, you cocksucker?" I was in no mood to be coy. "I know they're here."

"Truly astonishing . . ." Agent Marks exclaimed as the thick doors of the Suburban were closed after the other agents had situated themselves. "I give you some credit on however you figured out that they are being held in Camp Verde. That is federally classified information. Although I'm sure it was fairly easy to realize that we were in fact the ones that abducted them from you, I mean, after we tried to kill you and all. But I must say, Mr. Wyer, that you have been about as slippery as a greased fish, especially after your little escape from Jane Street."

The Suburban started to roll.

"You're damn lucky, is all I think." Agent Marks didn't bother to buckle his seatbelt as the other agents did. No one bothered to buckle me in either. "Actually, you are nothing less than incredibly fucking lucky, but as you can tell, your luck just ran dry. And although your family is indeed here in Camp Verde, there is no way in hell that I'm going to give you the pleasure of seeing them. However, the thing that I will give you is a bullet. Maybe even a couple of 'em. How does that sound?" He was smiling immensely, and I wanted to bash his grinning face in with my handcuffed fists.

Agent Marks pulled a pistol from his suit and cocked it with his left hand, as the driver hit the pedal and drove us past the plane and off the runway. I tried to thrust my arms forward toward Agent Marks and grab his gun, but strong arms held me back. The agent on my right crushed his elbow into the side of my head, momentarily dazing me.

"Sit still," he said in an echo.

I had forgotten how scared I was of being killed by the agents as I ran from them that foggy night in New York, but the elbow strike and the cocked pistol were grim reminders.

Shit, he really is going to shoot me as soon as they are out of range of everyone from the airport. No witnesses. Why in hell do I go with them so peacefully? I might have had a chance to get away before they loaded the plane. Huxley told me that it would work out though, and I listened to him, and I am going to die because of it!

Agent Marks pivoted to face me, shifting his arm to aim the gun directly at my head. His bold teeth leaked through as he smiled again. "I'll tell your family you said hi," he said as the agents firmly held me, and he brought the muzzle of the gun to my forehead. "Or more accurately, good-bye."

I closed my eyes.

Suddenly, Huxley spoke in my head, just as I was expecting in the end, "*Ask him about the Picasso Project. Ask him how it's going. Ask him now.*"

As Marks's gun pressed between my eyes, I could feel the cold, unforgiving metal circle of the barrel. I had no idea what Huxley was talking about, but I definitely had no time to get details.

"How is that Picasso Project going, Agent Marks? Going as well as expected?" I said, preparing to be interrupted with a flash of the gun, wondering if my last words would be a broken sentence that even I truly didn't understand. Immediately, the pressure of the gun eased from against my skull.

"What the fuck . . . did you say?" Agent Marks looked entirely dumbfounded. He had removed the gun from my head but kept a few inches from my face. My comment had definitely made an impact. Then he asked the taller agent on my right, "Did he say what I just thought he said?"

"I believe so, sir." the agent replied, equally surprised, but maintaining better professionalism than Marks.

Huxley quickly began transmitting thought to me, arranging the details of the "Picasso Project" in my head, and within seconds, I knew very much about an experimental operation gone wrong.

"Yeah, the Picasso Project," I started again, a little more confident in what I was saying. "Technically called the 'Piccolo Project' until things went wrong, really wrong, and people started nicknaming it after the abstract artist. And I'm sure you, more than anybody, Agent Marks, can appreciate why."

Agent Marks sat there for a few moments, staring blankly at me. His gun wavered aimlessly in the air. I could tell that he still wanted to blow my brains all over the rear of the large Suburban, but my words had stopped him from doing so. At least for the moment.

"I give you credit for that one too, a lot of credit. But you obviously don't fucking know what you're talking about. You can't."

"I can't? Oh, Agent Marks, I think I can. I know I can." I flashed him the biggest, most confident smile I could muster. This aggravated him, as I knew it would. I felt somewhat powerful, even though it had been almost moments since I was nearly made into a puddle of flesh.

"I should exterminate you right now, I really should. But you continue to pull information out of your ass, and it somehow doesn't seem to stink. How can that be? How could you have known about your family being held here, and about the Picasso Project? How can a little maggot like you know these things? And even if you do, why should I care? Why shouldn't I inject some lead in your head?" With that, Agent Marks ground his teeth together and leveled the gun back between my eyes. I knew that he was once again ready to pull the trigger.

"Because I can help him. I can help your brother," I said quickly, staring into the barrel. Huxley was telling me exactly what to say again. "If you let me live and return my family to me, your brother will be fine." I had now stopped smiling and looked him directly in the eyes.

You're right though, Agent Marks. I am pulling this directly out of my ass, and I sincerely hope that you don't really know that.

The gun lowered a little more, and I relaxed a little more as it did. His eyes blinked and wandered curiously, then he twisted the bulk of his body back into a forward sitting position in the front seat. He returned the gun to the holster hidden beneath his suit. "Turn the car around, Greg, we're going to Sindex," Agent Marks said, rolling down his electric window. "Uncuff him, boys," he said then, as he pulled out a cigarette. He leaned over and pushed the cigarette lighter in, waited patiently until it popped back out, then stuck the end of his smoke into its bright orange circle. A quick gust of smoke escaped his lips as the cigarette lit. He inhaled deeply.

The car was stopped, and we changed direction. "Well, tough guy," Agent Marks resumed after a few drags of smoke "Since you seem to know so much, I'm going to be nice today and give you a chance to live. Hell, I'll even give you your family back. If you help my brother, of course. We'll consider it a trade, your family for mine."

The handcuffs were removed from my wrists, which I immediately rubbed.

"However, if you don't help, and you are lying about this, which I can only imagine you most certainly are, I will see to it that you are tortured so slowly and with such precision that pure agony won't even begin to describe what you feel." He leaned back in the leather seat, and it bulged from his weight. "I promise that you will be left raw and kept alive to live the rest of your tortured life that way." I could see the muscles of his large jaw work as he spoke. His large cheeks expelled fine mists of dirty smoke that drifted around him for a moment before snaking out the window. "I hope for your sake, Mr. Wyer, that you didn't just let your mouth write a check that your ass can't cash."

I was truly in the thick of it now. In the grease, in the grime. Waddling in filth with conniving beasts that wanted my head. I had an awful taste in the back of my throat, not even aware that I had taste buds there.

I just want my family back.

Of course I had no way of knowing how to help his brother, I barely knew anything about him, but I had just bought myself some time. And that was the one and only thing I needed right now, along with a miracle.

I didn't say much in the presence of such vile individuals, and it seemed that they too were also none too anxious to get a conversation going. The driver had doubled back and was soon cruising down a narrow dirt road somewhere in the middle of the Arizona desert, creating a wave of dust that curled behind us. Soon, the only visible manmade structures were telephone poles that ran alongside the road, and an occasional rusty sign. Everything else was sand and sagebrush as far as the eye could see. I wondered why this stretch of road wouldn't be perfectly accommodating for my murder, but realized that it was actually regularly traveled as many cars passed going in the opposite direction.

"So why did you have to take my family?" I asked finally, breaking the silence. "Why the fuck did you do all of this to me? I thought you were supposed to be the good guys?"

"We *are* the good guys," Agent Marks said through wisps of smoke. "You just can't see the whole picture. You never will. We had to take your family you dumb shit. Had to. Sorry 'bout it, but you are the ones that had to get hurt, in exchange for the millions that will be saved."

"Saved? You haven't tried to save a fucking thing. Every ideal you have involves sacrifice and bloodshed."

Agent Marks turned in his seat just slightly so that he could see me. His face looked bitter, and his greasy black hair glistened in the sun that shone through the open window. "Look, Leonard Caldwell, or whoever that guy was that you led us to, was probably the most powerful person the world has ever known. Or ever will know. Now, he may have been a savior of mankind, or helped the world in ways that we could not even imagine and all that prophetic bullshit, but he also could have demolished everything we know. Potentially, the information he knew could have brought an apocalypse. Yes, maybe he could have been the next Christ or Jehovah or Clint-fucking-Eastwood, but he also could have very well been everything but. He could have put everything to an end. And we could not afford to take that chance. And you, Chris, like it or not, were the only living link that we had to him. So that meant that we had to do what we needed to do."

"You had to take my family and put me through hell?"

"Yeah, we did. Tough titty. You didn't even know what you were involved in, and we decided that you probably were not about to just hand him over to us after he had saved your life so long ago. We needed you, Chris, and we needed you on our side. We needed you to think that he took your family, so that you would do anything to help us find him. So we pulled some strings. And it worked. Perfectly."

"You didn't even know him. You had no goddamned idea of what a great man he really was. You just blew his fucking head off."

"Yeah," Agent Marks said with a chuckle. "It makes it easier that way." He turned back around and finished off his cigarette. Then, suddenly, as I watched him suck upon the last of his smoldering stick of cancer, the voice of Huxley rang in my head.

"Okay, sit back and listen. I only have a small amount of time. The lady on the plane, you know the lady that must have thought you were crazy because you looked like you were talking to yourself, she identified me as being next to you the whole ride. She identified me as talking to you, although I know that she never actually saw me doing so, because I never really did. Anyway, the feds are taking me somewhere as well, so I'm going to tell you everything you need to know really quickly, hopefully before you get to Sindex."

How did you know that I was going—

"—Don't worry about that, like I said, just listen." Huxley then proceeded to tell me nearly everything about Sindex and the Piccolo project as I rode with the agents in silence along the barren dirt road.

The rest of the ride was of considerable length, and I estimated that took us about an hour to arrive at Sindex because Agent Marks had smoked exactly six cigarettes. I figured that it took him about eight minutes to inhale each individual smoke with a rest period of about two minutes between. He continuously shifted his girth in his chair if he was not smoking. I would watch him wriggle for a minute or two, wipe his brow, then find his pack of cigarettes in his shirt pocket and light another.

I waited anxiously for him to suddenly start vomiting blood across the leather dash and reel over lifelessly in his chair, or maybe even accidentally release the door handle and topple out onto the roaring road and under the spinning rear wheels of our SUV. And then with a large jolt as we ran over his enlarged carcass, the whole mess would be over. But sadly, nothing of the sort happened. The only things that flew outside into the road were his leftover cigarette filters, except for the last one in which he stomped out on the parking lot of the Sindex Corporation. Huxley had also stopped talking inside my head just before the Suburban had pulled in front of the Sindex building.

But he told me plenty. One hour of telepathic thought is equal to about a day of regular learning in a high-school classroom.

CHAPTER 17

Sindex stuck out worse than a sore thumb. The desert seemed to be interrupted with the presence of the overwhelming cement structure and black lake of its parking lot. Huxley seemed to have been simply cut off. I realized that if his thoughts didn't come back soon, I could still be in way over my head, even with my history lesson of the last hour. *My ass would definitely be bouncing a check.*

Part of what he did tell me was that the Sindex Corporation was a legitimate electronics company that housed a highly secured and secret F.B.I. black operations center below it. *"More secret than Area 51,"* he had transmitted to me during the ride, *"because people realize that Area 51 exists."*

Most of the government knew nothing of Sindex, including its own mother cell, the FBI. From what Huxley had instructed me, the things that do occur at Sindex aren't about aliens and spaceships, but instead "Doomsday Operations," or "dooms ops" for short. "Dooms Ops" focused only on projects that could conceivably bring about apocalypse.

At Sindex, they test theories ranged anywhere from mass nuclear fallout to the thermo-radiation needed to melt the polar ice caps and "drown" the world. The projects that take place here deal only with weapons that could entail the complete annihilation of the human race and possibly of all life as we know it.

"They are only interested in the things that can free us all," Huxley had quipped in thought.

As Huxley explained it through his projections, within the last ten years, the main focus of Sindex was almost entirely on a development known as "The Piccolo Project."

Huxley described the project originally starting with the discovery of the large book found in an underground tomb in the Middle East. It was the book that Agent Marks had told me about, the book filled with complex dots of blood.

The one written in Leonard's blood, and supposedly written by him.

"The Book of Life."

"***It was** written by Leonard*," Huxley had assured me somewhere near Mark's second or third smoke. "*He wanted to script as much of the information that was inside his head as he could. He did not want to just give the information out to anybody, so the book was written in code, along with twelve scrolls that each held a piece to completely cracking it. Some scrolls in Hebrew, some in the Iliad, some even in modern Japanese and English. It took many years, but the United States government was finally able to obtain enough information from the scrolls that they had collected, to partially crack some of the codes in the book. At least small parts.*

"*They discovered that the huge book neither preached of Jehovah, God, or any religious entity of any kind, nor provided a mathematical formula for all creation as some hoped and thought it might, but instead provided a formula for advanced thinking. The parts of the book that they decoded exclaimed that once someone rose to a certain level of this advanced thinking, they could discover any answer on their own. The book also mapped out alignments of our solar systems, as well as billions of other solar systems, as well as mapping out alignments of atoms that are inside each human's head. It then provided instructions on how to arrange and correlate the atoms inside our skulls to directly match any solar system, allowing any human the ability to instantaneously teleport to any position in the universe, in any point of time. If the billions of molecules inside the head matched up exactly with the stars that one could see from a certain point or position, that person would be immediately transferred there, into any position in all of the universe, into any point in time.*

"*The book detailed an extensive history of evolution, as well as the future of evolution, and described that once a certain stage of higher evolution has arrived, one will be able to correctly arrange the molecules inside his own head, mentally. Therefore one would then be able to transport himself anywhere.*"

According to Huxley, the book showed the beginning of the Earth, as well as the end of it, as well as how to evolve in order to transport somewhere else when the time came for the Earth to die. The government went absolutely mad. They had been trying to figure out how to travel through space and time for so long, and now possessed the instruction manual to do both, laid out right in front of them.

Traveling at the speed of light had now become obsolete, as the speed of thought was exponentially faster. But they would soon neglect one of the most important premises of the book: **HAVE PATIENCE.** The book instructed that it may take thousands upon thousands of years for humans to reach this state of evolution, but if one tried to prematurely reach the stage and teleport, it could result in anything from disfigurement to pure catastrophe. It also warned of the dangerous and devastating use of rearranging cranial atoms, foretelling that even simple misalignments can result in reactions equivalent to the force of a three and a half megaton hydrogen bomb.

"Basically, the destructive power that is concealed within the depths of one human can make the bombing of Hiroshima look like a mosquito bite," Huxley had told me. *"If one would decide to use it for that purpose. But remember, the creative power inside us holds tremendous dimensions as well."*

I thought about this as the agents led me in through the front sliding doors of Sindex. I was going to need to be pretty damn creative to survive this hornet's nest that I was entering, and to make matters worse, Huxley now hadn't communicated with me in over an hour.

Sindex was overwhelming and must have cost taxpayers a few pretty pennies to build. The main building was designed to function as a regular electronics company, complete with electronics labs, corporate offices, and pretty secretaries. High ceilings and skylights adorned the whole building, and modern light fixtures presented a warm illumination. Aesthetically, the place was spotless and painted in soft hues to make visitors feel welcome and calm. The main lobby was spacious and furnished with large prints of Renoir and van Gogh. Professional yet peaceful. The place was made to look as if it was a very successful large business, and nothing more.

The receptionists smiled gleefully as I followed the agents past their large desk in the entryway. We walked over marble tiling and through a large opening that led down a wide corridor, with offices on both sides. Soft fluorescent lights glowed overhead. We walked to the end of the hallway and came to a large elevator, where Agent Marks placed his large thumb on the down button. The down arrow came on, indicating that the elevator was on its way, but Agent Marks still kept his thumb depressed. A few seconds later, a blue light within the button glided under the tip of his thumb, scanning his print. He removed his hand as the elevator doors opened with their resounding "ding," and we all stepped inside.

Once within the elevator, Agent Marks stood in front of the floor buttons, and as soon as the door closed, he punched in a key code by pushing several floors in a particular order. Immediately after he finished, the soft white light of the elevator turned red, and I felt if I had suddenly been transported into the stark surreality of a photographic darkroom.

A robotic female voice spoke, "*Identification scan activated, please wait.*"

We all stood for a moment in silence. The elevator did not move. Then the electronic voice spoke again, "*Agent Tyson Marks, Agent Leon Vitesse, Agent Greg Woolen, and Agent Dartlon Gray identified. One subject, unidentified. Unidentified subject is unarmed. To proceed, push one. To lock down elevator at any time, press two. You have five seconds to comply.*"

Agent Marks pushed the first-floor button.

"*Thank You.*"

The elevator dropped swiftly, and the white lights switched back on. Agent Marks took a step away from the panel and stood with his large arms crossed in front of him.

"I am as anxious as you are to see how this all turns out," he said to me while continuing to stare forward. "But you realize that the place you are about to see does not exist. You were never here. Whatever the outcome." He turned slightly so that his gaze met mine, and the extra skin under his chin folded over his collar.

Nothing more was said for moments until the elevator came to a gentle halt. The doors smoothly opened and revealed the substructure of the Sindex Corporation. This time there were no paintings of Renoir or van Gogh on the walls.

"I will take you to the lab where my brother is being held, and I will call in any of the necessary doctors and instruments that you may need. Then I will give you six hours to show me significant progress on his condition," Agent Marks explained to me as we exited the elevator and began down the corridor in front of us.

"What, no grand tour?" I said with a smile.

He stopped still. "... I swear to God, I will cripple you right there at his feet if you don't fix him up, then I will cripple your family in front of you," he said indecorously. He continued staring ahead down the hallway instead of turning around to face me. He was deathly serious.

My smile faded quickly, and we resumed walking.

According to Huxley, the first experiments of the "Piccolo Project" had begun in the early 1980s, although some scientists involved believed that it was a big mistake. They pointed out that it was clearly warned not to try and jump ahead of evolution. But others, including a youthful agent Younglin, who had graduated as the valedictorian of his class at West Point, believed that if we understood the ways of manipulating the atoms of the brain, we had arrived at the correct stage of evolution anyway. So the project was given clearance.

In the early stages, cadavers were mostly used to study the brain more thoroughly in respect to the directions given in the book. But the cadavers remained almost completely useless, as they had no living, transferable, cranial atoms. So the project was forced to conduct experiments upon living specimens. Normally, the government is regulated against using humans for any type of mental or physical testing, but the FBI always has ways around the rules. Especially for such a secret operative such as this. So in 1989, a prisoner situated on death row signed himself over to be involved in highly classified testing, instead of being put to death. The prisoner's name was T.J. Huxley.

You? I had asked Huxley silently, while the agents drove.

"Yes, me. The one, the only, Timothy James Huxley. I had twelve days until I was to be put to death for a murder that I committed in self-defense, and a man came to speak with me late one night. He was with the FBI and had a proposition that I could not refuse. He told me that I could volunteer for 'psycho-schematic' testing, which was still in the early stages and came with a large amount of risk, or I could die in twelve days by lethal injection. He told me that I could have a few days to think it over, but I didn't need it. I volunteered immediately.

"So I stayed in prison for twelve more days, and on the day that I was supposed to be executed, they took me out of my cell and to the room where they lethally inject prisoners. They strapped me down and injected me with only a barbiturate that puts the prisoner to sleep, but never gave me

the potassium solution that puts someone to death. A doctor pronounced me dead, and I was hauled off to a hidden underground facility. But to the rest of the world, I had just been executed for first-degree murder. The reports were filed, and there were even witnesses to the event. I was pronounced dead at exactly three past midnight on August 4, 1989. The government had just traded a dead criminal for a live cranial test subject."

    The agents on either side of me dug their fingers into pressure points under my biceps near the elbows as we exited out of the elevator and walked me into the main hall. The substructure of Sindex was massive, and it resembled the interior of a large warehouse or enclosed stadium. Large hallways adjoined the main hall, each leading to sets of doors or labs.

    A smaller dimly lit passage also diverted from the main hallway, and I was escorted into it. As soon as we entered the exact point of the threshold into this smaller hallway, the temperature dropped immensely. I felt as if I had just walked into an arctic scene in the bad comedy that was my life. Each breath that escaped from my mouth was coated with a fine sugary mist. The doors that lined the walls of this hall were solid metal with toaster-sized squares of thick glass encased at eye level. There were also white numbers above the glass, and no knobs or handles on the doors with which to open them. Led by Agent Marks, the other three agents and myself arrived nearly at the end of the hall and stopped in front of the door with the number **1434-A** boldly lettered on it. Agent Marks stood facing the door for what seemed like a long time, then sighed heavily and stepped directly in front of it.

    "Open Alpha fourteen thirty-four," he announced into a small black circle directly beside the door's edge, a circle that I had not previously noticed. The door slid open with the sound of escaping air, and the agents released my arms. I followed Agent Marks into a chamber that lay out before us, a circular room that was only slightly illuminated by blue light. The three other agents remained at the entrance to the chamber, neglecting to follow.

    A large silver encasement with eight sides stood in the center of the room, thoroughly lined with thick glass on its perimeter. The encasement resembled a very wide pillar that extended from the ceiling to the floor, with a hollow area on the inside. The interior of this encasement was illuminated with a deep blue light that was so thick it nearly looked like a liquid, and it covered every inch of the open insides of the pillar. And there, standing directly within the deep blue, was a figure unlike anything that I had ever seen before, nor would I care to see again. The figure was male, naked and pale white, even while being shrouded in that cerulean light. His body resembled that of an extremely frail anorexic. His legs were touching the ground but were clearly incapable of supporting the rest of the body, as their entire width was no thicker than the wrist of a grown man. A large belt had been fastened around the figure's delicate waist and secured with black cables to the wall. The arms looked like malnourished ringworms, and dangled flaccidly from the sharp ridges of bony shoulders.

"However, the entirely unpleasant and sickly appearance of the body was not nearly as revolting as his head. The head was fastened within a large black cap that had various structures of thick cables protruding from the top of it. By my guess, the head itself was probably four or five times too large in relation to the rest of its body, and was exceedingly bloated in the areas above the lower jaw. In general, the head resembled a festering boil upon charred flesh, and had one exceedingly large eye that revealed no pupil or cornea, and seemed to be made of a pure white jelly. The other eye was entirely disfigured and in the wrong position on the head altogether, setting just askew of the rotted pulp that I believed was what remained of a nose. The figure's forehead had sparse displays of brown wiry hairs growing in irregular patches, and a large red bulb the size of a baseball expanded and contracted very slowly upon it, just above the right eyebrow. If I had not known any differently, I would say an actual heart had been placed just below the skin of the head and was desperately trying to pop its way out of the thin gluey membranes that coated its forehead.

I felt nauseous immediately upon seeing the thing before me. I bent over for a few moments and gagged dryly, barely holding my lunch back. The sour chemical smell of the room did not help.

"Yeah, he's not much of a looker," Agent Marks said after waiting until I regained some composure. "It's even pretty hard for me to really stare at him, but I know that my brother is still in there somewhere. At least I hope he is. And you'd better be hoping too because you have to give him a real good makeover."

Agent Marks walked over to the edge of the silver structure and tapped against the glass that held the blue substance and his disfigured brother. "Goddammit, what a fuckin' shame," he said quietly, " . . . such a shame. He had so much to live for, so much. Now he's just another statistic in the files of this Piccolo-Picasso bullshit. And he even volunteered for it, you believe that? He volunteered for this crap, to be a sun-dried vegetable." Agent Marks slammed his fist into the glass a few times, increasingly harder and harder each time. He placed his head against the glass after he was done, looking down with his eyes closed.

"Look, I don't much like you," he said after a few seconds, in softer tones. "Don't much like you at all. Actually, I wouldn't mind seeing you die right in front of me. But by some slim chance buried in hell that you can fix him, then there is that same slim chance that you'll live." He pulled his head from the glass and looked at me again. "I'll give you six hours. Six. That's it. So you better start pulling this miracle out of your ass soon. Or you'll look even worse than that thing that used to be my brother, and I'll keep you in a blender instead of a big blue—."

"It hurts when you can't help someone in your family, doesn't it, Marks?" I asked, cutting him off.

He stared at me. "Don't say another fucking word about family."

"Fine, fine, I won't. It's a pretty sore subject for the both of us though, huh? But since I know far too much about everything, what makes me certain that you won't just turn around and put a bullet in my head as soon as your brother is skipping around like a schoolboy again?"

"Nothing is certain. Only death," Marks muttered as he stepped away from the chamber that held his brother and made his way back over to me. "If you can actually cure my brother, then you are more powerful than I am, and more of a threat."

His head was tilted toward me, and his eyes and sly smile still shown barely from the shadows on the underside of his head. "Don't you get it yet? The only way that you get out of here is to do something that the best doctors and scientists in the world can't do. Fix him. If you can't do it, let me know. And I'll just put you out of your misery right now. If you can, then let's see it. Then maybe I won't kill you, maybe I will. But when you can't, which you won't, it'll be lights out at the ol' ballpark for sure." Agent Marks clasped his immense hand on my shoulder and smiled directly in front of my face, his jagged teeth gleaming, his wide nostrils expelling warm mists of breath into the cool air of the room. "—and the lights never do come back on again."

He continued smiling, a smile that is projected with so much emotion that it can only be threatening, after he finally removed his thick paw from my collar, then patted my back. "You've got another six hours to play tiddlywinks with my brother and maybe get him to be a little more social." The white air that was expelled from Agent Marks mouth as he spoke reminded me of his cigarettes. "See ya in a while, magic man."

He strolled on his thick frame toward the sliding exit door.

"Hey, Marks,"—my words stopped him—"if your brother has been in so much pain for so long, and is unfixable, as you put it, how come you don't just pull the plug?"

He turned around and chuckled cool bursts of air. His face still held a sneer that collaborated with a smile.

"Tried to, many times. Pulled the plug, asphyxiated him, injected him with every civilized death potion imaginable. I wouldn't let them put a bullet in his brain because he doesn't die, just lives on in more agony with every attempt at euthanasia. Slicing his throat will only mean that he lives the rest of eternity with the pain of a sliced throat." One last chuckle, one last burst of mist, and he turned around and punched his key code into the door.

I didn't say anything else and neither did he.

The door slid open, and he disappeared through it, leaving me alone in a cold blue room, with his overgrown grubworm brother.

I waited a few moments and then snuck over to the door, hoping that it had been left ajar after Agent Marks's departure. It was sealed tight. I peered through the small window, and from the angle that was visible through the glass, I could barely see Agent Marks talking to the three other agents in the hallway. I could not hear them, but I think I'm pretty sure what he was saying.

If anything happens, anything at all, do not let Chris Wyer leave here alive.

Agent Marks patted one of the agents on the back, as he had patted mine, and departed down the hallway, followed by the other two agents. The taller agent stayed for a few moments and opened a small compartment in the wall of the corridor. He pushed a few buttons, and the lights in the hallway dimmed around him. He then punched in a few more buttons and suddenly thin red lines crisscrossed the small hallway in intricate patterns. Lasers. They gave off a soft red glow and illuminated the hallway, as the regular fluorescent lights dimmed completely out. Then the agent closed the compartment and stepped away into the shadows, disappearing from sight.

I looked around the room to see if there was any possibility of a way out. I noticed a small ventilation shaft near the corner of the ceiling, but it was half my size. The rest of the room was completely sealed, not even a speck of outside light. No windows, one door.

Face it. There are only two ways of getting out of here, fixing this thing in the blue tank in front of you, or departing in a tightly zipped body bag.

I didn't even know where to start. Huxley had told me all about the experiments that went on here, but he failed to mention what I was supposed to do at this point. I walked over to the glass, not really looking up at what was inside of it. I pressed my hands against it, hoping that something would happen. Nothing did. The glass was frigid and icy to the touch. I left my handprints on the frosty pane, but it stayed intact, and the small bubbles on the other side continued to float softly. The large machine continued to hum at its regular pace.

Huxley, you need to start talking from somewhere, and quick.

I tried to remember everything he had told—*or rather thought to* me about this governmental testing. The ride over to Sindex was quiet only for the agents, for as we drove toward the dissipating Arizona sunset, Huxley spoke to me the whole time. Until he started speaking again, all I had to go on was the memory of what he had thought to me earlier:

"The government led me to believe that I would be a free man, completely pardoned of my crimes, if I only went through a series of simple mind testing. Simple mind alterations, actually. Minor experiments, not harmful in the least. This is all what they said, what they promised, but it wouldn't be the case. It had been a pack of lies. I had become a prisoner again, their prisoner, and a prisoner that was scared no longer of death, but of each passing day. I was soon to realize that I had made a terrible trade, and most days I had wished for death. It was at least a way out.

"I was detained in a huge underground facility, somewhere in the deserted desert of Arizona, and forced into daily rigorous testing. The testing started out normally, going through written procedures that focused mainly on mathematics. Then began the sensory training, which in itself was completely pleasant enough, with small bells in your ears and lights in your eyes. Then, for weeks on end, psychological testing was introduced, and I would soon become aware that this phase of the testing would be the start of a long trial of nightmares.

"They kept me up for weeks on end with electrical pulses and maniacal sounds of intermixing screaming, laughing, and high pierced notes and pitches, sounding like a mixture of fire alarms and wailing bed clocks. These shrill noises relentlessly blared down upon me, night and day, not pausing for a second. They were so loud, so deafening, that they blared past anything I tried to plug my ears with. I became dizzy with it after only a few hours, and then my head swirled and my vision blurred, and I toppled onto the cement floor of my room again and again, thrashing about wildly. This audio carnage carried on for days, and only when I had begun to dig my own ears out with my fingernails and bashed my head into the walls did they stop the testing. They wanted to see how long it took for one to finally decide that their sanity was more important than a part of their sensory.

"I had lasted two weeks under the deafening sounds, playing only insanity without rest. Others hadn't done as well as I had, lucky bastards, and were taken away from the testing. Where they went, I have no idea. But they went somewhere better. Anywhere would be better because the next phase of testing would get even worse.

"They began to operate on my mind, which I could not feel much at all due to lack of nerve endings in the tissue, but they messed with things inside my memory and my thoughts, and asked me questions about what I was seeing, hearing, or thinking. If I didn't cooperate they torqued at the nerve centers of my brain, and could control any pain that a human being can experience. I cooperated. And as I did, I actually began to see things. Think things. Feel things. Things I could never even imagine. At first I began to see mild hallucinations, which I could not clearly define as being real or illusion.

"I remember seeing a common housefly as a speck from across the room one second, and the next it had suddenly expanded to the size of an elephant staring directly at me with its huge circular fly eyes. I saw my own reflection in those eyes, divided into thousands of different frames, and in some frames I was a small child again, in some I was old, in some I was a woman, and in some I was smiling. I was smiling, as another housefly. Then the fly would shrink back into its normal size and still be across the room, after I had been hypnotized by its glassy stare for what seemed like hours. I could still hear its buzzing, clear as day, and the sound as it ground its wiry black legs together.

"I could still smell its scent. The scent of feces and putridity. Its essence. I could smell that it was a fly. But then, I watched in horror, as

the fly changed shape from across the room. It contorted and twisted, and its torso bulged out and crackled, and became larger. Its legs bent and extended out upon themselves, becoming longer and thinner. It lay there then after its transformation, lying listless as a small but horribly ugly black beetle.

"I watched it for days, until finally, it began to move. It rolled over, antennae twitching, and it started toward me. It moved ever so slowly, and it seemed like hours passed with each of its small yet deliberate steps. I could hear it too, as it came closer, and it made a sound as if it were chewing on something. Something soft, something watery. It scraped toward me until it finally traversed across the floor and to my exposed leg. Then it began to journey upward, over the hairs of my shin and up my thigh, staring me in the eyes the entire time. It steadily rose, and soon, it had come to my neck, then to my chin, then to my cheek. I could feel its tiny footsteps as they rose and fell upon my flesh. I could feel that it had come to my ear. There it paused for only a few moments, still making its chewing sound, and at last, began to crawl its way in. It nestled itself near my eardrum, and I could hear it scratching about, as it rooted for a place to lay its eggs. I could hear each one of its little hairy legs tread along the canal of my ear, and there was nothing that I could do about it. Then I heard the bursting of fresh larvae hatching, and soon felt the squirming of slick maggots as they burrowed farther and farther up into my brain.

"They were looking for warmth you see, warmth and food. And then, as they had driven me right to the point of sheer madness by nibbling upon the membranes of my head, a little here, a little there, they suddenly stopped. I felt them thrash about, then melt away into an oily fluid that seeped out of my ears and nostrils. It splashed out of me, gushed from my nostrils as diluted vomit sometimes does, and ran down me to the floor. There, it became hardened again, drying quite rapidly, and molded itself until it once again formed a small fly. The fly that it started as. But I later learned that the fly was only a figment of my own imagination. It had never even been there. None of that actually happened. Not the fly, not the beetle, or the beetle's birthing, nothing. It was all made up by me. They had forced my mind to create a disturbing hallucination, just to see if I could handle it, psychologically.

"Then the tests grew stronger, and so did the hallucinations. It was hard to discriminate what exactly was real. I was talking to someone through the paint lines on the interstate. I was communicating to someone in Texas, some rich cowboy, through the double yellow lines that ran down the hundreds of miles of highway that connected us. It was like playing that old game of telephone with two cups and a string, except the string was substituted for highway paint. The lines actually could transmit and receive audio, as a telephone does, if you just knew how to use them.

"'Girlies up there?' the cowboy asked me from somewhere dusty and barren.

'Them purdy ones with big titties and long blond hair?'

"'No, not here. I don't think that there are any here,' I replied into the yellow lines.

"'Oh. 'Cuz we got 'em here. Sure do, plenty of 'em . . . '"

Agent Marks had smoked his cigarettes, oblivious to the stories that were being told to me. The suburban drove on.

"Soon, the hallucinations increased more and more, until they had blended completely into my reality. But my reality was now multidimensional. I could see the world in layers. I could identify every piece of every layer that made up everything around me. In about two seconds, I could recognize each individual fiber in a person's shirt and tell you the exact length of the shirt if it were to be unraveled. I could tell you to the exact millisecond how long since your eyes had last blinked by calculating the dryness upon your pupils. I recognized everything. Everything had become sharper, all that was happening around me had become clear.

"After further testing, objects began to take on an entirely different look. There was no such thing as a line. Everything was made up of billions upon billions of overlapping points. The points inside solid objects were tightly ordered and stiff, and were organized into a very dense set, giving off the perception that the object was actually solid. The less solid an object, the less points that it contained. Of course I knew that these were molecules that I was seeing, but I wasn't really seeing them with my eyes at all. I was seeing them more in my mind. I simply knew that the molecules were there, and the more I realized that, the further my eyeballs were able to deeply focus upon them.

"I began to absorb the world around me, instead of simply seeing, hearing, and smelling it. I could see what the doctors were thinking, and I could even see their careful inspection of my own head, as they thought about it in theirs. I could see other doctors in other rooms, working on other patients like myself. Some doctors were stumped, some had started to become anxious and excited by the progression of their patient's progress. The Book of Life was studied repeatedly, and even though only a fraction of what was inside had been deciphered, they had come across a wealth of information that the human race would have taken centuries to achieve. Uncharted teachings that answered things that we, as humans, had only begun to question.

"But then things started happening, bad things. I remember the first explosion. It happened to a patient named Wiggs. The group of doctors that were working on him did not even expect anything amiss, as they had carefully uncovered many revelations on him. They had relocated thousands of his cranial atoms, and proved that some positions of the atoms allowed Wiggs to hear with an incredible ability. Some tests had gone to such lengths that an agent drove his car about forty miles to a grocery store near Phoenix, and was to whisper something when he locked himself in the bathroom. 'Yippee dee doo, screw you, and your hearing too,' was the little rhyme he had come up with.

"'Yippee dee doo, screw you and your hearing too? That was the best you could do?' Wiggs asked the stupefied agent when he came back two hours later.

"The higher ups in the government were not simply interested in how the testing was going, they were frothing at the mouth. The possibilities that were becoming available were astounding, and the operations on the correlations of cranial atoms had gone better than ever expected. Then the explosion. The compound where the testing was being conducted was underground and sealed room by room, as they knew of the warnings in the book that something could go wrong.

"But this wasn't your normal explosion. The doctors were doing only simple procedures on his head, when suddenly a wave of such heat boiled out from Wiggs's head and completely eradicated the underground complex. Nothing but charred earth was left, fifty-six-inch walls made of stainless steel and carbonite, which enclosed the complex, along with everything else, had been melted as if they were sticks of butter. Forty-three people were incinerated, not a scrap of teeth, bone, or personal items left. What remained of the complex was only warm air and a hole in the ground.

"Experts assume that if the sun could be condensed and placed on the head of a pin, its heat would melt everything within four miles. The heat from Wiggs's head had melted everything within two."

CHAPTER 18

I took a quick look at the thing inside the tank, and my eyes immediately removed themselves from the body concealed in the murky blue within. He was not getting any easier to look at.

Much less fix.

I sat down and concentrated.

Huxley, where are you?

No response from inside my brain, or from anywhere at all.

Come on, man, talk me through this like you said you would. I know you're out there, somewhere . . .

He wasn't there as the clock went past the first hour, and then past the second. Halfway through, I forced myself to stand up and go over to the tank and look inside.

I can't make him any worse. I can at least try something.

After close inspection of the tank itself, I discovered that a small keyboard and computer screen popped up from under a large silver plate located on the side. It asked for a user password. I tried, pushing everything that I could possibly know, or everything that I figured the FBI would use as a password.

1434-A,
Brother,
Piccolo,
Picasso—

—and similar things, but nothing worked. I tried cracking into it for another hour or so before I lost interest, then I sat back down. Maybe something that Huxley had thought to me held the password. I tried to recollect everything that he had projected to me as I had headed down the dirt road.

"Wiggs was the first casualty, along with his three doctors and forty others. The complex was completely ruined, as the heat expulsion had disintegrated everything within a two-mile radius, leaving a huge bowl in the Earth. The laboratory that I was being held in, however, was nearly

four miles away. I was in one of three labs that they had separated for the 'advanced patients,' and although everything had been quite shaken up, our sectors were still stable.

"The doctors nicknamed the three of us, the advanced patients, the only patients left, 'the Ascenders.' The reason was because our tests had now ascended from the principles of Earth to far greater equations in the galaxies above us. A patient named Onus, a patient named Brythers, and myself were able to calculate space/time equations within our heads, as well as constructing quantum theories that were far superior to any other theorem put down on paper by any other human before. Einstein, Plato, Stephen Hawking. All still in kindergarten.

"The doctors were no longer operating on us, as we could easily move atoms in our heads on our own free will, ten times faster then they could with their machines. Our intelligence had grown so rapidly in such a short time that the doctors no longer allowed themselves to be in the same room with us, as we could easily coerce them into letting us go. But we could not coerce the straight jackets off or loosen the cables that held us down. But it didn't even matter. We were all a million light-years away anyway, even if we were physically inside a glorified cage. The three of us were able to communicate through our minds for some time now, and it was like a group party line telling each other everything that we saw as we separately investigated vast parts of space. What we had come to know was simply amazing.

"Brythers was the first to go. He was the first to rise, as we named it. To rise was to teleport. I remember studying ionic patterns from memory when he thought to Onus and me.

"'I'm sure we'll see each other again, and until that moment I will miss you both. Right now, however, there is somewhere more inviting.' That was all he said, and then he was gone. I could feel his absence immediately, and I knew then that he discovered some sort of wormhole inside himself, and disappeared into the reaches of the universe that even I could not fathom. He had lined them up, as I put it. He had aligned the molecules in his head to match the stars of a distant solar system, and had been teleported there in an instant. He had risen. I hoped someday soon I would follow him.

"A thunderous impact emerged from the inside of his skull, shaking the very belly of the Earth. A radiant light also blasted out in an ellipse miles long, but this time, contained no heat whatsoever. Only light of the brightest variety that I could ever even conceive, and even as I had *the lids of my eyes sealed tightly, I still felt if I was staring directly into a welder's torch. I believed for just a moment after the explosion that I must have certainly been blinded by the intense light that burned fiercely even through my eyelids, but as I opened my eyes, I could see even more clearly than before. I cannot fully describe it, but everything seemed to stand out distinctly from everything else, but at the same time, blended neatly together as one.*

"The doctors described everything within a hundred yards of Brythers's chambers to be wiggling when they first arrived. Wiggling like everything was made of a soft shaking gelatin. And everything looked fuzzy too, they had said. The area was gradually increasing into higher shades of brilliant white as they neared the core of the actual mind explosion. They noticed that the areas of shadow seemed to be stenciled in, as everything else around the shadows appeared to be cleanly burned. But structurally, nothing was actually burned at all. As they neared the actual door to Brythers's chambers, they were then visually puzzled to an even greater extent. They realized that everything had become blank. The whitest shade that could possibly be.

"There were no darks, and all shadows had completely disappeared. No contrast on anything. It seemed as if everything had been stained in absolute white, and there was nothing more. It was hard to even see definitions at all, as the white outlines of any object blended against the white of everything else. Everything appeared like a painting upon a bleached white canvas, painted with only titanium white paint.

"The area was sealed, and all the patients were moved to an entirely different building altogether. I believe that there was an immense fear of radiation poisoning from the situation, as many of the doctors quit, and the area was completely shut down. Chernobyl was still fresh in the government's mind, so nothing was left to chance. But to tell you the truth, I loved it. For the first time in my life, I had felt truly warm, bathed in the radiant white that had gushed from the intelligence of my fellow patient. I didn't want to leave. That was radiation of pure thought, not of a debilitating kind that the government believed it to be. The whole area was coated with the depths of such a wonderful mind, that it made my own thoughts rush through me with an elevated power every moment I stayed there. My intelligence had risen dramatically after the explosion, and I was able to convince the doctors and technicians that it was harmless to continue experiments within the fallout area of the mind explosion. So we stayed in that building for two more weeks.

"However, it was decided that operations were to be relocated, contrary to anything I had to say, because construction on a state-of-the-art facility had been completed, with impeccable timing. The building was constructed mainly to specifications that the doctors had taken from Onus and myself. It was fully equipped with machines that were incredibly advanced in medical and scientific technology, increasing precision in mind alterations and decreasing the errors with those procedures. But with the new building came new policies. Both Onus and myself were considered threats to the security of the project, as we could convince anyone to do as we said using our ability to read their minds and manipulate our words perfectly into their heads. We were no longer allowed to communicate with anybody, but instead to remain to be studied and nothing further. Personal contact was completely prohibited. It had been noticed how easily we were able to infiltrate the minds of the less intelligent, and it was deemed that we could easily overturn the project and possibly the whole governmental system if we continued to be unregulated.

"Onus and I were both given heavy sedatives called Tryunicamine, about twenty-four times the dosage of one hundred milligrams of morphine, because our brains could easily overpower the affect of any typical drug. We were then taken to opposite ends of the new facility. The drugs were designed to knock us out cold, as one-third of what we took would put an elephant to sleep for weeks, but they merely made me feel as if my mind had gone numb. I simply could not think with any clarity. When my thoughts finally resumed to normalcy, I realized that I was being housed in a circular cell that had a diameter of about forty feet. The room contained nothing, except for IV's that ran to my arms and supplied me with nutrients and a large conductor that ran from the ceiling and attached to the cerebellum and frontal lobes of my brain. The conductor was there for two reasons.

"First, it was able to generate electrical activity of my thoughts into details that were inputted into a large mainframe computer. The computer translated my thoughts into written words, diagrams, and/or visual/audio, but about 90 percent of what I thought on a consistent basis could not be rationally deciphered by it.

"The second thing that the conductor did was measure the electrical activity of my brain. Normally, the electrical output of the typical human brain is anywhere between ten and fifteen watts, depending on the state of consciousness. About enough to run a flashlight. At that time, my brain generated an average of about seven thousand watts, or seven kilowatts. About the same output as two car batteries. The conductor was designed to regulate my electrical impulses and basically inject Tryunicamine anytime my cerebral activity rose above ten kilowatts, decreasing my synaptic firing and reducing my brain's electrical activity back to normal levels. They did not want me exploding into space like Brythers had done.

"Soon, after arriving in the new facility, things really began to change. The doctors that once monitored Onus and myself had been replaced by soldiers. The conductor made it nearly impossible to think in an elevated state as I had done previously, so I could only read the minds of the soldiers outside my door for short periods of time. It took me about three weeks of mind reading to discover what was happening inside the facility.

"Supposedly, new advancements had been made by the scientists that reduced the time it took to completely restructure the molecules in the brain. They were presuming that they were now able to make their patients evolve quicker, and hopefully learn more from them as they advanced. Onus, Brythers, and myself had been test subjects, guinea pigs, and what they had learned from us had been priceless. But we were still 'convicts' in their eyes, and could never be trusted. Our feedback could be misleading, and our evolution was deemed as a threat to national security. Onus and myself were now expendable and were to be, once again, put to death. But they realized that Brythers was still out there somewhere, and they had no idea where he was exactly, or what he could do.

"They estimated that he was probably far more powerful than they could conceive, as he was free to let his mind expand exponentially. So they had decided to first try and locate Brythers before putting us to death, as our executions may warrant strong repercussions if he were to become aware of them.

"They increased both the security, as well as the operations. They felt they needed to move quickly. The government decided to bring in high-ranking soldiers to operate on instead of criminals. Their experiments for mind alterations had gone flawlessly with the criminals, but they needed patients that were 'trustworthy and compliant.' Twelve voluntary officers were selected and soon had become the new subjects for what was deemed to be the second phase of mental evolution, and the Piccolo Project had now truly begun.

"The objective of half of the new patients was to evolve and travel to six different directions into the universe. Remember, there are six main directions when you travel three-dimensionally, like the faces of a cube. One of the patients would teleport up, one down, one east, one west, one south, and one north from the Earth. They were free to determine where to go specifically, but were instructed to try and find new plants, animals, elements, compounds, medicines, extraterrestrial beings, or practically any existence of other life that would help the whole of the human race.

"The other six were to locate and attempt to destroy Brythers if at all possible. Brythers was more than just a loose end, he had become the single biggest threat to national security. He was a threat because of his knowledge. What he knew already, and what he could know soon. They had no way of determining how intelligent he had become, and how powerful, and that was all the more reason to exterminate him. He needed to be stopped. He needed to be silenced immediately, at any cost.

"The doctors believed Brythers to be somewhere in the Neiurthomine galaxy, roughly eighty million light-years away. It was a galaxy that had discovered by Brythers himself, in his own mind, roughly two weeks before his disappearance. He had deducted that the Neiurthomine galaxy had sixteen planets, one of which could support life. His schematics showed that the galaxy contained two suns, both of which were more than twice as large as our own, and may have looked to an observer to change color throughout the course of a day on the smallest living planet, a planet he named Hewron. Brythers believed that the atmosphere of Hewron, composed of rich oxygen and small amounts of nitrogen and a gaseous compound that existed only there, would actually become thickened by the heat of the suns. Brythers explained that this would form a filter that would regulate the temperature to stay between fifty and ninety degrees on the planet, night or day. It would also make the suns appear to shift through the colors of the rainbow as they passed across the horizon. Much like the horse in the *Wizard of Oz*. Beautifully subtle.

"The scientists believed that they had the coordinates of the stars for the placement of the six patients on Hewron, and the doctors believed it would take them about a month to do the correct math and schematics, and another month or so to surgically operate on the patients to transfigure their cerebral molecules. They would try to project all six patients to Hewron simultaneously, giving them the opportunity to take Brythers by force. It had taken me eighteen months to get to my intellectual level, the majority of that advancement being because I had elevated myself. Yet I was still unable to project into the universe, although the conductor attached rudely to my brain made it impossible to do so. Even so, I was not quite to that level yet, and I knew it.

"Brythers was an exception. He fully understood himself, and his own mind, and accelerated very quickly to the point where he was able to rearrange the atoms in his head and transport. Just like that. Some people are thinkers and some are stinkers. Some can comprehend most anything, given time, and some just don't get it. Period. You were born to play basketball or you weren't. Simple as that. You were born to be a genius, your were born to make a difference, or you were born to watch the ones that can. It is inside, or it isn't, and it comes with the package.

"But it had still taken Brythers over a year to do so. The new patients were going to try and teleport within a month. It was completely absurd, and it went against the main premise of the instructions for the procedure in the first place.

"Three weeks had passed, and I could feel intelligence seeping in from the next rooms. I knew that advancements were definitely being made, but I could not tell how much. It was still incredibly hard to gain any information from the soldiers guarding me, and I knew that there was no way of getting my mentality through the thick encasement of the conductor, as I had repeatedly tried to foil its mechanisms without progress. I truly was a prisoner again, as I was forced to think as I had once done. Within boundaries. I was no longer able to picture the network of nebulas in the Sinne galaxies, or watch the workings of a supernova that is ten light-years wide. I was unable to discover new creatures or new colors just by imagining them. I was normal again, and it was severely disappointing. I was forced to sit in a circle of a room, thinking about the simpler pleasures. My family, or my old friends, or my life.

"There was to be no more mental escape, and the magic in my head was prohibited from release. The black cables and large mess of wiring that ran from the ceiling into my skull served as a wall, and no matter how high I jumped, climbed, dug, or pushed, it was unfeasible to once again find myself on the other side.

"Yet the energy continued growing more intense from the other rooms. The conductor definitely did not block that. I could feel intelligence all around. They had to be getting close now. I had remembered how Brythers had felt to me just before he escaped. He was above me somehow. Above everything, and sending waves of power down to the rest of us below. I almost felt as if I was a small child again, maybe looking up to my father, just knowing that I was safe. Knowing that whatever I needed, anything I needed in the whole world, he could help me with. He would know what to do. He would know. Just as Brythers knew.

"I could feel the same security, the same life force, even through the concrete that separated our rooms. It was almost like a warm breeze blowing through an open window in the middle of January. Reassuring.

"The days passed, and somehow, the warmth that I was feeling from the other rooms had begun to just slightly change. It had an icy edge to it. It was no longer pure warmth as it had been with Brythers. It was tainted, and it contained a tinge of something else. Something wrong. Something that should never have been there, something that should never be involved with pure thought. It was like a sticky film, a putrid layer that had begun to settle around the building and the energy inside. Yet, there was no way I could communicate that to anyone. I could not warn a single person of what I knew was about to happen. I tried to wave my arms and yell at the guards that stood watch outside my door. But they ignored me, as they were supposed to. Then I tried to send my thoughts out to anyone, but of course the conductor shut my brain down as soon as I tried.

"So I struggled in my circular room, struggled to communicate, and that is the worst feeling in the world, I will attest. It is worse than anything else. If you were to ask any mentally handicapped person what it is that really expends them, they will all tell you that they just wish for once that they would be able to tell someone else what they really think. What they really feel inside. As long as you are able to express yourself, you will always be free."

"The icy tinge grew to a crescendo, and the whole essence of what seeped in from my surroundings had become dirty. I felt myself grinding my teeth many times as a reaction to the filth I constantly felt all around me. The experiments had taken a dreadful turn, and as far as I knew, everyone but myself were completely unaware of it. The operations continued, and continued to burrow themselves farther and farther into a filthy hole. I had become sick from the absorption of the illness around me, the illness of unnatural thought. I could only wiggle uncomfortably strapped to my conductor with my muscles constricting tightly to my bones. It was almost as if I was locked in a gas chamber, and the *dreadful yellow stuff was now burrowing into my lungs even against my strongest efforts to expel it. I had cramped up completely as I seethed with negativity, and when I thought that I could bear it no longer, I felt the explosion.*

"*Now this explosion was completely unlike the first two. It expelled no heat or light whatsoever. Instead, it was an explosion of darkness, an explosion of abhorrence. With Brythers, everything had become lit, extremely white. With this explosion, everything had become dulled, and seemed to wither everything just slightly, like an elderly flower. And this time, it had a domino effect. As soon as the waves of the darkness carried through to other rooms and other areas, it shut everything down. Everything. It was basically a supercharged electromagnetic pulse, or EMP. Nothing moved once the darkness hit it, nothing at all, whether it was electricity or brain waves or the pumping of blood. Nothing had motioned after being swept over by the explosion. An explosion of deep freeze, without the cold.*

"*To my understanding, the explosion originated from a room three doors down from mine, from a patient named Jenson Marks. Jenson was a natural leader and won many medals in the Marines. He had volunteered to be a patient for the experiments and had clearly shown the most progress. He is also the younger brother of your favorite agent, Tyson Marks.*

"*This changed everything you see. Things had been going very smoothly for months, and the doctors and scientists were nearly convinced that they had everything in order. Early on, patients had become epileptic if the procedures went wrong, but that was the extent of the damage. Once more, experiments were made, and more information was obtained, mostly due to Brythers, Onus, and I, epileptic seizures became nonexistent and progress was made. With that progress came confidence, and with that confidence came arrogance.*

"*The doctors started believing that they understood the astronomical patterns of several galaxies, and more importantly the matching of those galaxies to molecular patterns in the human head. Most importantly, or disturbingly as it may be, they believed that they could also make the correct surgical operations in accordance with those patterns. The new twelve patients had all seemed to react very well to mental experiments, and had been evolving without the slightest incident. Jenson had actually evolved the fastest, and the doctors already had twenty trillion cranial molecules rearranged in his head before it erupted on them. He was nearly there, nearly to the point of being able to transfer to the designated point on Hewron. They only had to rearrange three billion more.*

"As I said, the explosion basically knocked everything out, instituting a complete energetical shutdown, restricting the movement of everything. No electrical activity, no atomical activity, no activity of anything at all. Just as if someone hit the pause button on the VCR of life. The doctors, scientists, soldiers, patients, and anyone else within the proximity of the dark blast were instantly captured motionless, and are probably still that way now. They will probably be that way until the day they die, if they aren't technically dead already. They, basically, are living mannequins. Unable to move, speak, breathe, or even think, and they now just simply exist. But there were three exceptions to the absolute stillness, three cases that were unlike everyone else in the facility. Onus, myself, and the center of the black explosion himself, Jenson Marks.

"I really can't specify how the waves of darkness felt to the others when they were hit, but it felt to me as if someone had chiseled into my head with a hammer and crudely hacked and sawed without the slightest precision, leaving a gaping hole of exposed nerve endings. Believe me, the worst migraine imaginable does not even begin to compare. I realized after the fact that the pain I felt was a mental collapse, at least a partial one, that destroyed about ten billion brain cells. It was a massive brain hemorrhage that should have killed me, if not for the conductor that was attached to my head. It took the majority of the fierce energy brought about by the blast, and basically short-circuited, saving my life in the process. The same with Onus. I was finally free of the mechanism, but had lost a lot of mental ability and was unable to think clearly at all, nor would I ever be able to think as brilliantly as I once had. The worst part of it was not the pain, but the fact that it was now impossible for me to ever be able to teleport anywhere, as I no longer had enough mental cells to match up with the stars of any galaxy."

"I found myself stumbling around the circular room in which I had been confined for so long, after somehow dislodging my head from that dreadful contraption that hung from the ceiling. It was still smoking and sparks occasionally jumped from its muddled wiring as it dangled loosely. I took a few minutes to regain my composure and recognize my surroundings before I went to the air-locked security door. There was a keypad next to the door that obviously required a password to unlock the air seal, but I somehow knew that the door would simply be open, so I dug my fingers into the crack of the door's opening and pulled. The door was heavy, but it began to slide open immediately. I was able to open the thick frame and slide out of the small opening that I created and into the main hallway.

"The power was all off, but the hallway was dimly lit by outside windows that lined the ends of the corridor. My head was still reeling, like I had a severe hangover, and I walked hazily toward the south end of the facility, where Onus had been kept. I needed to know if he was all right. He had become my closest friend since my arrival, even though I had only physically met him once.

"I passed examination rooms and patients' quarters on the way, and what I saw inside of them was basically the same. The occupants were stuck in the exact place that they must have been when they were hit with the blackness. Some still standing, some sitting, some lying peacefully in their beds. A doctor here examining papers on his desk, a scientist there on the toilet reading the new Popular Mechanics as he did his business.

"The first room I went into, the rest I did not. There was a petite female patient in that first room getting dressed, or undressed as it might have been, wearing faded blue jeans and white socks. Her small chest was bare, and her arms were looped within a small white bra that rested just below her shoulders, covering her collarbones. Her small head was cocked to the side, as if she had just heard the immense sound of the explosion from down the hallway, not even being able to react before she became forever constricted. She was the first victim I saw of the blast, so I entered her room and went up to her, almost hypnotized by her artificial look. She was pale, more so than any living being could possibly be, as if she had a reverse suntan. Her skin and hair almost had a transparent look, and I almost thought that if I stared long enough I could see right through her. Even the color of her revealed nipples were paper white, matching the rest of her skin. And her eyes were completely blank as well, white throughout, with pupils that once may have been a wonderful soft blue or brown, now as blank as the rest of the whites of her eyes.

"I touched her, cautiously, for just a brief instant. I had to. I had to see if she might just jump alive again with the caress of something that was as she had once been. Alive. I immediately wished that I hadn't. Her skin had the same consistency of Elmer's school glue, and soiled the end of my fingertip. She seemed to now be constructed of a paste, yet still felt warm to the touch, as if she had been put in the microwave for a few minutes. Yet she was a living façade, and the warmth about her wasn't generated by anything living and organic, instead, it was a torridity that resembled the radiation of uranium. It made me feel ill, and my head ached. I turned and left her there, stuck in a pose, her delicate fingers daintily holding the straps of her bra as if she were a lifeless mannequin in the window of a department store.

"The other rooms held the same results. Pasty white caricatures of human beings, all stuck doing something, resembling life-sized dolls. And as I walked steadily on, I only looked in the passing rooms, but did not dare enter them, and wondered if I would find Onus the same way. Wondered if he, too, was now only a plastic shell of himself. But I came to Jenson's quarters first, and there I found myself faced with something more intensely chilling than anything I had ever seen in my life. Jenson had become a being of pure suffering. Something living in utmost despair.

"He was in a far corner of the room and surrounded by four doctors in their bleached white suits and as solid as stone. The frame of his body had been drastically crippled, I could see that immediately. His legs and arms had been withered and furrowed, and were merely attached by shredded tendons and limply protruded from his frame. The whole of his body was blackened, and as the former victims I had seen appeared to be made of a thick white paste, Jenson looked to be covered in a fetid black tar. His head was now greatly disproportional, four or five times its normal size, with different parts bulging and bubbling out, and other parts caving back in. He was still moving just slightly, slithering rather, as he lay in a festering heap on the ground. He sat in puddle of his own fluids, some of it blood, most of it black sludge of which I could not recognize. And I could hear a faint sound emanating from him, even beyond the door, a rasping of air, a sound like the hiss of a snake. It was him desperately continuing to breathe.

"Although horrified, I stayed at the edge of his room. I was unable to even try and move. My feet seemed to be secured in a tub of set cement. I watched him. His engorged head swayed back and forth, his neck and shoulders unable to completely steady it. His arms wiggled at his sides, the disfigured stubs of his fingers clenching and releasing and clenching again, making knotted fists. Then, as I watched him, the oily black substance that covered him looked as if it had begun to drip or melt off. It began to run down his body and pool around his groin and thighs, and as it did, it tore away flesh along with it. Whole layers of skin peeled right off of him at a time, mixed with that disgusting syrup, *revealing auburn clumps of muscle and contorted paths of arteries and veins. Everything inside of him was displayed as his skin pealed away. Red and purple paths of blood were still being pumped to and from the heart, back and forth, instead of spilling out unto the floor. I figured that without the skin, his innards and juices would all come gurgling out, but they stayed intact and continued to function quite normally, under the circumstances. As the black slime slipped from his body, tearing away his egg-white skin underneath, Jenson let forth a howl. It was a mixture of nails being dragged across a dry chalkboard and the shrieking of an impious hyena, enraptured in pain and agony. It was a sound that was excruciating for one to even hear.*

"The pain in my ears from his torment snapped me from my daze, and I decided that I needed to leave immediately or I would vomit. I realized that he was in dire need of help, but I also knew that there was nothing I could do for him. Nothing. I could possibly have devised suitable medical treatment for his intolerable condition with my old brain, but with my regressed intelligence, I had become powerless to help. I wouldn't have even known where to begin."

I looked at Jenson inside his blue tubing encasement and felt the exact same way.

"So I covered my ears instinctually and resumed walking down the hallway. Toward Onus. I could still hear the screaming however, and could not quite tell if it was actually him that I was hearing, or if his morbid yells were still just echoing in my head. So I began to jog, then sprint, away from the room filled with white jell-o-dummies of doctors and the incessant agonizing yells of Jenson Marks, who could never be the same again. Who could never again be purely comfortable. The audio tests that I went through before my mind alterations were horrific to endure, but his screams were twice as intense. And I was fairly sure that they may never stop ringing in my head.

"I scrambled down the dimly lit corridors as they twisted and weaved before me. I was losing my mind. I raced past the other rooms in the same state, as a furious drunkard, with no intention of even glancing in at the morbid scenes that I knew were there. The hallways contracted and expanded in front of my eyes, and I wondered for just a moment or so if I might actually be detained within the bowels of hell. I made my way toward the end of the building as quickly as I could navigate through my delusions, and finally came upon the room of Onus.

"I stopped outside his closed door, wondering if I should even dare to venture inside. He could be like the others, like the doctors and scientists, frozen in time and as lifeless as a stone. Or maybe, I might find him with his insides out, and his outsides in. Or worse, he could be like Jenson Marks, tortured and withering in his own terrible spasms of pain and wiggling directly on the other side, a human version of a worm with its skin being ripped from it. There was no way I could have helped Jenson, and there would be no way that I could help Onus either. I did not know if I could tolerate seeing yet another person in that kind of agony. Especially a dear friend. I did not know what to expect, but I pushed through the door anyway and stepped forward.

"His skinny body was still connected to the large black conductor, and he dangled limply from it. He was clearly unconscious, and his long arms hung at his sides, his bony fingers spread evenly apart. It had been the first time that I actually saw him, for we had communicated in our heads but never officially met. Mental pen pals, if you will. 'Damn, he is just like the others, stiff as a brick,' I thought immediately. But then I realized that he was not sickly pale white, and his muscles were not locked in a fixed position but instead seemed relaxed, as if he were sleeping. I rushed to him. His body was warm to the touch, but with life, yet I could not stir him.

"'Are you dead, Onus?' I remembered asking to myself. 'Did you die on me too?'

"And then I heard Onus all around me, or maybe just inside my head. 'Of course I'm not,' he replied. 'In fact, this is the first time that I have truly been alive. My thoughts have exploded out of my body, my soul independent now, and I am no longer encased in a physical shell. I will tell you that it is simply the most incredible feeling that one can possibly have.'

"'Where are you?' I had said aloud. 'What happened?'

"'Evolution happened, Huxley,' he replied. 'Evolution. I have leaped millions of years forward, have experienced millions of years of advancement. And where am I now? Everywhere. Yes, everywhere. See, humans still think with their minds, but don't realize that thinking itself is the key. True evolution is the advancement of thinking, and nothing else. After billions of billions of years, as creatures evolved from *one-celled organisms to apes and then to humans, the course of thinking also evolved. Creatures got smarter and smarter, and began to change after doing so. Alter shapes, alter size. Their bodies changing ever so slowly to accommodate their expanding minds. To evolve. So then, what is the next step from human form to the next level? What will we evolve into next? And when we will start doing it? The answer, Huxley, is that we will grow smarter and smarter, as a human race, until our bodies just are unable to keep up with our minds. Our bodies are like a cocoon in a way, and after billions and billions of years of evolution, we will simply grow out of them. We will have matured and have become an elegant butterfly, anxious to spread our illustrious wings. We will have become thought itself, you see, we will have gone to the top of the ladder, from the created to the creators. There is no such thing as good or evil, God or the devil, or heaven and hell. There is only and always will be thought. Pure thought. That is what creates everything, and it is what will create everything again and again. That's how the universe works, dear friend, that is how the lights are lit and how the winds blow. The cycle of thought. And thought was once all there was all that existed, the foundation of everything. Pure thought was just drifting around in an abyss, creating things from itself, just by thinking about them. As more things were created, those things, those plants, those animals, those humans, had the ability to think too. And as they processed thought, even more things were created from their thinking. The universe then had become a snowball rolling down a frosty hill, gathering speed, momentum, and mass. Gathering thought. The more creatures that were created, in turn, created even more. Multiplication by contemplation. When you think about something, anything, it becomes real. It creates itself from the ideas inside your head. Maybe right here on Earth, or maybe on the dark side of the moon. Maybe whatever is created appears eighty trillion light-years away, but believe me, Huxley, it appears. Thought is expanding to such a degree every second, that it has become a whirlwind of absolute creation, making the universe infinitely wide. Being the universe itself. And soon, every creature, every being, will evolve in great proportions, until they have become pure thought themselves, starting the process all over again, from where it began.*

"*'Physicality is a temporary brilliance, Huxley, a nice place for your soul to rest as you evolve, but obsolete in the long run.' Leonard found this out when he finally reunited with his body as Leonardo da Vinci. He had gone there and was able to actually witness his own rebirth, which* was a very fine thing to see. He witnessed himself be born about three hundred years after he had died. Quite a show. And at once, as soon as the baby cried with his first breath of air, Leonard walked across the room in someone else's understanding body and touched his own arm. He then transported into himself once again.

"It was different than he expected. Once inside his own shell, his own body again, Leonard realized that his mind had started over as well. His body was not just an empty case as he thought it may be, but had a consciousness in it. The consciousness of himself, as a baby. So like the rat in the dank prison cell, Leonard shared one body with another mind. Two souls in one. It was not as disturbing or as uncomfortable as it had been when he shared the body of the rat because the baby was still himself and thought just as he did so long ago. An earlier version at a later time. But the baby had started over, and so it was his own mind, just demoted, un-evolved. It was like meeting himself as he was in the past. Seeing the world through his own eyes again, yet not thinking nearly the same. Not quite that simple anymore. But he learned to grow with himself, himself inside himself, a brain all his own now twice as strong.

"After speaking that, the voice of Onus simply disappeared, and he hasn't spoken to me after that day. I stood around his room, talking loudly, begging for him to tell me what I was to do, where I was to go. But the only answer I received was silence."

And your brain was too weak to teleport with him? I asked, in the Suburban with the agents at the time.

"It always will be, unfortunately. I'm still able to do many things, many things that normal people cannot, such as project and receive thought as I am doing now, but I will never be able to rise. Because if there are 20.2 zillion stars that you can see from a point in the Cerfiluna galaxy, then the brain requires at least that many molecules to transport there. Each one of those molecules needs to line up exactly in your head as each one of those stars line up from that certain point. If you have one less molecule than required, tough luck. Close, but no cigar, as they say."

But you can have more than required? I asked him in my head while Agent Marks tossed a cigarette out the window.

"Oh yes, the more the merrier. The more you have, the more opportunities are provided. There are that many more galaxies, that many more points in the universe, that have opened up to you."

But I thought that if you think about something, it becomes created instantaneously. So why didn't you just create yourself a new galaxy with only a few thousand stars and go there?

"Much easier said than done. Yes, if I think about something, bam! it becomes created immediately. But stars are navigational tools, you cannot simply create a new set. Stars are there to direct you to a specific point. They are like addresses in a way. You can create a new house from the foundation up. You can build it completely from scratch, but the house will still be on Seventh and Main. You see?"

Yeah, but how did you find me? How did you know that I would be here?

"As I said, my mind still works quite marvelously, so I can read your mind like a children's book. I knew where and when you received that letter from Leonard, and I knew when you encoded it for yourself. I knew that you'd be here, Chris, and I know that you play an important part in this. I know Leonard, and have glimpsed at a part of what he has become. I knew that it was me that was supposed to meet you here, Chris, to guide you in the right direction. I knew this because Leonard knew it when he wrote you, and the rest goes without saying. I was propelled to be here, just as you were, but what propelled me was in my own heart, as opposed to yours being on paper. But Leonard, certainly, was behind both."

CHAPTER 19

Apart from the occasional murmuring of the coma machine in front of me, everything was silent, as it had been for the past five and a quarter hours. The lump in my throat had begun to thicken, correlating with my deepening fear.

I have forty-five minutes.

I felt as a prisoner on death row must feel, like Huxley had felt, scared to death of death itself, but also, in a weird way, anxious. I had accepted the fact that there was absolutely nothing I could do to alter the thing that was once known as Jenson Marks, and so I also accepted the fact that I was going to die. I almost wanted it to be over with. Huxley hadn't communicated to me since the ride over to Sindex, and he wasn't going to. He would have done so already. He would have done something at least, told me something. Something must have happened to him.

I had exhausted everything I could think of about trying to alter Jenson Marks in any way. Hell, I couldn't even open his damn cylinder for Christ's sakes. Put a fork in me, I was done. All I could do was watch the clock wind down. Wait until the buzzer sounded.

An A for effort there, big shot, at least you put up a fight.

I had made a game of it after all, a real barn burner. I sure had. It started bad, but I had really come back, regained a lot of ground, but then, deep in the fourth quarter, I blew it all to hell.

I just hoped that Agent Marks wouldn't really torture my family like he had threatened, but I had the feeling that he probably wasn't going to. He didn't want me around any longer, so I figured that he would simply pop me a few times and that would be that. He would probably get some medal of honor for killing the madman cop killer of New York, and retire happily with a thick pension. His brother would still be slightly more than a vegetable, but I'm sure he was used to that fact. I was devastated by the fact that I would never see my family again, and I would die alone, not in the arms of my wife or a loved one. Nobody would ever be there for me, and I would never be there for anyone else as well, ever again.

I honestly wanted to help Jenson. As I saw him floating in the cylinder, his enormous head horribly disfigured and non-proportional, I imagined the pain that he must have endured for years. I would never wish that upon anyone, even if it were a person who was related to the person inflicting the greatest pain I had ever endured myself.

I sat there, on the cold tile of the circular room, staring directly into the thick sapphire that surrounded the withered body of Jenson. Hoping for a miracle, knowing that I would get none. I watched as small white bubbles drifted upward to the top of his tank, like bubbles rising in a can of soda, and wondered how this world would be without me. I was going to miss it all.

What about my family? What would become of them? They had to be scared to death already, as they were probably being held in a room that was similar to mine. *Similar except for the big blue encasement of a malformed ex-marine.*

Hopefully, they were being taken care of. That was all that I could wish for. With all the money that the government was spending on these treatments and the Piccolo Project, they should at least be able to provide my loved ones with suitable accommodations and decent meals. They have no part in this anyway. Never did. Although the only thing that I really did to get in this mess was to meet some kid in high school, I would still take any amount of torture to ensure that my family was safe.

Twenty-five minutes.

All I could to do was wait . . . and wonder what the next step was.

Death, most likely.

The last step.

What you do means everything in the end. It means everything. How you feel is who you are.

And who exactly was I?

What impact did I leave here, on this Earth, what did I do that was truly important?

What was my purpose?

A morbid thought suddenly occurred to me, and I realized that it was stupid and pretty vain, but I couldn't stop thinking about it.

How many people were going to show up at my funeral? Who was going to show up to pay their respects? Especially since I was now known and would die being known as a hardened cop killer, a man that had no mercy for a constituent of the law. Who would know that these were false claims? Who would still believe in me after I was dead and could not tell them my side of the story? Who of my friends were really true friends? How long would it be until I was completely forgotten?

I guess when you know that death is looking right at you, gazing upon you with hungry eyes, all you can do is look back. Stare right into its ugliness, expecting it. When death is anticipated, one is likely to only think of it with their last remaining minutes of life.

Seventeen minutes.

But why was I just simply giving up, especially to that bastard Marks?

I had been fighting so hard to save my family, and running for so long just to save myself, why was I about to roll over now? Why the hell am I fucking thinking about who was going to show up at my funeral? Christ, man, pull yourself together, you need to live. NEED TO. You still have two beautiful girls that are awaiting your rescue. And you are going to allow them to not be saved? You're just giving up? You're going to allow Marks to win?

My mind was slapping me awake again, talking to me, like it had done so long ago, when I got into that wreck with Leonard.

With Leonard.

Then it finally occurred to me. It became clear then, right at the end. I needed to talk to Leonard, not to Huxley. Huxley was there for support, for advice, and he had given me all the advice that I needed. He was merely preparing me. I had been looking for details in what he told me to get out of here, but what I had failed to realize was that he gave me all the details I needed.

The details of how to get Leonard *in.*

He had been telling me the answer to beating this thing all along.

"The mind of man is capable of anything. Use your best judgment, use your mind, and anything can happen."

Yeah, I was still anxious, and the reason that I was anxious was because the game is still being played. I still had hope.

We can always still win.

Yes, we. All this time sitting here in the blue chamber, I had forgotten. I had forgotten that I wasn't playing by myself, that it wasn't just me against the world. I was on a team. The best team that had ever been assembled. Leonard was there with me, with us, the team captain. Or rather, the coach.

Eight minutes.

I had to hope that I still had a chance.

Time to throw the Hail Mary. Time to win.

Actually, I must say, I did more than just think for the last few minutes before Agent Marks arrived. And I did more than hope.

I believed.

I believed that I actually could pull this out. I believed I could actually live through this whole ordeal, and save my family in the process. But most importantly, I believed in Leonard. I believed that he was real.

I believe in magic.

The boy that I met in high school was only a part of the real Leonard, and could never be forsaken. The real Leonard wasn't a silent skinny kid that dropped me notes. The real Leonard wasn't the guy that got his brains blown out in front of me either. The real Leonard could look like anything that he wanted, it was up to him. But that Leonard, the omnipotent being of free thought, was the Leonard that I was believing in. Believing that he would come through for me, that he would make it all, make everything right.

The room was still incredibly cold, and I began to really notice how my warm breath escaped my lungs and twisted its way into the air in thin wisps before disappearing. Yet even after disappearing from sight, I knew that my breath was still there. It was still floating around me, carbon dioxide mostly, and becoming one with the atmosphere. Proof of life. Proof that I was still living.

My breath, my thoughts, my mind—all still existing. It was weaving its way all around the room now, yet remaining invisible. Remaining unseen. But it was there. And so was Leonard, invisible yet present. All around, or maybe just over in one corner. You could never really tell. Just as you don't know where your breath travels, where it is concentrated after you breathe it, you never really know exactly where Leonard is, or how much of him is there at all.

Two minutes.

I stood up from the tiles and took a few steps to the blue canister that held the dangling Jenson Marks. "Sorry that I couldn't help you, partner, God knows you need help worse than I do, but I think that the cavalry is on its way. I hope it's on its way." I had no idea why I said that into the encasement, but I felt bad for him after being locked in the same room with him for six hours and witnessing inhumanity at its worse. I would have liked to help him myself if I could have, to save myself and my family, but for his own sake as well. But I, maybe the both of us, knew that it was going to take a miracle.

"I have a feeling that you are still there, underneath all your disfigurements, and I have a feeling that you know about Leonard too." I continued talking to him, in soft tones. Pleading for him to believe that he could make things better, that he could come alive again. To believe that life was certainly more powerful than death. To believe in what I was believing. "You have to concentrate with me, Jenson, and I think that we can change all of this. I think that if we can get Leonard here, we can go back to being normal again."

The machine in front of me gurgled, but Jenson Mark's papier-mâché resemblance of a living body didn't move in the slightest. I stepped away and looked again at my watch.

Nine o'clock.

Time's up.

"Okay, Jenson, game time," I said aloud, trying to sound as energetic as I could. Trying to prep him up, prep him right out of the coma that he was in, but really trying to persuade myself that anything could happen. "Let's hope for the best, let's win this thing." My words sounded phony somehow, like a stubborn coach telling his players that there was still a chance, a great chance, although he wasn't quite sure that there was a smidgen of a chance himself.

Tyson was late, not that I really cared, but he was ten minutes late.

Hopefully, he committed suicide after finally realizing what an immoral pile of shit he was. Or maybe his cronies finally developed a sliver of dignity and decided to kill him themselves. Or maybe . . .

He was just late.

I decided to move around to the other end of the blue tank, so that I could see the door and witness his arrival if he did ever decide to show up. I have always felt uncomfortable with my back to the door, but that's another story dealing with aces and eights. I also realized that if Tyson busted through the door, firing a storm of bullets in my direction, that they would have to go through his brother. Maybe, just maybe, he would think twice about jamming his finger down on the fully automatic trigger and lighting up everything in the room.

I circled around the tank, arm extended, with my right index finger touching the glass as I did. The glass was perfectly circular, almost a work of art but definitely fine craftsmanship, and I now realized that it seemed to be warmer to the touch. Or at least my fingers were not leaving a trail of warmth on the misty pane.

I quite distinctly remembered placing my hand on the glass earlier and leaving distinctive print. It had looked unfinished, and not quite the actual look of a normal hand, as handprints most often do, but this one was even more unusual. The common handprint looks empty mostly just above the palm, because obviously the hand is higher at that point, so it leaves less of a trace when lain down. But as I pulled my hand back from the chilled glass, the print that it left looked exactly like my regular hand, in every detail, except for one. The hand was smaller, like the last digits of my hand had not shown up. It had almost looked like the hand of a young teenager, or a large child.

The glass *had* gotten warmer. I moved all around to the other side and situated myself just beyond the edge of the blue tank and could see the door on the other side of the room perfectly through the blue thickness. I crouched there, peering through the colorful encasement, and fixed my eyes directly on the small rectangular window in the door and waited. Waited for the blackness of the hallway outside to suddenly become illuminated, giving me the sign that the agents were finally here. I watched the blackness outside for quite sometime, and yet it continued to stay just that, blackness.

The hall lights still aren't on, agent asshole, and you should have been here thirty minutes ago.

The back of my neck had begun to sweat. I wiped it with my hand.

I kept talking to Jenson, not really looking up at him but past him.

"Believe, Jenson," I might have said.

"Please believe with me."

I could still see his fingers and his ivory back out of the corner of my eye, but concentrated solely on any potential movement twenty feet in front of us at the door. I had seen his back already, and already had it lodged in the back of my mind. I could see in my head quite clearly, how the jutting bones of his ribcage almost seemed completely exposed, and the sharp ridge of his black spine almost seemed to burst from his barren skin, like a range of mountains tragically cutting through a white, barren Earth. His skin was transparent and displayed many blue and red veins and arteries, which probably still flowed although his body was essentially dead. It was sickly chilling, at the least. I had spent the last six hours discovering exactly what it looked like, I did not look any more. So I stared forward, diverting my eyes past him at all times, but still, I continued talking to him.

"Okay, my friend, use that mind of yours in there, like a telephone call. Call somebody up, somebody that can help us. Somebody that you might have met in your mind travels through space before it all stopped. I know that you've seen many things and learned many things. Huxley told me all about you. He told me that you were brilliant, the quickest learner, the quickest one to evolve in your highly selected class. So I know that you must have seen some things,"—my hand squeaked across the blue glass—"things that will help us get out of this jam."

I concentrated on talking to Jenson, almost if just to break the impending silence. As I did, I realized something else. My breath was no longer visible as it had been. I was speaking without expelling a warmer breath into a cooler air. It was also warmer in the room as well, it wasn't just the glass. The sweat on my neck, as I wiped it away again, could be only partially generated from my fear. It was getting hotter, period.

Maybe Tyson, the big bad agent, increased the temperature of the room before coming in. His big brass ballsie-wallsies are just a bit sensitive to the cold.

The room was cold in here when he arrived with me, I remembered that too, so it couldn't be Marks. He had looked like a charging bull at one moment, in a cheap blue suit, because his nostrils had been flaring that white mist. He was visibly breathing, just as I had been ten minutes ago. Yet somehow, the whole room had become heated, if only by a few degrees.

My underarms had now joined the perspiration team, and warmth seemed to also be revolving around my head as well. The room was actually becoming stuffy. And Agent Marks had still not shown his *fat* face. Was he not coming? Was he just leaving me in here with his brother, maybe until I starve to death? And then, just when I thought for sure something had happened, and he wasn't going to show, the rectangle on the door turned from deep black to a soft yellow. The fluorescent hall lights outside had just come on. Someone was coming.

It took a few seconds before he actually arrived, and yes it was him, to my disappointment. His large bulk of a head suddenly appeared in the rectangle as he peered inside. He was smiling as he looked, his square gapped teeth as large as ever, and when he finally saw my position behind his brother's tank, his smile increased drastically, forcing the extra meat on his cheeks to bunch around the corners of his pulpous lips. I could not hear him from outside, and maybe he didn't even speak. But I could quite clearly see him mouth the words: "I see you!" through the window as he lightly curled his fingers in a childlike wave. His eyes cut away from me for a split second, but his crooked smile did not fade at all. He was punching in the key code to the door.

The door slid open in a whir of compressed air, and as he entered, I caught a brief glimpse of two agents waiting directly on the other side. "Hey there, pretty boy! Good ta see ya again!" He was deliberately talking cute, like I was a child. "It's been a while, huh? Golly gee, I really fuckin' missed you!" He was loading his black pistol, popping cartridges into the chamber with both hands, smiling gleefully. "I hope you had a fine playtime with my brother there because it sure doesn't look like you did anything more than that." He finished loading the gun and released the chamber with his thumb, allowing it to pop forward.

"Yep," he said, looking into his brother's blue hollow, "he looks pretty damn much the same. Too bad, that means that you are about to change appearances a whole helluva lot." He started walking casually toward the blue encasement, toward his brother and me. The other agents stayed. "Probably won't be winning any beauty pageants I'm bettin', if they even have beauty pageants at the morgue."

Tyson stepped directly in front of the large blue cylinder directly across from me, and his round face was coated with the blue light that escaped from Jenson's chamber, as he looked up at him. "Whaddya think there, brother? Should I spare this lousy fuck? If you tell me to, I will. I'll spare his pathetic worthless life. I will, I promise. Just say the words right now." Tyson stood there, staring up for a few moments into the ocean blue silence, posturing, but of course, Jenson did nothing but remain limp and lifeless.

"Okay, brother. Looks like that pretty much settles it then. Not much disagreement from you. I think you made the right choice. Time to exterminate your playmate." Marks sank his gaze into me. "He definitely looks like he needs a bullet or two to play with now. Oh hell, you're right, I'm feeling generous, maybe I'll give him five or six. Maybe even reload and give him a second helping?"

Marks made his way slowly toward me.

"Whaddya' think? . . . Yep, me too."

I moved behind the encasement as he advanced. He crouched and looked through the blue insides of the canister. His eyes met mine, and his smile broadened once again.

"You know, Chris, for a second there, after you told me shit that you could never have known about what is going on here—well, for a second, I must say, I started to believe you," he spoke from the other side. "I believed that maybe you could fix my brother and get things back to order again. Fucking crazy, isn't it? And then, we caught my old friend Mr. Huxley coincidentally on your plane. We slid a skullcap on him, a device that our doctors came up with a few years ago, something that Huxley never had the experience of wearing. Shuts down all brain functions, except for involuntary actions of course. Basically a paralytic shot into the head, turning any subject into a slobbering, blabbering retard."

Marks stood back up and started walking around the perimeter of the blue encasement, waving his gun, as I continued to keep my distance on the other side.

"Did you kill him?" I asked.

"No, no. Ha! He will probably wish for death though. He truly does hate that monitoring system that they latch into his brain. But that's where he is headed again. Probably much more rigorous testing will be applied this time, psychological torment, his favorite variety."

"How do you sleep at night?" I asked him. "Don't you see what the government has done to your own brother?"

"My brother knew the risks. Sure, I feel bad that it had to happen to him, but Huxley and Leonard and all of them need to be stopped. For the well-being of our country, so that we *all* can sleep at night."

"They are trying to help humanity to elevate and unite us all!" I replied from the opposite side of the tank.

"Is that what Huxley told you? When you rode with him on the plane? Maybe while you drove with us here, inside your head? That they all want to help out the world? That's a fucking joke, too bad you are too stupid to get the punch line."

He advanced, I retreated, and we revolved around his brother and spoke, as if it were some sort of dance. "It's not that hard to piece this puzzle together, Chris. Huxley obviously told you about the Piccolo Project, probably filled your head with sweet sentiments. Probably told you a story about how they are going to save the world, and bless us all. Sounds like a fucking God complex to me."

Marks tapped his gun against the glass as we both rotated clockwise.

"Tell me, in all his mental stories to you, did he explain that he is a criminal? That he was found guilty of stone-cold murder?"

"It was self-defense," I stated.

"Self-defense? Please. That reeks of lies. He killed the guy that was fucking his wife, in the first degree. Should we just sit back and allow a man like that, with no remorse of care for humankind just become a demigod? I wouldn't let that motherfucker tuck my children in at night, much less alter the future of our world."

The large mass of his body looked slightly distorted as I viewed it through his brother's glass, as if I was watching his approach in one of those carnival mirrors. I still saw his distinct smile when he met my eyes. His smile seemed irregular as well, as I viewed it through the glass, much larger than normal. It resembled the grin of the Cheshire cat.

Then I saw it, as I watched Tyson advance toward me. As I said, the white fingers of his brother were just barely visible out of the corner of my eye before, and I was almost completely sure, yes, nearly positive that I had seen what I thought I had seen. Out of the corner of my eye again.

Jenson's delicate white fingers had moved.

My eyes had been focused on the approach of his brother, but in my mind, I saw Jenson's fingers quickly twitch, if just slightly.

I had made it nearly one hundred and eighty degrees around **the** tank, retreating from Agent Marks, but the other agents stepped through the door and brandished their weapons, cutting me off from retreating further.

"Goddamn, it is really fucking hot in here." I could still see Agent Marks through the glass, but he was coming around, nearly into the open. "Do you realize that? It should be cold, should be frigid in here, helps my brother's brain continue to be preserved. Or what is left of his brain." Agent Marks was at the corner of the tank, five feet from me, and I could clearly see his gun no longer obscured by the glass. "I'll have to get the temperature corrected. Get things back to being Arctic in here. But I need to take care of just one little thing first. Gotta have your priorities, Chris, don't you agree?"

His body came out from behind the blue.

"The reason that it is warm in here, Agent Dickhead," I said, frantically, trying to buy some time, "is because your brother is turning. Becoming alive again." The words had slipped from my mouth, unconsciously, and I wasn't even really aware that I had spoken them until after I did.

"Oh, is that a fact?" Agent Marks asked with look of disbelief on his face and a large tinge of sarcasm. He had passed the edge of the tank, and nothing was left between us. "Let me guess, my younger brother is all better now, the only exception is that he just looks the same. The only exception is that his head is still an exploded mushroom, and his body looks like he is a worm that has been left on the fishing hook for too long. But this time tomorrow, he'll be up and running and playing flag football and drinking beers with the guys. Right?"

I said nothing but began to think. To project thought, to project ideas through the dark blue glass and into the brain of Jenson Marks.

You are alive, aren't you? I saw your fingers twitch. I saw them, and you twitched them. You most certainly did. You are alive. The room is warm because it is warming up to you, isn't it? You are changing, aren't you? You will be alive again, alive and well. And we both know it.

Tyson progressed, and my back became pressed against the wall of the room. He raised his arm slowly and pointed his gun at me. I crouched in the absence of a place to go, and he looked down at me. I could almost feel his shadow looming over me, but I tried hard to only stare at his brother's encasement.

My mind was racing, thinking a rush of things by itself.

You are ready to come back, ready to think again, ready to live again. Ready to love and be loved. You have seen Leonard, I know you have. And you have helped invite him here to help us both. Haven't you?

Tyson brought the end of his gun down upon my head, pistol-whipping me to the floor. I didn't even see it coming. I reeled and slammed against the tiles, turning on my back and laying flat. My temple throbbed, and I stared up at the ball of the man that leaned over me. He was no longer smiling.

"I'm glad I killed Leonard," he whispered, but loud enough for the other agents to clearly hear. "And I'll be glad after I kill you. Maybe I'll help your wife mourn your loss, if you know what I mean."

He aimed the gun at my head again as I sprawled on the floor. "Yeah, you're innocent, I know that's what you want to say. But, Chris, you really aren't. You wanted to help Leonard, you actually think that he was a good man. But Leonard was a fucking infection, and could have taken all of us out. Could have destroyed the whole world, maybe the whole universe and all of creation. He needed to be stopped, and I'm glad I helped do just that."

"You and your government are the things that need to be stopped," I said, my senses spinning.

"No. No. Leonard wrote the book. Leonard gave the recipe for destruction. Leonard. No one else. The thing the government did wrong was to believe in Leonard, believe that he was all knowing, believe that that Leonard held the key to the survival of the human race. Believe that we could teleport to distant planets. They did wrong in believing in his fucking lies. That's all. I don't blame the messenger, I blame the goddamned message."

"The message clearly told you to hav—"

"Yeah, yeah. Have patience. Bullshit. The human race is ready, we have to be. The Earth is gonna end soon, don't you fucking realize that? Our world is gonna come crashing down, and we can't do a damn thing about it. We had to take that chance, Chris, because we are all going to die anyway. Apocalypse is not going to wait for us to get ready. But what we thought would help us, the changing of our molecules inside our heads to match up with distant solar systems, is actually what will ultimately destroy us. Faster. It will enable everyone that ever gets a hold of that information inside that book to become walking bombs. They will try and mold their mental molecules to evolve, but instead they will become disasters waiting to happen. If that book were ever to become public, or if any of the information inside of it became public, we would have three billion people walking around the Earth with the potential of detonating their minds at any time. Detonations that equal that of a nuclear explosion. Three billion atomic bombs going off, Chris. Three million Hiroshimas. The end of everything on Earth, as we know it. The only things that would be left might be cockroaches and steaming craters in the ground. Apocalypse. Plain and fucking simple."

"That is not what Leonard intended, and we both know it."

"No. That is where you are wrong. *Wrong*. That *is* what he intended. The formula for complete obliteration, and he wrote it down for all to see. He wanted people to try and teleport so that they can help destroy mankind. But he failed. We have the book, and we have all leaks to its information. And after I put a few rounds in your head, all the leaks will be plugged. The information will not get out. The world will not end. Because of us. Not because of you."

"What about Brythers and Onus and Huxley? They still know everything, they will spread the knowledge. They will spread the word of true evolution." It was getting really warm in the room, I realized. It was getting downright hot.

Tyson seemed to be sweating profusely now too, but he laughed at my comment about Onus, Huxley and Brythers. "Fuck them. We caught Huxley and are about to turn his mind to that of an insect, and hopefully we can pull all his legs off while we're at it. Then we'll put him back where he loves to be, strapped to his machine. He loves it there. We will make sure that he carries out the rest of his life there. They have more tests to run on him. Tests that, this time, may not be so pleasant."

"But you'll never catch Brythers or Onus, we both know that, and they are the biggest leaks you have."

"Brythers is gone, you shit heal. As is Onus. Never coming back. They exploded into space, sure, but have no help on getting back. It would be infeasible. He would have to remember the positions of each star in our sky to make it back to Earth. Impossible. And we tested them, just in case. We took their family, just like we took yours. Used them for bait. A long time ago. They would have come back by now, to try and save them. Just like you are trying to do. But whatever may happen, the end result will be the same. This whole deal will remain airtight. You will be dead, Brythers and Onus will be gone, and the Piccolo Project will never have existed. And no one will know any differently."

The place had become an oven, and I knew that Agent Marks was thinking the same thing. His brow was producing a swamp of sweat, and he loosened his tie with his empty left hand. His gun was locked directly at me, I could see the round hole clearly at the end of the barrel. We locked eyes, we had come to the end, and we both recognized it.

Anytime now, I will be dead.

"Well, well, Chris. It has been a blast talking with you and all, a real treat observing your lies and your act, but I need to go get something to eat. Say hi to Leonard for me when you see him in hell."

I distinctly heard the click of the hammer as it slid backward and I closed my eyes.

And then the most unusual thing happened in a split of a second inside my head. There was a voice, a distant voice, faintly speaking deep within the recesses of my brain. A voice that I had never quite heard before, yet a voice whom I knew. It was the voice of Jenson Marks.

"You're right. I am still alive," it said, lighter than the whisper of a butterfly. *"Things are going to change. Starting now."*

The world felt different then, in that very moment. Time slowed, and the energy in the room changed. I felt myself breathe in, and hold it. I knew something very powerful was about to happen. I felt it in my guts. But what it was exactly, or if I would die before I had the chance to see it, I was not immediately sure. In my mind, I could actually see Tyson's plump finger pulling back on the trigger, applying pressure, but releasing that pressure just a millimeter or so before the gun would have activated and sent a bullet through my brain. Something had stopped him. Something that he saw out of the corner of his eye. Something moving.

His brother.

Tyson kept the barrel of the gun focused at my forehead, but his eyes wandered just briefly. He had seen his brother jerk.

I had seen it too.

His brother's hand convulsed just for a fraction of a second. His lifeless fingers bowed, and within the cool blue color of the tank, Jenson shuddered.

Agent Marks turned his head toward the tank, and his gun dropped a few inches. His eyes fixated on the tank.

Jenson stayed motionless. Then just as Agent Marks was about to resume his attention on executing me, the tank moved again. Jenson's thin white legs kicked against the glass, and his arms stretched and pulled at the empty blue around him. His whole body, ripped awake again, suddenly began to thrash about. Bubbles stirred throughout the tank, and ripples of activity splashed inside.

Tyson lowered his gun, mesmerized.

Jenson's movements were spastic and furiously awkward, but they were movements nonetheless. He still looked quite unnatural, and it almost looked as if his rapid movements might cause his withered body to shatter apart like old glass. "Get Agent Younglin in here now!" I heard Tyson say to the other agents at the door as we watched what was transpiring before us. "Holy shit. Hole-E-shit!"

The heat in the room had become intense, yet it felt wonderful. I could feel a drastic change, a change not just inside the blue liquid cage, but all throughout the room.

Energy.

This was a feeling that I had never experienced before. It was a radiation that seeped from the wriggling white mass in front of us, through the aquatic tones of the canister, and into my blood. It was warmth and joy and bliss and happiness, but most importantly, intelligence, which could be physically felt. It floated all around me, infiltrating my pores, my essence. I felt as if I were being slowly filled with an unknown liquid that coated my insides with everything pure. A ten-gallon shot of Pepto-Bismol made from a mixture of pure uranium and love. I had never felt as good in my life. I had been nearly empty before, lived parts of my life that way, but now I felt full, I felt energized.

I rose to my feet, and Agent Marks and I simply stood transfixed in front of the glass. The color inside the hollow was changing too. It was becoming a bluish greenish light purple, and was mixing and swirling all around like an old lava lamp set at six thousand rpm. Agent Marks, as if hypnotized, holstered his gun and placed his hands against the glass screen and gazed deeply inside. I couldn't see it, but I knew he was smiling and happy.

Jenson swiveled around, no longer flailing violently. Instead, he simply rotated. A light began to grow from within him, as if someone was adjusting a large orange flashlight underneath his ribcage. The light was growing in brilliance by the second. And I watched as it changed him.

The pallid skin of his fragile arms slowly retrieved a more natural tan, and the ridges of bone underneath them sleekly reformed into symmetry. His extremely long, incredibly thin fingers retracted in on themselves and moved naturally. His bulbous elbows evened, and his arms curved back into shape and aligned with them. His chest and legs swelled like the filling of helium balloon animals. Muscles melded together and began to create definition in his limbs, shoulders, and abdomen as rich blood pulsed through them. His skin smoothed itself, and it looked like peanut-style peanut butter changing to smooth style as it became evenly applied all over him. He moved his arms and legs about gracefully, stretching them, loosening them from their tight molds. He spoke to me, briefly inside my head, and I think he might have said the same thing to his onlooking brother and the other agents.

"Only now am I truly being born."

And then there became a source of the ardent orange light just beneath the skin of his large misshaped skull. It began faintly, like a flicker of a candle, but grew to an intense glow, soon highlighting the room. Agent Marks and myself looked on, enraptured.

A memory suddenly came to me.

"Look at the fireworks, honey!" my mother said to me, on Fourth of July so long ago. *"Aren't they beautiful? Aren't they the most beautiful things that you have ever seen?"* She pointed her soft fingers up into the sky, toward a large shower of aerial electricity as we sat huddled together under a blanket in the town park. She pointed again, as more went off. *"Oh, look at that one! The big gold one with the white frizzles! And that one there! See it?"* I watched her movements and the way the fireworks reflected off her face. My mother's excitement captured me at that moment more than the fireworks did. I knew she loved me completely and unconditionally, and always would. *"Oh, it's so beautiful! It's so beautiful, Chris!"* Her face glowed from the lights above her. Her eyes gazed longingly up into the brilliant night, and she was young again.

The transformation of his head took a few minutes, and was very smooth. The big lumpy white ball that was settled at the top of Jenson's head began to mold evenly over the burning light. The irregular clumps of hair that lined it thinned and magnetized toward the ridges above his eyes and into a curly head of hair and thin eyebrows. His bony cheeks and malformed jaw shifted, creating a chiseled, balanced chin with large, even lips. His teeth aligned perfectly underneath, returning to their original position from the erratic placement in his swollen gums, which they had held for so long. His right eye had been located halfway down his cheek and once resembled a cue ball stuffed crudely into its surrounding socket. Now, the eye reduced itself in size and slipped comfortably between his lids, and a green pupil formed inside the vacant white of his eye, like moss growing on a golf ball. His eye then slid its way up his newly reformed cheek and nestled directly under the ridge of his skull. There, it blinked normally again.

He smiled, the same smile his brother had, but genuine. Effortlessly. There was nothing sinister about it, as his brother's had been so many times. Jenson spoke again, inside my head.

"Leonard is here. Here with me. He says hello, to all of you."

The room was completely silent, yet even in my head his voice was like a pin drop. Tyson was silent as well, and that normally required a cigarette.

"I am leaving soon, but must communicate something very important before I go. I will never really be leaving anywhere, or leaving to anywhere for that matter. Instead, I will be everywhere As Leonard is. And Brythers. I will be free thought without a true body, but inside the body of everything at the same time. I will be the whispering winds and the gently flowing waters. I will be the light from the sun and every blade of grass growing to catch it. I will be in the past and in your memories. I will be here at this exact moment and every exact moment of your present life. Yet, most importantly, I will be in your future. I will be what you may someday become. I will be human evolution in the greatest way. I will be your next step. Our mentality is what divides us, what separates all the species of the universe. Not our physical bodies. The final step you must understand is to live outside the body, outside any confinements or boundaries, and live within everything together as eternal thought."

The intensity of light grew within his chamber, originating from his perfectly sculpted head, and the whole of Jenson's body seemed to be a single beam of energy. I realized that the cords that once held him up had vanished completely, yet he was still suspended in the midst of his glass encasement, levitating.

The air door on the other side of the room slid open, and Agent Younglin burst in, the coattails of his jacket wisping behind him. Both of his dark hands cradled his revolver as he rushed through the door. He made it three or four paces inside, then stopped and stared into the blue canister with the rest of us.

"Everything—" he spoke hesitantly, his voice shaking. "Okay?"

"Yeah, everything's fine," Tyson replied, not glimpsing in his partner's direction at all.

Meanwhile, Jenson spoke aloud, without moving his lips:

"There will be a series of letters sent to you, Chris, letters that will detail and thoroughly explain every part of Leonard's ancient book. They will finally allow humanity to read the Book of Life. These letters will show the whole human race how to evolve correctly, and how to discover everything there is to discover. These letters will explain how to think sharper than Albert Einstein and play music better than Beethoven

and create more fantastic things than Michelangelo, collectively. These letters will uncover every secret to the universe and whisper many, many new ones. These letters will be everything to everyone. They will be the answer to it all. Yet, they will only be sent to Chris, and only he will know where and when to pick them up. If anyone harms Chris or his family in anyway, the letters will immediately cease."

There were so many questions I had just then, but I stayed silent. It was the right thing to do. It was not the time to talk, but to listen. Both Agent Marks and Agent Younglin remained quiet as well. We probably all figured that the questions would all be answered sooner or later anyway. So we simply watched the rest of the fireworks.

Jenson floated over to his brother, completely engulfed in sheer white light. He pressed his hands against the glass, and his brother walked over to the glass and matched his on the other side. I heard nothing aloud, it stayed completely silent in the room, but I'm certain that Jenson spoke only to Tyson. They remained there looking at each other for a few short moments, and then Tyson, with his face lit up from his brother's light, smiled. He smiled a sincere smile as well, one that seemed to light up his face even more. He smiled up at his brother, and then his brother, being wrapped in that terrific light and pressing his hands against the inside of the glass, smiled back.

Then Jenson softly ascended back into the inner hollow of the glass tubing as gleaming trails of light began to swirl around him. His body began to melt into one fantastic prism of brilliant yellows, golds, and whites, and he twisted around inside himself, fresh beams of light streaming through the blue liquid of the tank and piercing everything. It began to get too bright to look directly at him, and so I slightly diverted my eyes. In the briefest of moments before I did, it seemed that his face was rapidly shifting through and instantly becoming many different faces, each molding into the next and the last one.

I saw the gleaming eyes of my father while he laughed, or the pouched look that my mother would display just before she kissed me on the forehead. I saw my brother in there, smiling as he did when we threw the baseball out in the backyard.

Happy.

I saw my wife and daughter for just a fraction of a moment as well, smiling and molding into one. They resembled each other's beauty as only a mother and daughter can. Their mixture then shifted into the large face of a young agent Marks to the slim face of an elderly agent Younglin, then into the soft folds of the face of a child. All shifting in fractions of a second. Tyler Cunningham appeared, laughing, his face and lips grew thick in fractions of a second, becoming the larger lips and face and body of Sunshine's, her dark skin lightening again to become the skin of the lady behind the counter at the police station, then she became Sally Deevers, then my grandmother, then my grandfather. He winked at me, then was a small child, growing rapidly, shedding through faces of both infant boys and girls, then through elderly women and men. Eyes waved through rich colors and smiles jumped from grins to smirks to laughs, then to smiles again. Hair colors changed, the thickness of eyebrows changed, lips and noses and chins and eyes and ears and cheeks and skin changed. Billions of different personalities and appearances blurred by in that instant.

The whole series of faces must have only lasted less than a second, but it seemed to last forever. As the faces flashed by, each as interesting as the next, I knew that these were the faces of everyone, every single person that was alive or had once been alive in this whole world. Trillions of faces, faces of us all. They were all different, but at the same time, exactly the same. And then, the faces slowed, until they briefly finished on one. It was the face of that small kid that had once pulled me by my arm from a drowning car, the face of the fragile kid that I once bullied in high school. I could still distinguish his soft face even though it was surrounded by intense white light. It was the face of Leonard Caldwell, young and full of life, and gone in an instant. Gone in an intense shimmering flash that rippled from the tank and across the room like a tidal wave from the ocean. It whipped me back on my haunches, although I felt no real force pushing against me. It was simply an overwhelming emanation of brilliant warm light.

The three of us stood in silence for minutes, staring into an empty tube. Our clothing looked as if it had gone through a wash cycle of bleach, and all of our visible hair was white. The hair on my arms, on my face, on my head, pure white, and each one of my hairs were standing up, as if I had just put my finger in a socket.

The room looked as if it had just been freshly painted in the brightest shade of white that was possible, and there was not a single point in the room that dabbled at all in shadow. Even my moving body cast no shadow on the sharp white tiles below, but somehow I could still see definition. I simply knew where things were, even though it all looked the same. The glass tank that housed Jenson for so long still stood completely intact, and the thick blue substance that had been inside had cleared, resembling water in a cup. The room was humming. I could not hear it, I could only feel it. It was vibrating through my bones. The room was absolutely humming with concentrated energy.

Jenson was gone. He had risen in front of us all, and proved that the feds didn't kill Leonard, and that they never will. The feds hadn't won or lost, but had merely been another pawn in the game.

We all want to be the driver so badly, but we all will always be buckled in the backseat. We may jabber the ears off of everyone in the huge car, on which roads to take and the fastest thoroughfares and where to find the cheapest places for gas and such, but we are, and will always be, passengers. What we don't understand, and never will, is that the car we are in, this immense car of life, cannot be steered in a certain direction or navigated down a certain road or highway. In the whole scheme of things, it is not us driving the car, it is the car that is driving us.

"You probably ought to see your family now," Agent Younglin said from across the room after we had stood there for some time in disbelief. Slowly the colors had begun to appear again, gradually adding hue to our hair and clothing and features, painting the canvas again.

"Yeah," I spoke back to him, dazed, finally pulling my eyes from the glass case that had been the epicenter of the explosion that we had just witnessed. "As soon as possible."

"They're about a ten-minute drive from here," Agent Marks said after first clearing his throat, "so, I guess—I guess that—"

"—we should get going," I finished for him.

"Yeah, get going," he said in an echo.

The five of us somehow managed to exit the room.

CHAPTER 20

I don't really remember walking back up and out through the lobby of Sindex, or the drive to the facility that they had kept my family in. But I will never forget seeing my family again.

They were waiting for me in what looked like the lobby room of a dentist's office, and met me by a small table that nearly overflowed with magazines. They rushed me in laughter and tears, and I hugged them both tight, real tight, never ever wanting to let go.

I had been lost without them for so long. Now I was whole again. Rebecca squeezed my leg when I first saw her, but I picked her up and kissed her head. I never cried before, at least like this. I have never felt my body release so much love, never feel so much relief. The tears streamed down my cheeks, tumbling from my eyes, and I let them.

Rebecca's eyes were as big as saucers, but she said nothing. She was my flesh and blood, she didn't need to. She grasped my neck, her little head buried in the nape, and held. I could feel her excited breaths, and her small arms gripping me with as much strength as they could muster.

My wife was fairly speechless as well, although after we kissed, she whispered, "only the heart can see the future, so I knew that I'd see you again," and held me in her eyes. We stood there for what seemed an eternity, and anytime I need to feel uplifted, anytime I need to feel happy, I picture the way it was just then. The way I could feel my daughter cling to me as my lips met my wife's, the emotional completion that all our family, the three of us, shared.

I am going to live happily ever after. We all are.

I closed my eyes then as I held them in my arms, and I can close my eyes whenever I want to hold them in my arms again. The darkness behind the lids of my eyes is no longer threatening. The darkness that once brought about dreams of wicked forests and the darker realms inside the hearts of all of us has been tamed. The darkness everywhere, in fact, has become quite meek and will never scare me again. No more trees with crooked fingers, and no more running through the shadows of dirty alleys. It has been replaced by warm brilliant light; light that helps us think, helps us help each other, helps us see, helps us grow, helps us love, helps us live.

I returned my family to our home, and returned our home into a home again. I quit my job, figuring that I no longer needed it. I still had a lot of things that needed to be settled with the FBI, and to this day, I probably still do. Actually, they probably have a few things that they would like to settle with me too, but we will get to that. I want to say a few things first.

Agent Marks actually turned out to be a real nice guy, if you can imagine that. Something inside of him changed on the day that he saw his brother sprout to life again and burn fantastically away into the air. I realized that he was an inverse reflection of me, or vice versa.

I had become a bully, so long ago, due to my brother's death. He had stopped being a bully because of seeing his brother be reborn.

Maybe the real Tyson Marks finally came alive when his brother did. Or maybe he was always there, just waiting to be revealed. He had driven me to my family on that day, apologized to my face as he led me to the room that they had been held for just under a week, shook my hand and left me to see them. He then, as he says, went immediately to the director of the bureau, handed over his service pistol and badge, and quit his job as well.

I talk to him from time to time, and he is doing well. He now has a family of his own, a rather large one from what I've heard, three boys and two girls. That suits him well, I think. He lives in Southern California with his wife, kids, and dog because he wants to be by the sea.

"Something about the movement of the thing and the size. But mostly it's about the color of it, Chris. I'm pretty sure that's it, and I'm pretty sure I know why I like it so," he explained a while ago when I talked to him on the phone. "It's a beautiful thing to see every day, feels good to be around."

I still don't really have the longest, most heartfelt conversations with Tyson, there is still a lot of awkwardness between us, and we both know it. But he seems happier now, and he seems to understand me, and I seem to understand him as well, regardless. Everyone must try. Forgiveness is power in meaning. The wall between us is slowly being chipped away with each telephone call, which happens about once every three months. He still feels horribly guilty about our past, and usually apologizes one way or another each time we chat. I usually tell him that it is water under the bridge, to brush it aside. I tell him that I have forgiven him, and quite seriously, *I have*.

He is on a better level now, and happier because of it.

"The stars are the most appealing, Chris, don't you think?" he asked the last time we talked over the phone. "I'm addicted to them. Got a high-powered telescope a few months back and haven't turned on the TV since. I just like to look, see if maybe, just maybe, someone is up there staring back. And each night, as I gaze up into the twinkling heavens, even though I never see any of those stars blink at me or anything, I realize that someone is."

Times have changed, for us all. Agent Younglin stayed on the bureau for quite a while longer, but he too retired prematurely. From what Tyson informed me, Younglin retired and became a monk about three years after the whole ordeal, but my theory is that he just wanted to be by himself deep in the mountains of Tibet. I don't talk to him on the phone at all, like I do with Tyson, but I'm sure that I will probably communicate with him sooner or later. He never really talked much anyway. He had always seemed a bit more withdrawn than his larger partner had been, so I guess living in solitude in a holy place suits him as well.

Some might say that just from looking at me, I probably hadn't changed much at all, besides getting a bit older. Yeah, on the outside, I'm basically the same. I'm still a slightly overweight, middle-aged man that likes to watch *Monday Night Football* and occasionally work on his golf game. I might be caught from time to time fixing up the siding on the house, or giving it a fresh coat of paint during a cool fall afternoon. Or I might just be busy tossing the football around with some of the kids in the neighborhood or maybe walking with my wife along the ridge above our house to catch a sunset. If you compared me before the journey to me after, you would probably think to yourself;

Yeah, Chris Wyer hasn't changed much at all.

I will agree; my routines are still basically the same as they have always been. I still wake early for a cup o' Joe and a read of the morning paper and the letters I retrieved from the night before (none of them have been scrolled in blood, I may add). I still often watch late-night television with my wife on the couch and still make jokes that only I seem to laugh at. I still make "pasgetti" on Wednesdays, although I rarely would use that word seeing that my daughter is a bit more mature than she was back then, growing into her own woman, now making "pasgetti" for the ones she loves. She is brilliant, top of her class throughout her school career, and is always hungry to learn more, which makes her brilliant in the first place.

She still has a lot to learn, I assure you. We all do.

I still very much enjoy the simple things in life as I always have, good music, good moods, good friends. I still think one of the forgotten pleasures of life is reading a good book in your most comfortable chair or having a conversation with someone that really knows how to have a conversation. It's not the little things that make life good, it's the culmination of them. It's not who you know or even what you know, it's the fact that you are able to even know at all.

Yes, it's true. I seem to be the same old guy, just living in a brand new day. But what no one knows is that on the inside, I am changing dramatically every passing second.

I believe the change really started on that day that I saw Jenson evaporate, but maybe it was even before then. Maybe I have been slowly changing my entire life, and it was on that day that I merely recognized that I was. But the real part of the change, the real important part, the flame of my general transformation came from reading the letters.

The letters. The letters that have told me just about everything. Oh, what fine letters they are.

On the day that I recovered my family, I had a few things to deal with, as I said earlier. Things had changed for the FBI on that day as well. They could no longer kill me, and we all knew it. In fact, they wanted me to live as long and as comfortably as possible, as I was again their only link to Leonard Caldwell and his information.

What about the gigantic book of dots and braille?

I can hear you saying to yourself as you read this, *the feds still have the book, they still have all the information right there, the keys to the universe, all they have to do is decipher it.*

Right-o. The book certainly did hold the meaning of life, in the course of about ten thousand pages, I think it was, but as I said, it *did*. Past tense.

About the time that I was showering in the small hotel room in New York City, and dropping that letter onto the wet floor, watching the blood change into a separate code completely, the blood began to run from the ten thousand pages of the immense Book of Life as well. It completely dissolved, leaving the feds with nothing but a whole boatful of blank pages bound in a nice three-thousand-year-old antique book cover.

Sure, they had taken notes and photographs and scans and the whole shebang on the thing, really ran the cat through the ringer, but all of the journals and full hard drives of information and even small ideas written on the back of matchbooks about the book all vanished as well. It was though someone had gone through every bit of literature on the subject of that massive novel and scraped it off, clean. It, technically, no longer exists. All recordings of anything about it have been erased. It had been there, but not there anymore.

So that left me, Christopher Wyer, family man and your former friendly real estate representative as the only link to that massive amount of information. Christopher Wyer, who was about to be handed some letters that would ensure the establishment of mankind, and maybe the universe as we know it. Christopher Wyer. The one with the connections.

As I said, the FBI and I had some things to go over. They had lost their strong arm on my throat, but they had not lost their need to keep me controlled. I had not forgotten what had happened, or what was about to. They needed me, and I enjoyed watching them squirm.

Jenson didn't say anything about what I had to do with the letters, and no one asked him. Of course, the government felt that I should hand them all over to them, as a matter of national security, but I felt that it might not be a completely grand idea. Yet, I also realized that it probably wouldn't be a great move to store them in a shoebox under my bed either. Someone might come looking for them in the middle of the night, and that someone may not be so nice.

So we came up with a deal, our fine government and I. I most certainly specified a few things first. A few stipulations.

First, Huxley would be released from whatever incarceration he was in, given money to live very comfortably the rest of his life and basically get a gold pass to do whatever he felt like doing. I figured that he would want to spend a lot of his time thinking and looking up at the stars on his own private island somewhere. He would be forever unable to teleport to distant lands because of the inability of the molecules in his head, but

I wanted to make sure that the best of what this world has to offer was offered to him.

Brythers's family was to be released under the same structure.

Most importantly, the record of me being a murderer in New York City would also be set straight. This included that the late detective Tyler Cunningham being recognized as a national hero, and that the government take the bad heat for what happened, in whichever method they chose.

These were all introductions to the real contract, I suppose, as the meat of the thing was really about the letters, and the processes in which they would be handled. Whenever I would receive a letter, I would be the only one to read it, unless I decided otherwise. The letter would then be personally taken by me, escorted by twelve fully armed agents, to an underground bunker at an undisclosed location. Here's a clue: Colorado Springs, NORAD.

At the "undisclosed" location I was to open a laser-, temperature-, and movement-secured triple vault system using only my keys along with a matching set. The other identical set of keys that were needed to unlock the doors would always only be in the possession of none other than el presidente himself. Yes, it started with Clinton having them, then Bush Jr. ("Jumbo" as I liked to refer to him), Obama, (our wives have lunch together quite often), then . . . well you know the rest.

So like old golf buddies, the president and I would shake hands, shoot the shit about the Red Sox or something meaningless, and simultaneously turn our matching keys in their matching locks. I would then drop the letter off in a date-sensitive safety deposit box, lock the doors up tight, and call it a day—but not before I picked up an envelope of my own from the FBI. An envelope that contained an undisclosed amount of money.

A helpful reminder from the government for me not to run out into oncoming traffic.

The only stipulation that the government made was that I was not to tell a bit of this to anybody, until the right time came, until the public was ready to deal with it all.

Have patience; a certain book had said.

So I decided that the patience idea was fine. I signed a few papers dealing with disclosure provisions, and that was that. No alerting the media of what was going on, no alerting *Primetime Live*, hell, no alerting my neighbor's dog, but I liked it that way.

Patience, patience, patience.

We, as a people, are getting closer to being able to accept the truth, but I still think we have a ways to go. A lot of people could handle it, actually the majority of the world's population is ready to evolve, but there are still a lot of people that would hold things back. They would ruin it for us all.

Remember, I had made this deal with the FBI before I had even received even one letter. It was like Roger Clemens getting a multibillion-dollar pro contract, times five, even before he reached middle school, because a certain few just knew—*this kid is gonna be good*.

I figured that there might be a chance that I'd never receive a single letter at all, or maybe receive all of them but just be too stupid to figure out what, or more importantly, where they were. Nobody ever told me where I was to receive the letters, let me remind you, or when. There were no clues given to me by Jenson, or instructions at all. As I figured, if I was to end up without a single letter, it would not be very good. The FBI would probably wait for a long time, but maybe decide that I was worthless to them after so many years of me giving them nothing. Or perhaps decide that I was holding out on them, and put a bullet in my skull anyway.

I had the feeling that a UPS man in a brown uniform wasn't just going to show up at my door every week or so with a package from Mr. Leonard, so as I signed those contracts, I was actually sweating it quite a little bit. I was wondering if, once again, I might just find myself back on the chopping block.

I signed those documents because I had a stronger feeling that things were not going to turn out that way. The whole deal felt good. Everything seemed to be on the right path. I knew in my bones that the letters were going to find their way to me, in some way or another.

The next day, I flew home with my family and thought about it all. Thought long and hard, and relished the fact that I was going home again, safely, with my girls.

We arrived home, and to tell you in complete honesty, although you may find it hard to believe, I didn't care about the letters at all. I focused on family and home and happiness. I splurged on dinner for anyone that wanted to come along, and I bought my father a Jaguar (the car, not the animal). He has always wanted one. I had money, and I had everything in my corner. I was living, and I wanted everyone else to live as well.

I didn't buy several different houses or anything like that, as most people do if they have the means. The home I had in Durango was just fine. I had helped build it, had loved it for so many years, I wasn't about to call it quits. I wasn't about to just sell the old girl off.

Rest assured, though, we traveled. If there was somewhere I wanted to go, or my family wanted to go, we went. If it meant pulling Rebecca out of school at the time, so be it. Culture is a very significant lesson to learn anyway. If it meant that only my wife and I wanted to seclude ourselves in the middle of the Ozarks with a supply of my food, our books, and her lingerie, I was all over it. Or sometimes my girls instituted a "no-testosterone zone" and took off somewhere without me to go shopping and flirt with Spanish pool boys. Hey, whatever yanks yer crank. Life was simple, life was good. But life is only the class, love is the lesson.

Then, about three years later, the first one arrived. I sensed immediately that it had. I was sitting on the back porch, sipping a root beer, and listening to a good friend of mine, Sand Sheff, play his guitar through the stereo system inside. Sand is, and will possibly always remain, a mystery to the world. Hopefully his music will be discovered and recognized regardless, even if genius often finds the best places to hide.

It hit me right there on my patio seat, smacked me like a bag full of marbles. It was a blinking light that went off in my head.

The letter has arrived.

I knew then, too, exactly where to pick it up.

Rebecca's first word wasn't mama, or dad-da, or cat, or dog. Both my wife and I were there to witness her first word, and we both looked at each other in such amazement as Rebecca sat up and spoke it so long ago. She was playing with a green ball in the middle of the living room, surrounded by us when she stopped suddenly. She looked up and casually pointed to the elm tree outside with her chunky little fingers.

"Twee," Rebecca said, clearly.

My wife, covered her mouth, wide-eyed. I remember.

I think I laughed.

"Say it again, Becca!" my wife said, obviously overjoyed. "Say it again!"

But Rebecca went back to playing with her green ball, as if nothing had happened.

It had come back three-sixty, as it always does. If you travel far enough one way, you will sooner or later come back to the point you started from. The point that I started from, at least dealing with this whole scenario, was that mysterious letter from the person with the same name as the author of *To Kill a Mockingbird,* Harper Lee.

I won't go into great detail at all of the novel, but recommend it highly. I have read it probably twenty times now. However, during parts of the book, the main character Scout (which is perfectly fitting somehow, may I add) finds hidden treasures within a knothole in a tree in her backyard.

Rebecca's first word was a direction, and I knew it in that moment. She had been an instrument, even as a toddler, to show me the way.

The elm tree.

Cathorine and I had even put up a rope and tire swing on one of its first large limbs for Rebecca to screw around on, although I think I swung on the old tire more than she probably did. The tire has since been long gone, but the large tree, that glorious thing, aged well and stood strong.

I removed myself from the back porch and walked over to the elm, and gave her a pat on the bark of her sides.

I knew that it had to be right.

"Harper Lee," I said aloud. "I wouldn't hardly believe it."

I walked around to the other side, and sure enough, there it was. Never was there before, I'd put my word on it, but sure as saltwater, there she was. A knothole, just like the one in the book. It was about the size of a football, gaping open right in front of me, nestled into the tree just like it had always been there.

I reached inside. There, my fingers came across the crisp paper of an envelope. I pulled it from its bore and brought it out into the afternoon. It was neatly sealed but contained no script on the cover. A blank letter, addressed from no one, addressed to no one. No **Harper Lee** scrawled down as the return address, or an inkling of writing that displayed who it was for. But I knew. I knew it was for me, and I knew whom it was from.

I opened it and pulled forth a folded piece of crisp white paper within. I immediately recalled the familiar handwriting. It was the same handwriting that I'd first seen so long ago, in a classroom from my past.

HELLO, OLD FRIEND. GOOD TO SEE YOU'RE DOING WELL.

That was it. No further instruction or explanation or code.

Just saying hello. Just checking in.

This letter would only be the introduction to what was bound to come. I would get another feeling about a week and a half later, and again I went to the hollow in the tree. By the way, the hole in the tree stayed completely vacant, I'm quite sure, unless I had one of my feelings. Then, as soon as I did, a letter was waiting for me just inside, like clockwork.

The second letter that I pulled from the tree was really the start of it, I must say. That was when it all became magical. The second letter was an exact copy of a certain children's book that most of us have all read, and not one sliver of it isn't simply brilliant. The things that can be read in that children's book some people will never be able to understand their whole lives. The title of it alone made me laugh out loud. I took the letter into my house like a child receiving a birthday gift.

The letters would come about twice a month, sometimes more, sometimes less, but there would always end up to be twenty-five of them at the end of the year. Some of the letters were massive, measuring hundreds of pages that would take me two or three weeks to read. Some were smaller, more concise, maybe even having one large mathematical equation in them, or a truly complicated yet fascinating diagram. The letters would always be found in that elm in my backyard, when I felt that one was there. Always plain white envelopes.

The things on the inside of those envelopes were nothing but miracles. Nothing but raw intelligence of the greatest magnitude condensed into letters specifically written for me.

Each time I read one, I felt as if I was staring straight into the heart of God, watching it as it pumped gigantic pulses of blood through the universe. The pulse of life.

After reading the letters, I did as the government wanted me to do. I took each one to Colorado Springs, maybe had lunch with our chief executive, we put our fingerprints against some sensors, said our names into a microphone that analyzed pitch, had my eye quickly scanned by a laser, turned our keys simultaneously, and I dropped them buggers off. Another day at the office. I was paid handsomely for this.

I received the letters for twenty years.

Twenty-five each year.

That leaves a grand total of five hundred. Each one I read meticulously, most at least twice, some ten or more times. After reading them, I would usually be unable to do anything for a few hours but recover. I would only think of what had just been given to me. Some letters I would actually breakdown and weep, actually cry, from pure elation. These were the letters that showed the power of creation, making me a witness to the true power of love.

They have ended now, a little less than a year ago. I am certain. I feel that there is closure, and that is a good thing, even though I'm a little sad. My brother said that he always felt a little bad after he saw a great movie because he knew that it was over, and he would never get to see it for the first time again.

The experience of something good, something real, always includes that sadness, but that is part of what makes it great.

The last one that I received I pulled from the elm at exactly nine in the morning on Christmas Day. Rebecca had come back into town that day, having a small break from a clustered college schedule, to spend the holidays with the family. We had already opened our presents and eaten a wonderful breakfast of sausage and eggs. The world was covered in a fresh blanket of thick snow and a thicker blanket of joy. I had diverted from my family that morning to sip my coffee outside and catch a few breaths of the brisk December air. I stood outside for a moment, watching the steam slip from the top of my cup, when the feeling came into me, such an incredible feeling.

Another one is here.

I smiled a little as it hit me, and I could live immersed in that feeling and never complain again.

I put my winter boots on that were near the sliding glass door, secured my robe a bit more tightly about my waist, and clumped out into the smooth snow. The elm looked as if it had been dipped in sugar, and if I were a thousand times my own size, I might have mistaken it for a fancy treat and gobbled it up. Instead, I walked under the slope of snow-covered branches and around to the other side of the trunk, where the hole kept itself.

I reached inside and brought out exactly what I expected. I opened the white envelope and found only a single page within. This was unexpected, for the only other one-paged letter that I had received in the previous twenty years was the first.

I unfolded the page.

> ONCE YOU FIND ALL THE WAYS TO LOVE LIFE, LIFE WILL FIND ALL THE WAYS TO LOVE YOU BACK.
>
> GIVE YOUR FAMILY A KISS FOR ME.

I stood there, ankle deep in snow. It was all I could do. The most magical things in this world are the simplest ones. Moonlight, whispers, smiles, music. True poetry is simple poetry. True life is a simple life.

"Thank you, Len," I said aloud, but mostly inside my head. "Thank you for everything . . ." I knew he was up there, above all the snow and the clouds that make it. He was up there, and I knew that he was listening.

I folded the letter in half and placed it back in its envelope. As I resealed it, I noticed the tree. The hole was gone. The hole had rendered itself shut, in only a few seconds, healed like a cut heals in the skin. The bark ran down along the length of the trunk without a hint of any slight rupture ever existing. It was complete again, unblemished, just as I had remembered it being so long ago. No more void. No more cavity holding marvelous things.

It was then that I knew: the letter I held in my hand would be the last one.

After I had finished examining the bark of the tree, I trudged back along the path I had made in the snow and went inside. I took my time. I had to. There is nothing in nature that is not simply breathtaking. I noticed my breath, as I tramped along. It was being chilled by the surrounding air and forming temporary clouds of its own. It made me remember of a time long ago, a time when I was being pulled from my own wrecked vehicle and on to a muddy embankment. A time when I was being saved. My breath was cool then as well. I almost felt like I should cry, like it would have been the right thing to do, but I refrained.

Rebecca was sitting comfortably on the couch, body engulfed in pillows, and I went to her and gave her a large kiss directly on her forehead. Her forehead is larger than I always picture it being, and her hair longer. She is taller than I always picture her being, and older. I always picture her skipping along the sidewalk, her hair in ponytails, flowing behind her. I picture her riding her bike unsteadily, just learning. I picture her trying to escape from me, the dad-shark, while I swim at her underwater. I picture her sleeping after her birthday, exhausted, face clenched in a pose that shows she is dreaming of wonderful places.

She is only those things in my mind, in reality she will never be those things again. She has become a grown woman, I realize, certainly a gorgeous creature, carrying on her mother's legacy.

"Merry Christmas to you too, I guess," she said, slightly perplexed. "What was that for?"

"Just paying some respects, that's all. To the important things." I left her to her couch and her confusion, and went to find Cath.

Cathorine, the beautiful.

She was in the kitchen and looked as if she were expecting me. She always seemed to have a look like that. She can always sniff me out. It's a look that tells me she knows exactly where I was and exactly where I am going. Maybe all women possess the same look, but she has crafted it. It may be another biological trait designed to drive men wild; or drive them insane. One or the other, or a mixture of both.

Cathorine, however, was no ordinary woman, and did not even pose a resemblance of one. Angels are simply not on the same level.

I didn't say anything to her, and she didn't say anything to me. There is really no need for words anymore. We say everything with our eyes. We always have. I realize that talking with Huxley on the plane was not the first time I had fully communicated without words, not nearly the first.

Cathorine and I had it down to a science the first time we saw each other, and had been connecting that way ever since.

I walked to her, as she smiled innocently, yet certainly slyly, and she reached out to me. We kissed, and quite possibly, at least in our minds, we have been kissing ever since.

For the longest time, however, a question gnawed at my brain.
Why me?
Why had Leonard done all this for me? Why had he selected me to be the one to receive these letters, why had he saved me on so many different levels? I had bullied him in high school, and he came back to save my life from a sinking car. Just for starters. Why would he have done that? Surely I was not the best candidate for the good of humanity. Why did I then deserve to be told the secrets that were written neatly in the letters that I had received? Why me?

So I did some research, but mostly I talked to Huxley. Huxley was always a wealth of information, and usually answers to questions I had streamed into my head in the sound of his voice if he was feeling generous. Although, he preferred me to find my own way. But since the question—*Why me?*—persisted in my thoughts, Huxley decided it was fair that I should know.

"Leonard was very concerned about the re-emergence of his own body, surely. That was his key to maintaining eternal life," Hux explained to me, from Bermuda, one night as I ate dinner with the girls. Cathorine would often look at my quizzically while I maintained these discussions telepathically with Hux, but never really mentioned anything.

"But he also promised himself that he would do whatever it took to ensure the security and well-being of Fitzgerald's future as well. Which meant tracking down Fitzgerald's re-emerging body as well."

Old friend.

Cathorine sees my large warm smile emit from apparently nowhere.

"You like your potatoes tonight," she asks, as a statement, as only women can do.
"Completely," I respond.

"You see, the body and the soul depart each other upon death, the soul dissipating into the air to combine with the massive expanse of other souls everywhere, the body dissipating into the earth, waiting to be joined with another soul. Imagine that the body is a cup, and the soul is water. The cup can be refilled, but the water will never be the same water, unless in Leonard's case. The cup gets thrown out, trashed, broken, and destroyed, decayed by death, then gets reformed over the years and is re-shaped again, into a different looking cup, and scoops up another cupful of soul from the pool."

So basically I'm a regeneration of Fitzgerald's body? But not his soul?

"Well, yes, and no. You are a regeneration of his body, many times over, but we all are basically the same water, the same soul. The souls are in a sea, an ocean, infinitely wide and deep, and there will never be enough cups to drain it. Every time something living is born, it is filled with all of us. The thoughts you are thinking right now, the conscious awareness of yourself, is what everything feels. You are only encased within your body for as long as it stays physically alive."

Then the process starts all over again.

"Yes, for eternity."

So when I'm born, everything is born in a way? When I die, the world dies with me?

"For whom the bell tolls. John Donne."

What?

"No man is an island, entire of itself; every man is a piece of the continent, a part of the main. If a clod be washed away by the sea, Europe is the less, as well as if a promontory were, as well as if a manor of thy friend's or of thine own were. Any man's death diminishes me, because I am involved in mankind; and therefore never send to know for whom the bell tolls; it tolls for thee . . ."

My mind was silent, it had gone somewhere deep, maybe even deeper than Hux could see.

"Leonard loves you more than anything else in the world. Leonard was irrevocably alone until he met you, when your body was Fitzgerald's, and you took him in. You saved him from torture and burning many, many years ago. Even though you were crippled and blind and near death, you shared everything you had with him. You saved him and became his greatest friend. Fortunately for you, Chris, you are the first one he found."

The first one?

"The first reemergence of Fitzgerald's body. It takes anywhere from two hours to one hundred years for a body to re-emerge, obviously the longer it takes the harder it is to find it."

But Leonard has evolved enough that he can finally track me down?

"Let's say his mathematical abilities in calculating probabilities are fairly strong now, yes."

I could almost hear Hux doing that chuckle of his, in my mind.

I still go out to the elm tree occasionally, although I probably won't get a chance much in the future. I just like to hang out there, under the looming limbs of the elm, it's a wonderful place. Sometimes I run my fingers along the sides of the tree, or over the point where the knothole once used to be. Just to check, to make sure there is not a secret door or anything. There is not, I know it, nor will there ever be again.

I'll be leaving Durango, I think, to travel around, see some sights. There are quite a lot of things I feel I need to do. A lot of things that I've always wanted to see, a lot of places that I've always wanted to go, and now I'm being afforded the opportunity. I'd imagine that the FBI has probably gotten a bit suspicious of my dealings, as I haven't seen them in over four years. I have given them no communication whatsoever, and more importantly, no more letters. Not even the last one. That one stays with me all the time, and I read it every day. At times, I almost think that it has the most to say.

I have gotten older, much older, even from the point when I first met Tyler Cunningham and Sunshine and Huxley. They have become warm distant memories, attached to a point in my life in which I was confused and scared. A point in my life when I needed them the most, and I thank them every day for being there.

I sincerely believe that my adventure has truly only just begun. Yes, the FBI will probably be on my tail soon, if they aren't already, looking for me to help them figure out all the letters that they have compiled. The secret is in the sauce, in the preparation. They will never understand. But the FBI is of no concern to me whatsoever. I have learned to run faster than they could ever even imagine, and to places that they will never be able to find. I somehow have a feeling that they won't even try. You see, they see me as an old man now, too elderly to cause much of a stir, and they really only wanted the information from me anyway.

They have nearly all of them, four hundred and ninety-nine of them, to be precise.

If they ever could catch up to me, which they certainly could, I still would not worry. For the knowledge in the letters is what is truly important, and if you understand that knowledge, then not only will you understand how to *rise* through space and time, but also how to stop hate and killing and violence.

Stop elimination.

Instead, we will look at the world in a much different light, and go about doing things in a much different way. We will no longer strive to start war, but to cease the very idea of it completely. We will fight famine and poverty instead, worldwide. We will concentrate on the unity of all people, of our collective well being, strengthening our collective consciousness in the process. We will learn to evolve, without corporate or political agendas, all people will be accepted and included in this evolution process, regardless of age or wealth or creed or race. Inevitably love for all will be the only thing that will remain important. We all will be socially cognitive human beings, evolving to the next level, as one.

There is so much out there to be explored, I'll tell you now. The human race knows just a scratch from off the tip of the iceberg, just enough to get under the cuticle.

It will come to us all in time.

Have patience.

The world will end, sure, but I think that we will be prepared by then. We will be prepared to go to other worlds, or simply create other worlds of our own. There is plenty of good to go around.

If someone ever told you that there are only seven wonders of the world, they lied to you. I'll tell you that there are about six and a half billion of them. One in each man, woman, and child. We all have the power to change the world, each one of us, with each of our breaths, in each of our minds. The power is not the spoken word, or even the written one, but the things that scramble around somewhere inside of each of us, which words can't begin to describe in the first place. It is the power that connects us all. We are all the dreamers, the seekers, the contemplators of marvelous things; and in doing so, we become the creators of the marvelous things in the first place.

As I said, the hole in the elm tree is gone now, sealed up as if it had never been there. However, a window has opened, my friends, a window to the next level. I see the window, and I'm going toward it, and quite steadily. For I believe that I haven't yet reached my peak, my crescendo, my highpoint, but I'm anxious to get there. Knowledge is simply an invitation to further knowledge, keyholes that will inevitably reveal more keyholes. The dream within the dream. I am certainly anxious to see what develops in this life of ours; to see where everything goes. Life is certainly such a marvelous thing. I want to reach out and grab as much of it as I can.

Made in the USA
Coppell, TX
28 August 2024